# Philly MC

# A Kavanagh Story II

## Jim Wills

Carswell House Books

FIC Wills

Wills, J.
Philly MC.

PRICE: $24.03 (3559/he    )

Cover Design: ArtPlus Ltd.

ISBN: 144955668X; EAN-13: 9781449556686

Printed by Create Space

*In Memoriam*
Edward E. Gibbons
Teacher, Scholar, Friend,
"Stranger Fluttering on the Grate,"
*Carpe Diem.*

And for All Those Who Didn't Make It,
Especially the Brothers, Charlie and Mike,
*Requiescant in Pace.*

*Philly MC*, the second of the Kavanagh stories, is fiction. Inevitably, though, some incidents, people and places in it are real enough. Where necessary, names have been changed, locations altered, and times shifted to shield the blameless, ignore the less than innocent, and watch the author's back shown on the front cover of this book.

At the close of the first novel in the Kavanagh saga, *A Few Men Faithful*, Sophia Kavanagh asks her husband, Danny, if he's going to throw the last of his pistols over the side of the ship taking them into North American exile. He tells her, "Not just yet, my love. There are still Devlins in this world. Back there, over there, even here at sea." He turned out to be very, very right.

Thanks, Frank, Gerry, AJ and, posthumously, Bill, for your help with stuff historical, musical, structural, and other. In particular, Ted Wood was a generous friend and an enormous help. Bobbi Speck, my editor, was sensitive, encouraging and demanding, as she should be. The dappled woods and hissing surf of Dutch Boys Landing offered me the necessary peace.

JTW, January 2010

*Turning and turning in the widening gyre*
*The falcon cannot hear the falconer;*
*Things fall apart; the centre cannot hold;*
*Mere anarchy is loosed upon the world,*
*The blood-dimmed tide is loosed, and everywhere*
*The ceremony of innocence is drowned...*

*But now I know*
*That twenty centuries of stony sleep*
*Were vexed to nightmare by a rocking cradle,*
*And what rough beast, its hour come round at last,*
*Slouches toward Bethlehem to be born?‡*

‡W.B. Yeats, "The Second Coming," 1920.

# CHAPTERS

# 1. "The Centre Cannot Hold"

"Goddamn thing never works," I said to myself. The Triumph Tiger had a mystery problem I couldn't find, so I was losing money. Hose let me go flat-rate: I got half the labor charges and the shop got half. Sometimes it worked; sometimes it didn't. If it didn't, I had to fix it for nothing. Bikes like this one didn't help the paycheck at the end of the week. The college kid owner said it would break up at around 3500 rpm, but only when the motor was hot.

"Hey Hose, I'm gonna take this pig for a spin to heat it up and see if I can find out what the owner's beef is. Back in ten." Hose was at his bench, cursing a Royal Enfield, and he just waved one hand to me without turning.

I thrashed the bike pretty hard, shifting it no higher than third gear. Sure enough, it started to break up just like the customer said. I beat it back to the shop, tossed the bike up on the center stand, pulled off the cover and put a timing light on the points. The cam pin must have been out of round just enough. Under the flashing white light, I could see the wobble. "Hey, Hose, check it out. I think I found it."

Hose was a good teacher. Didn't get involved unless I asked him. Now, he strolled over and looked. "That's far out, Jack, I woulda guessed a bad coil, but you never know. Better change the whole thing and ride it again, just to be sure."

I bent my head down beside the tank to take a good listen to the motor. When I looked up, the Breyers Ice Cream truck was already half way out of the alley and backing up fast, twenty feet in front of me. Looked like Freddie Devlin at the wheel, grinning like a maniac. Couldn't really tell; he had a full beard. I went down, hard, to avoid t-boning it. My bare right elbow slid along the asphalt, then my leg got tangled in the rear shock, and I did a somersault. The mint leaf of the Breyers sign on the side came at me in slow motion; the slogan said, "Eat Breyers All Ways." "Yeh, right," I thought, "like through the ear, maybe," as I put out my right hand to push it away. Then the lights went out.

Next thing I knew, I was on a gurney in the Emergency Room of Philadelphia Hospital. Mom was there with Hose, and Dr. Ray was talking to them. He was muttering some-thing about baseball. As my head cleared, I could hear him better. "The concussion is serious enough he'll need blood thinners for a while. The abrasion on his elbow will take a long time to heal, but there's no break. The fracture in the forearm is only a greenstick. There's another problem, though, and it's a lot worse.

"Ah, I see my patient's awake. Jack, it's Dr. Ray. I'm afraid I've got some bad news for you, son. You're going to be okay in a while, but your shoulder has been very badly smashed, and we'll have to operate to put it back together. You'll be able to work a little in about eight weeks or so. We'll operate in a few days, once you're stabilized. Just sit back and enjoy our famous hospital food in the meantime."

Hose leaned over, hatchet face close. "Truck was stolen, Jack. Cops don't know or won't say who lifted it. We should talk about that when you can think again."

I saw her face surrounded by a halo: about thirty, dark, pretty, Semitic, in her starched nurse's cap and uniform. The bib didn't hide how busty she was. She rolled me over on my side and seemed to swab my right cheek for a long time before she gave me the injection. Who was it that said, "Jack, them nurses is always horny, and they know just what to do?" Must have been Jimbo. Right, it was, just like him, too.

The operating room table room was covered with the most beautiful silver tools I'd ever seen. I was up on my good elbow looking at them. "Hey, doc, what's the saw for, huh?" "Didn't you have a shot son?" "You betcha, I'm right outta my gourd." Then the ice man started up my left arm. When he walked into my chest, the dreaming started.

I was standing in the narrow side aisle of the church waiting in a long, squirming, scratching line of kids for my turn in the dim little confessional with Father McLaughlin. Jimbo was way up at the front, pulling on a girl's ponytail. Typical, when I think back.

The priest always smelled like White Owl Cigars on the other side of the dark oak screen. He knew who I was. He knew where I lived; how much my father made at Eddystone, down on the Delaware River; what grandpop thought of priests. I'd better tell, just like the nuns said, then I could get outside.

I had to say something. Make it up. Must be something. Remember the words, do your penance, get out. Hurry up.

Christ, why did the girls take so long?  Were they really bad in secret?

"Bless me father, for I have sinned.  It's been two weeks since my last confession.  I had impure thoughts, talked back to my mother, played doctor with a Protestant girl in the park and didn't do my homework on Tuesday."

"Jack, remember that Protestants aren't like us.  They have no morals.  Say four Our Fathers and three Hail Marys."

I could feel the disdain, almost hate, coming through the screen—tense, electric.  He cleared his throat, and a thick stink of sour White Owl came at me.  "I hear, Jack, that your father and grandfather had another donnybrook with the Devlins down at McGarrity's Saloon.  This is the third time.  I've warned your father, but your grandfather and your uncles are beyond salvation.  Now I'm warning you; it's never too young to start with people like you.  The Kavanaghs have no business with the Philadelphia  Brotherhood or the *Clann na Gael* or whatever it's called these days.  They're godless men.  You, young man, have only one mission, and that's to be the best, most obedient Catholic you can possibly be.  That's the only cause you'll ever need.  Is that perfectly clear?"

"Yeh, right," I thought, as I pushed the heavy oak door open and bolted into the sunshine outside, "I'm Irish. It's just like granpop and dad say: 'Stand up for what's right, and there'll be a line-up of guys ready to knock you down.'" Granpop always added, "especially them goddamned dagos."

His large, round gold watch and its thick chain were at the corner of his woodworking bench. Granpop picked it up and pushed the stem with his mangled right thumb to open the lid. He peered at it closely with his good eye; that made the deep scar seem even deeper. It ran up into his hair, divided his left eyebrow and dented his cheek, just below the eye. Inside the lid was the inscription he read to me many times as I sat on his lap in his big, scratchy, horsehair chair in the parlor: "From all your friends in Cork No. 2 Brigade. Good luck in America, Danny, 1924. Soon or Never." The gold watch chain had a heavy square fob from the Philadelphia soccer club he played for when he first came over. It was dark bronze, had a trophy on it and said, "Moyamensing All Irish, League Champions, 1925." In that chair he told me many times about how he was beaten at Boland's Mill in Dublin during the Easter Rising—rifle-butted in the head by a British soldier, over and over, left for dead. They shot his oldest brother, too, Jack, same name as mine. The other brother, Mick, saved his life on a Triumph motorcycle he always called "Trusty." The stories always made me proud and angry at the same time.

"Danny? Jackie?" granmom was calling down the basement stairs. He turned to me: "This ain't no union job, I'm thinkin, but these two working guys need a break. How about a Coke and a sandwich there, helper? This Kavanagh surely could use a cold beer. Alright, my love, we'll be up in a tick."

Granmom was in the kitchen, humming *Ave Maria* by the coal stove. "Danny, Father McLaughlin will be by for the tithe later. Do we have any whiskey in the house for him to have his tipple?"

"The tithe is always due, it seems to me, my dear, and the good father is always thirsty. I'll step out later to get some, after we two men have finished down below."

"Humph. And you aren't, I suppose? Don't you dwaddle when you go out, now. It's only the one drink you'll be having. And, just for today, stay away from Joe McGarrity and the *Clann*." "Christ," he said under his breath, "not bloody likely, bloody priests."

Back in the basement after our ham sandwiches and vegetable soup, we started again. He tested the dovetails with his finger and said with satisfaction, "This fresh lot of horse glue sets up fast, Jacko." He reached under the bench without looking and pulled out a wooden plane with a blade like little steps. He clamped a board in the vise and used it on three of the edges to make a molding. "Could be a tad sharper," he muttered. He seemed to have the wood cut out for the brass hinges in a flash. The brace he used to drill the screw holes was made of rosewood with brass inlay. The tiny, spoon-shaped bit made a scratching sound as the coils of wood came out.

"Now, you just hand me those screws there, boyo, one at a time." He let me screw the last one in myself. "There she is," he said proudly, as we both regarded the finished box with professional eyes. It was about two feet long, a foot wide and eight inches deep, like an old document box. "We're artists, that's what we are. It's a shame it's dying out, Jackie. Everything has to be all metal these days: ships, cars, skyscrapers, railroad carriages, even the locomotives are steel now instead of good old black iron. Bloody Hitler. It ain't right, but there's no sense fretting. Just a few finishing touches to go."

From the rack on the wall, he took a round mallet with a black head, v-shaped chisels and then lifted some little crooked knives from a fitted box. He quickly penciled a shape in the center of the lid and started tapping and carving away, bending over so close to his work I couldn't make out what was happening. Clean little chips flew out in all directions. My eyes widened and my mouth opened when he backed away. Like magic, there was a deeply carved medallion of vines and leaves and flowers. Right in the middle were my initials: "J S K," and the date: "1948."

"There you are, my fine young lad, a box of your very own to keep all your precious stuff in forever and a day. Maybe I'll add a lock. Just might be I could find you a treasure or two around here someplace." He looked around vaguely and then wiped his mouth on his sleeve. "Sure is dry work this. Up we go then."

The bartender swung me to the floor, and I couldn't see granpop anymore. I sipped the root beer and watched him serve drinks.  There was a big black cash box on the shelf underneath, a baseball bat and a shotgun with two short blue barrels and curlicued hammers.  "It's loaded, boy, hands off." I snatched my hand back.

I could hear shouting and scuffling, and then granpop's voice, very level and gruff: "Devlin, I swear to God, if I have to turn you upside down and shake it outta your pockets, I will.  Right here in front of all your pals.  Is that what you want, then, you Free-State asshole?  The *Clann na Gael* will spit on your money and your shadow. You'll never be able to hold your head up in this parish again.  That is if I leave your thick head where it is and change my mind about knocking it back to the ould sod.  If you were from Inniskeen instead of Tipperary, you wouldn't be breathing now."   Then his voice dropped so I couldn't understand it.  The men at the tables started talking again, a few  laughs rang out. A separate argument—loud—started right in front of the bar.  I peered around the corner of it to see.

The man with the very red face shouted, "Dammit, ya blockhead, it's right in fronta yer nose," stabbing his finger at the *United Irishman* from New York in his hand. Costello says it right here: 'The principle objective on which we agreed was the ending of partition.' That's good enough for me. Anybody who doesn't support the Brotherhood now is a bloody Free-State traitor. It's war now, ya dumb shit. It's the only thing the Brits understand. Maybe we lost the Civil War, but we ain't gonna lose this one. De Valera might be the prime minister of the Republic, but he's still a traitor, just like the Devlin over there. All they want is the status quo, not a free, united country."

The bartender lifted me back up onto the bar. Granpop was there with a full glass in his hand. "Yer one tough customer, Danny Kavanagh. That was smooth and quick as grease. I thought old Devlin was gonna shit himself. Too bad, though, it woulda been grand to see the skinflint with his heels in the air. Did you get it all, then?" Granpop nodded, grinning tightly: "Every last cent."

"Have one on me, Pat, and wrap up a bottle of the Irish for us to take away. Never can tell when the priest might stop by for a tipple." Paddy snorted and said, "Sure, Danny, sure."

On the way out, we stopped at a bunch of tables pulled close together, the men talking low. "Bless my immortal soul, it's Joe McGarrity, himself," granpop said as if he was surprised. "You're the very image of sedition." They shook hands like old friends. Granpop pulled out a chair and sat down; I stood proudly at his side. "Here's big Jack's boy, little Jack, come to stay with us for a bit." Mr. McGarrity shook my hand gravely, man to man. He was a dry, sick old man, once tall, with a black Derby hat on the back of his head. "Aha," he said, "I do believe I spy a future Irish Volunteer. Never you worry, young Jack Kavanagh, we'll come for you when the time is right. We always need good Republican hearts that don't flinch—like your granpop here, and your uncles." He pointed to the white flash in my hair and turned to his cronies: "See, here, lads, the boy's got the touch of the banshee on him. We should send him to sea. He'll never drown, at least." They laughed. Then he raised his voice: "What we don't need is any Free-State cowards who agree with partition." His tone lowered once more: "How about Big Jack, then, Danny?"

Granpop shook his head. "No, not the boy's dad. The other two lads are with us, anyway."

"Good men, those. Have you talked to the young dago?"

"I have. Castesi's boys will have the gelignite ready for us in one week. Then we can ship it over. I've had a letter from brother Mick in Armagh; the border plans are being laid as we speak.  It'll take time, though. What about Devlin, Joe?  You sure he's really from Tipperary like he says?"

"Sure as we can be. Not to worry, Danny.  We have him and his people covered.  He doesn't know a thing."

After lunch was the dreaded, boring Religion class.  At least they let us grab a smoke outside the cafeteria first.  We all hated that class, even the Polish guys from Frankford. Brother James, the pushover, stood behind the desk and told us, "Today, we have a very special guest to help us with the works of Saint Thomas Aquinas that we've been puzzling over.  Father Thomas O'Neill of the Jesuit Order has graciously given up some of his valuable time to enlighten us on the ten proofs for the existence of God.  Listen carefully and think about your answers."

O'Neill was the perfect jevvie.  About forty, fat and sleek. Some worried spinster served him hand and foot in a stuffy rectory somewhere.  She shined his shoes, washed his underwear, took the food off the table if it wasn't perfect and cried in the kitchen after.  He was a big, self-important, balding man who sweat, and we could all tell he was born right. Jesuits always are.

It was the usual stuff. Aquinas knew all, saw all, had a pipeline to the Almighty and had the ten proofs engraved on his forehead by the holy finger. The priest started asking the questions, direct and stern. He got to me. "Let's see," consulting the list in front of him, "it's Kavanagh isn't it? Well, Mr. Kavanagh, I understand your brother is in the seminary with us, and," looking around the class, "he has a *fine* future as a Jesuit. Now, tell us, Mr. Kavanagh, just how many angels can dance on the head of a pin?"

I didn't want to answer, but I had to. He was drumming his fingers on top of the desk. Jesuits never gave you time to think. It was one of their best tricks.

"Well, Father, none, I think."

There was a very loud intake of breath from the student desks, a kind of "I knew he'd screw it up" noise.

"Yes, I see, we have a wiseacre among us today. Very amusing. Exactly why would you say that, Kavanagh?"

"Brother James always says to think about the premise, the thing the question's based on."

"And so?"

"And so, Father, I deny the premise."

He looked at me very directly for a long moment, red face set, mind working. There was restless movement in the desks. The big electric clock on the wall buzzed.

"Good answer. Next boy."

After that, they didn't bother calling me into the tiny room during retreats anymore. Guess they figured a vocation was out for me.

Near dad's steel bench at the refinery was a tall drill press standing on the floor. "Let's see," he said, "we need a clearance hole of an inch and nine-sixteenths. Jack, scoot over to my box and find the right drill, willya? It'll be in a gray metal index, second shelf down. They're all marked by size. Don't forget the cutting oil; it's in the can with the devil on it, Red Devil Cutting Oil it's called."

I went over to the cabinet to look for the stuff. Dad had taped up black and white photographs on the inside of the doors: mom in her wedding dress, smiling radiantly; mom and dad on a Fourth of July at Steeplechase Park on Coney Island before they were married, dad mugging with a little flag on a stick draped over his shoulder; granpop and granmom smiling shyly in the little Fishtown back yard; me and Mark and Matt standing on the stoop on Hope Street in the Hopalong Cassidy duds we got for Christmas, double-holster gun belts and all. Then the yellowing *Bulletin* article: "Pep Boys Pull It Out in Seven." I was some proud of the Philadelphia American Legion League championship trophy I had at home. I pitched the winning game, and the team all signed the game ball for me. It rested in the box granpop made for me, next to his watch fob and some other precious stuff "forever and a day."

I found the drill index and the right size, grabbed the oil and looked down at the devil's face grinning at me from the can. "Found em, dad, I'm commin, I'm commin," I called to him.

He adjusted the belt that controls the speed of the quill and went to work. Hot, shiny coils of steel erupted from the holes in a choking haze of Red Devil Oil. Later, we clamped the rod in the vise, and dad brazed it up. The brass flowed so evenly that when the joints cooled they looked like pictures of rippling lava turned to stone in *National Geographic*.

"You can handle it," he said, handing me the flaming torch and the thin brass rod. "Remember, it's just like soldering a water pipe, only hotter. The brass is like a glue, not a weld, where the metals flow together."

I tried to do it just like he did. It was a mess: hot brass bouncing off my shoes, bumpy little spots of braze in the joint.

He laughed, but it was a gentle laugh. "Don't worry, Jack, it takes a lot of practice. Look closely, now, and I'll show you just how it's done."

Black glass goggles on, our heads bent close over the vise. He heated the steel washer until it turned a pale gold. The flux dissolved into the joint with a flash of acidic smoke, and the brazing rod glowed cherry red with a crust of black just before it turned molten and started to run under the torch. Dad backed the flame away a little and used the pressure of the gas like an invisible hand to push the brass ahead of it, all around the joint.

"Okay, now you do it." I did. The flow pattern wasn't perfect, but the joints were filled. "Not, bad," he said, "not bad, young brazier Jack. Now, we should be gettin the hell outta here." He looked at the watch on his wrist, "Christ, 3:15. We really gotta get a move on before the foreman shows up. Here," he said as he threw me the keys, "hustle out and get the car and drive it in while I sweep up around here."

I was a truck when it came to the 100 yard dash, but I ran like hell, just the same.

Sitting on the sofa with your arm strapped to your chest is pretty boring. The paper gives out really quick, and it's tough to read a novel, even Joyce, or mainly Joyce, with your head full of pain killers and blood thinners. All you can do, really, is stare out the window at the row houses across the street that look just the same as yours. You go into a waking dream; without trying, the memories, the echoes, come. One, though, I don't think was a memory, unless it was bred in the bone.

There were three of us. We all had South Armagh accents. It was raining and dark. Our breath made steam in the air. In the distance, far off, the rattle of a machine gun. We were kneeling in the muck, looking through a gap in a hedge. Each of us had an old Webley pistol, just like the one Cary Grant carried in *Gunga Din,* just like the one granpop used to have when he was in Dublin. Across the road, the customs shed was in flames. The Royal Ulster Constabulary had taken five more of us prisoner. One at a time, they made each man lie, face down, on the road and, laughing, shot him in the head before moving on to the next one. Something granpop told me? Something I read? Don't know. What I did know, somehow, was that this scene made me who I was.

The other was definitely a memory, clear and sharp. I must have been about eight or nine. Me and dad and Mark drove down to Connie Mack Stadium on a sunny Saturday to watch the Philadelphia Athletics lose to the White Sox. Matt didn't come. He was over at church practising the organ with mom. Dad didn't seem to mind, but sometimes with him it was hard to tell.

Lehigh Avenue had meters on it, so he parked the Ford up behind on Stella Street where there weren't any. As we fell in with all the people walking toward the park that loomed like a dark, berthed ship ahead of us, we passed three men standing together. They had butts hanging from their lips and denim jackets slung over the shoulders of their white T-shirts. The one with the green sunglasses had a pack of Lucky Strikes rolled up in his sleeve. On the backs of their heads, they wore pilot's hats with winged wheels in the center.  Lined up at the curb were three massive, shiny motorcycles, with fringed leather saddlebags.  My mouth was open, "Catchin flies," granpop called it.  Mark didn't care about them.  He ran ahead of us to look at some soldiers in uniform.

After the league championship game in '62—hotter than hell—by the stands dad was talking to two men in heavy suits. Face red as an apple, he held his thick, rope-muscled arms tight against his sides with his big hands balled into tight fists. He spun away from them and walked over to me.  "See those assholes, Jack?"  "Yeh, the nuts in suits.  What about em?" "Stay clear of them if I'm not around.  They're *Clann na Gael*. Trust me; they'll break your heart."

## 2. Curve Ball

"Hiya, dad, how ya feelin?"

"I'm fine, kid, fine. Matt just left; came down from the seminary. Mark's been here, too. Why haven't you been over yet? I'm not gonna die, ya know. Take the trolley tomorrow. It's Saturday, and you won't have much to do at the gas station in the morning."

"Okay, dad, I'll make it. Promise."

His voice sounded weak, tired. The heart attack was massive, and Dr. Ray said he'd had quite a few before, but never said anything.

Mom didn't wake me, so I slept late on Saturday. I seemed to feel worn out all the time. When I got to the bottom of the stairs, I could see them all in the living room: mom on the sofa, staring straight ahead, listening; Matt in his black junior priest suit, his look almost pleased; Mark in his uniform, jaw set; Uncle Joe, Uncle Mark, and their wives and kids. Granmom was fingering the white beads of the rosary blessed at Fatima; her lips moving to the Hail Marys. Father McLaughlin was standing in the kitchen doorway, smiling, sipping coffee, gossiping pleasantly with Mr. Flaherty, the undertaker. Two men I didn't know leaned against the wall with beers in their hands. Their dark suits were heavy. Nobody had to tell me who they were. You could almost smell the gun oil on their hands. I ran back up the stairs and into the bathroom. Once the door was shut, I just couldn't stop laughing, then the blood red haze came over my eyes and I punched a hole in the plaster. Didn't go back down until the bleeding stopped and the haze drifted into the back of my skull.

The funeral mass took too long, and Father McLaughlin almost didn't make it through. The church smelled sickly of thick incense. The priest walked down the aisle and put his fat hand on dad's copper-colored casket, expensive, fancy, paid for by his union friends. The black vestments were embroidered with silver thread, and the white of the surplice underneath was blindingly pure.

Big Jack Kavanagh was a fine man and a good Catholic. God has his own plans for him, just like he has for each and every one of us. It pleased the Lord to take Jack home to Him, so we should not mourn, we should not grieve, because the ways of God are mysterious. As mere mortals, it might seem hard to us. As mortals, it may even seem unjust. But as Catholics, we know nothing could be further from the truth. We are not privy to God's plan, and it is not for us to presume to fathom his goodness and love for us. God, in his wisdom, has taken Jack Kavanagh home to heaven, as he will each and every one of us, but only if we believe in and obey Holy Mother Church. It is to the Church that you must turn for guidance and understanding and interpretation of all that appears mysterious in God's ways. Only within the bosom of the Church can we count on salvation. Nowhere else. I repeat, *nowhere* else. Only as true Catholics can we enter into the kingdom of heaven.

The priest was just warming up the sales pitch, but I was going to strangle him first. I could hear granpop's voice clear as a bell: "Priests and the women they control, Jacko, they're our crosses to bear." I sat in the front pew with Matt on my left and Mark on my right. Matt had a smiling, hypnotized look on his face. Mark's jaw was set, and I could tell he was pissed, too. I just couldn't hack it, and I was on my way over the pew.  I was just as big as Mark, six two, but he'd been through a lot of training and was in incredible shape.  Just as I started to move, his big hand shot out and caught my fore-arm.  The grip was so tight, I thought the blood would stop flowing to my hand.  He leaned over and whispered, "I'd like to get my hands on that fat throat, too, Jack, but it ain't worth it.  Dad's gone; that's it.  Who gives a shit about what the priest says?  All we gotta worry about is mom and granmom.  Member what dad said: 'Button yer lip and keep the peace until the time comes.'  It's a wise thing to remember.  Retaliate when the time is right for victory."

He didn't let go of my arm until we got up to walk behind the casket.  Outside, Matt said to the steel gray sky: "What a beautiful sermon."  Mark looked at me, wide-eyed, and I looked at Matt.  "Bullshit," I said.  Matt's stare told me he knew I needed professional help.

Uncle Harry sat at the upright piano.  Granmom brought it over in '56 when granpop was killed in Ireland, and she gave up the place in Fishtown.  We called him Uncle Harry, but he wasn't really; he was an O'Faolain, granmom's cousin.  As usual, there was a glass of the Irish nearby. He was about sixty, a skinny, bald, red-haired, sandy man with a beak like a ball peen hammer and a soft, breathy Tourmakeady brogue. In the family, it was gospel you never talked religion or the IRA with him. He hated priests just as much as he loved and supported the Brotherhood and the Democratic Party. Around the piano stood Uncle Mark, bombed, and Father McLaughlin, very red in the face. They were singing along with Uncle Harry; all three had good tenor voices.

Uncle Joe was sticking to beer, so he was in pretty good shape in the kitchen. Father Liam, granmom's brother, was sitting at the Formica table, drinking tea. He was close to eighty, and the older he got, the less he washed. I think he only had one black robe; it was shiny and spotted. He was a monk from the old country, but the Redemptorists shipped him to the States a few years before for some reason or other.

Uncle Joe wasn't sober and he wasn't drunk, but he was into starting trouble. It was one of his greatest strengths. "So, Liam, Uncle Harry tells me the British interned you in Long Kesh. Just marched right off Sandy Row into the Clonard and pulled you out. That true?"

"Aye, it is, Joseph. May God forgive them."

"How long were you in for anyway?"

"It was eighteen months and three days."

"What was their excuse? I mean, arresting a seventy-five year old man of the cloth seems kinda stupid, even for the English."

"Oh, well, they had this notion that I was using the monastery to store arms that came through the Gap of the North in Armagh. Your father's country."

"They didn't charge you with that, did they?"

"No, they did not. They didn't charge me with anything, thanks be to God, because lying is a mortal sin."

"Aw, come on, Liam, you're not tellin me it was true?"

"About the arms, you mean? Oh, aye. We lost a bit of fine gelignite that day. Come sit by me, and we'll talk some sedition. Young Jack, you join us too. It's time you learned your history. Get him a beer Joseph and me a dram, and give me your cigarettes." Father Liam shook out a Camel for me. I packed the end on my left fist, just like dad.

Mom's brother, Germy Donahue, had come in from Brooklyn for the funeral; her parents refused to set foot in Philly, and they never could stand dad, alive or dead. They were what granpop called "Free-Staters." In Ireland, they supported the Anglo-Irish treaty that partitioned the North; in

New York they were for a political solution to Northern Ireland. "Bloody traitors," granpop used to say, "force is the only thing the Brits understand."

Germy was in the living room, near the open door to the kitchen. He was a short, balding, black haired man with a tremendous beer gut and a New York accent so thick sometimes I couldn't understand him. Now, he was drunk as a skunk and talking loud: "The Kavanaghs will never learn. We're Americans now. All that shit about 'fightin fer the faith' is long over, and we have no business in Irish politics anymore. Just look at the Devlins. They got it right. The hell with the IRA and their fundraising thugs. We'd be better off thinkin about how to keep the niggers in their place. Anyhow, we've got bigger fish to fry and better jobs to get where the collars are white, not blue. Stop livin in the past. Get on with it. And try not to be so fuckin stupid."

The two men in the heavy suits were making for him, but Uncle Joe was out of his chair like a shot. He reached around the door jamb and picked Uncle Germy up by the lapels. He carried him to the back wall of the kitchen, by the back door, and slammed him up against it.

"Jack, shut the door, quick, and don't let anybody in until I say."

I heard my brother, Mark, on the other side of the door: "Stay out of it, priest. It's none a yer bizness. You two guys relax. We'll take carea this. Sit down, Matt, there's nothing for you to do now. The men will take care of it."

Uncle Joe turned back to Uncle Germy, whose feet were still off the floor, and held him up so their faces were very close together. Through his teeth, he said: "Lissen, you little prick, you *do not* talk like that about this family. *You* do not talk that way in front of the women. You *do not* come here and show disrespect to the best man that ever was. *You*, fuck face, do not talk down to any of us, you lace curtain Irish asshole. You wanna forget who you are, that's your fuckin business. We don't. Don't you ever mention the Devlin name in front of me again. If Big Jack was still alive, he'd pull your head off like a chicken. If my father was alive, he'd kneecap you for badmouthin the cause and suckin up to the Devlins. Those two *Clann* guys out there would be pleased to put a bullet in yer gut if we asked nicely. Me, I'm just gonna take you out the back and kick yer fuckin ass. Then, if ya can still walk, you can hop on your bike and get the fuck back to New

York. *You* will never show your face to me again, if ya like breathin for a livin."

Uncle Joe opened the back door and kicked Uncle Germy down the stairs to the laneway and followed calmly, a set look on his face. Father Liam sipped his Jameson slowly, rolling it over his tongue, a serene look on his face. "Ah, Jack, your grandfather was a grand man of the old sort. It's not over with the Devlins just yet, even the ones from Tipperary." Father McLaughlin pounded on the kitchen door: "Let me in. This is absurd." I looked to my grand-uncle. He shook his head, smiling, so I held my shoulder against it until Uncle Joe came back. He was out of breath, and his knuckles were skinned, but there wasn't a mark on his face. He went to the refrigerator, took out a Piels, sat down and nodded for me to open the door.

Everybody was gone. Only me and mom and granmom were left in the living room. Granmom was rocking back and forth, her arms cradling her sides. She was keening lowly in the back of her throat. I don't think mom moved the whole night.

Minute after silent minute passed. Without dad, none of us knew what to say or do or think. Outside—or maybe in my head—the clatter of hooves on stone, the whistle of high tide, wind driven. Wasn't the first time, wouldn't be the last. I parted the Venetian blinds; the street was quiet. My head felt hollow. Finally, mom turned to me, her face off-white, grainy, like the newspaper: "Jackie, I didn't tell you but his insurance lapsed. There'll be some money from the union; the school might give us a break on tuition; maybe something from granpop's fundraising friends. Matt can't help, and neither can Mark, right now, so you'll have to get a better job than the one at the gas station.

"Mr. Dubinsky stopped by. I couldn't invite him or Irene to the funeral, of course, because they're Jewish. He wouldn't come in, of course, but he did say he heard they're hiring at a new motorcycle shop down near Rising Sun and Old York. It's somewhere around the hospital. You've always liked them, and maybe you can get something better. I guess college is out for a while. I'll probably have to sell the house and find something cheaper."

"Okay, mom, I'll go down there tomorrow. We'll be okay. Promise. I'll drop out if I have to."

"No, your father wouldn't have that. No, no. Finish up." She paused, looked straight ahead and cocked her head.

Without looking at me, she said: "Did you hear it, Jackie?" Her eyes seemed to have sunk into her skull.

"Hear what, mom? Uncle Joe? Yeh, he was great. I know Germy's your brother and all that, but he deserved it."

"No, I mean the banshee's knock. Your granmom heard it in the cemetery. I heard it here, but I didn't tell Father McLaughlin. He wouldn't approve."

"The hell with what the priest says, mom."

She blessed herself quickly: "May God forgive you this day."

The shop was on Schiller Street, just south of Tioga, near Rising Sun Avenue. The sign outside read: "Rising Sun Triumph❖BSA❖Norton." The place used to be a gas station, but somebody put an extension out the back to make a bigger shop. I wandered in and looked around. About ten feet away, a very thin, tall man in black jeans and T-shirt was standing at a bench with his back to me. An engine was apart in front of him. I stood and watched, until he said without turning. "Hey, man, something on your mind? Speak, prophet, or forever hold your peace."

"Yeh, lookin for a job. I'll work any hours you got on anything you want."

His accent wasn't Philly or New York or Irish or Southern or anything I'd heard before. His voice was flat and low, and he spoke slowly. He turned. His thick, black hair stood straight up from his flat forehead. The cheekbones were unusually high; the black eyes slightly slanted, almost invisible eyebrows. The skin on his face was the color of coffee with cream, large pockmarks covered his neck. He was about thirty, had a scraggly goatee and might have been Puerto Rican or Mexican. He looked me up and down, slowly, expressionless.

"Well, you're big enough and strong enough, that's certain. You're pretty young, though. Got your license?"

I reached for my wallet with a nod.

He held up a flat, oily palm: "Desist. I believe you. Ever worked on bikes before? Can you ride one? What kind of work have you done before? Do you have a name?"

"Name's Jack Kavanagh. Live over near Olney. Work part time at a gas station up on Ogontz, but I gotta make more money than that. I can braze, and I'm good with my hands. I been crazy about bikes since I was a little kid. One a my uncles used to ride an Indian, but, no, I can't ride one and never worked on anything but junky Fords.  Please, mister, I really need the work.  I'll do anything you got."

"Relax, man, calm yourself.  Breathe from the diaphragm; you'll live longer.  As the great poet Moondog once said to me: 'Slow down, traveler in the night, and the destination will come to you.'  It's true I need help.  It's true you need work.  The question remains: do these two truths agree, revolve like the Tao, or conflict?  These are deep questions that only the poets can resolve.

"Yes, I'll call Allen in New York tonight to get the Ginsberg on the situation.  In the meantime, you will see against the far wall four crates from the shrine of motorcycledom, Great Britain, birthplace of my phoenix, my Vincent Black Shadow.  Above them on the wall, you will also spy a crowbar and a hammer.  I assume you know how to use those implements without damaging the contents or yourself.  If you would be so good as to open those crates and begin rudimentary assembly, I will see to it you get paid for your efforts. "

"That mean I have a job?"

"It does.  I can always tell when the karma is good.  You will start at $2.50 an hour.  Once you get good enough setting up the new machines, you'll go on piece work. You'll make more bread, and I will get the new bikes on the showroom floor faster. Do you have any tools of your own?"

"Some from my dad, but they're mostly too big for this kinda work. What're the hours, anyway?"

"But fleeting moments in the continuum, my son. The poet said, *Carpe Deum*, umm, *Diem*, yeah that's right. I don't insist on regular hours around here—restricts the mental juices. I'll get you a key so you can do your set-ups when you want. It doesn't matter in the scheme of things. Of course, we must learn to ride, and we must have a helmet. Mustn't we? That's the only rule. Wearing a lid is the best way I know to keep your brains and your shit together at the same time. Choose a good one from the case in the showroom. You can pay it off as you go. You will need your own tools if you plan to make a living at this. Fortunately, I have a compatriot who is very lucky at finding things that fall off the back of the Snap-On truck."

He wiped his hands on an orange shop rag, came over to me and offered his hand. As we shook, he said, "My name is Jose; some people call me Hose. I answer to both, but I prefer Hose. My girlfriend, Chica, says it's more descriptive.

The hands are good, Jack, you'll go far. That flash in your hair is a bit on the white magic side, don't you think? By the way, why do you wear it so short? You look like a soldier."

We were in the alley out the back, dumping the drain oil into the gravel. It was 6:30 on a Saturday evening in July, the first summer after I graduated from high school. The air was so thick with burnt oil fumes and humidity, you'd think about heading for the nearest storm drain to puke. Hose said, "Young warlock, Kavanagh, I think the end of week ritual is in order. Let us move into the shadow of yonder trash bin and partake of some communication with the gods and poets of Ireland. Perhaps we will hear some horsemen pass by, or maybe the banshee will float past. Just kidding."

He opened the plastic sandwich bag, stuck his nose in it and took a deep sniff. "Ahh, reminds me of a Jamaican sunset. Here, Robin Roberts, take a snort of sun, surf and miracles." It smelled like perfume; the tight, little, gray-green buds looked like clumps of mown grass left in the sun to dry. Hose took out some Zig-Zag papers and rolled a skinny joint. He took a drag, held in the smoke, then let it out slowly. "Yes, there are hoof beats in the air, but they're friendly. Here you go, Jack, have a toot."

The smoke was so thick, acrid and sharp I almost coughed up a lung at first. As we passed the joint back and forth, my mind seemed to go into first gear, and the words we spoke echoed in the back of my skull. We were sitting on top of the trash bin. Hose was singing: "'There is a house in New Orleans, they call the Rising Sun. It's been the ruin of many a young man. And, God, I know I'm one.' ‡ Well, Jack, how's the baseball gig going? Broken wing any better?"

It seemed to take a long time to order the words. "It's okay, I guess, but I don't think we'll win the championship again. Lost too many good players. Mostly the draft. Course, I don't get much time to practise with all the work I'm doin. No fastball left, anyhow. All I can throw is junk to set up a little cutter."

"Would such a life attract you, Jack? Beat up bus trips from Louisville to Syracuse to dusty whistle stops in nowheresville? It's a fine thing to see the land, but maybe not just that way. I know you dreamed of pitching in the majors,

‡*Song: Traditional/Alan Price.*

but it's a long, slow road for all but the best. Besides, young warlock, you're a marked man with that flash in your hair. Magical. Do your brothers have that?

"You have the instincts to become a fine mechanic. I've never seen anybody take to the innards of a four stroke engine so quickly. What that means, in the end, is that you'll have a very portable and valuable trade, so you could go anywhere and find work. Mexico, Canada, England, Europe, Ireland, they're all at your feet once you have a bit more experience.

"That reminds me; I have a book by my buddy Jack you have to read. It'll teach you everything you need to know about being on the road. Are you pitching next weekend?"

"Not startin, no, because I pitch Wednesday night over in Torresdale. I get a week's rest. But the coach likes me on the bench for long relief when it's needed."

"Make an excuse. Instead, we should head to New York for a weekend of musical and intellectual stimulation. You have too much rock and roll in your head, Buddy Holly, and it's time you heard some good old blues and folk. If I hear *Poison Ivy* one more time, I'm gonna go bonkers. An acquaintance of mine, one Dave Van Ronk, will be playing in the Village. His fingers are magical. His voice is like gravel falling out the back of a dump truck. I'll take Chica on the back of the Shadow. We'll disconnect the speedo on one of the new Bonnys, and you can ride it. Why don't you ask Rene of the profound Semitic face and great knockers to join you?"

For some reason, it all sounded incredibly funny. I couldn't stop laughing. Hose jumped off the trash bin, went into the shop and came back with two Pepsis and an enormous bag of potato chips. We munched away silently for a few minutes. The salt tasted like a dive in the Atlantic, the Pepsi bubbles exploded on my tongue.

"Yeh, Hose, I could ask her. Might be fun. Let's see what I can do with the coach."

"Far fucking out. A done deal. What's up with the hero, Jack?"

"He just went back. Tells me we have to keep the commies from taken over the jungle."

"He believes that? Thought he was too smart for that jive."

"So did I, Hose, so did I. But sometimes he's like my old man. Hard to tell what he thinks."

"And the future Pope? What's his excuse."

"Oh, man, don't get me started. He's my brother and all, but I sure can't stand that 'I am the word' shit. I always thought Jesuits were assholes; now my brother's one. Weird."

"Now that, Jacko, I agree with entirely. So, come on, what's the answer?"

"What answer? Oh, yeah, no they don't have the white mark. Only I do."

"Where? You're going where?" mom asked.

"Up to New York with Jose, mom. We're gonna go to a concert up there and stay with some friends of his. I'll be back later on Sunday. Talked to the coach, and he said I needed some time off, anyway. It'll be fun, and I haven't had much lately. You haven't either. Why don't you take the test and get your license, finally, then take granmom down to Margate for a few days later on? Or I could drive you down. Maybe I could come up with the money."

"Oh, Jack, I don't know. It looks like the house will sell, so we'll probably be taking that little place up in Manayunk. Maybe the money will be there for a few days downashore, but I'm not sure right now. Jose does seem like a good man, even though he isn't really an American; he's certainly been a good teacher to you. I guess it'll be alright. How will you get there?"

"Dunno. Maybe Jose's truck or maybe the train."

"Just be back by Sunday night. Shouldn't you get your hair cut first? And remember, no beer, even though it's legal at nineteen in New York."

"Okay, mom, okay. Sure."

"Where you going now?"

"Over to Irene's and see how she's makin out."

Mom wrinkled her nose. "She's always liked you, Jackie, but wouldn't you be better off with a nice Catholic girl?"

"Aw, cut it out, mom. We're just friends." I wanted to go to New York, had to go, for fun and to find out just what was going on in Ireland, and New York had the only Irish-American papers worth anything. Dad wouldn't have liked it if I went to the *Clann* in Philly. Since he died, it seemed really important for me to find out whether I sided with granpop and my uncles, or dad. Took a long time.

## 3. "HOUSE OF THE RISING SUN"

Hose locked up the shop at 2 on Saturday afternoon, and we took off. Chica looked over at me with a wide grin on her lovely Puerto Rican face. Her arms were tight around Hose. We were heading north, up Roosevelt Boulevard to the Pennsy Turnpike, then east across the Delaware River at Bristol to connect with the Jersey Turnpike. As we drove toward Manhattan, I could feel Irene's arms around me; her breasts flattened against my back. The Bonneville was okay, but it was stock, and I knew I wouldn't be able to keep up with Hose if he made a move. The big Vincent wasn't even breathing hard at 70.

We got through Newark, the dump, fast enough so you could hold your breath most of the way. When we got to Jersey City, we turned east on Pulaski Skyway and headed for the Holland Tunnel. The air was pretty clear for a change, so the view of Manhattan from the skyway was incredible in the late afternoon summer sunshine. We took the slick ramp down to the damp tunnel entrance. Inside, it always looked like the Hudson River was just about to flood it. The lighting was terrible, so I pulled off my green face shield and stuffed it in my denim jacket. The traffic was heavy, and the air stank like the inside of a carbon-filled muffler. Stop and go in a tunnel on a motorcycle can make you feel pretty woozy, so it was a relief to get out onto Canal Street. We turned north on Lafayette, between Soho and Little Italy, then cut over to First Street and First Avenue.

We pulled up on the sidewalk and got off outside what looked like an industrial building from the thirties. With a magician's flourish, Hose yanked an orange shop rag from his back pocket and carefully wiped a film of oil off one of the hot heads of the Vincent. "Here we are, a wayside inn for weary travelers. This is my buddy's place. I have a key, so let's make ourselves at home. After we hit Bleeker Street tonight, we'll have to secure the iron, but they're okay here for now. Let us regard the Big Apple and dig the worms. In we go."

You had two choices: down some steps into the breeze-way and the bottom floor, or up the steps to the second, third and fourth floors. The place had been used for something like garment making, but now it was chopped into shotgun apart-ments. The hallway smelled like the mens in a Jersey road-house. Beat up galvanized garbage cans with apartment numbers on them lined the wall. Hose pounded on the door of Apartment 1 and yelled, "Open, innkeeper, your guests have arrived bearing gifts of frankincense and myrrh." No answer, so Hose opened the police lock in the center of the door with his key. "Wheels is a night person, so maybe he's still crashed or maybe he's practising up in Harlem. Aha, a new wrinkle, must have been more break-ins nearby; Wheels has cleverly installed another lock. Have no fear; this situation can be remedied." He took a thin piece of plastic from the inside pocket of his black leather jacket, slid it between the door and the jamb, and slipped the second lock. The bar of the police lock slid in its frame as we walked in.

Except for the refrigerator, the business parts of the kitchen hadn't been used for a very long time. Paper containers of Chinese food leaked grease on the table. Empty quarts of beer stood in the gruesome, shallow sink. The tall windows were just above street level; they looked out over our bikes and across the street. We walked through to the living room; it was a jumble of beat up armchairs and pillows; a guitar, books and copies of the *Village Voice* littered the floor. There was a Heathkit stereo and hundreds of records stacked on shelves below it, large speakers to either side. On one wall was a torn poster of Karl Marx.  Leaning against the wall below it were two 2x6" boards about twelve feet long, the edges joined together with cleats to make a plank. A large oil stain in the center of the floor had been sprinkled with Oil Dry. The bathroom was in a sort of temporary cardboard closet, like you get from U-Haul to move your clothes in.

Hose took a quick look around.  "His bike's gone so he must be out visiting. Young Jack and my Biblical Irene, dig this, we must observe the rules of the house.  Through that door is Wheels' and his old lady's bedroom.  Behind that are two more rooms.  You two can have the one all the way at the back. You'll get a great view of the airway.  Chica and I will occupy the one in the middle.  The heat requires that the doors remain open at night. Etiquette requires that you become blind and deaf when coming though other people's domiciles heading for the can.  Other than that, we have the run of the place.  You guys settle in; I'll step out and pick up some sandwiches and beer."

Outside the kitchen windows, a gentle rain of black ash began.  It lasted about forty-five minutes as the sun declined and shadows took over the streets.   Around 6:00 Hose said,

"Children, let us regard the Wall Street parade that is about to begin. I give it five minutes more or less. "

Across the street was a building much like the one we were in, except it had chintz curtains on the windows. Cabs started dropping off men in narrow-lapelled Midtown suits, brushed snap-brim hats and shiny shoes; they walked in, one after the other. "It will take a while for them to prepare, but we'll be able to catch the show before we split for the Village."

Now Irene, my 'Ruth amid the alien corn,' James Joyce here is familiar with legends and rituals, but I don't think you are. I will begin one now that will amuse you as a new experience. Do not fret if you begin to feel a bit strange afterwards; that is the point."

Hose took out the sandwich bag and the Zig-Zags. Irene's eyes were wide when she looked at me, but I just smiled and nodded. Chica put on a record. Hose said, "It's a Robert Johnson tune, Jack, *Last Fair Deal Gone Down*, sung by Muddy Waters. After, we will sample some immortal Van Ronk." He took a couple of quick tokes, passed the joint to Irene and started rolling another. She took a hit and passed it to me. Her hand was rubbing the inside of my thigh, just below the zipper on my black jeans.

"Yes, young lovers, there will be world enough and time for that, but first we must dig the conga line. It should be about time for the first arrivals to sashay out and depart for their sundry haunts."

The big windows were wide open, but the air wasn't moving. The small fan only worked sometimes. Outside, they minced down the steps in twos and threes, hailed cabs and waved to their friends hanging out the windows. They looked like part of the maraca number in an Xavier Cougat movie. I was looking for Carmen Miranda. Irene started it, then the laughters got us all. Chica stood in the tall window, pulled up her T-shirt, put both hands on her big, black bra cups and called, "Hey, Chiquita Banana, don't you wish yours were real like these?"

The one with the feather boa laughed and called back, "Not me honey, I've got what the boys really want. You just get your big, tough motorcycle men to give us a ride on those bikes. We'll show them a really good time. I'd just love to have that big black machine between my legs." He grabbed his crotch through the skirt and looked up in ecstasy. "Oooh, Rita, you saucy bitch," lisped his partner in the purple sheath and blond wig, "you're such a silly fabish, and you're sooo easy. Come along or we'll be late for the party." In the windows, their friends laughed and waved and whistled. They jumped in a cab and sped off, waving their hairy, bangled arms out the windows.

Rene was choking, but when she finally got it under control, she asked Chica: "Aren't there laws against that? I mean, they don't seem to care who sees them. Don't the cops do anything?"

"Honey, we're not in the fifties anymore, and this is New York. You don't get out enough. You ever been down at 13$^{th}$ and Locust in Philly late on a Saturday night? It ain't much different. Sure, the cops raid the bars once in a while. Maybe beat up a couple for kicks. Maybe shake em down for a few bucks. Mostly, they ignore em. Course, the wives and kids up in New Rochelle, think the girls across the street are working over the weekend on some important deal. It's their business, I guess, but they sure are funny." She imitated the exaggerated walk, hips swaying to the stereo.

The laughter started again. Hose passed around the second spliff. "Hey, my Philly Maria, it's your turn to step down to the corner and pick up some more beer and some pickles and some chips and some sour cream and stuff. We have a ways to go before we head out to the Gaslight.  Put on some BB King on the way out. You two lovebirds head for your room, but no later than 8:00, okay.  We gotta be over on Bleeker by 9 or we won't get a seat.  I'll keep the tunes coming to maintain the mood."

The first thing Irene did when I closed the door was pull up her T-shirt and hold the white lace cups of her bra, just like Chica.  Then she reached behind her, undid the hooks and fell back, laughing, on the rumpled mattress on the floor.  This time we didn't have to stand up, and I didn't have to pick leaves out of her hair before we walked home from Hunting Park.

Around 8, we found Hose in the kitchen rolling another joint.  We passed it around, but I took it easy because I'd never driven high when I didn't know where I was.  It was a good thing we didn't have far to go. We went out on the pavement, kicked the bikes over and drove across the Bowery and Broadway to the West Side.  The exhaust pipes were very loud, and Rene was heavy against my back.  We parked near Washington Square in a line of motorcycles on the pavement.  In the square, somebody was playing a flute.  Slowly, we strolled down Sullivan, hung a right on Bleeker and headed for MacDougal Street. The sidewalks were packed with hipsters and poets, college kids from NYU, tourists looking up a lot, street people looking down and beat cops looking around.

The Gaslight was about half full when we got there. It was a narrow, tiny little place, with round tables and bentwood chairs. We took a table pretty near the stage. The air was already thick with tobacco smoke. Hose ordered iced mocha javas all around. The crowd was mainly younger than Hose, but older than me and Irene, mid- twenties, Chica's age. The men and women, black and white, bent to each other and spoke intently across the tables. There was a murmur of conversation, the odd burst of laughter, but mostly it was quietly serious. A thick set man with a sandy full beard threaded his way among the tables, pulled up a chair and sat down with us.

"Hose, my main man, how are you, oh exile in the wilds of Philly? Chica, my darling, you remain lovely as always. It's great to see you both. I hope you don't have a heat problem with the narcs anymore, Jose; the management definitely would not approve. What do I spy here, two of the younger generation come to be educated about real music?  Or are you two robbing the cradle?"

"We're both very cool just now, Dave.  The heat is off for the moment by the way.  I'm just keeping my head down in southerly climes for a while.  This is Jack Kavanagh, fledgling motorcycle mechanic at my place, and his dusky damsel, Irene Dubinsky.

Jack, Rene, meet Dave Van Ronk, tonight's headliner, finger picker extraordinaire and Folkways recording artist.  Dave, who's the front man tonight?"

"We got lucky.  It's Son House; I got him to come down from Rochester for a few weeks. Sam Charters will be on washtub with me as usual, and a young friend of mine, Bob Dylan, will play harp.  It should be an interesting couple of sets.  Any requests, young visitors?"

"Give it up, Dave, they'll ask for the Everly Brothers or the Coasters.  You can do one for us, though, how about *Yas-Yas-Yas*.  It'll be like old times."

"My pleasure, Hose.  Why don't the four of you come over to my place after the last set?  They'll be a lot of old friends around, Hose, and Chica can hold court and drive the men wild. Jack and Irene will have to fend for themselves, but it looks like they'll leave with the one that brought them."

Son House came on. He was bent and shrivelled and didn't have many teeth. The lyrics lived rather than known, the thick, cotton picker fingers pulling impossible notes from the cheap guitar, the hush of the crowd were unlike anything I had ever seen or heard before. Rene's mouth was open; so was mine. Across the table, Hose leaned back in his chair, smiling.

After House finished up, Hose said across the table: "Ahh, the Delta gods are smiling down on us tonight, warlock Jack. He's not even sixty, but he looks a hundred. Treasure up this night, both of you. Now, how's about another mocha java? Unfortunately, they don't sell beer, and the food's as lousy as it is pricey."

Van Ronk was a technician. His guitar was precise, perfect. The songs weren't out of any book I knew about: *Duncan and Brady, Black Mountain Blues, In the Pines, Careless Love* and a lot more. Hose was right; his voice was like gravel sliding on steel. Next to him on stage the skinny kid with the frizzy hair looked like he'd eaten a dozen week old oysters, but he played a pretty good harmonica. The guy on bass was a riot.  At the end of the last set, Van Ronk said to the crowd, "I'd like to do an old favorite for an old friend of mine in the crowd, his bewitching girlfriend and their two acolytes.  It's about a confused chicken and goes like this:"

*Mama bought a chicken, well she thought it was a duck,*
*Put him on the table with his legs sticking up,*
*Now in comes Sis with a spoon and a glass,*
*And starts dishing out the gravy from his yas-yas-yas.*

*Mama, mama, take a look at Sis,*
*You know she's out on the levee and she's dancing like this,*
*Well now, come on in here Sis, and come in here fast,*
*And stop that shaking your yas-yas-yas.*

*Well, the old folks do it and the young folks too,*
*And the old folks show the young folks just what to do,*
*Well now you shake your shoulders, you shake them fast,*

*And if you can't shake your shoulders, shake your yas-*
*yas-yas.‡*

When we got to the sidewalk, the air was a tiny bit fresher than inside the Gaslight. We ambled over to Washington Square, found a dark spot under the trees, away from the arch, and passed another joint around before we started for Van Ronk's apartment.

We never did see Van Ronk. Very few people were sitting down, because there just wasn't room. The spade dude with the beret and cigarette holder was saying with a lilt, "Well, now that Kennedy is in, you'll see what happens to the brothers in Southeast Asia. It'll be cannon fodder time, just like it always is." Across the room, the blond woman in sunglasses said, "I can't agree. Ferlenghetti has much more to say to *me* than Whitman ever will. Next, you be asking me to read Melville, again. Really!" Near her a fat man in a full beard proclaimed to the room: "Zionism is not the problem. It's the Russians, goddamn it. They've lost their Leninist

‡*From "Dave Van Ronk Sings, Volume 2." Folkways Records,*
*Album #FA2383, 1961.*

vision.  Hoover has no reason to target them; they're both visionaries.  We're the ones living in a police state."

Me and Rene squatted against the wall near the door. "Jack, can you think?  I can't."  I shook my head:  "My brain's stuck."

Across from us, the harmonica player did the same.  He stared into space, looking lost and mad about it.  Hose and Chica moved among the crowd shaking hands.  Many of the men hugged her hard.  She was loving every minute of it. Guitars started on the far side of the room.  We couldn't see who was singing, but we could hear the words because the crowd quieted a bit.

It was a black man's voice, deep, low and rich:

> *There is a House in New Orleans*
> *They call the Rising Sun,*
> *It's been the ruin of many a poor boy,*
> *and god I know I'm one.*

Hose and Chica made their way toward us.

> *Oh mothers, tell your children,*

*Not to do what I have done*
*Spend my life in fear and misery*
*In the House of the Rising Sun.*

"Chica, keep the Shadow running, while I go upstairs." We were on the pavement on First Street again. Hose sprinted up the steps, threw open one of the kitchen windows and slid out the plank. He beckoned to me with a grin: "Put it in second, Jack, and just chug on up here. I'll catch the bars; no sweat. Just remember to duck under the window frame."

I was stoned enough that it seemed funny, not dangerous, even though I knew if I stalled or lost my balance there was nowhere to land but in the breezeway below. Hose grabbed the bars at the top of the plank; we lifted the Bonneville onto the floor and parked it next to a Harley Sportster. "You should see Wheels do this stunt, man, he doesn't need help, just comes in full bore and stomps the rear brake when he hits the floor. Anyway, you hold for me now. I'll send the girls up, first."

"Hey, man, what's happenin?"

I turned to see a black guy in his forties. Wheels was about five six, 160, had wire rimmed glasses on the end of his nose, and his head was shaved clean as a cue ball. His voice was rough, cigarette hoarse: "I know it's a drag, man, but you leave the iron on the street in this neighborhood and there won't be nothin left but smokin bones in the AM. Dig what I'm sayin? I do believe Jose is on his way."

The Vincent was at least as heavy as the Harley, and we lifted it down from the windowsill and parked it in line in the living room.

On Sunday, I drove up to the Bronx by myself. I found out where to go before I left Philly: some of granpop's guys. First, I stopped into the Phoenix Bar for a beer and to ask where I could find what I was looking for. On the ride back to Philly, I had copies of two newspapers stuck in my waistband. The first was *An Phoblacht*, the IRA's Dublin mouthpiece; the second was the *Irish Voice*, published in New York. Later, it seemed to me that they really were speaking different languages, and I had to find out how to read both.

I'd been expecting it a long time, even though Matt was in the priesthood, Mark was already doing a tour in Vietnam and I was the last son. The letter came from The Selective

Service System: an Order to Report for Armed Forces Physical Examination. It said, simply:

> You are hereby directed
> to present yourself for
> Armed Forces Physical
> Examination by
> reporting to Local Board
> No. 327, 2266 Butler
> Avenue, Philadelphia,
> PA, on Nov. 3.

At the bottom, it read in bold capital letters:

> **IF YOU HAVE ANY PHYSICAL OR MENTAL CONDITION WHICH, IN YOUR OPINION, MAY DISQUALIFY YOU FOR SERVICE IN THE ARMED FORCES, BRING A PHYSICIAN'S CERTIFICATE DESCRIBING THAT CONDITION, IF NOT ALREADY FURNISHED TO YOUR LOCAL BOARD.**

Well, mental for sure, probably physical. We had a kind of family meeting about it. Granmom sat in the corner pretending to read her missal. Mom said I should be proud to serve the flag. Matt cleared his throat importantly and observed to the room, "Perhaps it will make a man of you, finally." Only Mark, home on leave, grim, tanned, tired, didn't seem to think so. "What for? We're not gonna win. Besides, they won't want you. Lucky, because you don't wanna be a soldier, do ya?"

There were about twenty of us milling around in the Selective Service office at the Legion. They packed us into a school bus with Cyclone fence over the windows and drove us up to the Armory on Broad Street. There must have been a thousand young guys like me wandering around. Some wore glasses so thick they bounced into walls. Others tried to carry purses along with them. Everybody had a story to tell why they weren't suitable to serve in the jungle. One kid had lost his left arm, and he said to anyone who would listen, "What the fuck am I doin here?" I was having Arlo Guthrie delusions.

About fifty of us sat at desks in a classroom for the tests, Jimbo McDevitt on my right. Freddie Devlin was up at the front. He turned in his desk, glowered at me and gave me the finger. There was a blue swastika tattooed on the back of his hand. At first, I shrugged at him. Far as I was concerned, all that was over a long time ago. Then I noticed from the pale skin on his face that he had shaved off a beard. "So it really was him in the Breyers truck," I thought. "I'll find that bastard after."

A big, shave-headed top-kick with lots of stripes marched in: "You boys lissen up. This here's an intelligence test. We know who you college boys are. If you fuck this up on purpose, you'll be in Nam so fast it'll make yer candy asses squirm. You long haired fags'll get the same treatment. You'll be on point first when the time comes." He grinned in my direction.

The test was a joke. There weren't any words, just pictures. In the left hand column might be a wood screw. In the right hand column was a choice of a hammer, a wrench, pliers and a screwdriver. We had to mark the right tool with an X.

Later, we stripped to our skivvies and stood in a large hall in long lines. Military doctors poked and prodded and told us to drop our drawers and spread our cheeks so they could have a close look.  One of them poked around at the scar on my shoulder. We got dressed, and one at a time went into little cubicles with army blanket walls.  Inside mine, a lieutenant with lots of spit and polish and razor sharp creases in his shirt sat behind a wooden desk with his head in his hand. There was no chair for the victim.  He looked up briefly, saw the stack of papers in my hand and frowned.

"All right, boy, let's see whatcha got.  I get so mucha this bullshit, I'm downright sick ta death.  Whatsa mattah wit you people, anyhow?   You should be damn proud to serve yer country, not weasel out on some sick ass excuse."

He swiped the papers from me with a roundhouse and looked through them lazily, his head back in his hand again. Then he started to pay attention, going back and forth in the pile a few times.  He looked up at me steadily with a mixture of disdain and pity.  "Son, in the Armed Forces of the Uuunahted States, we ain't got no room for long haired fuck ups and damaged personnel.  Only the best are allowed to serve.  You ain't fit even for latrine duty cause a them pins in yer arm.  Get out."

I gave that white-trash Arkansas share cropper Mark's best snap salute.  "Out, get the fuck outta here, before I call the

MPs," he growled. I turned on my heel with a grin and took off. Outside, the looks of worry, fear and downright revulsion were legion. Freddie Devlin seemed to have disappeared, but, still, I had an uncomfortable feeling I was being followed. I shook it off. On the way home, I sang to myself:

> *And I'll take my short revolver and my bandoleer of lead,*
> *I'll do or die I can try to avenge my country's dead.*
>
> *I'll leave aside my Mary, she's the girl I do adore,*
> *And I wonder will she think of me when she hears the rifles roar.*
>
> *And when the war is over, and old Ireland she is free*
> *I will take her to the church to wed, and a rebel's wife she'll be.‡*

Jeeps and Nate, the two cops who shook us down every week so we didn't get tickets, came in one afternoon in mid-

‡*Off to Dublin in the Green*, Anon.

January. Me and Hose were putting up some more peg board to hold the shop tools. They were in uniform and didn't look very friendly.

Big, sloppy, lots of free beer fat stuffed into their Philly cop storm trooper gear—black leather, tassels hanging from their gun belts, spit-shined riding boots. Rizzo's raiders.

Nate, the spade cop, stood in front of us, while Jeeps, the pasty faced Italian, went straight to Hose's tool box. He opened the bottom drawer, rummaged around and pulled out the sandwich bag. "Okay, Jose, we got you good this time. No use tryin to buy your way out again; we got orders. Just come along peaceful and nobody gets hurt."

Hose was up on the ladder. When he climbed down, he said to me very low as he passed: "Tell Chica, Arizona."

He was out on bail: $50,000 for possession for the purposes of trafficking. He wasn't a dealer. I knew it, and the cops knew it. Somebody dropped the dime on him, maybe to settle a score or make points in the precinct. I didn't know, and Hose didn't say. "I'll go down hard when I'm convicted, Jack, so I have no choice but to split. I talked to Nate on the way downtown, but they wouldn't let it slide, wouldn't do a cash settlement." I'm headed for Arizona tonight. That's where my people are from, but only you and Chica know it. You're welcome to come with me, if you want, but I don't think you'll leave your mother behind, will you?"

"Hose, you know I can't do that. She's got nobody, except me right now."

"Right, loyal to the end, young nobleman. Just be careful with it; it could bring you down. Dig this, then. Here is the phone number: memorize it, get a tattoo but don't keep the paper. You need a place to hide out, come. If you call, only say, 'Warlock for Ramirez,' nothing else, except a number where I can reach you. The hearing's not for a month, so Chica will sell what she can, pay off where need be before the sharks move in and then join me in the desert. Here's a hundred for you to tide you over. Oh, yeah, one more thing."

He went over behind the crates of new bikes and dragged out a heavy cardboard box. "Open it, mechanic Jack, it's for you. I was going to keep it till your birthday, but times they are a changing."

Inside was a brand new Snap-On tool box, the big, red one with all the graduated drawers. "I hear through the grapevine that they're hiring over in Germantown. Get your young ass over there in a week or so. Don't go hourly, stay flat rate.

You're ready.  Oh, and by the way, Jack, close your mouth.
It's a bad habit."

# 4. BROWNIE'S PAROLE

When you're a kid in Philadelphia, you play basketball during the winter.  Playgrounds from Torresdale to Fishtown, Germantown to South Philly, are full of kids learning the perfect turn-around jump shot, left jab and one-two combination.  I went to Immaculate Conception, where the nuns taught us how to see the world through Catholic eyes, made us buy pagan babies to save their souls and showed us ours in the *Baltimore Catechism*.  We were all like empty milk bottles—pure and clear—until terrible sins like playing with yourself put little stains in there and then you went to hell. Far as I could tell, then, we were all goners.

We were the lucky ones.  All the others—even the Episcopalians in Radnor—didn't have a chance.  They were against us.  Always would be. We were right. God was Catholic. We owned heaven. They couldn't stand it, so they kept all the money.

The nuns used clickers to make you do everything.  They'd get behind you and let you have it right in the ear.  Click— march, two by two, boys in one line, girls in another. Click,

click—kneel down in the dark wooden pews and breathe in the incense till you felt like passing out. More clicks and out to recess to play B-ball. Those clickers stay with you; they were hard, made out of oak turned on a lathe, and they came down on your head with a "thok" if you really screwed up. The only good thing you can say about it is at least there was some kind of order then.

Sister Asumpta had beautiful blue eyes that kind of smiled sometimes. Her pale, sad face looked out from her white and black hood. Her starched white bib spread like a pure paper moon over her black habit. She had more eyes in the back of her head. Janie had hair on her lip, but she had bumps on her chest. You better not get caught dropping your fountain pen so you could look up her uniform. That meant serious shit from the priest and a lot more in your milk bottle.

We played in the Catholic League and went to alien neighborhoods like Nicetown or Juniata Park to play other teams. The ref was always a priest. He'd stab you in the breastbone with his fingers when you mumbled "asshole" under your breath after he called you for a foul.

If you lost, you could always take on the other team in a real game with no priests around and no foul shots—on your home court where you knew just what the backboard would do to a bank shot. Lose again and you could show who was best with your fists. The Micks against the Pollocks, Puerto Ricans against the Wops—whatever. Didn't matter. We were all Catholics—right? Except for the Devlins, of course. They just couldn't forget. I seemed to be making a career out of beating the shit out of Freddie Devlin. He just couldn't get enough, on the court or off. His fat little brother I ignored when he mouthed me from half a block away. They had an older step-brother, but he was away somewhere. Anyhow, they lived in Kensington, so I didn't see them all that often, but Freddie did seem to show up at odd times, like he was following me.

At the playground, we found out how Frankie got laid—just twelve, too—when he got picked up hitching by a thirty-two year old blond. How Ricky from Mount Airy climbed a tree to peep in the convent windows at night. They caught him. He was never heard from again. And we wanted to believe. I was good at that, the wanting. Like almost all the men in the family, never was much for believing in anything other than a united Ireland—bred in the bone, I guess.

Sometimes I had to. I knew that Georgie blew himself up with the blasting caps he stole from the quarry shed when he visited his aunt in Jenkintown. The day before I saw him behind the church bending over a pile of them on the grass, a lot more in the pockets of his yellow windbreaker. At the funeral mass, Father McLaughlin stood in front of the closed casket in his black vestments. He was really mad and told us about how they had to pick Georgie up in a bucket after, so we all had to be better Catholics.

Games on the old court went on when we first started high school. Same rules. One day we lost to a pick-up team from Our Lady of Sorrows on Henry Avenue. They cheated. They had black kids. We wanted another game. They accepted. Even on our turf they were too fast and too good that Saturday afternoon. I scored ten points and got a bloody nose standing up for Jimbo. The other guy got fifteen and not a scratch.

Later, me and Jimbo headed for Wellens Avenue and Hoagie Heaven to get a Coke and some grease. Freddie Devlin came at me out of a doorway and got me good with a right to the temple. Then we were rolling around on the sidewalk like a couple of kids. I'd beat him up so often; I guess I wasn't taking it seriously until he tried to knee me in the balls.  Then the red fog took over, and I went kind of nuts on him.  Snapped out, as they say on the street.  Good description: a switch clicks in your head and you lose it. I straddled him and punched his face about twenty times— hard.  Then, I grabbed his hair and beat his head on the pavement.  The more I did it, the better I felt.  When he was really out of it, I stood up to kick his head in.  Jimbo was on me from behind, pinning my arms, yelling into my ear.  "Jesus Christ, Jack, that's enough, man.  Don't kill im. Yer one crazy shit, no lie."  The fury came fast and went fast.  It was always the same with me.  Jimbo spat in his face as we walked away.  The last time I saw him was much later, during the test in the Armory.  Probably drafted.

Hoagie Heaven was a tiny, narrow, long little place, a closet stuck on the end of a row of old buildings made of the gray fieldstone with little, sparkling flecks of mica you see all over Philly.   Gerry owned the place.  He was about thirty, a Harp with a red nose, faded red hair and splotchy orange freckles. He liked the work and the kids.  Didn't have any himself. Made his money frying hamburgers, stuffing hoagie buns full of salami and provolone, slinging soda.  Nice guy.

Drank light rum and coke all day. Didn't tell you what to do; when to go home.

It *was* heaven—private and safe. I learned to smoke Camels there, just like my dad. A counter on one side had the chrome plated swivel stools you used to see. The long mirror above the soda fountain featured greasy post cards from Flagstaff, where Gerry's brother lived, and one dark dollar bill held on with peeling, yellowed tape, fuzzy with greasy dust. Along the other side were booths covered in red Naugahyde worn smooth by generations of little Catholic asses. On the back wall were two pinball machines—a sure way to fill your milk bottle right up.

Bobby was there that day. He was an older guy, about seventeen, and he was famous in the neighborhood. He dropped out of school, stole cars and went to Camp Hill Reformatory, out near Harrisburg, the state capital. The skinny dark guy that sat across from him with his back to the wall wasn't local. He was nervous and ugly; hair shaved close like a soldier; his little black eyes darted around; couldn't tell how old he was. Bobby called me back to their booth. Jimbo stayed put in the front; just shook his head.

"This here's Lights," Bobby said, "but up at the Hill we called him Brownie." I stuck out my hand. Brownie took it, then pulled back like he stuck his finger in the toaster. "Brownie's been in an out since he was twelve. You should see him open a parkin meter—perfect. Lissen, Jack, we got a little job set up for Saturday. Make you a few bucks. We got this liquor store over on Wadsworth Avenue. Mom and pop joint. Old fart's at the cash. Piece a cake. Interested? All you gotta do is lookout. We do the rest."

"Nah. Gotta work. I don't show, my mom'll kill me." I did need the money, though. Brownie sneered: "Shit, man, if his momma won't let him, we sure don't want im. But I'll tell you what, buddy, you just keep your fuckin mouth shut, you hear? I'll find you if you don't, and I don't forget a face."

The *Philadelphia Bulletin* reported it:

### Savage Killing

Two juveniles, Robert Strong and James Lightbody, both with prior convictions, entered the Quik Liquor Mart last Saturday night for the purposes of robbery. After taking money and liquor, one of them, allegedly Mr. Lightbody, savagely beat the proprietor, Irv Weinstein, 65, to death with a baseball bat. The police inform us that when asked why, Mr. Lightbody replied, "He wouldn't shut up, so I hit him till he did."

"It's about time you showed up. It's been three days. Where have you been? Granmom's been worried sick."

"Just out, mom, stuff to do. Nothin to worry about, honest. Here's some money. I'll keep it commin. It's time I got my own place. This one's way too small for the three of us anyhow. And I won't be wakin you up in the middle of the night when I get home anymore. No sweat. I'll just drop off as much money as I can at the end of every month. How's that, huh?" She was crying.

"Those people you hang around with. They're dangerous. And the women. I'm scared if you go out on your own, something bad will happen. Don't."

"Sorry, mom, mind's made up. See ya."

After Hose split for Arizona, Nate and Jeeps paid a lot of attention to me. They'd be parked outside my apartment early in the morning or late at night, wasn't sure how they found me. They'd just sit there, watching, drinking coffee, eating donuts. I'd wave, and they'd stare. I didn't go anywhere near

Rising Sun Avenue, or Hose and Chica's old place. I knew where she was before she left town, but I only talked to her on pay phones. After that, they stopped following me around; at least I thought so. Somehow, I was sure somebody was tailing me; in better moods I wrote it off to paranoia.

Hose was right; they were hiring in Germantown. I landed a flat-rate job at Germantown Cycle. After the years at it with Hose, I had a bit of a rep. The bucks were good, enough to keep me and mom and granmom going. At the end of the month, I'd stop by their little house in Manayunk at night and push an envelope through the slot. Some guys even started asking for me by name. The owners noticed. A lot of outlaws hung around that shop: Bandanna, Jersey Devils, Vagabonds, a few Hells Angels. They were scary people, but they were okay to me as long as I did my job and didn't jack up the bill. They tipped heavy if their bikes ran right: ten bucks or maybe some tools right off the back of the truck. If you needed anything really nasty, they were the guys to see. That's where I got the high-quality switchblade I kept in the back of my tool box. Cops like Jeeps and Nate you just couldn't trust, even when they offered. It would always come back as dues you had to pay. It was better to reserve debts like that for important occasions, like speeding tickets.

Those 1 Percenters were really serious about attitude, staying dirty and smelling bad. Took the name, proudly, from some cop who said something like: "Only, one per cent of motorcyclists are scum." They were mean, too, but it was their way of showing class. It was none of my business, but I couldn't stand choppers. "Hardly Ablesons" we used to call them—hardly able to run. All you had to do was open one of the engines. Looked like the inside of a 1930s tractor. Slow, too, unless you threw money at them. I fixed them, but own one? Never. I took my Bonneville apart, stripped off the chrome, made it fast, made it light and painted it black. Wrote "Trusty" on the tank in small white letters. Did it for granpop, because he escaped the from the Dublin General Post Office during Easter Rising in the sidecar of a "Trusty" Triumph driven by his brother Mick. I got my AAMRR license and dreamed of putting on full leathers and hitting the tracks from Daytona Beach to Mosport. Just like Hailwood at the Isle of Man.

Iron Mike was an Angel; one of my regulars and always broke. First time I saw him, thought I knew him, but it was probably just his fat Irish face under the greasy full beard. He was a classic outlaw right down to the Nazi stuff, the punched out teeth and the rival club's colors stitched to the seat of his jeans. His club wings were black—real class—most are just red because the guy only got initiated with a white girl. He was one tough dude, but he seemed fair and no bullshit. He owed me for a motor job I did on the side, and he walked in one day and said, "Hey, lookit, all the bread went for bail, but I got a primo Honda engine that'll plug right into that Yetman frame you got stashed. Whaddya say?" He looked at me with a lopsided grin that was both friendly and familiar.

Bonehead—I wanted the motor, so I didn't ask the right questions. Mike brought it in at night, and I stowed it under my bench to make fast later.

I should have been much more careful. Mike's boys were the slickest around. They could have the lock cut and your bike in their truck faster than you could unzip your fly in the gas station rest room. I should have stripped the engine down to an untraceable pile of parts, but there it was, serial number and all.

Nate and Jeeps walked into the shop about a week later. They knew just where to look.

These guys joined a cops-only MC club, and now they always wanted parts and work for free. One of their buddies, Ratzo, told me once, "Yeh, we always wear our guns when we're out ridin. Drives the country cops crazy. They pull us over. We flash our badges. Them farmers just don't know what to do. Funny shit, man." They all lived in their own, very strange, space.

Nate, the big black cop, walked up to my bench and hit me in the gut—not too hard, just to get my attention. My hands went up, and he said very quietly, "Be cool, dickface, or we got you for resistin, too. Stay real still, and nobody gets hurt." Jeeps just stood there, grinning.

I wasn't connected; had no pull. All the money went for mom and granmom, rent, beer, and speed parts, so I couldn't pay them off with anything but a promise. It was a rough ride. They stuffed me in the back of the van and drove downtown the way Philly cops always do: "Get outta the way, assholes." And they do.

At the station down on Spring Garden Street they tried the good cop, bad cop routine. Mostly, they were interested in Hose's whereabouts. I was all innocence on that one, and I wouldn't tell them where the motor came from. I couldn't; you just don't drop the dime: "Yeh, yeh, got it from a dude owed me money. From New York. Never seen him again. How'd I know it was hot?" Not good enough.

"Listen, Jack, don't be a fuckin melon farmer. We want Hose." This is Jeeps, the good cop—for now. Nate was playing with his nightstick. "Just get us the details, so we can be friends and make a livin. This beef ain't a pinch a coon shit. We drop it right now if you cooperate." Funny they didn't have a clue about Mike. They weren't getting any info, period. Besides, I had to stand up for what was right. Always did get me in trouble.

I tried to keep it from mom as long as I could, but once it hit the papers she went nuts. The trial was a joke. The lawyer the state gave me couldn't defend his right to cross the street.

Judge Whitlock told me to stand up: "Ordinarily, Mr. Kavanagh, in a first offence case like yours, I would offer you a choice of incarceration or the Service. I see from your record, though, that you're 4F, so the Army is out. Furthermore, the arresting officers have convinced me that you consort with known felons. Therefore, I have no choice but to find you guilty as charged of receiving stolen goods and resisting arrest. I sentence you to eight months in—let me see—it will have to be Holmesburg Prison because of space restrictions. Guard, take him away. Next case."

As his gavel came down, I thought, "Holy shit, Holmesburg, they shouldn't send me there on a first offence. It's for real hard guys. Good thing I'm not pretty the way cons like and good with my fists. I'd better be." I heard granpop's voice again: "Don't ever get locked up, Jacko. People die inside for no reason. Just look at my friend Joe McKenna."

They took my shoelaces, my belt and my hair. It had to be a mistake; they put me in the zoo—the crazies and lifers range. I shuffled down the row and looked over the railing to the concrete floor four floors down. The old screw whistled a Johnny Mathis tune and tapped the beat on the bars with his stick. I didn't get any respect, because he knew I wasn't connected. "Tough biker, huh? Looks like one a yer own dropped the dime on ya. Got some real winners for you, honey, two real hard guys. You'll have lotsa fun. Better you should have rolled over for Jeeps. Here you might roll over cause ya have to."

We stopped in front of cell 547, and the guard nodded down the range to another one in a glass booth. Click, the door slid open. Click, it closed. The cell was narrow, maybe six by ten, with a white ceiling, hospital puke-green walls and a gray floor. The smell of disinfectant was heavy. There was a sink, a seat-less toilet; pictures of body builders taped to the walls; on a narrow shelf some official-looking reports, a TV; a bunk bed, three high. Nobody was home. "So, it was Mike," I thought. "Why?"

The door clicked and in walked two guys who'd shout prison at you if you met them in a seminary. One was forty, paunchy, a fringe of hair above his ears. Very neat, clean and starched in his prison blues. Comfortable. He was in control. The other one was wiry, dark, early twenties, in a strap undershirt like a South Philly wise guy. His little black eyes looked like a Doberman's; the long hair was combed straight back, held there by a perfect red bandanna around his head. He had "lots of ugly on him," as they said then: tattoos, some professional, some not: on his left biceps was "Mom" in a heart, the letters dripping blood, a swastika adorned the hollow of his throat, a red and blue dragon climbed his right arm, "Love" and "Hate" were spelled out on his knuckles, the letters, scars, done over and over with a razor blade, dyed with boot polish mixed with cigarette ash.

They stared me up and down real slow, smiling. The older one had seen enough and climbed to the top bunk. The younger one crouched against the wall. "Hey, Deac," he said, "Think I know im." He turned to me: "You know a guy named Strong, honey? Good with cars? You used to hang out over near Olney—few years back? Don't con me, man, I don't forget no faces."

I nodded. "Yo, Deac," Brownie said, "This dude knew we was gonna take that old fart at the liquor store. But he kept it quiet. Diddn ya, babycakes? That was real smart, cause if you diddn, you wouldnn be standin here now."

"You awight for now. Name?" "Jack," I said. "Dig it, Jack. Me and the Deacon, we know what's happenin inside. You just do like you're told. Keep your mouth shut like I know you can. You might even get outta here a virgin. But maybe old Deac here wants to be your sugar daddy. Hey, Deac?" The Deacon grunted, "Too big."

Brownie laughed through perfect teeth. His dead black eyes stared, unwavering, straight into mine. "Anyways, you come along to the party tonight. He's only eighteen, just in today, the prettiest little Italian piece you ever did see. We gonna welcome him to Holmesburg. You cummin, right? We wouldnn want you to miss out and maybe talk to somebody you shouldnn."

There were six of them in the storeroom with the new kid. I was at the door, the lookout, so they said. I got in one black guy's face and said, "Hey, man, why don't you chumps let the kid alone." I got beat pretty bad until Brownie stepped in. He turned on me with a snarl, "Lissen, shitferbrains, in here you stand up when yer told, not before. Got it?" When the kid started screaming, I puked on the floor. They were in there a long time. It was a noisy party, but nobody complained.

Over the next few weeks, my cellmates studied hard for Brownie's parole. He was due for review, but the chances weren't good without an angle. Theirs was Judy Brocklehurst, the psychologist. They were smart. They knew the con. They had time, and they took it.

Some dope, cigarettes, muscle, sex, changed hands, and they got a profile on her better than she had on Brownie: voting record, attitude towards prisoners, journal articles, address, license number, family, daily routine. It was all set up. Long before I got there, Brownie started on the model prisoner scam. He got religion ("Not too serious, you gotta be believable"). He talked at all the rap sessions, took the programs, even learned welding.  Between them, Deac and Brownie worked out just what Judy Brocklehurst wanted to hear, and they gave it to her, slowly, a little at a time.  There was no advantage in hurrying.

Brownie stood in the cell, smiling thinly, his jaw muscles working like he was chewing steel gum: "You see before you, gentlemen, a reformed man.  A tribute to the penal system.  The answer to recidivism.  I'm on my way out because I'm ready to become a productive member of society.  Deac, you woulda been proud, man, little Judy came through so fine.  She took it all, man, right down her stupid throat."

Sanity was becoming an issue.  I took to going to the library to read and hide out.  One Saturday, the prison librarian sat down across from me.  There was no one else at the long wooden table.  "Name's Pat," he said, "Pat Johnston.  Heard there was a certain Jack Kavanagh inside on some bogus stolen goods wrap.  Guy with a white flash in his hair, when he has any. That you?"

"Yeh, what's the beef?"

He was a short, fat, little old man with pure white hair; his yellow, pipe tobacco stained teeth showed when he laughed.  "No beef, brother, just wanted to introduce myself.  Would your grandfather happen to have been, rest his soul, one Daniel Kavanagh from Fishtown?"

"That's right. How'd you know?"

"You been in twenty years like I have, you'd develop your sources—inside and outside. Let's just say I know some people that know you and your family, Joe McGarrity for one, may he rest in peace, and I knew your grandad in the old days. We raised a lot of money and moved a lot stuff from the Navy Yard to Dublin in those days. He was a saint, a hero, a grand man of the old sort."

"Thanks. He was—and then some."

"I've seen you in here pretty often. Anything particular you want to read? Looks like you have a taste for the Irish in you. Maybe I could help? I can even get stuff from outside if you know what you want."

During my entire sentence, he fed me more books on Irish history than I ever knew existed. From them I learned that granpop's "Emmett, Fitzgerald and Tone, Parnell, and Pearse, Clarke, Mac Diarmada and Connolly, McSwiney and the rest" were more than saints. In my eyes, then, like him they were heroes, patriots. Right, justified and killed for their pains. They stood up and got knocked down. Even, and maybe most of all, the Protestant Parnell. His life taught me in detail what I long knew in legend: the fight had nothing to do with religion; country, land, not religion. "Right, Jack," Pat said. "All that 'fightin fer the faith' horseshit comes from the priests. It's supposed to keep us under their thumb." If Parnell hadn't been hounded down like he was, the troubles in Ireland never would have happened. I was firmly with my granpop and uncles, but my father's refusal to join them troubled me deeply. No resolution, just anger.

Then I started on more recent times. The old splits, the old feuds, brother fighting brother, seemed to get even worse. Just like the Irish Civil War, just like granpop and the Devlins, I guess. It all looked so confusing, so useless, somehow; even the fiftieth anniversary of the Easter Rising and the Bodenstown commemoration of Wolfe Tone's suicide. The Irish papers were full of speeches that seemed to set the factions at each other's throats. Pat started feeding me IRA stuff just off the boat. It didn't take long to figure out that all the Sinn Fein hot air about "uniting the workers of the world" didn't have a lot to do with a united Ireland. It was pretty far from Christoir O'Neill at Bodenstown in 1949: "The aim of the IRA is simply to drive the invader from the soil of Ireland and to restore the sovereign independent Republic proclaimed in 1916." Fair enough, but I couldn't hack the socialist manifesto.

Pat had a plan for me, no doubt. We talked a lot about the need for force on the border, in Belfast, against the Royal Ulster Constabulary and the Protestant clerics whipping up the marching boys. I was unsure about the need for killing, dead set against a workers' paradise, certain about an end to partition. I was some confused. More so when Pat told me he shot a Philly cop in the eye robbing a bank for money to send to the heroes at home. He was very calm about it. "Orders," he said.

When I wasn't hitting the books, I started writing letters to anybody, just to keep going. Mom and Irene, of course, but I couldn't chance any to Hose and Chica; no address anyway. I took Penny out my last year in high school—we went to her senior prom together. Got her address and wrote. She came to see me a few times. Good kid. Mostly, I just kept my head down, didn't hear anything, didn't see anything. I was just waiting, trying to stay safe.

Mom visited once, but she couldn't stand it, couldn't do anything but cry. Rene came and said, "Jack, we've always had a good time together, but we'll never be anything more than friends, will we?  Besides, I got into Brandeis for pre-med, so I'll be moving up there in a week or two.  My father would kill me if he knew I was here.  I hope everything works out, but I have to go now.  Try to find the right path.  You're intelligent enough, but maybe too crazy, too angry. If only you weren't so beautiful."

Then the letters came: one from Mark, one from Matt. Mark's was postmarked Da Nang.  It was long, rambling, confused, very unlike him.  But he did say, clearly, that he thought Vietnam was a lost cause, "no return," as he put it. Just as clearly he told me he was going to re-enlist: "The army's my home now. Going Airborne soon as I can."  Matt's was very short, stiff, right, just like him.  After he told me what a lost soul asshole I was, he wrote in his polished Palmer Method nun's penmanship: "I'll never forgive you for what you've done to my mother.  Confess your sins and reform." Sounded like somebody I never knew.

Brownie came to see Deac every visitor's day.  Deac never said what they talked about, except that Brownie had a job as a welder up in Fox Chase, where Judy Brocklehurst lived.  I was damned sure he told me for a reason.

A month later and Deac was snickering over the newspaper. "Check out this shit, Jack," he said as he threw me the *Philadelphia Bulletin*. The article was a short one, on a back page:

### Prison Reformer Disappears

Prominent penal psychologist and prisoners' rights crusader Judy Brocklehurst vanished from her Rhawn Avenue home on Thursday. There were no signs of a struggle. The police have no motive and don't suspect foul play. Her husband, Jonathan, who was away at a dental conference at the time, says she would never leave home without telling him where she was going. The police are looking for a beige Mercedes, Pennsylvania license 62VEJ35.

Deac's eyes were shining. I knew I was a dead man if I went to the screws about it. Me in the shower with a shiv in my back wouldn't help anyway. I did talk to Pat, though. All he said was, "Oh, yeh, that animal. Leave it with me, Jack. I'll take care of Brownie all right."

The next piece was on the front page:

### Gruesome Murder in Fox Chase

Police found the badly burned body of prison reformer Judy Brocklehurst after answering a call from the manager of Fox Chase Welding on Sunday. A police spokesman would say only that she appears to have been tortured. Acting on what they call "reliable information," they are looking for a recent parolee from Holmesburg Prison, James Lightbody, a.k.a. Brownie, who was employed at the welding shop and was known to the deceased.

The third *Bulletin* article described the bust:

### Torture Suspect Caught in Camden

James Lightbody, suspected killer of Holmesburg Prison psychologist Judy Brocklehurst, was apprehended at the Travelers Rest Motel on Camden's Atlantic Avenue on Monday night. Lightbody put up no resistance and told police he was confused and didn't remember anything. Forensic experts are examining the Brocklehurst's Mercedes found in the motel parking lot and the welder's tools discovered in the trunk.

I was walking toward the library when I got grabbed from behind. Two guys held me up against the wall while Deac put the shiv against my jugular. It was made from a ground-down file; the cross hatching was still on the handle. "You been spillin your guts, jelly baby?  Maybe we let you bleed real slow so you can watch yourself die."

"Yo, Deac.  Check it out man.  I coulda got Brownie busted years ago—but I didn't.  What makes you think I did this time?  What's in it for me?"  I could feel the fury rising in me.  If the red fog took me, I was dead.

As he thought about it, the pressure of the knife on the vein lessened, then it came back, hard enough to cut the skin.  I felt a dribble of blood rolling over my collarbone.  "Yeh, maybe not, but who, who did it?  Brownie had more work to do on the outside.  They took him too quick.  Somebody inside had to drop the dime.  Gimme the name, prick."

"I don't fuckin know nothin, Deac."  I started to get righteous on him, pulling away from the two guys he had with him.  "You think I dropped the dime?  That's how I got in here fuckhead.  Don't forget it."  It was Pat Johnston for sure.

He turned from me in disgust: "Yeh, right.  Jerkoffs like you, chump, are just too fuckin pure to be true.  Watch your back, pussy."  The two guys let me go.

The trial was all over Channel 10, WCAU.  John Facenda's bloodhound face stared out from the screen.  His rug didn't fit his head.  Deac was glued to the box.  The defense was insanity. The prosecution wanted life with no parole. A reporter stood outside Holmesburg in the rain and talked about how the death penalty wasn't the answer. They copped a plea, and Brownie got life with no parole for twenty-five years. Either way, it didn't matter much. Deac wanted Brownie back once he took care of business on the outside. Brownie wanted inside until next time.

I just wanted out. Guys like me get caught in the gears; then they're spit out. Deac was inside because he wanted to be; it was heaven for him. Guys like Brownie are rabid dogs frothing at the mouth. They tear you up for fun—in the joint, on the street. It's the fear they like. The manipulation. The power. The rush. They have no souls.

It wasn't such a bad day when I got out, two weeks early on good behavior, though it was damp and cold the way only Philly can be. At least the sun was shining. I walked for miles along the Delaware, under the bridges—Tacony-Palmyra, Betsy Ross, Benjamin Franklin—through Wissinoming and Bridesburg, past Port Richmond and Fishtown. I stopped on Indiana Avenue to look up the steep steps at the narrow little rowhouse granpop and granmom used to live in, trying to think straight about him, my uncles, dad, the old cause. No luck. I ended up down at Penn Treaty. On the streets were torn open garbage bags, smoldering mattresses, shopping carts, trashed cars halfway down the bank, rubbies in bombed out easy chairs screaming at the sky. I looked up and to the right where that old Quaker, William Penn, in his green suit and hat, surveyed his dream from the top of City Hall.

There was enough wind to make white caps on the blue-green water. In midstream, the tugs hurried down the current. Across the river, Walt Whitman rested in his Camden grave. In my back pocket was a dog eared copy of the O'Brien's *Life of Parnell*. Below the "Property of Holmesburg Prison" stamp inside were two pencil inscriptions from Pat Johnston. The first was expected: "*Éirinn go Brách*," "Ireland for ever." The second was a surprise, "*Tiocfaidh ár lá,*" "Our day will come." I had enough money to make it to my mother's place in Manayunk and pick up my toolbox and the oak box granpop made for me in 1948. Somehow, over eight months it had become very important—vital. Paying my dues with Mike, strangely, didn't seem that necessary anymore. Penny's phone number was in my jeans. What I really needed right then was a hoagie and a whole bottle of milk.

# 5. Circus

The Norton Commando was pretty new, but compared to the Japanese and Italian motors I had been working on recently, the engineering and the inside of the engine looked so simple and primitive I wondered what made the British think anybody would buy such a bunch of mismatched sand castings. In the trade, we called these dinosaurs, "the bikes with hinges in the middle." Not something you'd want to lean into a corner at speed. No wonder the Japs were beating the Brits back to their island. Made me feel good. Still, if you were in the service end, they were great, because they were always broken. Somehow, Trusty the Bonneville was beyond the Pale.

Next bench to mine belonged to Vultch. He was so black, his skin looked blue. Drove a fat old Harley FLH with a jockey shifter down by his right boot. Had a stiff left leg from a flat-track crash up in Bethlehem years ago. Really wore one of those winged-wheel fifty-mission-crush hats and an ancient black leather motorcycle jacket with all the useless zippers. On the back, somebody with no talent had drawn a gawky vulture in green house paint crushing a Triumph in its too large talons.  He was working on a Harley Sportster, using large tools, singing his only song: "Battery acid and a rat tail file. Do dah, do dah. Battery acid and a rat tail file. Yeh, she loves me all the while.  Honey, oh, baby mine."  There was no doubt he had memorized every one of Marlon Brando's lines from *The Wild One.*

Around him, Luci, the fifteen year old spade street kid, made it look like he was sweeping up.  He would only work if he didn't get his clothes dirty or sweat up the doo-rag tied around his head under his wide-brimmed Jimmy Cagney hat. The only difference from Cagney's was one side of the brim was rolled, the other absolutely flat. Luci made sure it stayed like that, taking it off to admire it, adjust the look, and use a small brush to take off the dust about twenty times a day. He was even more particular about his shoes, spit-shined, pointy-toed fence climbers or black Converse All-Star high-top sneakers.  He had that perfect street strut: left arm stiff, left hand in a fist, right arm swinging across his body as he did the strand down the street.  Very cool kid.

Vultch's real name was Barnabas.  Funny name for a black guy. He was a genius.  Nuts, but a genius.  He worked only part time at Fairmount Honda. Just to keep his hand in, I suspected. Mostly he machined tiny parts out of exotic metals for NASA.

My bench was all the way at the back of the long, narrow shop. It used to be the ground floor of an old brownstone. Now it was like a mine tunnel, the only outside light coming from the garage door chopped into the front of the building. The floor was rough, patched concrete.

It kept you going, looking up from your work to see Vultch gimping around in the square of daylight, shouting his head off, singing his tune. He loved Harleys, hated everything else, like Hondas and BMWs. Something about God and the war. I was deep in the Norton's prehistoric bowels, cursing designers of water pump motors, when the phone rang. I made a grab for the receiver with a greasy hand, giving just a bit more character to a phone made fuzzy with overspray from the paint booth. Pete, pill head and parts man extraordinaire, was on the line. With a snicker, he said, "Yo, Jack, got a weird one for ya on line 2. Says he got your name from somebody down near the airport." "Right, Pete, but where's Julie? He shoulda took the call." Julie was the shop and sales manager. "Ya got me, man. Probably takin target practice. Come on, pick it up. I got parts ta count."

It didn't surprise me much that a new customer would ask for me by name. Besides speed work, I had a rep for fixing odd-ball problems, but I wasn't prepared for what I got. I could understand most of the city's five or six different accents, but like most people from Philly I was on my guard right away when I heard a foreign accent: New York, Boston, Atlanta, London, whatever. This one, though, was European. A Hungarian, maybe. Maybe Polish.

"Hullo, I been told you fixes old motorcycles, right?" "Yeh, right, whatcha got?" With a lot of mistakes and questions and backing up, I got out of him that he had an out-of-production Honda, the kind the Japs made before they got it right. The body style was copied from DeSoto, or Studebaker, or Nash, sometime in the fifties. It was what mechanics call a rat bike.

"I be over now," he said and hung up. I threw the phone in the direction of the cradle and went back to work, hoping he might forget about it or lose his way in the maze of tenements and torn up streets around 13th and Fairmount.

I forgot about it at least. It was lunch time, so I locked up everything I owned to prevent the lighter than air problem tools have when you aren't looking at them. Vultch stalked over. He moved with a kind of step, jump, slide that was a cross between Chester in *Gunsmoke* and Gabby Hayes in some old western.

He put his arm around my shoulders and picked up on the story he had been telling me ever since I first met him. "I saw the light, Jack, just when I got into the Lehigh Tunnel, up on the Northeast Extension of the Pennsy Turnpike. Summer time, hotter n hell, stop and go. The fumes were somethin awful. It was like a bright light in the darkness of error." Now he had religion, so he said, and at night he'd tape little pamphlets—the ones that look like they're printed on brown paper bags—to my tool box. Bold type said things like "Repent," "Jesus Is Your Only Friend." Stuff like that.

I made the mistake of going to his house for dinner once, up in Norristown, on the edge of farm country. His silent, tiny, washed out, skinny little wife was the color of a Hershey bar. She made green Jell-O for dessert and a cake that tasted like cardboard with "Revelations 1:11" squirted on top of the white icing in that red decorator junk you should never eat. Later, some very unhappy looking Bible thumpers showed up. "Join in, Jack," said Vultch, "We're gonna read some verses from the good book and exorcise all that pagan stuff in your soul." I left.

Vultch believed that anything made in Japan was the Antichrist. The shop had a promotional poster of a Honda Superhawk on one wall, and when he was really into his prophet mode he'd load up the air hose with a used spark plug and shoot at it, sharp end first.

All the shop people ate lunch together, so me and Vultch stood waiting by the door looking across the alleyway out on the garbage filled vacant lot we used as a practice dirt track during the day and street people drank in at night. Trashed sofas with the stuffing coming out, Formica tables with rusty chromed legs, refrigerators lined up in a short but tricky course. Only problem was, Julie used it to plink Castrol Oil cans with whatever gun he had with him. The combination could get dicey.

Claus was the BMW expert. Originally from Hamburg, he was six-six in his socks. Began as a bulldozer mechanic and was famous for quick fixes using big hammers. He worked in a little room off the main shop with Charlie Murphy, a quiet, wiry little Irish guy with bad teeth from the Bogside in Derry. Except when we went out together at night to find a bar with a decent rock and roll band and talk Irish politics, he didn't have much to say for himself.  Good thing Charlie didn't talk; Claus said enough for both. He had a voice like a howitzer and cursed a lot in German. He was a poet, too, "*Die runtz die puntz, und stinkt und schwuntz.*"

They showed up with Luci, so we walked around the corner to collect Pete.  The parts department was in another old house: fenders and gas tanks in the bathroom, engines in a bedroom, electrics in the parlor—all that gear in a house that was probably pretty fancy once, with its plaster medallions on the high ceilings and deep moldings around the large windows. Those were the days when Philly was under control, in one piece, had order from within.  Well, okay, sort of.

As usual, we found Pete counting parts.  He knew just exactly how many of everything he had.  Maybe it was the reds he popped day and night, but he did love those parts like an accountant loves a sharp pencil.  He didn't appreciate it much when we used any, because then he'd have to change his totals. Washers were his favorite: "See that box, man? No, not that one, the other."  I was looking 5 degrees to the left.  "It has 453 10 mm washers in it."  His chicken chest was always hidden in a T-shirt that would have strangled a human. Pete was our reliable pipeline to secret factory information.

All together we gimped and strutted, jumped and pounded, over to Wallace Street to Lily's Bar and Grill. It was a fancy name for a certifiable fire trap. Inside it was dark, smelling of stale beer, grungy, turn of the century, brown embossed tin walls and ceiling. Under the blue glare of the twenty-six channel television, everybody was in a sort of shaky truce: motorcycle cops, bikers, shopping bag ladies, locals, spades with pints of rye in their back pockets and cutthroat razors on strings down their backs.

Lily was the fattest woman I ever saw, black or white. She smiled all the time, probably to show off her gold front tooth with a white star of enamel left as a decoration. I often wondered where she got clothes that huge. How about monster bras? Humongous underpants? Anyway, she did a good business, mostly because of the baseball scoreboard given out by Schmidtz beer that had long rows of numbers chalked on it that didn't have anything to do with baseball.

When we walked in she was laughing and slapping one of her huge cheeks, "Goldie, you ain't never gonna get as much lovin as I got."

Pete was mysterious over meat ball sandwiches and Bud on tap, telling us about the coming of the mighty Honda six-cylinder engine. Vultch raised his eyes to the ceiling and said like a TV evangelist: "The end is nigh," adding," We could always fuel-inject the sucker." Claus just chewed. Charlie's mouth was open as if he was going to say something. I looked, waited, but he didn't. Luci watched Lily with a grin.

There was nothing special about the dented blue Ford Econoline van parked by the shop door when we came back, except the Alabama license plate. In front of my bench stood the man with the telephone voice, looking a bit like Tony Curtis used to. The only problem was a fading black eye that had turned yellow-green. His once shiny Italian shoes matched the faded sheen of his frayed, gray sharkskin pants and the bright yellow of his knit shirt. He held one of the Vultch's pamphlets at arm's length.

Turned out he was a Hungarian who got out when the Russians came in. He explained that his bike had a funny habit of losing power at bad moments. "This is wery danger," he said. I nodded but didn't see why he was all that worked up.

"Okay," I said, "let's have a look." Here I was, surrounded by hundreds of normal, or at least near normal motorcycles, when the Hungarian wheeled the thing in. The little Honda was brush painted a vivid metal-flake green. The tires were gone, replaced by bolted up wooden circles made by some-body's uncle in the back yard. Rolling across the floor it reminded me of the sound track from *Ben Hur.* Norton Commandos began to look very modern.

"Wow," I thought, "this nut drives a bike with wooden wheels. Must have kidneys of steel." He came closer down the long corridor, but I couldn't make out his face with the light behind him. Only when he got to my bench and I saw that each wheel had a three-inch-deep groove lined with rubber did I begin to understand his power problem.

"Ah, look, ah...?" "Lintoff," he said. "Good, ah, well, look here Lintoff, just what exactly do you use this thing for anyway." It's always best to be polite with customers.

"Easy," he said. "Uh huh, easy." I replied. "Sure, bozo," I thought. "I ride it on the high wire in the circus. I am the great Lintoff, who rides above the crowd unafraid, without nets, seventy-five feet above the floor of the big top." The speech was boomed out to the whole shop without a hitch, as if memorized from one of those circus posters you used to see slapped on fences with whitewash brushes.

The shop was silent. Claus had followed the bike in from the street. He stood, towering over Lintoff, rubbing his chin. Charlie swung himself around the corner, his head perpendicular to the door post, big, gum disease grin on his urchin face. Vultch walked around the circus bike humming a low "do dah, do dah." Luci was gone.

"Look, Mr. Mechanic. I can't go on cause bike don't work. I have to go on. You fix." As he said this, his face darkened. It was not a request.

It figured. The thing just wouldn't fix. Years of bubble gum and baling wire repairs had made it a mare's nest. I couldn't figure out the electrical system. The pistons rattled around inside the cylinders like marbles in a coffee can. Pete told me there were only three oversize piston rings for it in the world. It made mysterious gurgling noises. Stove bolts held on vital parts, like the swing arm. Test riding was out of the question. The miracle was that it ran at all, but make it run right I could not.

Day after day, the Lintoff phone calls came in. Most of what he said I couldn't understand; each time he sounded more and more like Bella Lugosi playing the count. Enough was enough. I wanted to roll it out into the street on Friday night and leave it for the termites before I took off with Charlie to head for Kensington and McDougall's Saloon, an Irish bar that had brought in a traditional band he wanted to hear.

I'd heard of the joint but never been there. Word was, under all the hustle and happy Paddy, stage Irish stuff, sometimes it was a pipeline and meeting place for IRA sympathizers, granpop's old *Clann na Gael* boys. Any other time, they might have anything from a rock and roll bar band to strippers. It was time I went to find out more. Charlie had been at me for a long time about it. "You can't turn your back on it, Jacko, can't be done. Your sainted granpop was right. Some day you will have to choose."

The place was packed when we got there. Seemed every second guy looked like a member of the grim heavy suit brigade I knew since I met Joe McGarrity with granpop. Somehow, me and Charlie got a booth to ourselves before the band came on. Two friends of his joined us, Sean and Mike—heavy suiters for sure. The fingers on Sean's right hand were busted up really bad. Made me wince. Almost looked like somebody broke them deliberately, one by one.

They were buying, and one of them plunked the first bottle in a long line of Jameson on the table. They had Philly accents, sort of. You'd have to be brought up Irish to know they weren't native born.

The band was called "Blackthorn," four guys from Ballyshannon with the traditional flat drum, the Irish squeeze-box, a penny whistle, a fiddle and a mandolin. They were possessed, those guys, making more noise in the jigs and reels than a symphony orchestra. One of them had that perfect Irish tenor, and the ballads made me choke up, no doubt about it.

Charlie's buddies were on a mission to get me right plastered. They were doing a great job. They pumped and pumped about my family, my schooling and, more than anything else, my job. Sean said, "Now Jack, how can you sleep at night, you, a Kavanagh with Republican blood in your veins and Republican thoughts in your head, fixin motorbikes made by the Brits that raped your country?" Through the haze in my head I thought, "Motorbikes, what a tip off." Out loud I shouted over the music, "Don't think so, Sean. Seems to me they're made like shit, so they're always busted. I make a buck and have the satisfaction of knowing they don't know what they're doin."

The last song of the last set started. When the tenor started belting out "Off to Dublin in the Green," half the men and women in the crowd stood up. So did I.

> *I am a merry ploughboy, and I ploughed the fields all day*
> *'Till a sudden thought came to my mind that I should roam away*
> *For I'm sick and tired of slavery since the day that I was born*
> *And I'm off to join the IRA and I'm off tomorrow morn.*

I probably looked some stupid, weaving, mouth open, chest pushed out like a Scot when the piper hits the first sour note. I don't remember how I got to my apartment that night, but I do remember that all four of us were blood brothers.

The Saturday morning call was very clear, for Lintoff at least. Just what I needed with a whole battalion of infantry marching across my tongue in muddy boots. "Lissen, son of a bitch Mr. Mechanic. You fix by 1:00 or I come with my friends to fix you."  I thought of Paul Newman in an alley with his hustler's fingers broken, or maybe Sean.

Lunch at Lily's gave Vultch the umpteenth opportunity to tell us about the evils of the overhead camshaft. "My friends, only our Father has the power to give orders from above. We—mere mortals—should be content to give orders from below.  That's why Harley-Davidson has stuck to the moral push rod engine and Harley riders make such good Christians.  All those who like machines with overhead cams—you know who you are."  His finger stabbed in my direction.  "Beware the fate of atheists and give up on bikes made by them little yellow fuckers."

I was slouching against the garage door around 1:00, just coming to, sucking on a Camel, when the Econoline came roaring around the corner.  Lintoff's face was dark, with a frozen smile. His knuckles white from strangling the steering wheel.  Tires squealing, he rammed it into park with a grind while it was still moving.

Out he jumped, leaving the door swinging on its hinges.  At the same time the van's back doors banged open and the whole circus piled out, like something from a kid's pop-up picture book: the strong man with a ridge of muscle between his eyes, wearing a red and white T-shirt that would've fit Pete; the midget with a big stogie between his teeth carrying a kid's baseball bat and wearing a Tyrolean hat; the ringmaster with his teeth taken out for the event; the lion tamer with plastic sideburns and skinny moustache; the giant ready for an audition in a James Bond flick.

There was some justice in this. "Bizarre Bikers Duke It Out with Weird Circus Types." What a headline in the *Inquirer*. For news, sure would beat out the crime count ("Eleven Murders on Saturday"), the mayor's last speech ("Influence Peddling Denied"), how the umpires beat the Phillies once more ("Umps Dump Us Again") or the coming out party at the Cricket Club ("Wedgie French Was Divine in Satin").

I backed slowly into the darkness of the shop, not turning my eyes away for a second, ready to reach back for the switchblade. They followed me in a knot until they were lit up from behind like a scene from *The Invasion of the Body Snatchers*.

Inside it was very quiet. Vultch mumbled, "Remember therefore from whence thou art fallen, and repent," as he picked up the air hose with one hand and loaded a spark plug with the other. Claus clumped in with a ballpeen hammer almost as big as the one I had of my dad's hanging from his enormous fist. Charlie appeared, silent and frowning. Julie arrived with his Castrol pistol—a WW II 45—stuck in his belt. Luci circled Lintoff, eyeing his shoes like a bandido from *The Treasure of Sierra Madre*. Pete bounced around the corner as if his feet were on springs yelling, "Wait, wait, not yet, wait till I see."

Everyone was ready to go, fists clenched, noses open as they say on the street, when Charlie spoke up, very calm. "Now, now, children. There's no sense in the violence. What'll it get ye? We're all of us brothers after all is said and done. I'll buy the beer, and then we'll all kiss and make up." The last bit was such a weird idea that everybody stopped dead. Maybe we all saw at the same time just how stupid the whole scene was. I doubt it, but for a moment nothing happened.

Then Vultch, grinning, dropped the air hose to the concrete, coiling and hissing like a Diamondback. Humming, he gimped over to his tool box, scooped out a stack of pamphlets and started handing them out. "Salvation, my Philistine friends, has to do with multi-speed transmissions and the tubular frame. Begone you relics of the dark days of wandering in the wilderness and kick starters. Arise, the new age of technology and electric starters."

This was just strange enough to prevent any serious death from happening. Luci said to the midget, "Hey, bro, yo lid needs a brush. Use mine." Pete asked the strong man, "You gotta tell me. Where do ya get your shirts?" Lintoff stared at me. I stared back. Maybe Vultch's nutty sermon sank in, because we started talking about the best new bike he could buy for his act.

Julie sold Lintoff a new Honda 160, and I adapted the wooden wheels to fit so he could make his 8:30 performance. With a great show of gulping emotion, he gave each of us a guest ticket, "You my good friends. You come see Lintoff in greatest show under canvas. Free, for nottink, my pleasure. Maybe someday we put act together—all of us."

We passed a few hours and a few beers at Lily's until it was time to head to the circus. It was set up on a weedy vacant lot next to the police car pound on Route 95 that leads south to Marcus Hook and Wilmington. A sagging, beat up galvanized fence surrounded the pound, but it wasn't high enough to hide the piles of crushed cars and the tall conveyor spitting shredded steel into a tangled, rusting pile. The circus wasn't big or famous, no Ringling Brothers glitz, just lots of shabby trailers, bored, frumpy animals, popcorn stands and canvas.

We parked our bikes in a knot, looped chains around them and threaded our way through the midway. Barkers called, trailer-trash dancers beckoned, the freak show looked inviting. But we headed straight for the big top that wasn't really very big. Nearby, I heard a Harley engine. It revved and quit.

Inside, it was packed, smelling heavy of elephant shit and too many people in a hot tent. The lion tamer ran through his really terrible routine: lots of whip cracking by him, T and A from his assistant, but not much action otherwise. No matter the lions were ratty, old, on drugs and couldn't jump anymore. No matter the strong man wasn't the strongest. No matter the giant wasn't much bigger than Claus. We knew these guys; it was special.

We really wanted Lintoff. After the clown act, the ringmaster, teeth in this time, appeared in the spotlight to a tinny fanfare from the PA system. Resplendent in his shiny tailcoat and waxed moustache, he boomed out:

"Ladies and gentlemen, the moment you've all been waiting for, the moment of truth, of life and death." Beside me, the Vultch intoned, "Amen, brother."

"The Wanninkopf Circus has the esteemed pleasure to bring you—for your amazement and edification—that hero of the Prague Spring, that defender of democracy, that daredevil of the high wire, that confidante of presidents and the crowned heads of Europe—the grrr-reat Linnn-tofff and his beautiful assistant, Marta." Marta's bit was said very quickly. "As you can see, there is no safety net, no protection from sure death, as Count Lintoff rides his powerful motorcycle on the high wire, some seventy-five feet above us."

"More like forty feet," I said to Vultch, "and Honda 160s ain't powerful." "Shh," from him, "Believe, my son, you gotta believe." Charlie snorted and shook his head at that one.

The spotlight whipped to the clowns holding open the curtains at the far side of the ring. Lintoff was old-world courtly as he made his stately entrance into the big top. The spotlight picked out the red sequins of his shabby jump suit. Holding his hand was a very black haired woman—well past it—with breasts the size of Lily's and a phony twenty-two inch waist. It was a wonder she could breathe. She was crammed into a matching, minimum type bathing suit that showed lots of cleavage and cheeks. The crowd loved it.

The drums rolled scratchily from the speakers. Up they climbed, with just enough hesitation every few rungs to make it look difficult. She was first; behind, he focused on her rear end, no small task, and then turned to the crowd with a brilliant smile. The clowns acted out disaster from below, running around with their arms out.

When they got to the platform, Lintoff looked around as if to say, "Think that was cool?  You ain't seen shit."  Marta put one hand on his sleeve, and with the other invited us to regard this phenom of daredevilhood.  No getting around it; she was acting just like the blond bimbos with long gloves and pointy bras in those dumb black and white Chevy television ads from the late fifties.  What an intro; it was sensational.

Lintoff picked us out in the guest seats, bowed deeply and gave us a backhanded wave, just like the Queen of England. "Awesome, man, awesome," said Pete very fast.  "Yeh, just check out those knockers," from Julie.  Claus mumbled under his breath, "*Marta, meine Liebschen.*"

Another, more tightly focused spotlight appeared on the sawdust floor and followed the midget as he wheeled in the little Honda. He clipped on a rope, and the light stayed on the bike as it ascended to the platform like magic. Marta alternated between Lintoff and the bike with her General Motors demo. Her job became more demanding as she steadied the bike. With a look in our direction that would have made Buster Keaton proud, Lintoff pressed the electric starter, and the bike purred. "Have to work on more noise," I thought, "Megaphones would do the trick."

Another drum roll from the speakers, and the perilous journey began. After a few well practised tries, backing off and shaking his head, Lintoff finally put both wheels on the wire. It sagged alarmingly. He swayed a bit, then rode to the middle of the line and stopped. The crowd groaned. There, after a few near fatal adjustments, he raised his hand as if to say, "No, I will defy gravity and not go splat on the floor. I am Lintoff."

The crowd said "Ahh" as he began to move again. This time the dominance, the power were there, and he made it across. Lintoff dismounted to another "ta da" from the speakers. He raised both arms in victory; Marta did her new Chevy number from the other side. They climbed down from their platforms, pausing to accept the cheers from the crowd.

Reunited in the center ring, they held hands as they bounced from sight between the canvas curtains. The spell was broken.

"Man, with a tent like this I could start my own travellin church. Whaddya think, Jack?" "Vultch, you're a sick-ass, crazy, bible-thumpin coot." "Jack, my son, I knew you cared."

Only one of us didn't make the show. Luci refused sullenly. Most of us roared out from the circus, away from the pound and the dry flats filled with dusty cattails along the Delaware, going to whatever home or bar or bed we had. I headed back to the shop. Luci was leaning alone against the brownstone. I pulled up, put down the sidestand and shut the motor off. "Hey, Luci, what's the problem man? You missed a good show. Wanna ride somewhere? Smoke a joint?" He looked down at the hat in his hand and stroked the brim softly, gently, "Shit, man, shit. Don't have to go to no show. This whole fuckin place a circus. Fuckin honkey ass mothafuckas." Our eyes met; his were empty of recognition. On the next block, I heard a Harley engine, idling, in need of a tune up.

It was time, anyhow. I started the bike and headed for Manayunk. When I got near mom's place, I shut the motor down and rolled along the narrow, dark street to her door. The greasy envelope held enough cash to keep her and granmom going a while longer. It fell through the mail slot in the cheap door and hit the hardwood floor with a crunchy thud. On the ride back to my apartment, the thought that I needed to make more money was with me even more than usual. It made me tired. All this crazy shit made me tired. Sure, some of it was funny as hell, like tonight, but there was no pattern, no reason, no goal beyond a buck. Not good enough.

# 6. Toot's Last Big Hit

The Northeast is just like most of the other zones in Philly: big, spread out around the rivers. When I was in high school, on Saturday nights we'd drive there from Olney up tree-lined Roosevelt Boulevard with the killer traffic circles at Pennypack and Oxford in Jimbo's red Olds 88. We were headed for Saint Timothy's to boogie with the Italian girls. Even in grade school, he always liked to fight. At the dances, it didn't matter who it was; he'd move in on a guy's girl and start swinging when he was challenged. I spent a lot of skin getting him out the exit before the priests showed up. Standing up to get knocked down again. Guess I'll never learn. Except for Freddie Devlin; him I could always smash. In a strange way, I kind of regretted it when he dropped out of sight.

Jimbo'd jump in the car whooping. "See that, Jack, I smoked that sucker. Nice tits on his chick. Coulda made it to home with her, buddy. No sweat." He was a crazy man, especially after a couple quarts of beer. Seemed like second nature to stick up for him.

There's nothing unusual about the Northeast: street after street of narrow rowhouses, mom and pop stores, the delis and hoagie joints, turf cut up like Sicilian pizza. Rectangles for the Pollocks, the Italians, the Irish, the Ukrainians. The Italians and the Irish liked each other least. Spades stayed in North or West Philly—healthier that way for everybody.

Those neighborhood guys protected their turf, proudly, fiercely, young guys and old heads alike. They'd be out on the stoops on Friday nights in summer, drinking quarts of Schlitz in paper bags. They knew who they were. They didn't know you. "If the boys wanna fight, you better let em,"‡ the song goes. Smart move.

Each slice had its own bars. You could get good sandwiches and okay beer. Some were strictly neighbor-hood. At 5:30, the old man stopped in after work for a quick shot of Canadian Club and a Piels with his pals. Later, young blue-collar guys came in with their girlfriends to watch the Phillies, Eagles, Warriors, boxing, play 8 ball, work the juke box. They flexed their muscles, shouted at each other about what being American meant, agreed on the Russians, Vietnam, faggitts, college boys, Castro. Some were more or less open to anybody as long as you weren't

‡Group: Thin Lizzy; album: "Jailbreak;" song: The Boys Are Back in Town; label: Virago, 1976.

black and didn't put a move on the wrong chick. It's impossible to figure out the rules unless you grow up with them. Walk into the wrong place, though, and you'd find out quick.

Some places, like McDougall's, had live entertainment sometimes, like when I went there with Charlie Murphy. It was on a side street off Bustleton Avenue. Square, two storeys of cinder block painted battleship gray. The flat roof was covered with tar and pebbles, split orange clay water pipes capped the false three foot walls that surrounded it. You could get to it by climbing the iron fire escape in the alley out the back. "Up on the roof," the song said for a reason. If you could stand the smell of hot tar, it was a good place to hang out when the Philadelphia summer humidity got stuck in the Delaware Valley, between the Pocono Mountains and the Atlantic. June to September, it was a smelly wet blanket that stuck to your face and smothered you.

McDougall's was a real classic: small, barred windows with flickering beer signs up high on the walls of the first floor. You couldn't really hear the bass from outside, but you knew it was there because your eardrums thumped. The parking lot was full of bikes and the shiny Chevy Bel Air convertibles Italian guys like. Dark. Prime spot to get laid, settle a beef, make a score. Some of the local boys leaned against the cars, drinking some beer, shooting some shit. The IRA contingent had taken the night off.

Toot wanted me to meet him there. Strange. I didn't really know him all that well. He didn't explain why, and he definitely wasn't Irish, more like Jewish. But, then again, he was a strange dude. Drove over from my place on Germantown Avenue on the Yamaha road racer I'd been building. Elegant. Slick. Fast. Very black, very illegal on the street. No mufflers; super loud expansion chambers instead. Hung on some lights. Dealer's plate from the shop. No sweat from the cops. I was connected since I started working for Mr. Castesi at Five Points in North Philly. They knew me around there, so they didn't bother pulling me over. Anywhere else, all I'd have to do is show the "Castesi's" patch on the back of my work shirt, and the cops would get real polite: "Yeh, okay, buddy, take off, but try ta keep it down on my beat, will ya? Say hello to Mr. Castesi for us."

The door to McDougall's was thick and heavy enough to need a shoulder to push it open. Inside, it was bigger than most but the usual. Long, dark wooden bar on one side.

Formica tables with chromed legs in the middle. Booths on the other covered in dark red Naugahyde. The dance floor looked like an ash tray. The dingy stage was empty, except for a tripod with a dog-eared blue sign, "Introducing Cristal and Pearl," in silver sequin letters that shined a little through the smoke when the front door opened. The "Air Conditioned!!!" sign outside lied.

Toot was nowhere to be seen, so I sat at the bar. The bartender slouched over and marked me. Irish towhead with a "What the fuck do you want?" look on his face. His tight white t-shirt said "Triumph" in blue letters. There was a lot of noise from the fat, bearded outlaws in the corner booth with their women: young, slender, pretty, busty. Never could figure that one out. I looked at them closely in case Iron Mike was there. He wasn't. They were Jersey Devils, not Hells Angels.

Somebody put on Hendrix, *Are You Experienced?* Red and green spots lit up the stage. Two girls in cheap nighties came out: a blond wearing one the color of cherry Jell-O and a brunette in a white frilly number. The blond had a boa constrictor around her neck. Big sucker, maybe six feet long and as fat as your biceps.

They got into it, the Hendrix burned out blues haze. The nighties came off. The bras. They danced alone, not touching each other, eyes fixed on the wall across the floor. Nobody paid much attention, except for the rubby art critic down front with ten draughts on his table.

The brunette was very young, pretty, thin, small breasted. She danced like she was new at it, or embarrassed, or bored. The blond had a plain face, but a body like one of those Rodin statues in the garden over on Ben Franklin Boulevard. She was a pro, and she had the snake. He was on the floor by now, and he started coiling up her leg. His head disappeared between her thighs just as they joined. "Can snakes hear," I wondered? His head popped out from behind her hip, swaying, tongue flicking in and out, then slid up between her big breasts. Even the outlaws shut up and started paying attention.

I got an elbow in the ribs and turned to see Toot. "Took me a long time to train George, man, but I think he digs it now."

"George who?"

"The snake, asshole. We needed somethin to make the act better, see, so I got George. Cristal, Pearl and me been together a long time. We needed a steady way to pay the rent, unnerstand, so I showed her how to dance with the snake. Only problem is sometimes he crashes if you feed him too much. No way to wake him up, either. You should see me tryin to catch rats behind the apartment, fuckin goofy. The neighbors look out with real big eyes, then pull down the shades. It's a hoot." He imitated their eyes.

Toot was one spacey freak. Somewhere between thirty and forty. Six-four, two hundred and twenty lumpy pounds. His frizzy hair something between blond and no color at all stuck to his skull in ragged patches. His clothes were so cheap he could have been a street bum or a university kid who bought his clothes at Arties on Wadsworth Avenue. As he talked, he scratched his scraggly pale beard with one hand and sipped his beer with the other. None of his movements seemed to go together. He was like Ginger Baker, the drummer with Cream, playing the solo in *Toad*—arms and legs all going in different directions at the same time, to different beats.

The band that played during the break was no account. Some guy called Bruce somebody or other, a short, skinny kid from Perth Amboy, New Jersey, with a lousy drummer and sad-ass lead guitar. Nothing any good ever came out of Jersey, my dad used to say. He was right on this time.

Cristal and Pearl came back on later. George looked fried, but the crowd didn't seem to mind. They'd had enough trips to the can for a joint and enough beer to make them like just about anything. The rubby art critic was passed out sitting straight up.

We went up on the roof together to wait for the girls' last set to end. He pulled out the hash pipe, and we had a few hits. Just my luck. Hashish hits me like a sledge hammer. Cristal and Pearl came up. We had a few more hits. Great. I managed to laugh my way down the fire escape by following Toot's balding head as it bobbed in front of me. Pearl, the blond, climbed on behind me; it was a tight fit for two on the Yamaha's racing saddle. I didn't mind. Even through my leathers, she felt good, soft, supple, against my back. I pulled her arms around me for safety and patted her hands to tell her it wasn't personal. She seemed startled by that. I could feel her jump, anyway.

I concentrated on the tiny tail light of Toot's outrageous purple chopper. It was very important, that little red light, as we roared through the empty streets.  It couldn't go out or I would.

We seemed to be doing 80, but none of my bikes ever had speedos; a tach was all I needed.  It was the dope.  We were probably doing about 25, tops; I was only reading 2000 rpm in second gear.  We stopped ten feet before we had to at red lights.  Getting rolling again took a lot of doing: "Left foot up on the peg, now pull in the clutch, make the foot work to put it in gear, let out the clutch, and, stupid, turn the goddamn throttle." I was some stoned.

The apartment was as weird as Toot.  The door sill was right at ground level, and we drove the bikes straight in.  It was 3 in the morning.  The neighbors must have been dead, scared, deaf or so wired it didn't matter.  The living room had no furniture, just a bunch of pillows, a white shag rug, a stereo, a black light.  Toot leaned the chopper over on its chromed side stand in the middle of the room.  I made for the wall to lean my ride against it.  There were sayings smeared on the walls in day-glow paint:  "Go stoned."  "The world ain't shit."  "Do it now."  Stuff like that.  The paint shimmered and glowed in the black light.

"See that rug, man, not a spot on it. Whoever said Harleys always leak should be shot and pissed on."

Cristal carried George in a burlap bag; he squirmed around in there. Her teeth were capped, and the black light made them look gray. Toot cued up a stack of records. "They call me Doctor John, the night tripper," sounded like it was coming from the bottom of a deep hole in the ground.

Toot turned to the girls, "Okay, we're home. Clothes off." Holding the bag at arm's length, he whispered, "Come on, Georgeoh, it's feedin time for the workin stiff." He disappeared into the bedroom. Pearl looked at me, then Cristal. They shrugged and started to strip slowly. Or at least I thought it was slowly. I sat on a pillow and couldn't move. Even my eyes were stuck. I couldn't raise my head, just watched their clothes pile up on the rug.

Toot came back. He had a hookah for us and his works for him. He unwrapped the tin foil from the hash; it was beaten into a flat strap and very brown, almost black. "Turkish," I thought, "no wonder."

He turned his left sleeve up slowly as he watched the girls. Pearl cooked up the smack in a bent spoon. I watched the match flame under it. Toot did his own shooting, choosing the vein carefully, tapping it with two fingers.   Cristal tightened the belt. It was a big hit: five lines.

"Shit," he said, as the snow went to his brain.   "So fine." His head dropped off to one side for a minute, or maybe ten, couldn't tell.

I heard his voice, low and far away.  "Hey, lookit, I don't bring my buddy home to be treated like some kinda animal. Take carea him."

Pearl cradled Toot's head on her large breasts.  He nodded in and out of life.  Cristal smiled her gray smile as she started to take my clothes off.  She was so gentle, so sweet, I put my hand on her cheek to tell her it was okay; wasn't necessary.  She shrugged it off and kept going. So very light and small and young.  I had the strangest flash in my mind's eye of Toot as a skeleton, stripped of flesh, bleached dry white.

I first met Toot a few months before at Castesi's.  Motor-cycle shops are always pretty much alike—rows of junkers in the back that never move, ancient Oil Dry underfoot, the indelible grease only bikes make, no ventilation, worse light.

This place wasn't any different, maybe lousier, but there was a lot of warranty and tune up work to be done on the British bikes they sold. That's why Mr. Castesi hired me.

Castesi's British Connection sounded good, but it was only a big, ugly Quonset hut rejected from some abandoned Army base in North Carolina or somewhere. It was just like an oven when the sun was out. It came out a lot that summer.

Mr. Castesi hired me away from Fairmount Honda. He offered me 60 percent of the labor bills instead of 50. That made it easier to come up with mom's envelope at the end of the month. The fact I wouldn't get any more tickets was a big draw. There were special relationships. Half the wise guys in the city belonged to his family. Good connections. Great protection when you drove as fast as I did.

I was spooked when Pete the parts man told me he was on the line. "Yo, Jack, you been bad or what? I got the mob on line one for ya. Pick up, now, man, now." I could hear granpop's voice telling Joe McGarrity in his saloon: "Castesi's boys will have the gelignite ready for us in one week. Then we can ship it over." On the phone, Mr. Castesi said he wanted me to meet him down in South Philly so we could "have a nice lunch and talk." Everybody in Philly knew about the place, Palumbo's Cabaret-Restaurant.  On their way up, singers like Buddy Greco, Frankie Avalon, Bobby Rydell, Bobby Darren, Fabian, even Eddie Fisher used to hang out there.  It was a kind of rock and roll shrine for white guys.  I wanted to see it.  Besides, it wasn't like I could refuse somebody like Mr. Castesi.  Not just stupid, very unhealthy.

Palumbo's is on Catherine Street, a barn of a place with hundreds of tables.  I circled it a few times on the Bonneville, looking for a place to park, until a big guy in a silk suit waved me into the loading zone right in front.  He didn't say anything, just led me through the place to a private room at the back.  Castesi looked up at me with a smile when I walked in, feeling awkward in my black jeans and leather jacket.  He moved his hand slightly and the three guys at the table stood up and walked out quickly.  The room smelled like veal and power.

Mr. Castesi was a big  sofa of a man, about sixty.  His face looked something like the picture on the box of the Mr. Potato Head toy you got for Christmas, all bumpy and warty.  The little hair he had left was very neatly trimmed, the clothes were casual but expensive, including the South Philly wise guy signature knit shirt with the funny round collar.  He wore a thick, plain wedding ring on his fat finger and a heavy, chunky gold wristwatch that probably came from Vegas.

"Ah, Jack Kavanagh, please have a seat. An Amoretto to start? It's good for the appetite." He was very pleasant, even courteous, asking after my mother and grandmother as course after course hit the table. He sure did know a lot more about me than I knew about him. For dessert, we had Cannoli and Strega. Then came the espresso and business.

He handed me a cigar and lit it for me with a tortoiseshell lighter. "Now, Jack, you probably wonder how I know so much about you. First of all, I make it my business to know who's good in the trade. You have an excellent reputation. I hear you're a stand up guy. I think we can do some very nice business together, maybe long term. You looked surprised when I spoke of your family. You shouldn't. My family goes back a long way with yours. As you probably know, your grandfather and I did quite a bit of business together. His people needed certain products I could provide. Your uncles stay in touch, too. They have always treated me with respect, so I would like to return the favor. You're not in the same line as they are, I think, but we can work together on the motor-cycle side. How about it? You'll definitely make better money than you are now. By the way, your good friends Jeeps and Nate will find out right away that you're working for me. Same goes for the rest of the cops. Deal?" he said, holding out his pudgy mitt. I shook on it. It was a good one, I figured then. More bucks meant I could keep mom and granmom going without sweating so much. It seemed right, too, appropriate, like finding the last piece of the jigsaw puzzle under the table: no picture, just a swirling cloud.

I depended on my hands, but I had this family thing about them. It was like they were out there at the end of my arms and sometimes they weren't quite mine. They might have been on loan from somebody else. They did stuff; I watched. The forearms were always mine, though, and when I worked the veins stood up proud. Heredity, I guess, just like granpop and dad. I think dad was the same about the hands, except the last time I saw him in that stupid-ass casket, all pleated fake satin crap. His hands then weren't right.

My first day at Castesi's I opened the Snap-On toolbox Hose gave me, spread out British Standard and Whitworth wrenches on the steel bench top and went to work on an older Royal Enfield that leaked oil like a sieve. Made a mental note to call the number he gave me and use the signal. It had been too long. The work order had only two words: "Fix leaks." Brit bikes always leaked, but it was a matter of volume. You needed a tanker truck behind this one to keep it full. I yanked the engine, hauled it up on the bench and watched my hands take over.

In Philly, you learn on the street to watch your back or duck a lot. Some people, like me, are born with a sixth sense about trouble, alerted by the soft brush of a feather on your neck, touch of an angel's wing, to ward off the muggers and the crazies. That's why I got out of the joint in one piece. There was something else, though. Started in again after I got out—a feeling like I was being tailed, set up. I was smoking a lot of dope then, so in my straight moments I shook it off as paranoia.

This day I sensed a presence behind me, then the sudden chemical sweet smell of a Mars Bar that's been on the shelf too long. Something large behind me was breathing injection molded chocolate at my head. It spoke: "Man, I'd give my girlfriend—hell, both of em—for veins like that."

Without moving I said, "Okay, who's gonna do the transplant?" I turned, wiping my hands on an orange shop rag. There was Toot. It wasn't the long sleeved shirt in the hot shop, it wasn't the non-stop candy. It wasn't even the runny nose, the sniffing and slurring. It was the eyes—the bleary, unfocused eyes with the dirty whites—that told me he was a long-term junkie. No doubt about it. Funny thing, Toot turned out to be a great mechanic between highs. The kind of guy who looks at a motor, sniffs it a bit and knows what's wrong. That's a gift. I had it, too. It didn't always work; there was always Lintoff's circus bike.

As June passed into July, we got to know each other. Toot suspicious; me knowing you can't trust a junkie. The other guys in the shop, Rico and Jesus, the two Puerto Ricans who worked part time for a burglar alarm company; Geets, the Japanese specialist; and Jerry, the two stroke expert and stereo freak, didn't have much to say for themselves. They worked like hell in the morning, smoked grass for lunch in the paint booth out the back, laughed a lot at nothing and dropped wrenches in the afternoon. I only smoked at night.

Toot's habit was big but not out of hand. Uppers for wake-ups in the morning, two lines for lunch, a little taste in the afternoon, more later. I could always tell when he'd had a hit. He'd stand there, swaying, head rolling around, his eyes closing slowly and with a sigh almost sexual he'd dream himself away. Then he'd come around and start working. Just like that, now down, now up: shouting, mumbling, destructive, waiting for the fault line to open all the way in his personal earthquake.

Toot rode the real thing, a purple metal flake Harley knucklehead with chromed everything, an extended springer front end, a tiny front wheel, ape hangers. It was impossible to drive. I tried once when we switched bikes. He looked hilarious laid out on the long black tank of my Yamaha, his Mexican serapé billowing over his back as he held on to the short clip-on bars. I probably looked just as stupid, all in black, trying to keep the Harley's front wheel on the ground. Mostly, though, I drove Trusty the Bonneville; much more civilized for street riding.

He loved that slow, ugly Hardly Ableson even more than the undertaker's flower car he sometimes carried it around in. Those were his only real passions, beyond smack.

We took to going to Francey's on Lehigh Street for lunch. It was a dump. What really happened was I'd have a cheese-steak with sauce and onions and a few beers to wash it down. Toot would rave on about whatever was staggering around in his soggy brain. We sat in a booth on one of those Philly days when it's so humid the sweat rolls down your back and between your cheeks, your hair feels too heavy and you can't take a deep breath. The table was covered with empty draught glasses and greasy paper plates transparent in the middle.

"Toot, you know that shit's gonna kill ya, don't ya?"

He stared at the table top for a long time, trying to focus those garbage-can eyes, then snorted: "Lotta death goin round, man. I'd rather go stoned than straight. Look at Ray Charles. He's been a shooter forever. All you need is enough money and clean works. Didn't ask to be here. Don't matter, anyway. You gotta learn, man, it ain't up to you. I don't want nobody to save me. Know what I'm sayin?"

August began. That's when I met Cristal, Pearl and George at McDougall's. Things changed after that; he decided we were buddies. I guess we were. One night he took me in the flower car along Passyunk down by the

Delaware, where it smells like chicken shit and nothing grows along the river banks. The air must creep up from the chemical factories in Marcus Hook. It's so thick you can chew it. He parked near some train tracks on a dead-end road covered with broken glass and burned out cars. Reaching over, he opened the glove compartment, proudly showed me his silver 45 automatic with the pearl handles and told me how he paid his dealer by pulling B & E jobs with what he called his associates. This from him was trust.

He took out his works. "Just look at this shit, man, so much goddamn talc. It's been stepped on so bad I can't get much of a rush off it. Wanna try? Just a skin-pop, Jack, save the main line for later." For a junkie, sharing dope is as close as you'll ever get to friendship.

"No thanks, Toot, I'll stick to the juice for a while," and took a pull from the pint of Jameson. Relieved, he rolled up his left sleeve, then his right. The veins were a road map through a Laotian jungle, dark, collapsed, sick; the needle marks bombed out towns. He gave up and, looking in the rear view mirror, injected himself under his tongue. Spit dribbled down his chin. "Best spot there is. Cops never look for tracks under your tongue. Course, between your toes ain't bad, but

I'm ticklish. Did I tell ya?  Cristal thinks yer sweet.  You believe that shit, man?  Women are weird."

"Whatsa matta, Jack, don't you like me, or what?"  "Nope, it's not that, Judy, yer a good kid.  Nice body.  It's just I'm tired.  Why don't you catch some sleep.  We can make it up in the morning."  "Man, you are one strange dude.  Think too much.  Cute though," she said and turned over.  I kissed her cheek.  Judy was a pretty Irish redhead from Kensington, waitress at McDougall's.  I knew her a while, and after the bar closed one Friday night toward the end of the month, it seemed like a plan to both of us to come back to my place. Problem was, I just couldn't get interested in the girls I knew. Sex, sure, most of the time, but that was it.  They didn't seem to have personalities of their own.  I looked at her pale body as she slept.  Her large nipples were pink.  It was like I was watching her from outside the room.

I stayed wide awake, staring at the shapes on the water-stained ceiling that shifted every time a trolley went by on the street.  Judy didn't move when the phone rang.  It was Toot in his mysterious mode. "I'm in the booth right across the street.

Be down in five minutes." The girl slept on. I didn't wake her. I didn't have anything worth stealing, not that she would have. The oak box granpop made for me was very carefully hidden.

He was slouching in the dark doorway of The New Christian Church of Christ Jesus; really it was only a store-front where black people dressed in starched clean clothes sang on Sundays and were yelled at by the minister. "Party time," he whispered, starting the chopper with a roar from the straight pipes that shook the church windows. I climbed on the back, and we headed down Germantown Avenue to Broad Street then onto Snyder and the docks. Under the fierce, blue-white street lights we flew down the slick old cobblestones past sagging fences, scrap yards, loading bays. All of it mutated out of the ground, fed by nuclear fallout. Thought I heard an echo behind us. Another Harley motor? Maybe. Maybe not.

We wove in and out of the warehouses, some empty and wrecked, some still working, covered with crude, gang turf graffiti. We stopped in an alleyway near a moored boat. It was very still, so quiet you'd think nobody else was left alive, anywhere. Small points of light gleamed from the flecks of mica in the damp, black slate sidewalks that were laid down 200 years ago when Philly was an important port.

The freighter was big, fat bellied, abandoned, sinking slowly into the oil slick water. "Amphora" was painted on the bow. Rats rustled and squeaked in the gray, dusty brush. I thought of rat teeth. We went up the rickety gangplank to the high stern, then down into the guts of the dead ship. Toot held up his flickering Zippo as we ducked through doorways and under broken pipes and trashed wiring; the junkies had stripped everything worth selling for scrap. The place smelled like low tide.

At last, we came to a long steel gangway that led down to the floor of the dripping hold. At the far end, about forty feet away and twenty feet below us, was a smudge of murky light that lit up peeling walls streaked with dark rust. We slid down the slippery ladder, stumbled through the garbage and broken glass, and walked into the light. Ranged around the slimy walls, sitting on packing cases or stalking up and down were Toot's associates. The smack freak nodding out. The dealer, high on coke, talking a mile a minute, closing a sale. The glow of the pipe lighting up stoned faces. Further off, a hooker on her knees. The sharp smell of decaying iron, the perfume of hashish, acrid grass smoke, the choking odor of old piss all mixed up with the greasy smudge from candles and Sterno cans.

Toot was home. He walked up to a pimp in a red velour hat, bought some Dexedrine for me and some Methedrine for him. Mine was pills; his he cooked up and shot. We both kept talking till just before dawn, about anything, everything, nothing. Toot had the last words, "You gotta understand, the world ain't shit. Men, women, ain't shit. Takin a dump feels better than sex. People, countries, armies, mothers—they ain't worth shit, don't mean nothin. This is what there is," taking in the hold with a disjointed wave of his arm. "You're a stand up guy, Jack, but it won't do ya no good, might just get ya snuffed, too."

Coming down from a speedo high is not nice. By Monday morning I was just getting unwired, but I still felt like my feet didn't touch the ground. "Gettin too old for this crap," I thought. I let my hands take over to fix the Triumph gearbox that lay in an oily heap on my bench. I didn't notice Toot come in until he slid a paper carton of coffee across to me.

"I got the word over the weekend, like from up there, ya know." His head jerked back for emphasis. "I'm gonna kick. I mean it. No more smack. Too expensive, lousy quality. Besides, it's startin to be for teenagers and yahoos from Levittown—fuckin suburbs. Christ, it's awful. So I'm gonna kick. Whaddaya think?"

"Sure, Toot, sure. Smart move, man." I'd heard it before. Not just from him;  from the white collar tourists looking for a score downtown to the South Street winos balled up in doorways with empty bottles of Thunderbird next to them. Only one thing is for sure, they never do.

After that Toot started shooting Methedrine like it was heroin. This you don't do. Smack doesn't attack your body; it just fries your brain. Meth is like an alien parasite in a space movie. It gets into your chest and eats you from inside, heart first.

I used to teach dummy junior mechanics about electricity. It was necessary, because British bikes used electrics made by Lucas, "The Prince of Darkness," as I called the company. I'd hold up a piece of melted wire and say something like: "Think about this wire like a sidewalk. A buncha da boys from one neighbahood are runnin down it, fast. Everything's okay if nobody gets in the way, right?  But what's gonna happen if a buncha guys from anudder neighbahood start runnin at em from the udder direction?"

"Duuhh," they'd say. "There's gonna be a fight?" one of the brighter lights would pipe up.

"Correct. They'll be a collision and a burn out. So don't screw up the polarity, okay?"

It was the same with him. Real quick, Toot went from a big, lumpy, chocolate-fed, small-time hood to a scrawny, speed-propelled paranoid. His teeth fell out, his gums bled, the little hair he had came out in clumps. He didn't show up at Castesi's. When he did, all he could do was blabber, couldn't hold a wrench, couldn't concentrate on anything for more than two seconds.

The late night calls started in November as the summer trade slowed to a trickle. He talked, I listened: "Yeh, I'm into electronics. Takin this radio apart right now to see where the sounds really come from. It's a puzzle, man." He never put anything back together. I took to putting the phone down for an hour or so to have a beer or take a shower. He never noticed.

Then he got into leather clothes. "Dig it, Jack, me and the girls are gonna rake in some serious bread makin bike duds.

You'll be the manager of the company.  All the black stuff will be named after you.  We're gonna call it the Black Jack line."

What really happened was that Pearl gave him a sharp brown leather vest.  He started decorating it with brass grommets, first a few, then more and more and more, until it was more air than leather.  It must have fallen apart, because he stopped wearing it.

The last call came at 4 in the morning on a rainy Tuesday in the middle of December. There wasn't enough work at Castesi's by then, so I was driving a tow truck for a gas station on Lehigh.  I got a commission for bringing one in on the hook.  That night, I didn't get off until 2, and I was tired, groggy as hell and pissed off that I wasn't making enough money.  Not good, with mom's winter heating bills on the way.

"Listen, man, you gotta help me.  I got bad trouble; only you can do it."  Toot sounded scared, like somebody wanted him dead.  He gave me an address near Moyamensing Prison.

Sometime, the little street was a good blue-collar place to live. Now it was run down, battered, like the people inside the beat up houses.  The house was 1920s, jerry-built brick, with broken windows in the make-shift porch somebody with pride but no talent put up once. The porch door and the main one stood open to the damp cold.

Inside, it was overheated from the radiators at full blast; air very dry. The living room was littered with half empty pizza boxes, candy wrappers, dirty socks, beer bottles, an empty crib. The television was on, but the sound was off. I'd seen the commercial for Blue Cheer a million times. Bodies were strewn around like they just bumped into something and fell down: on the floor in the middle of the room, a girl about fifteen, wearing only stained panties; propped against a wall, a fat man in his fifties with pizza sauce on his strap undershirt; in the doorway to the kitchen, a pearl-pale woman about twenty-five in a gray slip wearing one fuzzy pink slipper; on the lumpy couch, two skinny young black guys in shorts holding each other. They were alive, just waiting until the time came.

"Yo, Toot," I called and got a cracked, feeble answer from the second floor. The other inmates didn't budge.

"Up here, man, hurry up, hurry up."

I climbed the stuffy, narrow staircase and found him in the bathroom, sitting in gray underpants on the edge of the unused tub. He couldn't have weighed more than a hundred pounds. There were angry red needle marks all over him, from his freckled shoulders to his yellow toes.

"Great, man, great. Glad you're here. You gotta help me. I can't get the belt tight. Found the fuckin vein, but I can't get the belt tight. Look." He took the needle in his right hand, put the belt in his mouth and tried to pull with pulpy gums. His hand quaked like he had malaria. He was crying. "It don't work anymore. Shit, man, just look at this."

I watched my shaking hands reach out and pull the belt tight on his tiny arm. It was the least I could do. He stuck himself once, twice, three times: "Gotcha, mothafucka."

The plunger went down. He smiled, closed his eyes, slid to the floor and died. Not a sound, no resistance, not a whimper.

Nothing was left of the Toot I knew in that pile of bones. As I knelt and put my fingers on his cold blue jugular to make sure he was dead, I saw his pleased, relieved, peaceful face. What little color there was left in his skin had drained away, and against that crummy linoleum floor he looked like a translucent piece of greasy paper blown against your legs in a burger joint parking lot. I closed his garbage-can eyes and took off. Nobody downstairs saw me leave.

I didn't call the ambulance until after I was back in Germantown. Did it from a phone booth, just to be safe. Didn't leave my name. Tore the phone out as I left. The city gave Toot a tag on his toe with a number on it and put him in the ground somewhere. I went to the apartment, but Cristal and Pearl had moved, no forwarding, and they didn't strip at McDougall's any more. I smashed a window on the flower car and took Toot's 45 and a box of shells; not for protection, I could get a gun very easily if I wanted, but to preserve a piece of him, some memory of a life, no matter how sad. As far as I could tell, he didn't have any relatives or friends, except me. I never did get his real name, and didn't look for it. He didn't ask to be here anyway. I thought about that a lot—then. Figured I didn't, either. What for? Anyway, I put the pistol in granpop's box.

Sometimes—in the anarchy of time—an accident or tragedy occurs that starts things happening as they should. I was sitting by myself in a booth at McDougall's on Sunday afternoon in early spring. After the waitress brought me a beer and yelled out my food order, she beetled over to the bartender, and he headed for the phone. The place was just about deserted. The only full table near me had two guys and two girls in their twenties. One was wearing an Army uniform. They were talking and laughing over shots and beers. Looked like the soldier had just gotten back from his tour. A welcome home party. I thought of my brother, Mark, and wished him safe. Matt's jevvie letter to me in prison came to mind. I spit out the thought.

Hard to miss Sean and Mike when they walked in later, mostly because they had a knockout black-Irish colleen with them that could've stopped traffic. Sean gave me a wink, walked up to the bar and got a bottle of Jameson before they headed over.

"Now, then, Jacko," Mike said, "you're a grand sight. Shake the divine hand of Mary Daugherty from Derry." I liked that part. Sean started in. "I'm to say hello for Charlie Murphy. He's up in New England on some important business for us; says he'll be around to see you before too long. We hear you changed jobs. Smart move, that. Never hurts to have some muscle at your back." Both of them dropped the not so authentic Philly accents.

"Exactly," from Mike, as his shot glass hit the table. "Jack, the Kavanagh name means a lot to us, right up there with Joe McGarrity and the Philly *Clann*. We know you haven't exactly followed the path of your grandfather and your uncles yet, even though you slip the odd fifty to the cause and spent your time well in Holmesburg with Pat Johnston. We think, maybe, now's your time to make a decision."

An argument started at the soldier's table. They were all pretty drunk. "Don't be an asshole, Billy. Just because you been in Nam don't make you no expert. We're Americans. We gotta bomb those bastards inta the ground. Otherwise, they'll be takin over. Sweartagad, I get so pissed of wit you vets. Ya go over there, smoke a buncha weed and come back talkin like some faggit college boy peaceniks." The soldier looked into his beer, shook his head slowly and said like he was tired, "Oh, well, I guess we're just fucked, then."

"Please, God, don't let it end too soon," from Sean. "We still have much to learn from the Viet Cong, bless their pointy little heads. Anyway, Jack, like Mike was saying. We think you might want to listen to a small proposition we have for you. A bit of adventure, travel, night life, the ladies, maybe vacations in the Middle East could be arranged. But, then, Mary should be the one to lay it out for you."

She covered my hand with hers. Her eyes were deep, deep brown, like mahogany. I went into a hot melt when her breathy voice began, the banshee song of ages past. "The lads tell me you keep up with the news, North and South, and that's a fine thing. What you can't know is that there are big plans being laid. When Ian Paisley's bastards started the blood in Armagh, the Army decided to take the battle where it belongs—the North—and then to England itself, but that won't be for a few years yet. What we need in Britain is a sleeper we can trust, one who will act for Ireland when the time comes. How would it be if we got you a nice job in Manchester or Birmingham, say, where you could work away at your motorbikes for a few years? You'd be a model citizen, married to a model woman, myself it would be. We could slip down to London, weekends, and do the clubs, the King's Road, Carnaby Street, whatever you fancy, Jack. You're a fine, big, handsome Irishman with the touch of the Faery on your head, so it would be no trial. As much or as little as you fancy—all around."

I sat back, chest punched. Sean poured me a shot using his left hand because the right was so mashed, and I downed it in one. Joe McGarrity was right, so long ago. Finally, they had come for me. Finally, I had to choose. I sipped the beer chaser slowly, trying to think in a straight line.

Sean stuck in, quick: "Now, of course, we'd be very willing to sweeten the deal for you. Nothing tastier than revenge. If you need our assistance with the Devlin business, we'd be more than pleased to help you out. Nobody would ever know where the hit came from. Trust me."

"Say, what?" from me. "I got no problems with the Devlins any more. Ain't seen any of them for years."

Sean and Mike looked at each other with raised eyebrows but said nothing, so I let it out: "Look, you guys, are you sayin I'd have to kill? Set bombs? Stuff like that? Sorry, but I'm not your man." In my head, I could hear Toot, see him dead. "I was brought up to believe in one thing for sure, that Ireland should be, will be, united. But that don't mean killin to me. What it does mean is that the majority should rule the country, all of it. The British should go back where they came from, and the troubles will stop once the nutbars in the Bogside and Sandy Row sort themselves out. I think Sinn Fein should recognize the parliaments in Dublin, Stormont and Westminister, then get to work on a political end to partition. That's not my grandfather or my uncles talkin; it's me and my father. I don't want nothin to do with no workers' paradise or Marxist-Leninist anything. Not because it's communist, socialist, whatever, don't get me wrong, don't care. It's because it's all bullshit—their side, your side, this side—all bullshit."

Mary shook her head sadly. "Ah, it's a democrat, then, is it? Too bad. We could have had some fine times together, Jack. The time will come soon when Sinn Fein has no power atall over the Provos. Still in all, no harm done. We thought we had our man. We didn't. I'm sure it goes without saying that this little conversation never happened." She gave my cheek a pat before they left. Across from me, the soldier had passed out on his arms.

## 7. "HELLHOUND ON MY TRAIL"

Dad drove the beat up, two-tone 1950 Chevy coupe across the Delaware on the Tacony-Palmyra bridge, tires thrumming on the metal grid in the center span. Now we're heading southeast on 73 in Jersey, on our way to Route 30, "downashore," as Philly people say. It's crowded and hot, with my mother, Matt and Mark, granpop and granmom all crammed in on our way to Margate for the day. I'm sitting on granpop's lap in the back. I have to pee, but dad doesn't stop except for women, so granpop holds the milk bottle for me, chuckling with granmom, the soft way the Irish can. Matt turns to me with a sneer.

We're driving through the Pine Barrens, east of Atco, where the piney truck farmers live in shacks back among the creeks and scrub bogs. One by one, printed signs reel off Burma Shave rhymes. Dad grunts every time Matt reads them out proudly, precisely. Sloppy hand written signs advertise monster tomatoes and cantaloupes ahead. These I can read. We don't stop until a sign says, Toms●Lopes● Clams ☞500 yds." Dad likes clams.

We pull over on the pebbly shoulder next to the ram-shackle stand. In the shade of the lean-to roof, the vegetables on the shelves are blinding red and green and golden. Ragged little kids run around. Dad picks out a dozen clams and hands the money to the skinny lady in the faded house dress who cuts her own hair. He pulls out his pocketknife and shucks and eats them on the spot. Their tongues lick out as they're opened. Mom buys tomatoes and a cantaloupe for our picnic on the beach. "Corn's not so hot," she says.

The road's a two-laner, so the going's slow on summer weekends when you get away late. I start bitching, so granpop starts with the stories. He's got millions. We're passing yards where they store road materials; one has a mound that looks like a cave. "You know who lives in there, boyo?" I nod, but he goes on. "The sand man lives in that cave. He's made out of sand, only four foot high. Legs like fireplugs, pine branches for arms and a head like a big soft melon. No eyes, just deep, deep black holes in his head. He's the one who puts sand in a little boy's eyes so he can't help but go to sleep. Your lids get so heavy you just can't help yourself." I twist in his thick, hairy arms. I've heard this one

before, and I'm not going for it, so after a while he tries
another angle to shut me up.

"Look out across the pines, my lad, can you hear him
keening like the banshee?" I frown and shake my head; this
is new. "When the wind's just right, you can hear him. I think I
hear him now. It's the Jersey Devil. He's half human, half
devil. His human mother tried to put him down when he was
born, but she couldn't. He flew up the chimney and
disappeared.

"He's been shot many times, but he can't die. He can fly on
wings like a bat, but much, much bigger. Has feet like a goat,
the head of a horse, the teeth of a bear, the devil's tail and
huge claws like nothing on earth. But mostly it's the eyes,
Jackie, red and yellow as coals they are, boyo; hot enough to
burn your skin. He's been seen many times, flying just above
the pines or perched on the roof trees of people's houses.
Not just around here, either, but in Philly and Delaware, too.

"Mind you, that Jersey Devil, he's a mean one, make no
mistake. He sees everything with those hellhound eyes,
knows everything. Mostly, he snatches chickens and dogs in
those claws; then he takes them to his lair and eats them right

up. But, sometimes, little bad boys just disappear forever. Nobody even finds their bones.

"Should we let you off here and pick you up on the way back?  Might be dark by then."

I lower my head to my chest and shake it. The bottom lip starts to go, and the bawling begins. The backs of dad's ears turn red as he twists his big hands on the wheel and stares straight ahead, rigid as a Welshman. Mom says, "Dad, now you just cut that out right now.  You're scaring him with that nonsense. Next thing, you'll be telling him about the Kavanagh banshee knocking for all to hear when one of the men passes away." Granmom blesses herself.

Granpop's got it right, though.  He comforts me in his soft brogue, rocking back and forth, humming *Spanish Lady*, and I drift off to sleep.

Next thing I know, we're crossing the rickety bridge over Egg Harbor.  The tide's out and the flats are a sticky, stinky mess of mud and sand.  We turn south to Margate, and I can see my friend, the fat wooden elephant, painted for the circus, standing on the sand. It's a small, quiet, uncrowded little town geared to families; no tacky, jammed, carney boardwalks like

Steeplechase Park, Wildwood or Atlantic City, where mom and dad met at a Benny Goodman show on Steel Pier.

Mom spreads out the blanket and lathers everybody with Coppertone. Dad curses the umbrella: "Goddamn thing never works." Granmom sets up the beach chairs, and granpop takes off to find some bargain Jersey beer.

Me and Matthew and Mark race for the elephant. I look up, squinting, into the sun. She's huge. We jump up the stoop, go in the little door and climb the creaking wooden steps so we can look out at the ocean through the cobwebbed window in her side. It smells like hot dry rot, but the spiders like it. So do we.

Matt reads the sign, "Danger, Rip Tide," so on the way back he tries to keep Mark and me out of the surf and on the wet sand. We ignore him, mostly. We leave perfect white footprints behind us that disappear as the thin, foaming wash of ocean rolls over them. Little birds on long legs scoot about, needling their sharp beaks into the sand. A lone seagull with a yellow beak and pure white and coal black feathers stands on one orange foot looking out to sea. Mark runs to my mother and says, "Mom, mom, there's a beautiful big bird." "Yeh," I say, "let's kick it."

We eat tomatoes and cantaloupe and hot dogs and Coke. We build castles with moats, throw clam shells at each other and get blisters on our freckled shoulders. Around us, the other day-trippers from Philly and Camden do just the same.

Downashore on an August Saturday means a long drive home, so near sundown dad herds us, gritty, sunburned and screaming, into the Chevy for the hot, slow ride back to Hope Street. On the way, the sand man gets me, and I dream of the banshee in her long white robe and hear the Jersey Devil wail.

"Dig it, Jack, got some good news if you ain't busy."

"Pecker, what the hell do you want?"

"Yer motha, man, like always. Lissen, got a line on a party down on Walnut Street tonight. Figured two dangerous, good lookin bike dudes like us could do some serious damage with those University of Pennsylvania chicks. Sound good? Got some deadly weed from the club, man, righteous deadly. Right outta Cambodia."

"Not doin nothin. Why not? I'll meet ya at Five Points about 8. We'll have a toot, grab some munchies and spin on down."

"Far out. Just got back from the pines, man. Got some great tomatoes and a lope."

"What? You tellin me you're bringin that stuff to a party fulla college chicks. You really are a piney, man. Too goddamn inbred fer yer own good."

Pecker snickered and went hillbilly on me: "Tell ya, Jack, my sisters're good enough for me, so they gotta be good enough for a bog-trottin dumb-ass like you."

"Yeh, yeh, yer mom, too. See ya then."

Now what was his angle, calling me out of nowhere? I'd known him a couple of years; not that well—a few beers together down at the drags at Atco, that sort of stuff. Mainly, he stuck close to his club. Then it made sense. This was outside the club and the rules, and the Jersey Devils MC came down hard on broken rules. If he went to a college girl party with me; it was my idea, not his fault. Besides, because I fixed some of their rides and sped them up, I had a courtesy card in my wallet that gave me some rights not to be hassled. He knew they'd believe him if he used my name. Still, what was he up to? Lookin for a new old lady? Slummin? Maybe the club ordered him to reel in a college girl to pull a train. Might turn out to be a ridiculous night.

I had a little trouble getting the sidestand down, or maybe it was my foot that wasn't working. Finally, I gave up and leaned the Triumph up against the wall of the brownstone and turned to Pecker. The weed really was Cambodian, opiated and powerful as hell, and it didn't make him look any better; his head seemed very large, kind of lopsided. He was five eleven and thin as a dry cedar fence rail. The dead white skin of his face, where you could see it, was deeply pockmarked. His full beard was very black, like his long hair that was neatly squared off behind and greased back flat on his skull. The eyes were very pale grey. A small silver cross dangled from his pierced right ear. Then, that was a statement, not a fashion one either.

"Whoa, man. You don't smell any better, do ya? Coulda dressed for the occasion." His denim jacket was stiff with grime.

"You know fuckin well I ain't allowed to wash my colors, Jack. And I can't afford those fancy horse boots you got on. Let's have another hit before we go in."

I took it very easy as we passed the joint back and forth, taking small tokes and not holding the smoke in very long. A soft early July breeze rustled the Sycamore leaves along Walnut Street. The noise seemed louder than the traffic. We were out of our territory, up in West Philly, across the Schuylkill River, on 42$^{nd}$ Street. Once, this long row of tall brownstones had people with names like Lippincott and Biddle. Both sides of the street sure looked that way, stately and quiet. The wide black slate sidewalks had sparkling specks of mica that would not let go of my eyes. I raised them very slowly to watch Pecker extinguish the smoldering roach on his tongue before he ate it.

He wore the regulation sleeveless Levis jacket over his leathers. An outsider, I was never allowed to witness an initiation, but I had no doubt it was true every member of the club pissed on a new member's colors. It reeked like the can in a Jersey roadhouse. On the front, the red flying wings, the SS skull and crossbones pin, the 1% patch that yelled outlaw at the washed world, the Iron Cross, all were part of his status in the club. The red, white and black Jersey Devil screaming on the back gave me a color flashback of granpop's story, but

I shook it off as one of those eerie things that happen when you're stoned.

The attached, three-storey brownstones were broken up into apartments for university kids with daddy's money coming in regular. Right off the sidewalk was a one-step stoop; it had a pattern in worn, white marble diamonds surrounded by a blue rectangle. Pecker pushed one of the buttons set in the entryway wall. Right away, there was a buzz and the lock clicked open. "Not too safe," I thought, "but what do college kids know? All some of them seem to be good for these days is bitchin and tryin to look like us. Pecker should be a hit."

The apartment was on the first floor, off the long, high-ceilinged hallway that ran down the left side of the building. Inside, there was very little furniture and no rugs covering the shiny hardwood floor of the large living room. The only light came from the kitchen, where guys in chinos and blue button-down Gant shirts stood around a new garbage can full of Screamin Purple Jesus, that mix of Chemistry lab alcohol and grape juice that really will make you wail.

Along the living room's far wall was a kick-ass Kenwood stereo, 100 watts a channel probably; too bad they were playing folk music. Pecker looked at me and mouthed, "Pete Seeger?" I shrugged and looked around.

There were a few tie-dyed pillows scattered about along the walls, grabbed by the early birds. Maybe thirty people in the room, two-thirds women. I hadn't seen so many plaid skirts and gold blanket pins, Bass Weejun penny loafers, knee socks, cashmere sweaters, pearls and Jackie Kennedy hair since a high school dance. Looked like a Republican convention in DC.

Hanging out under the poster with the peace symbol were some SDS types in bell bottoms and Peace Now! T-shirts trying to look hip, but the women were wearing bras and the hair wasn't right. The guys wore their hair long, with beaded headbands holding it back. They were all very clean. Still, there were some good lookin chicks. Seeger sang "Little boxes all the same." You could hear it clearly because the noise had died down, and everyone in the room was staring at us. It was only for a moment, then they turned back to their friends, embarrassed.

Pecker didn't lack stones. He just walked across the room, sat down on the floor with his back against the wall, spread out his bag of piney munchies, yanked out his jack knife and started slicing. I got the laughters from the weed. Pecker turned to the blond next to him and said, " Hey, check it out, this stuff's really fresh, right from Jersey. Want some?" I couldn't help thinking of Arlo Guthrie's lines in *Alice's Restaurant*, because she stared at her loafers and just started sliding away from him along the wall. He munched away happily, tomato juice running into his beard, right out of his gourd. I laughed out loud.

I wandered over to the stereo and started checking out the records. It was time warp stuff: Ink Spots, Kingston Trio, Joan Baez, Buffy Saint Marie, Beach Boys. I pulled out a Jim Kweskin's Jug Band record, mostly because it had a picture of Maria Muldaur on the jacket.

Then I noticed her coming right toward me like an arrow through the crowd, an astonishingly pretty girl about twenty-two, with tended black hair and understated Ladybug clothes. She stood close, looking past my shoulder. I'm six two, so she must have been five eleven at least. She smelled of Coté. "Do you like Kweskin?" she asked with a small, tight smile.

"Yeh, not bad. I'm kinda partial to Hendrix and Cream, though. Any a that here? Shame to waste this stereo."

"We go to the Main Point to hear Kweskin whenever he's there.  Ever been there?"

Her hair fell across her eyes from the neat part on the right side of her head.

"Nope, Main Line's not my turf.  Mostly I hang out at McDougall's in the Northeast.  Ever been there?"

"No, I'm from Bryn Mawr."

We listened to the music for a while.

"You go to the university?"

"You mean the University of Pennsylvania?  No, not really. I just finished my archeology degree at Swarthmore.  Do you ride?"

"Yeh, course.  Why dya ask?"

"It's the boots, I guess."  And smiling, "Horses?"

"No. Bikes.  Motorcycles.  On the Bonny tonight."

"Oh, I see.  I've never been on a motorcycle.  Might be fun. What is it like?"

"It's how I make a buck.  Fixin em, I mean.  Ridin—it's like a sorta speed and freedom thing. You just go.  Do some racin, too. Course, it's a bit different if you're ridin two-up. Passenger's gotta stick to ya like glue and just lean with it.

Nothin worse than a passenger who tries to steer for ya. You wanna go for a ride with me sometime?"

Up came this football player type, a regulation Ivy Leaguer with the brown short back and sides. He was giving me the muscles treatment and the hairy eyeball. I laughed in his face. He got between us and turned to her with his back to me: "Honestly, you aren't really talking to this gate crasher, are you? Just look at him. Hippies! Really, sometimes I wonder how far you'll take this rebellious kick you're on. You should watch yourself. I certainly will."

"Oh, Chuck, you're so boring. You have your ring back, don't you? Let it go. I'm perfectly free to do what I want. I don't have to clear my every move with you anymore. Just bug off, please."

He turned to me with a look like I needed to be shot and pissed on, then stomped off toward the kitchen. I snickered.

"I apologize for that. Boys like Chuck shouldn't drink so much. I'm Judith Earle, by the way," sticking out her hand so the charm bracelet jingled.

"Jack. Came with Pecker over there."

"Yes, we all saw you two come in. A bit unexpected. What kind of name is Packer, anyway?"

"It's Pecker. And don't ask."

Judith's perfect head went back as she laughed musically, hair falling away from her long neck. Her teeth were even, white, straight. A stray curl caught on her pearl earring, and she brushed it back in place with an unconscious, graceful little gesture. I looked at her quickly. Difficult to tell under the preppy clothes, but she probably played field hockey and was very tan at the end of the summer. No doubt she was smart. I tried to control the motor mouth you get after the laughters and before the munchies.

"He has this thing about hippies. Are you a hippie?"

I snorted. "Not me. Yeh, I see. It's the long hair and the clothes, right? Nope. Far as I know, hippies are counter-culture college kids with beads and mouth. They got back-up—money and stuff—so they can say what they like for a while. Can't say I understand what their problem is. 'Peace, love, drugs, man,' " I said, and made the peace symbol with my fingers. I focused on the black grease under my fingernails for a second. "I guess I'm just a blue-collar guy with underground connections. We're not the new guys in the neighborhood, they are. Seems like the hippies want to look like us. They always look like narcs to me. Don't think like us, either."

"What underground is that, exactly?" I nodded in Pecker's direction.

"Oh. Is he dangerous? He looks it."

"Not right now. We know each other. That's all it takes. Best, maybe, you don't ask too many questions about Pecker. I can handle him."

"Okay, change of topic, then. Tell me, do you think the war in Vietnam is a defensible idea? Should we still be over there?"

"Well, workin guys like me don't have much of a say. Buddies I used ta work with go, guys I went to high school with go, spades go. Some come back in body bags. Some shoulda. Don't guess it'll ever be much different. One a my brothers is in the Army, though, career soldier. He's already done one jungle tour. Now he's in Germany. Hope he doesn't go back." I paused and looked into her pale eyes. "I guess the answer is no, we shouldn't be there. This cost is too high, and there's no return."

"Have you been over there?"

"Nam? No way.  Down on Broad Street, the lieutenant took one look at my medical records and told me: 'Son, the Unnnahted States Army don't want no damaged goods like you.' "  I did the major's bit in my best Arkansas white-trash drawl.  I cleaned up the language for her benefit.

"What happened?"

"Nothin much, really.  Accident: concussion, messed up shoulder, pins and stuff, right knee's not so hot, either.  I figure they were worried if I got hurt at boot camp down at Fort Gordon, they'd end up payin for it for the rest of my life. And they didn't want to, so they gave me a 4F. That's about it, I think.

"Except, like I said, there's no return over there.  No cause to fight for. Maybe there isn't in Ireland, either.  Not as sure as I used to be."

"What's Ireland got to do with it?"

"A lot for people like me."

"I'll have to think about that one. Do you have other brothers and sisters?"

"Yep, one, my oldest brother.  He's a jevvie."

"A what?"

"A Jesuit, a priest, he teaches English at Fordham in New York. How about that ride?"

"You don't look 4F to me, I must say." A pause, and then: "Well, I am a bit bored. These are the same people I always see, you know. It's an interesting idea, and Chuck will be furious. But how do I know I can I trust you, Jack?"

"Honest Injun, Judith," I said, flashing the Boy Scout salute with my best smile, "you're in safe hands with Black Jack. No faster than a hundred, promise."

She circulated a bit, saying goodbye to her friends, then came back. I thought she wouldn't. Some of her girlfriends stared at me and talked to each other behind their hands. Chuck was ignored.

On the way out, I nodded to Pecker. He was trying to get close to another girl. He grinned, winked and gave me the finger as we left.

We headed for her parents' place in Bryn Mawr. I told her to wrap both arms around my waist for safety. Her look was doubtful, but she did it anyway. Took it nice and easy at first so she could get used to riding behind me, arms around me, body pressed flat against my back, thighs locked on my hips. She didn't have a lot of choice; bikes are set up that way.

The twin Dunstall performance mufflers sang deeply. She took to it easily, following my body as it leaned into the turns. Took the scenic route: over the river on Market Street by 30th Street Station, a spin around City Hall, scrubbing the side-walls of the Pirellis, then over to Logan Circle and up Ben Franklin Parkway dead center at the massive, brightly lit front of the Philadelphia Museum of Art up on the hill.

"Jack," she yelled, "this is perfect. I love it. Faster, please."

I twisted on a little more throttle, and the Bonneville lifted on the suspension with each shift in the straights and settled a little heavier before the apex in the corners. East River Drive winds along the Schuylkill River through Fairmount Park. It's a great road for a bike. We did the sweeper by Boathouse Row pushing 70, then geared down for the tight right-hander at the tunnel cut in the rock. The Dunstalls boomed for a moment as we flew through it. I could feel she was breathing hard against my back, her cheek on my shoulder. I looked down and saw a bare patch of her thigh where the wind had blown her skirt up.

I opened it up a bit more and we were doing a fine 80, sweeping through the turns coming up to the graceful old iron of Falls Bridge. Light was green, so I popped third gear, then dumped second, and dove a left-hander into it, the big Pirelli rear tire drifting slightly.

When we straightened up, I took a quick look over my shoulder. Her face was white. She tried to smile, but I could see that was enough. I let the Triumph thump along in third so Judith could catch her breath as we crossed to West River Drive. The night was fine; cool air whipping by the trees. The dope was in afterglow.

"You okay?" I shouted over my shoulder.

"Yes, fine. I got a bit scared back there. Do you always drive like that? Don't you worry about tickets?" She let go of me to adjust her skirt.

"Nope, faster. I'll tell you about the cops sometime." Her arms tightened around my waist again, more like a bear hug than anything else.

We wound along the dark secondary roads, the powerful Cibié headlight picking out a brilliant white, quartz iodine path for us. We passed Merion and Narbeth, then drove up into the scrub oak hills and hollows around Hagy's Ford. She directed me to a dead end road near Penn Valley School. The house was old, very large, colonial style, fieldstone, on a lot of ground. The rhododendron blossoms—white and pink—had closed up for the night. The trim had been freshly painted white, and the large, paneled red door had a polished brass knocker in the center. The house was set well back from the road. A semicircular driveway led to the entrance. A dark green Mercedes station wagon was parked off on the right.

I stopped on the road and shut the Triumph down so's not to wake anybody. The twin Dellorto carburetors hissed and popped as she settled down. We talked about this and that, and I was trying to figure out how to ask her out. Maybe she guessed, because she said, "Jack, my parents aren't expecting me home with anybody, so we should say goodnight here. Thanks, awfully. That was a lot of fun. Maybe we'll see each other again sometime."

"Hey, Judith. Can't I call sometime? Maybe we could go to the Main Point, or downashore or somethin?"

The front door opened, and her mother, I guessed, walked out on the flagstone porch in her robe, shielding her eyes from the bright overhead light to see what her daughter had brought home.

Judith was in a hurry now. "Okay, you can call me, but not here. My number at the dorm is TU8-6666. I'll be taking summer courses at Swarthmore. Thanks again, Jack, I enjoyed the ride."

She ran up the driveway, pleated skirt swishing over her bare legs, and didn't look back. She took her mother by the arm, led her in and closed the big red door. The porch light winked out. My mouth was open.

I repeated it to myself, "TU8-6666. TU8-6666. Got it. Well, I'm up the river far enough, might as well get back on my side. Gotta get a hoagie. Haven't seen mom and granmom for too long." The monthly envelope was in my pocket. I kicked the Triumph over; it started with a roar from too much throttle, and I headed for Belmont Avenue, Green Lane Bridge, and mom's place in Manayunk for the night.

"You mean to tell me, you can't be tellin me, you got that tasty college chick on the back of your bike and diddn score? What a supreme asshole, Jack. You need Pecker lessons, I'm tellin ya."

"Yeh, and you can fuck yourself, too. It just wasn't like that, man. I took her up to her parents' place in Bryn Mawr. That was it. Diddn even get to first with her; diddn try. You shoulda seen the place, Peck, buck city. I got a phone number, so maybe I'll call her. Just stop bustin my balls. How's it now?"

"Still breakin up, Jack. You gotta do somethin. Trophy run's soon."

We were in the pits at Atco Speedway for the nationals, and Pecker's Harley stroker had a chance. I got some aviation gas from a contact at Wings Field to give him an extra edge, but the high octane was causing problems. It wasn't a paid deal for me, but the beer was free and future considerations were understood. Besides, winning at the nationals on an engine I built couldn't do my rep any harm. Didn't have anything else to do anyway.

Six or seven beefy Devils with their old ladies and hangers on stood around us, drinking cans of Piels and crushing the empties on their heads. Their choppers were ringed to fence us off from the crowd. This wasn't really necessary, because everybody gave outlaws room. It was more their way of saying, "This is us. Over there is you. Don't forget it."

Around us were riders and bikes of every description: South Philly boys on Japanese stockers, college guys on black Nortons, Camden dudes on full chrome BSAs with apehangers, serious builders on punched-out street Triumphs with flat drag bars, full-time fuel dragsters on stretch-framed bullets. All of them gaga over the trophies and group pictures that went with a win. It's a "mine's bigger than yours" thing with drag strip types. Me, I preferred the asphalt road race tracks where skill and guts made the difference over laps of straights and Ss. Here you just got to the line, watched the lights, sucked up your nuts, cranked it on, dumped the clutch for the hole shot on green, hoped you didn't blow a shift and got to the quarter mile line first.

No lie, though, that 100 inch gas stroker had the horses. I made sure of that. I changed the jet size in the big single side carb, put in some colder plugs and thought that should do it. We hoisted the rear end of the Harley onto the rollers run off the back tires of Pecker's Ford pickup. I jumped in and gunned it until the Harley's slick was spinning fast enough to move those humongous pistons and con rods. Flames shot out the straight pipes as the stroker fired, so loud my ear drums just about met at the back of my nose. Sounded good, clean, shouldn't break up now. But if he stalled it in the chute, he'd be done. We'd never get it started again in time, and the track marshals probably wouldn't let us try.

I pushed him to the staging area and poured Clorox over the slick. Pecker nailed the front brake and popped the clutch. The square rear tire lit up and filled the air with burning bleach and blue rubber smoke. I pounded him on the back, and he let off. When I touched the tire, it was hot, tacky, perfect.

"Keep it above two grand on the line, Peck, or she'll stall," I yelled into his helmet. He nodded quickly.

I pushed him up to the line in the left lane, light tree to his right. Good spot, because traction in the right lane had been lousy all day. In the other lane was Tracy, a mechanic from Ambler I knew slightly, mostly by reputation. He was a first-class engine builder, but I'd never seen him drive on a drag strip. I nodded; he nodded, unsmiling. I slapped Pecker on the helmet twice; he looked to me with a grin, gave me the finger with his left hand, pulled in the clutch and jammed it into gear—ready.

I jumped over the rope into the pits. The marshal spun his arm in the air, faster and faster, and the exhaust notes from the two Harleys rose, thundering, in and out of harmony as their rpms came in and out of sync. The light tree started: orange, orange, orange, orange—green. The slicks lit up, smoke billowing, as the strokers shot from the get go. No red lights; a good start. As soon as he banged second gear, Tracy started going edge to edge on his slick, and he had to back off the throttle for an instant to regain control or dump the bike. Pecker was grease smooth, taking the engine to the red line, grabbing some smoke from second to third, then into fourth without a hitch, or the clutch, I noticed. He rolled it out, just touching red line in top gear and went through the timing lights ahead of Tracy by more than a bike length. "Another high quality Black Jack gear ratio selection," I thought.

"Ten point two-three seconds for the winner in lane one, ladies and gentlemen," came from the loud speakers. "Ten-five-five for lane two. Congratulations to two great competitors." There was light applause from the grandstand.

It wasn't a record or anything, but it was a respectable time and a solid win. Pecker stalled it coming down the return lane, so I ran out to push him in the last hundred yards. He was whooping. "Mothafucka, you see that, Jack, I smoked his ass, man. I blew his fuckin socks off."

For Pecker, this was as good as it got: winning for the club, thumbing his nose at the world. He got the trophy with the gold motorcycle and the plaque on the base. It was a lamp, too. He was right in the middle of the group shot of the day's winners, Devils colors proud.

In the pits, the Devils were going wild when Tracy walked by outside the ring of choppers. He looked me in the eye and mouthed "Fuck you," then stomped off toward his pickup. Sitting on the tailgate was a man with his back to me; he was wearing Hells Angels colors. Pecker sat on the Harley with the trophy strapped to the bars, just like the Marlon Brando poster. His buddies poured so much beer over his head it started boiling on the cylinder fins and running into his boots. He got off, grabbed an orange shop rag to wipe his face and came over to me.

"Hey, you assholes. Lissen up, you faggitts. We can't forget Black Jack, here. He's the builder, man, the best goddamn tuner in Philly."

I got whacked around a bit and the beer treatment. Then Pecker put a skinny hand on my shoulder and said, "Man, you're gonna get more pussy this day than you ever thought possible.  Hey, White Cloud, over here girl.  She's part Seminole, man, sweetest little thing around."

She was maybe eighteen, five two, spindly, slightly bowed legs in tight Levis, very large breasts in a yellow tank, no bra. The high cheekbones, brown, almond shaped eyes and long black hair said she might be part Indian, or maybe Italian. Who cared?  On her left shoulder was a small Jersey Devil tattooed in red.

"Cloud, Jack's done a great job for the Devils today, and he needs a class club reward.  Besides, he's got a little problem you can take his mind off of.  There's this college chick, see, and he just can't get in her pants."

"Fuck you, Pecker."

"No, no, Jack, *you* fuck *her*.  Off you go now."  White Cloud giggled as she looked me up and down.

All the Devils, laughing and pouring beer, pushed the two of us into the back of Pecker's Ford.  It had a fiberglass cap over the bed and a ratty mattress inside.  White Cloud, on her knees, pulled off her tank top then went for my belt: "Whaddaya like for starters, Jack?"

She was small, but she sure had stamina and imagination. We stopped to rest and the truck started to rock—hard—and the Devils chanted: "Go, Jack, go." The rocking stopped. The blacked out glass above the gate on the truck bed lifted and two hands appeared holding cans of Piels. Pecker stuck his head in, "Take your time, man, we got lotsa time."

I didn't show up for work until Tuesday, and the half-full tube of blue ointment Pecker gave me turned out to be a good idea. I felt like a crummy sleazeball. The old *Baltimore Catechism* thing again.

"Judith there?" I asked.

"I think she just got out of class. I'll check. Hold on, please. It might take a minute or two to find her."

I was in a phone booth under the elevated in Kensington, train wheels screeching above me as they ground slowly into a turn. I pumped in three more nickels just to be sure I didn't get cut off. Then I stuck my finger in my ear so I could hear better. "It's been almost a month," I thought, "wonder if she remembers me?" What a chicken. I was afraid to call earlier. Ducking the big "no."

I saw her once, briefly, at the Main Point. Kweskin and Muldaur were the headliners. I got there late, about 11, straight for a change, so I had to stand along the back wall of the crowded club. Mississippi John Hurt was on stage by himself finishing off his set. He wore his signature coat, tie and straw fedora, and looked like an ancient black mummy. Somebody yelled from the crowd, "Can you do some Johnson for us?" He bent to the mike: "Well, I usally just do my own stuff, but I guess it's okay, cause he died on August 16, 1936, so it's close enough to his anniversary. Here's Robert Johnson's *Hellhound on Ma Trail* for y'all. Caint play it just like he did, cause they say he sold his soul to the divil to loin how. Divil got jealous, so he pisoned him young. I'll do it ma way. Goes like dis:"

> *I got to keep movin*
> *I've got to keep movin*
> *Blues fallin down like hail*
> *Blues fallin down like hail.*

I watched his thick black thumb pick the base line like only he and Johnson could, then I started scanning the crowd, face by face. I caught their eye and waved to two old friends, Jesse Morris and Rena Weingrad, sitting near the stage.

*And the days keep on worryin me*
*There's a hellhound on ma trail*
*Hellhound on ma trail*
*Hellhound on ma trail.*

There she was, near the red Exit sign on the other side of the room, with a bunch of her college friends. Chuck was there, but not close to her. Their tables were littered with mocha java cups and cider glasses. They were all standing up, ready to leave as soon as Hurt finished.

*All I would need my little sweet rider just*
*To pass the time away, uh huh, huh, huh*
*To pass the time away.*

I started squeezing between the tables, kicking chair legs with my boots. They were very close together, so it was slow going, and people turned to say, "Hey, watch it, willya."
*I can tell the wind is risin*
*The leaves tremblin on the tree*
*Tremblin on the tree*

*All I need' s my little sweet woman*
*And to keep me company, hey, hey, hey, hey*
*my company.‡*


She was gone when I got over there.  I checked the full parking lot, but it was no use.

Somebody dropped the receiver, and it rattled in my ear. "Hello, who is it, please?"

"Hi, Judith.  It's me, Jack.  Remember?  We met at a party at 42$^{nd}$ and Walnut about a month back.  I gave you a ride to your parents' place.  I saw you across the room at the Main Point last time Kweskin was in town, but you were gone by the time I got there."

"Oh, yes, Black Jack, the underground motorcycle man with the long hair.  How could I forget?  Are you working?  It's so noisy I can barely hear you."

"No, it's the el.  I'm down in Kensington.  Lissen, I wanted to ask if you might want to, ah, go downashore this Saturday with me?  We could go to Margate, maybe.  It's a quiet family

‡*Robert Johnson, Hellhound on My Trail, ©1990, King of Spades Music.*

place. There's a nice little bar on the beach where we could have lunch. I won't go too fast, promise."

"Jack, you get full marks for brass, I'd say." There were a few ticks of silence. My finger was getting sweaty in my ear. "Well, I suppose, but you have to be on your best behavior; no swoopy turns. I'll be staying over with friends of my parents on Delancey Place on Friday night."

"Great. What's the address? I'll pick you up there Saturday morning at 7:30 so we can get an early start. Channel 10 says the weather'll be good."

"No, Jack, no. That wouldn't be—um—convenient. Why don't you find me at the south entrance to Rittenhouse Square? This time, I'll wear slacks."

"That's a good idea, Judith, but make em dark; they don't show grease."

A tinkle of the sunny laughter I remembered could just be heard. "Fine, Jack. Until then. Bye, bye."

I wasn't sure. She was so casual, so distant, so blue-book and Main Line, it was hard to tell if she'd show or not. "Nothing tried, nothing happens," as my dad used to say. I jumped on the bike and headed for Roosevelt Boulevard and Sears to buy some new black jeans. A bathing suit, I didn't have a bathing suit that fit, and a big beach towel, can't forget the beach towel.

# 8. Divination

The chicks in high heels on Manhattan's Fifth Avenue at lunch time are the finest. Times Square on New Year's Eve is the only place to be. The Midtown jazz bars were solid before they started closing down. But Fairmount Park was always better than Central Park; bigger, too. And New York couldn't beat Rittenhouse Square, either. Not that it's bigger or richer than the area around the Plaza on 5th Avenue, or anything like that. It just seemed older, more dignified, like it grew there on purpose to just the right size.

The Square is downtown. Nearby are little cobblestone lanes, like Delancey Place, only wide enough for a colonial carriage. The cast iron hitching posts outside the narrow, red brick houses have always been there. It's ritzy as hell.

I parked Trusty the Bonneville on the sidewalk on Rittenhouse Street side about 6:30 and sat on the low stone wall to wait. Anything before 9 is early on a Saturday downtown, so there were only a few blue rinse ladies walking little dogs and the odd junkie or two nodding out on the park benches. I looked at my watch: 6:40. Good thing I used Ajax and a floor brush on my hands; the palms were still a little wrinkled, but the calluses and nails were pretty clean. I jumped off the wall and strolled over to a cart on 18th Street. "Yeh, whaddya want?" the South Philly guy said like he was really pissed off. I bought a coffee and a soft pretzel with yellow mustard from him, and a *Bulletin* from the paper guy, then went back to my perch.

The paper had the usual bad news in it about the war. On a back page was a small article with the headline: "Battle of the Bogside." The byline was from *The Times* of London. The story was pretty short and two days old:

> Yesterday, 12th August, the Royal Ulster Constabulary charged a large group of unruly demonstrators in the predominantly Catholic area of the Bogside in Londonderry. A police spokesman said they were retaliating against a steady hail of bricks and stones coming from hooligans hiding behind hastily erected barricades. Many injuries were reported, but no deaths. This morning, the Bogside was covered in a thick haze of smoke from burning tires and vehicles. The fighting continues.

"So, now it begins," I thought. "Have to pick up a copy of the *Irish Voice* to get the whole story." Couldn't help thinking of the beautiful Mary Daugherty face down, skull split, on the Williams Street barricades. What about Charlie Murphy? Him too? He seemed to have fallen off the face of the earth, and I wasn't about to look for Sean and Mike to find out where he was.

The Vietnam news made my head hurt. Last time I saw Mark, home on leave, it wasn't good. He made Green Beret alright, but he was hurtin, damaged. Looked like he was on his way back to the jungle for a second tour. All of us, Mark, Matt, me, granmom and mom squeezed in around the round table in Manayunk for dinner. Like always, the arguments started. For once, I almost held my temper. Matt went at Mark when Mark said that Vietnam was a crock: "It's not the killing I mind. I'm a soldier. It's the unnecessary killing I mind in a country where we have no business." Matt told him with a sneer that he was disloyal, a coward. Mark stared at his corned beef for a second, stunned, then he looked up at him quick, mad: "Coward I'm not. I'm no robot, either, like you. Just because the President says it or the Army orders it, don't mean it's right. I don't believe everything I'm told. Can you say the same, Father?"

I started to say something, but Matt turned on me with a snarl: "You, you street bum, you've wasted yourself. All you care about is a rag-tag bunch of Irish terrorists masquerading as patriots. I'm a soldier of Christ. Your brother says he's a soldier of his country, though I'm beginning to doubt it. Tell me, Jack, what are you a soldier of? Ireland? You're just like your grandfather. I guess what you're wearing is the current street uniform, is it? Leather biker crap. You look like a criminal." Granmom's lips were moving to the Hail Marys. Mom looked at the ceiling.

He got me good though, no lie. No answer for that one, so I shot back: "Tell ya, Matt, you're a priest, okay, your choice. But you don't know who you are, turned your back on it. Must be tough. Seein that's how it is, how the hell do you know who we are, or aren't?" That shut him up. Made me sad to look him in the eye, because I could see he wasn't telling the truth about something.

Frowning, I put the *Bulletin* down and looked around at the fine, tall buildings. Not fifty storeys like New York, but just right. Somebody had a plan when they were built.

I saw her at the corner on 18<sup>th</sup> about 7:15. She was fresh and beautiful and tall the way I remembered her, but now she was very tan. She was the kind of woman who made men stand still in the street until their wives whacked them. The slacks were black and fit well. The blouse was very white, pretty, expensive. Her white deck shoes were new. In her right hand she carried one of those string bags you see in advertisements for holidays in France. No jewelry this time, only a small gold watch with a slender black leather band. Her breasts bounced lightly as she dodged a taxi coming across Rittenhouse. "Hey, honey, marry me, will ya?" the cabbie called out the window.

My mouth must have been open, because she said with a broad smile as she walked up to me, "Hello again, Black Jack. Catching flies?"

"Nope, burned my tongue on the coffee." Because it was dark at the party and during our ride, I hadn't noticed how very blue her eyes were.

She jumped up on the wall beside me. "Do you always wear black everything? Even the face shield on your black helmet is black."

"Goes back a long way to an old steam locomotive I saw with my grandfather when I was very young. And, well, it's, like, practical, ya know."  I didn't want to think about Toot just then, or even Hose.

"Doesn't show the grease?"

"Right, doesn't show the grease.  Or the bugs." I laughed, and so did she.

"How about the leather, Jack?  Is it a fashion statement? A uniform?  What?"

"Sort of, I guess, but mostly it's in case you fall at speed. Asphalt'll chew right through cloth, and it does nasty things to skin.  Asphalt rash takes a long time to heal, and the skin doesn't tan after it does.  Speakin a that, I brought you a jacket and a lid, just in case." I had a key to the shop, so I stopped on my way and borrowed a new Bell Star helmet from the case.  It was spanking white, with a clear plastic face shield. I bought the jacket from Webco in California, but it didn't fit me anymore.  The padding on the shoulders and elbows was held in place by diamond stitching.  That was the only decoration.  It had no sheen at all, was very, very black and very righteous.

She coughed lightly into her hand as she looked sideways at the jacket: "Oh, Jack, how thoughtful of you, but I couldn't, really."

"You ride to Jersey with me, you wear it. It's clean. Helmet, too. Here. I'm a good rider and don't fall much, not that it matters, but I couldn't take it if I dumped it with you on the back. You don't have to zip the jacket up. Please. Wear em."

She hesitated, then looked at me quickly: "Alright, Jack, just for you. Thanks for being so protective. It's cute. But they come off at the beach."

I truly hoped so.

I rolled her bag up in the beach towel from Sears and strapped it between the bars over the headlight shell. She was curious, and asked, "Won't you hide the speedometer?"

"Don't need one," I said, and lifted the towel so she could see the small, black-faced Smith tachometer in the aluminum frame I machined for it. It was a very trick, very pukka set-up. "It's okay, really, I know how fast I'm going by the gear I'm in and the sound the bike makes. Let's go."

I would have liked to go over the Delaware on the Tacony-Palmyra, like dad used to do, but we were too far south, so we headed east along Walnut, then up to Franklin Square and crossed the Ben Franklin Bridge into Camden. I don't like Camden much—it's a dump and I wasn't connected there—so we cut across the Copper River on Federal Street and headed for Maple Shade and Route 73. We were in the Pine Barrens, loafing along in light traffic at about 60. We flashed by the signs, "Toms●Lopes●Clams☞500 yds," the ram-shackle stands and the pineys who tended them.

It's tough to hold a conversation on a motorcycle. The exhaust noise isn't a problem, really, because it's behind you. It's the wind and the helmets, mostly. I tried, anyhow.

"You okay?"

"I'm fine, Jack. It's a lovely day. Not too hot yet."

"You keep holdin on, but you can relax a little." Her arms were very tight around me, and they loosened a bit. I looked down at her fingers locked together: no color on the nails, just clear polish and a recent manicure. "We're not in a hurry. You want to stop anywhere. Let me know." Her helmet was sideways on my back, and she nodded.

We were down around Ancora on Route 30 when Judith said, "Let's stop, I have to use the ladies' room."

"Right, we need gas anyway. Maybe we can find a coffee."

The flat-roofed station still had the faded red Calso sign nobody bothered to take down. I could almost see the old two-tone Chevy coupe next to the pumps and my dad asking for five bucks worth before he jumped out to check the fan belt. The old geezer didn't mind I filled the Triumph's tank myself. Most pump jockeys spill half the gas down the wax job on the tank and onto the hot engine, and I didn't like the smell or the fire hazard. Judith seemed to be taking a long time. I had seen the way the loafers in the folding chairs by the Coke machine looked at her when she went around the corner—hooded piney eyes moving without turning their heads—so I camped out in front of the ladies' room door.

The door opened: "Jack, really, you are sweet. Did you think I got lost in there?"

"No, just makin sure you can find you're way back to me without any surprise detours." Her blue chip eyes widened slightly, and her back straightened: "Now don't be silly. I'm perfectly capable of taking care of myself."

"Yeh, right."

As I jumped on the kickstarter, I looked over at the Coke machine boys. One of them showed a gap-toothed grin, slipped his eyes to Judith and pumped his fist back and forth. I dumped the clutch, and the rear tire spit sand as we headed back out onto Route 30. " Maybe we can pick up some fresh vegetables on the way back?" I nodded and pushed the bike to near 80.

The Egg Harbor bridge was still rickety, but at least the tide was in. It was a beautiful, sunny August morning, and the Atlantic sparkled like green mica. My old buddy the elephant stood there still, paint peeling off her tin skin, proud of making it so far.

I changed quickly and got to the beach towel first. Men's heads popped up from their towels as she walked toward me. Her one-piece bathing suit was blinding white with black piping around the scoop neck. It stuck to every contour and made her look even more tan. She was like a long legged Venus with arms. She wasn't stacked, exactly, but everything fit together so well, nothing out of proportion. She moved like she had no joints at all. I wanted her like no tomorrow. Sounds strange, but it wasn't just or only physical. She thought, had a brain, liked to listen, liked to talk. Way beyond my experience, and probably way out of my league.

She sat down, crossed her perfect legs and brushed the shining black hair from her eyes. With a bright smile, she said: "Jack, you're a very handsome man, rugged, my mother would say, but you really should lose some weight. You have wonderful shoulders and very powerful arms and hands, but the stomach needs work. Maybe you should swim at the club or something." She reached out and touched my hair briefly. "Your hair is very fine, like a baby's. Auburn is a very unusual color." She explored the white flash of hair on the left side of my forehead, then stopped and looked away. "The ends are split. You should have it trimmed. Perhaps I'll do it sometime."

She gazed over the families at play on the beach, out past the kids in the surf: "I've only heard about Margate. My family has a summer place up north at Bay Head. That's where we always go. Do you know anything about the elephant? Who built it? Why? It's very small and rather tacky."

She squeezed sun tan lotion from a white plastic Lanvin bottle and spread it on her arms. Then she handed it to me and rolled over for me to put some on her back. There were fine blond hairs on the skin between her shoulder blades. She felt like a ripe peach. I wanted to kiss the spot where her spine ended and her small, tight rear end began.

"Thanks for the training tips. Never learned to swim very well, but my father's mother told me I'll never drown, at least. That elephant is one of my oldest friends. We used to come here when I was young, before my father died—my father and mother, the brothers, the grandparents. When I was little, I thought she was the biggest elephant ever. Her name's Lucy; heard she was built around 1880 as a real estate office."

"Do the backs of my legs, too, please," she said into the beach towel. I went up them as far as I dared, using long, firm, massaging strokes. "Umm, that feels good. Why did your grandmother say you'd never drown, Jack?"

"You noticed the white flash in my hair?"

"Right away when we met at the party. It's very distinguished; it makes the color of your hair even more intense in this light."

"The Irish call it the 'banshee's mark.' It's a kind of spirit attached to old families with noble blood, they say. Kavanagh is such a name. I was born upside down with a caul—a membrane over my face. So was my granmom. She took mine away right after I was born."

"Humm, I've never thought of the Irish as having old families and noble blood. What would she want it for?"

"Ah, bedad, faith and begorra," I said in a stage-Irish brogue, "that'd be the heathen English commin out in the darlin girl." She tried to give me a backhand, and then I answered her. "I don't know about the caul, but I think my mother does. Anyway, the story goes that babies born like that are touched on the forehead by the banshee. That's where the mark comes from. We can't die by drowning because of it. If you want to get technical, I'm descended from Art MacMurrough Kavanagh, Irish King of Leinster, who fought the English King, Richard II, in the 1300s."

"My, you do read your history, don't you."

"Yeh, I had a lot of time to do it a few years back. And now I keep up."

"The banshee—that's a strange legend. Is there anything else to it? Does this ghost protect the family? Is it a male or a female?"

"Most of the old stories have it as a woman. Sometimes it's called the 'White Lady of Ireland.' It's a spirit, not a ghost. I guess you could say the banshee is indifferent. Not good. Not bad. It's like an attendant, or maybe a doorman. It just watches. The only other thing I've been told is that the banshee knocks when the oldest man in the family dies. My mother swears she heard the knocking when my grandfather and my father died."

"You don't believe it, surely. Is this some kind of Catholic thing?"

"Holy cow, not likely, Judith. It's from the old religion; pagan times, the church would say. I've never heard any knocking that didn't have knuckles attached to it. Can't say I don't believe it, though; can't say I do. The priests make out it's all bull, course, because it's outside their turf, and they can't control it. The old stories drive my brother Matt nuts."

She mused for a few minutes. "What did your father do?"

"For a livin, you mean?" She nodded, black hair shining blue in the sun. "He was a welder, down at the refineries in Eddystone. What's your father do?"

"Oh, he works in insurance in Center City. He started with the firm right out of Princeton. It's a family tradition, you might say. He's kind of bored with it now, actually, so he and mummy travel a lot."

The sun was climbing, and the heat from the sand made the air shimmer. We shared a Coke, ran shouting into the surf, dried off, talked, and dozed and woke and talked and dozed. Life was good. My head was spinning.

I was on my stomach, chin perched on my fists, hypnotized by the sound of the surf. She touched my arm lightly, and I turned. Our heads were very close together; her face was cradled in the crook of her arm. It was like a soft, warm china sculpture. "You don't have any tattoos," she said, her index finger lightly tracing the puckered scar on my shoulder, along a proud vein in my right forearm, down to the shiny white patch of asphalt rash that led to my elbow. "That's very good. I thought all bikers had them: hearts with mom in them or girlfriends' names, things like that. Does your friend have any?"

"What friend? Oh, you mean Pecker? I wouldn't call him that, exactly. Yeh, he's got enough ugly on him for everybody. I do work for him and a few of his club buddies, that's all. As long as they're satisfied, we get along. You gotta understand, Judith, I'm not one of them. If you get right down to it, I'm just a mechanic, a very, very good one. I'm not a club kinda guy. I'm not a 'biker,' either. Outlaw clubs like the Devils, Bandanna, Hells Angels, they're, ah, different. They have their own rules, their own way of doin things. It's very private and secret. If you like stayin in one piece, you just don't cross the line."

"Are they dangerous?"

"Yeh, armed and dangerous, big time. But don't worry about it. If they ever hassled you," I said with my best macho frown, "I'd take care of it."

She smiled and touched my lips to quiet me. I leaned slowly into the small space between us to let her know I was coming. She didn't move, and I kissed her lightly. Her eyes closed halfway, her mouth opened slightly and the tips of our tongues touched before she moved away. She looked right into my eyes, lids drowsy.

"Wow, your eyes are so green now, it's amazing. That's a bad combination: green eyes, auburn hair and muscles." I got to my knees and mimicked a Charles Atlas pose, popping the biceps. "Stop it." She laughed, turned, crossed her arms and propped her delicate chin on her hands and looked toward the ocean once more. "What do you want to do, Jack?"

"I have a notion that gettin somethin to eat soon might be a good idea."

"Notion? You do have some funny expressions, you unusual man, what's the origin of that one?"

"Comes from my grandfather. He was an Irishman from the old sod, and he used 'notion,' when he was lookin for a laugh or tellin little white lies."

"Did he ever tell you about the Easter Rising? I did a paper on W. B. Yeats in my junior year, and I read a fair bit about it."

"Yep. He ended up in the General Post Office, one of the Irish Volunteers that the English shelled to pieces. Nearly beat him to death. Escaped on a motorcycle. He—ah—did a lot of work for the cause during the War of Independence over there, and—um—then he had some problems during the Civil War and had to get out of the country. That's how he got to Philly. Why I'm here right now, instead of Armagh, I guess you could say." I definitely didn't want to go into what granpop actually had to do over there. Way too complicated. Scary.

"He was a fine craftsman, a great storyteller and a good man—tough but good. He had hands of steel. So'd my father. I miss them both sometimes. My grandfather went back to Belfast in '56. They shot him. My dad just worked himself to death for his family."

"Oh, Jack, that's so hard and sad. I'm so sorry. You really are unusual—and interesting. It's not a pretty story, is it, what happened in Ireland?"

"No, it isn't.  You're the first non-Irish person I've ever met who knew anything much about it.  It's still going on and likely to get a lot worse before long."  That was as much as I thought I should tell her just then.  But I really wanted to talk to someone like her about it sometime.  Had to.

"I was struck by the injustice of it all.  It didn't make any sense.  But I am beginning to understand about your hands.  Jack, what I really meant to ask you earlier was what do you want to do with your life?  Later on.  Do you want to go to school?  Start a business?  Settle down?  What would you want if you could do anything?"

"I think about that some.  I was on my way to college, but the money ran out when my dad died, and I never got around to it.  Anyway, I know this guy, Yvon DuHamel.  He's from Quebec, up in Canada.  He was tellin me in the pits at Daytona about these new things called Ski-Doos; they use motorcycle engines, but they run on snow with skis and tracks.  He says they're gonna to be big, even in racing.  Asked me whether I might want to go on the circuit up there."

Her laugh was musical.  "Jack, do you ski?"

"You kiddin me?  We don't get enough snow around here.  Oh, yeh, well, okay, so I don't know anything about snow, but an engine's an engine. And I thought maybe if it was any good, I might just move up to Canada sometime and open my own shop, with bikes in the summer and these Ski-Doo things in the winter. That way there's no down time between seasons. Lotsa draft dodgers have done it—gone up there, I mean. Lotsa space and clean air. No hassles, they say. Besides, Philly's crummy. I get tired of it."

"Yes, our worlds are very different, Jack."

I stood up and pulled her up next to me. She lost her balance in the soft sand and fell against me. I caught her elbow in a big mitt to steady her. We looked at each other, breath short, and kissed longer this time.

She put her tan hands flat on my chest and pushed me away playfully. "If you don't feed me soon, I'll just wither away." Holding hands, we ran laughing to the Salty Dog Café. We had to; the sand was so hot it made your feet hop. It was the only place close. I'd been there before; the food was standard issue, but the draught beer was always cold. Inside it was dark and cool. We slid into a booth and ordered burgers and beer.

"Oops," I said, "shoulda ordered chicken and ribs."

"Why would that be, oh noble Black Jack?"

"Well, you're the archeologist. I could cast the bones so you could read the future."

She slapped the top of my hand, laughed, and said, still smiling, "That's the worst joke I ever heard. Can I use it with my professor?"

"You bet, but I want royalties." She sipped water slowly and looked lost in thought. "Whatcha thinkin about?"

"Remember when you scared the hell out of me on East River Drive?" I nodded. "You said you'd explain about the police. What did you mean by that? I'm very curious. You seem to speak in riddles sometimes."

"Ah, the little ears are sharp," I said, imitating my grandfather. "It's a dues thing. I work for some powerful people. There's a rule: you do for them; they do for you. I put out for them, so I don't get tickets. Or if I do, one of my connections will make them disappear. It's more complicated than that, but that's pretty much how it works."

"What about here? Is it the same?"

"No, not in Jersey. I'm not connected here. Different families run Jersey, mostly outta Camden and Cherry Hill."

"What families? I thought we were talking about the police."

"I am. Let's drop it, okay?"

"Is that the way your underground works? How can you stand it?"

"Didn't say I liked it. It's just the way things are. Can we talk about something else? Like I said, I'm tired of it."

"Certainly, yes, have you ever been to Canada? How about Ireland?"

"Yeh, raced at Mosport in Ontario. It's outside Toronto. Pretty country up there: rolling farmland, dairy cows, horses. City's squeaky clean, and you don't have to watch your back on the street. Bumpy track, so I took a second. And, no, I've never been to the 'ould sod,' as granpop used to call it, but I have to go soon. Got relatives there."

When the food and the beer came, we talked some more about Canada, about her travels in England, about the summer courses she was taking so she could get on an archeological dig in Egypt next year, about this and that and everything. I got on a roll and told her granpop's Jersey Devil story. I knew it was corny *As the World Turns* stuff, but I felt I knew her forever. I was absolutely certain she felt the same way. We were eager to know each other quickly, heads close over the table, yakking. The food got cold. My chest hurt. I kept falling into her eyes.

Harley-Davidson uses a 45 degree opposed engine configuration. It gives the motors an unmistakably deep, throaty sound, even at a distance, more so when they're a lot of them. I was probably the first person in Margate to hear them coming.

In a few minutes, Judith said, "What's that noise, Jack. It's getting louder."

"Choppers, Judith, a lotta them. The boys are out on a club ride, I guess."

"Should we leave now?"

"No, they're too close. Just sit tight. It'll be okay. If they think we're runnin, they'll come after us for fun." I put my wallet on top of the table.

Most Jersey shore-town buildings are pretty flimsy: clapboard on the outside, curled up green shingles on the roof, cheap paneling on the inside. The walls of the Salty Dog started shaking and bottles rattled behind the bar. "About seventy-five," I thought. "They must be right outside." The noise started to lessen as the big motors shut down, one by one. Then there was the kind of silence that makes your eardrums hurt. I gave Judith my best casual shrug and "no problemo" smile.

About ten big Jersey Devils burst through the door and headed for the bar; two sported chromed German Wehrmacht helmets. The bartender was a young blond guy with a summer job; his mouth was open, and he looked like he had an underwear problem. The biggest Devil wore one-way sunglasses. He leaned over the bar to get in the blond guy's face and shouted, "Beer, asshole, now." The kid started filling pitchers as fast as he could. He was spilling a lot. The boys didn't use glasses, just tipped the pitchers, foam running into their beards and down their colors.

The big Devil was in charge. He turned around, leaned his back on the bar, wiped his mouth on his sleeve, took off his mirrored sunglasses and looked with a steady gaze at the silent people, booth by booth. The triple-row, chromed Harley clutch chain he wore as a belt was a deadly weapon in the right hands. Across from me, Judith was wide-eyed and rigid, hands in her lap. She looked at me with an imploring mouth. I smiled again as the big Devil growled at the room, "What piecea shit owns that Brit-bag Bonneville outside? It's in the Devils' way."

I jerked my head up and said, "Yo." His small, penny colored eyes turned to me; the whites were bloodshot and the color of coffee with double cream. Then he looked Judith up and down, stopping for a long time at her breasts. He walked over to us, his huge, hard beer gut hanging over his belt. The patch over the pocket of his colors said, "Zig-Zag—Prez."

"This bar's ours, fuck face. You leave your little lady behind and get yer skinny college-boy ass outta here." He spun to face the rest of the room. "Everybody else, too. Out, now." Cutlery bounced on the floor as they made a rush for the door. One guy about thirty-five wasn't having any of it. As soon as he said, "You guys can go to hell," he was surrounded, punched to the floor and stomped on by five or six of the boys. Then a snick and an arm came up in the Altamont pose. The switchblade was poised above the guy on the floor. A grinning, ugly face looked up at Zig-Zag for approval. Zig considered a second, then shook his head. The boys picked the guy up and tossed him out the door, blood all over his face, with his howling wife running after him. Devils pushed in to fill the empty booths. They started eating the half-finished meals. The smell was familiar and getting heavy.

We were looking right at the Jersey Devil patch on his back, the red, crude face leering. Below it was Zig-Zag's location patch: "Batsto Chapter." I was calm, but my voice sounded loud in the silence, "Yo, pal. I ain't no college boy, man. And my ride ain't no piecea shit, neither."

He spun back to us, spit flying, and put his big hands on the table. He was about my height, maybe forty. His long beard was the color of sand with a streak of white under his lower lip. He smiled, teeth clenched, nose open: "You givin Zig-Zag lip, sucker? I'll chew you up and spit you all over the floor. Then I'll take carea yer old lady right here on the table." His big fist came down on it for emphasis.

"Easy, Zig-Zag. Don't want no trouble. Pecker with you today?" I said and grinned. I had sized him up and wasn't scared of him. I could probably take him, but it wouldn't be easy, and the rest of the club would tear me apart and gang bang Judith on the floor. I couldn't take the chance. I opened my wallet slowly, both hands visible, pulled out the Devils' courtesy card and handed it to him. He snatched it with a roundhouse. "You ask Pecker about Black Jack, the tuner from Philly, man; I run with some of your boys."

Without turning, he growled. "Zeke, find Pecker. Get him here. Now."

One of the storm troopers took off from the end of the bar like he had a fire in his pants; he pushed the door open and yelled: "Pecker, hey Peckerhead, get yer ass in here. Prez wants ya." Zig-Zag looked at me steadily and said, "This a fake, jerk off, and it's yer ass." Judith's hand slid across the table and grabbed mine, hard. He noticed. He reached out without looking back, and one of the Devils put a pitcher in his hand. He drank slowly, watching us.

Pecker came in right away with White Cloud. All he wore on top was his sleeveless colors, every inch of his hairless chest and arms covered in tattoos, mostly sailing ships. He looked around and sized up the scene very fast. He walked slowly to the bar, picked up a pitcher and ambled over. "Hey, Zig-Zag, what's happenin, Prez." They shook hands. "Black Jack, ma main man, whatchu doin here?" He slid in next to me, and pointed for White Cloud to slide in next to Judith. He pushed the pitcher at me, and I took a long swig. I passed it to Judith and blinked my eyes to her. She took a sip and put it down, carefully, with both hands.

"Zig, you ain't got no beef with Jack, here. He's my bro, man. Member when I got that trophy at Atco?" Zig-Zag nodded, nose no longer open. "Well Jack, here, he built the motor, man, did the pits, helped the club out. Ain't that right Cloud?" White Cloud gave me a big smile and said, "Yep, Black Jack's the best. I'll vouch for him anytime." Pecker laughed. Judith noticed.

Pecker said, "You musta hearda this dude, Zig. Surprised you never met before. Works outta North Philly. He's cool, man, absolutely. Righteous, I'm tellin ya, knows when to keep his face zipped. Best tuner around. They're tight, him and his old lady."

That was enough for Zig-Zag. It was night and day stuff. He gave me the "you're one of us" smile and reached across Pecker to shake my hand. "Yeh, I hearda you, Black Jack, but I thought you worked outta downtown." He put the mirrored glasses back on.

"Used to. Gotta better deal at Five Points, so that's where I'm at now."

"What's with the Triumph, man? You should be ridin Merricun."

"I got lotsa rides, Zig. This one's good fer ridin two-up, know what I'm sayin?"

Zig-Zag turned to Judith. "Yeh, nothin like gettin onto a good saddle." His beefy hand covered hers for a long time. He turned to the Devils crowding the room: "Hey. Lissen up Devils. This here's Black Jack the builder from Philly and his old lady. They're cool with me. They party with us today, you hear? Hands off the chick."

"Solid, Prez," "You got it, Zig," from the crowd. I recognized a few faces. Zig-Zag walked behind the bar and grabbed a bottle of Seagram's 7 and four shot glasses and put them on the bar. He grabbed the bartender by the shirt, held him up so his feet were off the ground and said "Shoo" as he threw him toward the door. The guy couldn't get out fast enough. The Devils laughed, shouted at his back and pounded the tables.

Zig-Zag walked back over to our booth and put the bottle and glasses on the table. "Drink up, Philly Black Jack. Yer in the Devils' party now." His voice rose to a roar, "Now where the fuck is my fuckin beer. Where's my fuckin old lady?" He turned away and pushed through the crowd to the other side of the room.

"I owe you one, Peck."

"Forget it, Jack. I ain't paid all my dues to you just yet. Best to steer clear of Zig-Zag much as you can. He wigs out sometimes." Pecker turned to Judith, "Ya know, Jack's got motor mouth about you, honey. Just won't shut up. Now I get a better look at ya, I can see why."

Judith gave him a trembly little smile and stuck out her hand: "I'm Judith."

"Oh, yeh, I know, I know," Pecker said as he shook. "This here's White Cloud."

The booth was pretty small and the two girls were almost rubbing shoulders. White Cloud turned to Judith with a little jerk, and they touched hands quickly with the tips of their fingers. Judith took a fast glance at White Cloud's Devil tattoo.

Me and Pecker and White Cloud had a shot, downed in one, the glasses hitting the table with a bang all at once. Judith didn't touch hers at first, but I looked from her to the glass twice, and she took a sip. We chased it with beer. Pecker turned to me and said, "There's a big party up in the pines. Starts tonight, man. At my maw's place. I'm invitin you two. It'll be cool. I'll clear it with Zig. You got allies, bro, no hassles, unnerstand?  But lookit, man, don't wanna piss on yer parade, so we'll see you two lovebirds later."  He jerked his head at White Cloud.  They stood up and moved toward the bar.  The room was packed.  Somebody broke open the juke box and put on Steppenwolf's *Born to Be Wild* cranked up full tilt.  Then somebody fell against it, and the sound stopped with a long zip:  "You broke it, shithead, you fix it."

One by one, the Devils I knew came by and slapped me on the back.  Across the room, Zig-Zag looked around, smiling, completely satisfied.

Judith's eyes were the size of dinner plates.  "Jack, I don't believe this.  These people are animals.  I want to leave.  Now.  That Zig-Zag person scares me."

"No, we can't leave, not just yet.  We'll have to wait and see how it goes.  It's a gratitude thing with them.  You have to take what you're given and like it.  That's why I had to drink with them that way.  If we leave too soon, we're showin disrespect to the club.  They don't like that, and I'm not sure what would happen.  Could get ugly.  Member, I told you I'd make sure nothin happened to you?  That's what's on my mind right now.  I can get by with these guys on my own, but not with you here. You're just too beautiful. They've never seen anything like you before."

"Oh, am I? Who is this White Cloud woman? She seems to like you. Is she part of this 'take what you're given and like it' nonsense?"

I shrugged awkwardly, eyes down, studying the fork in my hand. "She's nothin to me, but it's not nonsense. It's their code, and you don't break it. This party thing worries me. If Pecker clears it with the Prez, we pretty well have to go. Here's the plan. You mighta noticed that their women don't talk much unless they're talked to. Just stick real close to me, kinda hang on my shoulder and keep quiet. We'll be okay. Promise. Sorry the day turned out like this."

She came over and slid in next to me, her arm pressing mine from shoulder to elbow, her hand in my hand on the Naugahyde seat. "Jack, on the beach was perfect. Maybe we can get back there soon? God, you're bold. Don't you fear anything?" Her face was lovely, forlorn as she looked around the room, dimpled chin trembling slightly.

"Jack, I think you might be the first truly honest man I ever met. So answer me. Won't the police break this up? I can't get involved in that. What about when they leave Margate? Won't they be stopped? They're doing a lot of damage."

I smiled into her eyes and kissed her quickly. "First off, Margate's small. There's maybe one, two town cops, that's it. If they're smart, they'll keep their heads down. Sure, they'll call the state cops, but I doubt they'll do anything except watch and hope it doesn't get too bad. They come in here, there'll be a riot. Remember, the Devils is a Jersey club. Know what that means?"

"They're connected?"

"You learn fast. Yep, they're connected."

I never liked rye, so I slid the bottle under the table when I could and poured most of it into the baseboard heater. They got the juke box fixed, and the Cream's *Sunshine of Your Love* was blaring, "Slow Hand" Clapton doing his magic on lead guitar. The Devils were getting hammered. Joints passed from hand to hand.

When the bottle was empty, I took it with us as we got out of the booth. We pushed through the crowd, my arm around her slender waist, and got to the bar. Casually, I threw the empty into the pile of broken glass behind it. I leaned over to Judith like I was nuzzling her and said in her ear: "We can't rush, but I think we can get outside. Take it easy." This time, she nuzzled me.

A hand grabbed me from behind, and I turned, ready to go, nose open, red fog rising. "Yo, Jack. Steady, bro. Where ya goin? Party's just startin," Pecker said. He was weaving a bit as he got between us and the door. White Cloud was draped all over him, with his elbow jammed in her cleavage. "Lookit, I talked to Zig-Zag. He says it's cool if you come over to the pines with us, man. That's fine, ain't it? We'll all saddle up when the sun goes down and head out. You ride on my right, kay?"

"Yeh, cool, Peck. Right now, though, I'd like a little blanket time with the old lady, know what I mean?"

"I can definitely dig it, yeh." He slapped me on the back with his free arm. "I'll find ya later. Have a nice time," he said with a leer. White Cloud tittered and rocked herself back and forth on his other arm.

Outside, there were close to a hundred choppers lined up on the street in front of the Salty Dog, metalflake and chrome gleaming. A wide swath of the beach was empty, except for a couple of Devils turning donuts on the sand. Others were jumping around in the surf, colors, jeans still on. One chick was topless.

We walked slowly, my arm still around her waist, until we got to our beach towel. I fell on my back with a long sigh. She knelt above me and said, "Thank you, Jack," as she came down on my chest. We didn't make love, but it was close in the murmuring heat and softness.

After a while, we headed silently down the beach toward the elephant. We were on the stoop ready to open the little door when I heard the rapid fire creaking and grunting from inside. We steered away and walked along the edge of the surf, watching the shore birds running ahead of it, beaks needling for a meal. Our feet made perfect white footprints in the wet sand that were swept away by the foaming wash of ocean. A single white seagull hovered motionless above us in the strong inshore breeze, wings spread, looking out to sea, black eyes gathering immensity.

The sun was lowering in the sky when we got back to the beach towel. All over the place Devils were crashed out in the sand, right where they fell. Judith asked, "What about this party? We don't really have to go, do we? I don't like feeling trapped by them this way."

"I don't like it either, but, yeh, we do. These guys have been drinkin and tokin a lot. We just make an appearance. They crash. We split. Simple as that." I tried to look sure of what I said. Pecker was walking toward us on the beach as she said, "You're a tough man, Black Jack Kavanagh, and I trust you."

# 9. "No Mortal Place at All"

Say what you want, a hundred choppers going down the road two by two at sundown is a grand sight. It's good feeling, too, when you're right in the middle of the pack, straight pipes roaring. It's a power rush, like you're Superman stopping bullets with your hand. I didn't think the Jersey state cops believed it, though. They were everywhere, sitting in their big-engined highway patrol cars parked on the shoulder, facing out on Route 30, watching us.

Judith held me tight, her pelvis up against me. I looked over at Pecker and White Cloud. He had his head thrown back—no helmet—a big smile on his face; his long hair was held back by a black bandanna. He turned to me and shook his head slowly, with a blissed-out look that said, "Man, it's a fine day to be a Devil." White Cloud was laid back on the sissy bar. He stabbed the front brake quickly so she mashed her chest into his back. He laughed when she punched him. Judith turned away and watched the pines flash by.

We turned right on 542. Four or five Harleys came from the back of the pack, blew by us and kept going: scouts, maybe, or decoys.  We were right in the heart of the pines in the Wharton State Forest.  Little piney towns whipped by: Westcoatville, Nesco, Pleasant Mills.  Sleeping dogs woke and yelped away from the tottery front porches as we passed; old people sat and rocked and watched, their heads still; teenagers looked up from the open hoods of their cars, beers in hand.  The pack was slowing down.  The first small sign read: "Mullica River," the second, "Batsto River."  We were down to a crawl, then a roll, front wheels wandering and motors revving with clutch levers pulled in, as we rode through Batsto Village.

Up ahead I could see somebody on the left side of the road waving a flashlight with one of those long red guards, like they use on airport runways.  We strung out single file as we turned onto a sand road with a hump of dead grass between the tire tracks and headed deep into the pines.  The night had come fast, and there was no hint of a moon.  The bouncing headlights ahead looked like spooks through the stunted trees. As the road wound along the banks of the Batsto, it became more of a path. Other tracks disappeared into the darkness on the right.  There weren't any signs.  We forded small streams and hit a few boggy spots. We must have gone about five, six miles when we came to a large clearing and stopped.

A bonfire was already roaring in the center of it, lighting up the chrome and wild paint of the choppers that had gotten there ahead of us. On the other side of the fire, set back in the scrub, was a small shack with a tarpaper roof and black fiberboard walls. Here and there smashed gallon cans had been nailed over holes in the walls. On the porch sat a skinny old woman in a rocking chair. She wore a faded house dress and cut her own hair.

I spread out the beach towel near the Triumph, and we sat down, cross-legged, out of the firelight among some pines. "Soon," I said to her, "soon." I could see Pecker moving around looking for us. He spotted me, came over and dropped to his knees. "Far out, man, this is my maw's place. She's up there on the porch." He handed me a fat spliff, and I took a long hit, holding in the smoke. We passed it back and forth among the three of us. Suddenly, he turned toward Judith. "Open your mouth, honey; I got a candy for ya." Before I could stop him, he grabbed her jaw and popped the sugar cube into her mouth.

"Hey, man, don't fuck around.  She don't do that shit."  I grabbed his greasy colors and shook him hard; his head rattled like a broken doll.  Over his shoulder, I could see her try to spit it out, but it was too late.  "What was it, Pecker, you piney fuck?  Not a microdot or STP, I hope."

"No way, Jack, Window Pane, medium strength.  It's a gentle trip, man, thought she'd dig it.  Honest.  Put some in the spliff, too.  Got some more for ya.  Want it now?"

"Not right now.  I gotta take care a her, thanks to you.  Let us be, huh?"  My knuckles were white against his colors.  The fury was there again, aching to come out and play.

He shook me off and stood up with his hands out at his sides:  "Okay, okay, no hassles, man.  I was just tryin to be friendly."  He backed away, then turned and stumbled off to the Devils around the fire.  His pickup was there.  Somebody jumped in and plugged in the eight track:  Arthur Black wailed out, "Fire, I think you should burn."  This thing was getting very out of hand. I wiped my hands hard on the beach towel. I turned to her.  She looked pale.  "Judith, please forgive me.  I wasn't fast enough to stop him."

"What's Window Pane, Jack.  Will it hurt me?  I'm really scared now.  Will they hurt me?"

"You know about LSD?  Well, something like it was on that sugar cube.  If you got enough of it, it will start to come on soon, about ten minutes.   You'll feel disoriented first, then you might start to see things.  You might feel, well, like you can do any kinda fool thing.  Fly, stuff like that. It could get very strange for you. Promise me you'll believe I'm here for you.  That I won't let you down. That I will protect you.  That I want to love you.  Deal?"  I held her face in both hands, gently, kissed her forehead, then smoothed her cheek.  The "love" part just popped out.  Surprised me.

"Can't we just go?"

"Not until I'm sure you're all the way down.  You couldn't stay on the bike stoned on acid.  Trust me."  I put her lovely head on my lap and threw my jacket over her legs.  I sat, watching the fire, stroking her hair.

The Devils were dancing around the fire, faster and faster, as the music pounded.  Red points of light from burning joints and pipes glowed in the darkness outside the ring of light. Some of the women started to strip, slowly, first the tops, then the jeans, then the panties, skin and triangles of hair flickering in the yellow light.  I thought I heard a low growl nearby, but maybe it was the dope. No doubt, I got some acid, too, but that was alright. Had it before; knew what to expect. The boys started on them: one woman lay on the sand and Zig-Zag did her right there. Another girl was spread-eagled on a chopper seat. A third bent over, holding handlebars in both hands. The Devils took turns.

I looked down at Judith. Her eyes were looking right at me, but they were wide, misty, unfocused. Her mouth was open, and she moaned lightly. She was out there, alright.

"Your hands are beautiful. Touch me."

Very lightly, I ran my hands over her head, her face, her neck, her ears, and she twisted slowly in my lap. She slid her hand down my arm, took my right hand and put it under her jacket on her breast. Rhythmically, her hand squeezed mine shut. She hadn't put her bra back on in Margate, and I could feel her thick nipple harden under the expensive white cotton. She moaned again.

"Touch my skin, Jack, my skin."

I unbuttoned her blouse and ran both hands over her breasts, slowly, again and again. They were very firm, like young cantaloupes; they didn't puddle on her chest. When I bent down to kiss them, she sighed, arched her back and came. It must have been a rocket, because her back stayed that way a long time. It was beautiful to see her face, like a Madonna in a vision. For me, it was odd, less exciting than just plain right. The dope again. Finally, she closed her eyes, smiling. I buttoned her blouse and went back to stroking her hair, hoping she could dream her way through it. About four to five hours, I figured. Mine was a mild one; multicolored, lighter than air, but still functioning, I thought. Bonehead again.

In half an hour, her eyelids started flickering rapidly, then her eyes popped open. She was scared, and I could see she was terrified by something she saw in her head. She started to kick and struggle, saying, "Get away, get away, what are you? I don't want you, get away." The kicking started to get violent; her heels made deep dents in the packed sand.

I had to do something fast to get her level. I stood her up. The Devils were occupied with themselves, and I don't think they even saw us. She was limp against me as I dragged her toward the shack. The old woman was still in the rocker. She watched as I helped Judith up the steps to the porch. She didn't say anything, just pointed to the patched screen door. I took Judith inside. The single room had an iron bed with an old quilt on it, a table, a chair, a potbellied stove and a coal oil lamp turned down low. It was poor as hell, but clean, swept out, looked after.

I laid her on the bed, pulled the chair over and put the lamp on the seat, turning up the flame. I got behind her on the bed so her head was on my chest, her legs between mine and she was turned toward the flame. Outside, the wind must have picked up, because I could hear it wail. "Judith, Judith," I said clearly but softly into her ear, "I'm here for you, but you have to help me. Open your beautiful eyes now and look at the flame. See the way it comes together, right at the tip. I want you to look right at that tip. It's real. It's all you can think about right now. Just keep looking at it."

I rocked her back and forth in my arms, singing snatches of Procol Harum's *Salty Dog* and humming *Spanish Lady* like granpop used to do. Her eyes were fixed on the lamp, and very, very slowly I sang and talked and rocked her back home: "Sand so white, sea so blue, no mortal place at all."‡ Outside, a dog yelped sharply twice, then quit. The wind was moaning in the pines.

"Jack, I think I'm better now. Do something for me?"

‡ Procol Harum; album and song: A Salty Dog; A&M, 1969.

"Anything, you know that."

"I want you to love me now.  Right here."

"That I won't do, not now.  You're not all the way down yet. Think about where we are, huh?  You don't want to know what would happen if they caught us.  Promise, though, you won't have to ask me more than once after I get you the hell outta here."

She turned in my arms so I could kiss her moist mouth. "Jack, I could fall in love with you."

We stayed like that for an hour or so, content to feel each other's heat.

Later, I said, "It's 4.  Except for the wind, it's been mighty quiet out there for a while.  We should go now if yer up to it, before any Devils come to.  Can you get up?"

She stood up, a little wobbly, but on her feet.  "Yes, Jack, I'm a bit light headed, but I think I'm okay.  My mind is fairly clear now."

"Let me see your eyes, love."  I held her face in both my hands and looked into them: the pupils were almost normal, but the whites were bloodshot.  "Okay, let's blow this joint."  I put everything back in place and turned down the lamp.  The old woman was still rocking on the porch.  Without turning around, she put up one finger: "Can you hear him wail? He's abroad tonight on the dark of the moon. Strangers aren't supposed to come here now. Beware him as you go. He can't cross the line at the Tabernacle and won't follow after that." She stared straight ahead. I looked at her face as we passed her. Framed by the chopped off hair, it was like stone lined by years and years of brown bog water trickling over it.

We crept quietly by the dying fire. The Devils were crashed around it in sleeping bags and blankets. The air was absolutely still, silent. She kicked a beer can, and it clattered away. Zig-Zag was at our feet, on his back; he grunted and turned over.

We got to the Triumph and pushed it out of the clearing and onto the dirt track. I pointed the bike up the trail, away from the way we came. She gave me a questioning look, and I whispered to her: "The cops or the Devils might have that way blocked, never can tell. I think we should go this way to be safe." She nodded agreement. I switched on the powerful Cibié headlight to guide us as we pushed. All around us were little split tracks like a goat or a fawn might make. Over to the right was what looked like a scrap of wet hide.

We got about 500 yards down the path when I stabbed the kickstarter and swung Judith on behind.  It was narrow, overgrown, not much of a road, and I had no idea where we really were, so we took it slow, in second gear.  Then, just beyond the headlight's range, I thought I saw something hop quickly across the road.  "Deer," I thought.  Then we both heard it, a high pitched wail, very close.  Judith had me in a death hug.  The hair stood up on the back of my neck and hoof beats of blood pounded in my ears. "Okay, okay," I shouted over my shoulder, "we'll be okay.  Just don't strangle me."  Her grip loosened enough so I could breathe.

Ahead about twenty yards, something large swooped across the road just at tree height.  "Hope that's an owl," I thought.  The wailing started again, and then I felt something sharp graze the top of my helmet.  Tree branch? Judith screamed.  I yelled, "Hang on," revved the Triumph until it was whining and took off.  Quick, tricky turns came up blind and fast.  I held my foot out, first left, then right, then left again, flat-track style, to kick the bike back up when the rear wheel slid out in the sand.  Under my leathers, the sweat ran down the small of my back.

We came to a fork, I hesitated an instant too long and the rear tire slipped out from under us. We came down hard. I pulled her up. "I'm okay, Jack, okay. Get it started, hurry."

The Triumph was stalled, on its side against a tree. The headlight was cracked but not broken. I picked it up and kicked and kicked and kicked. Flooded. Judith looked frantic. I twisted the throttle all the way so the carburetor slides would lift and get more air into the combustion chambers. "Dry, you suckers," I yelled at the spark plugs. There was loud hissing and cracking branches behind us. Suddenly, there was a thick, heavy slaughterhouse smell in the air. The engine sputtered and died, then fired with black smoke shooting from the pipes. She jumped back on, and we took off.

The intersection came up very fast, just after a sharp turn. The bike slid sideways when I nailed the rear brake too hard. Pretty good road surface leading off left and right. I worked the throttle to keep the plugs clear, looking for signs. Then we both thought we saw eyes staring at us from the top of a pine across the road. Judith screamed, "Mother of God, what is that?" The eyes were the size of golf balls, glowing cherry with a crust of black, like molten brazing rod just before it runs under the torch.

"Holy shit," I yelled, gunned the bike left, a rooster tail of sand spitting from the rear tire. We seemed to be in slow motion. I hoped I chose west. The eyes were rising into the air. The rear wheel squealed when we made it to the asphalt, and the Bonneville grabbed traction with a lurch, turning the bars to the right. I thought I saw a large, ragged bat wing at the edge of the halo from the headlight.

I straightened it out and gave that bike every last bit of juice it could handle, gear to gear. The pushrods rattled in their tubes every time I held it past redline. The rear view mirror on the handlebars was vibrating so much I couldn't make out anything in the pitch black behind us. And at speed on a strange road, I wasn't going to risk turning around to look. The road was empty, no street lights, and I was guessing in the turns. I was bent over the tank. My right hand ached from the death grip I had on the throttle. The carbs were all the way open, but I kept twisting, hoping for more.

We were going about 120, so the little sign came at me like a bullet. It took a moment to register that it said: "Tabernacle, Pop. 150." We cleared the village in a blink. I backed off the throttle, sat up straight, took a deep breath and patted Judith on the hands. "We're safe now, love. Pecker's maw said so."

We got onto 206, headed north, turned left on Route 70 and stopped at the Best Western in Medford. The manager was an old guy, and he came out of the apartment behind the desk rubbing the Corn Flakes out of his eyes. He was pissed off that I woke him, but he didn't grumble when I told him my wife was pregnant and wasn't feeling well: "We're from Philly, see. We were downashore for the day and started out on our way to Trenton to stay with her folks, but we took a wrong turn and got lost in the pines."

He squinted at me: "You been in the barrens tonight, young fella?"

"Yep, sure is dark and confusin in there. Somebody outta put up some signs."

"It's the dark of the moon, son. Best to stay outta there then. Didn't see anything strange, like, didya, huh?" He peered at me closely.

"Nope, nothin. Too dark. Just lotsa pine trees and bogs, man. Thanks for the advice. I'll remember it," I said, shaking the room key in my hand on the way out.

Judith was in the shower, and I was stretched out on the bed with my hands behind my head, staring at the ceiling. The water shut off, and she said from behind the door, "Did I really see that thing? Did you see that thing? What in God's name was it, Jack?"

"Nothin in God's name, that's for sure. It's been a strange night in a weird place. Maybe we did, maybe we didn't. We were both pretty stoned. I told you granpop's story this afternoon, remember? He told me about it many times. His description fit pretty well. Every once in a while, you see reports of sightings in the papers. There were a lot around 1909-1910, more in the thirties and some in the fifties, I think. It's supposed to be a hoax. The club's named after him.

"Whatever happened, it scared the livin shit—sorry—outta me. How are you now? You rode like a champ. Now that I think about it, though, I don't think we were in all that much trouble."

"Jack, you do have a tremendous genius for under-statement. I'm still shaking."

"Maybe we just plain outran the thing, but I don't think so. He beat us to the intersection, didn't he? And we were really movin. What I mean is I think we got chased off his turf. After all, we aren't club members, are we? We were trespassin. Nobody will believe us, you think?"

"Not a chance." She paused, probably drying her hair, because her voice was muffled. "I want to thank you, Jack, for not listening to me in the shack. It wouldn't have been good, there. You were right. I wasn't myself. But I am now."

The bathroom door opened, and she stood there holding one tiny, white motel towel over the front of her body; another one wrapped around her head like a turban. "When is check out time?"

"Eleven. We came in awful late, so I'm sure we could make an arrangement with the manager."

I reached over to switch off the lamp on the night table. "No, no, leave it on, please; I want to focus on you." She dropped the bottom towel and came toward me, a mischievous, crooked little smile on her beautiful face.

"Jack Kavanagh, you get in here right now. This is disgusting." There was heavy emphasis on the "gust" part. She didn't sound pleased.

It was October, and we'd been together steady since what we called our "Devil's Night." Her parents' place had a carriage house out behind with a large apartment up above, and we'd been staying there while they were in Italy, but they were back now. Finding places to sleep together was becoming a real problem. I didn't have the guts to bring her to my place, and I didn't have the bucks for back to back Best Western weekends. The decision to move in together was understood, not spoken, so I sucked up my courage, finally, and showed her my apartment. It was a three-room walk-up over Barney's Furniture Barn on Welsh Road in Bustleton.

I walked into the 1920s kitchen, and she said, "What in the world have you done to the sink?" I gulped and looked in. She was right; it was disgusting. When we got together, she was all I could think of, and I just forgot to finish washing the Norton motor parts. It was a single-cylinder 500 Featherbed ES, what they call a Manx Norton. I bought it, busted, for fifty bucks from a gas huffer with a nose problem. It was rare, a genuine classic from the old road race days, and would be worth quite a bit after I restored it.

The chipped white sink was streaked sticky slick black with oil left in the engine far too long. Next to the big, scored piston and connecting rod were the clutch chain, a heap of transmission gears, a hoagie wrapper and a cardboard coffee cup. The clutch was on the drain board, and it still smelled burnt. The cup had something green growing inside and black fingerprints on the outside. Water beaded darkly on the oil.

"This definitely will not do, sir. No, it just won't do. I'm not a cross between a Brillo pad and a mop. Not to put too fine a point on it, this place is a dump. It's impossible, and we aren't going to live here or stay here one minute longer, for that matter. Oh, and by the way, can you spell laundry?" She was laughing now, shaking her head wistfully.

I looked around. It really was a dump. Cheap, but a crummy dump.

We rented an apartment in Chestnut Hill, up at the end of tree-lined Lincoln Drive, just before Germantown Avenue turns into Germantown Pike and hits horsey country. It was the second and third floors of an old stone house on Roanoke Street. The big front windows on the second floor overlooked the tall oaks and small pond of Pastorious Park. It was airy and clean; we loved it and loved loving in it. I wasn't allowed to wash parts in the sink; I didn't mind one bit. The landlady lived downstairs. She had this beaming "Here's the young lovebirds in their nest, aren't they cute" smile when she came up for the rent.  The place wasn't a bargain, but Judith said firmly, "We split the rent; that's it, end of discussion."  So we did.

Yvon DuHamel was very bright on the phone when I called him in Montreal.  "You betcha, Black Jack," he said in his funny French-Canadian accent, "I'm workin wit Bombardier now.  I send evryting you need bout de franchise."  Judith was for it, too, and I was trying to save more money and make some plans.  Laying off the beer and the late nights helped, but I still needed more.  Always the money.  My gut was shaping up, too.

The letter came with a bunch of flyers and the phone bill on a rainy Saturday in November.  It was addressed to Judith.  She was out shopping, so I put it on the coffee table next to my pile of *Cycle World* magazines and Irish newspapers.  The return address said: "Cornell Institute of Egyptology."  I knew what it was and didn't look at it again.

I was sitting by the front windows listening to Jack Bruce belt out *Crossroads* when I heard the door bang.  "Goddamn thing never works," I thought.   I didn't turn around, just stared out, rigid as a Welshman, not focusing on the nearly bare trees in the park. She must have read the letter, because after a few minutes she put her arms around me from behind, nuzzled my hair with her nose and said, "Oh, honey, I'm so sorry." She smelled of wet wool and Coté cologne. I loved her, and I was going to lose her in a world I couldn't enter.

We spent Christmas Eve with her parents in Bryn Mawr. Chuck showed up drunk before dinner and quickly slammed out of the house and roared away in his MG. Her mother, Gwen Earle, stared at me a lot, kind of shocked. She didn't use my name and didn't say anything except what was required: "Oh, do have some cranberry sauce. It's from Fortnum & Mason." I don't think she breathed much that night; she had a very sour, sucked-in look about her. Judith's father, Roger, liked gin and tonic—a lot. We got a bit pie-eyed together, and by the end of dinner he was slapping me on the back in a "You're alright, jack" way that pissed me right off. Judith watched it all, sadly. Roger crashed early, so Gwen saw us off by herself with a lonely wave as we rode into the damp, cold night.

I gave Judith a wide-brimmed canvas hat for the sun, a fine, strong pair of khaki shorts, not too tight, the best stainless steel English garden trowel I could find, a brass compass in a leather case to find her way back to me, and a tiny, 18 carat gold Triumph Bonneville for her charm bracelet.

The first thing she gave me was a little green box with a gold foil "G" on top. Inside was a note: "Jack, my love, I've been collecting these when you dropped them from so many words, like doin and goin." Underneath were about a hundred little letter Gs she probably made on her typewriter and cut up. I ate a few so I'd start using them, I told her. In the big box with the heavy gold paper was the finest, softest, one-piece set of Italian racing leathers I'd ever seen—boots and gloves, too.

She left for Cairo in February. It was a two-year appointment. We wrote—all blue memories and private passion at first. Then came the day to day details about my work and my plans; her replies bitched about breaking her nails in the stony desert and problems with the dig. We even talked on the phone the following Christmas—unusual then. Her last letter came the second February. I was back living in the Northeast. It was much thicker than the previous ones. It was fine, just like her:

Jack, this is so hard for me. I've written this letter ten times now.

We had everything we needed then—just holding each other. I've never been with anybody who made me feel the way you do. You're only 27, but you're a man, not a boy. That's why. It was the best ever for me and probably never will be any better. I am so sorry to have to admit it to myself, finally, but our worlds are just too far apart, too different. Our roads were set in opposite directions before we were born. You have a white flash and loyalty to a cause, and I have a golden spoon and a career to build. I can't be you, and you can't be me. We can't change each other or what is. It won't work.

I never will forget you, or our "Devil's Night," the two days we spent in Medford, the quiet times in bed on Roanoke Street when you told me about your family—your grandfather's incredibly strange and tragic past—the lazy rides through Blue Bell in the fall when the leaves blew away behind us. I wear the little gold Triumph on a chain around my neck. It's my talisman against the evil out there.

I love you, Jack.  I will always love you.  "Promise," as you would say.  Please, go to Canada. William Blake said, "You become what you behold."  Don't let it happen to you. Get out of Philly, out of the underground, have your shop and behold far better things. You deserve it.

You never know, I just might come knocking on your door one day, looking for a fast ride in the snow. You're a good, powerful, honest man, my love, and at night when I think of your strong, beautiful hands I cry.

You are the funniest man I've ever met.  The boldest, the bravest, certainly. It was the boldness that attracted me first, until I saw your green eyes shining under your auburn hair on the beach at Margate.

You don't seem to have any idea of selfishness. You knew what I wanted, even when I didn't, and you gave it to me, over and over again, without fail.  You never said anything, but I could see it in your eyes that it pleased you so.  Any woman would be blessed to have you.  You *are* the best.  I'll vouch for you anytime.  Smile, now, please, for me, one last time.

Good bye, noble Black Jack Kavanagh. I know you'll always protect me. If ever I'm scared or in trouble, I'll just say your name, over and over to myself, like a prayer, and I'll be safe.

Please find it in your big Irish heart to forgive me. Please, please, for me, watch your back. As you said so many times, things can't always go wrong for you all by themselves. Be careful. My thoughts and my heart are with you, always.

Much later, I was in Kilian's Hardware on Germantown Avenue. I came up from Kensington on the way to Manayunk, and I stopped in to look for some knobs to match the ones in the kitchen of my apartment. I was building some new cabinets, and I was sure I could get what I needed there. It's the kind of place where you can find just about anything of any age in the little drawers and bins that line the crowded aisles. Sure enough, there they were, still in their oiled paper. "Must be from about 1910," I thought. "Granpop would be proud." I grabbed a can of Bon Ami, too, for the sink and my hands, paid for the stuff, and started to walk out.

Chuck, the asshole, was blocking the door, smirking at me. I pushed by him, but he followed me out on the sidewalk. It was raining. He had this phony accent that sounded like a mix of "Hahvahd Yahd" and Charles Laughton that really got under my skin. "Stop a moment, Jack. I must tell you that I heard from Gwen that Judith is studying at the British Museum in London. She's gotten into St. Hilda's College in Oxford for her Master's. I think I'll just pop over for a week or two. Should I give her your regards when I see her?"

I knew that if I hit him on the street the cops would come, and I'd do time. Instead, I imitated his accent: "Well, Chuck, old man, it's soo kind of you to offer, rahhly." Then I got very close to his chest, looked him dead in the eye and switched to Zig-Zag's voice: "Tell ya what, fuckhead, you ever get in my face again, yer dentist'll get himself a new Lincoln." Oh, did I ever want to cave his head in.

I put her letter in the white oak box my grandfather made for me in 1948. The wood turns darker every year, but the medallion with my initials in the center stays just as crisp as the day he carved it. I put it there to join the pocket-sized Prince Albert tobacco tin with his watch fob inside, one of his wooden molding planes, my grandmother's engagement ring with the red glass stone, my father's broken wire-rimmed glasses, the black and white photograph of the three brothers in their Hopalong Cassidy duds, a dirty Spalding baseball with "Champs, 1962" written on it in blue ballpoint, a dog eared picture of me and Rene, Hose and Chica, somewhere in Greenwich Village, the *Life of Parnell*, Toot's silver 45, a green felt scapular and a Miraculous Medal worn down to the brass on a chain that makes your skin turn green. I looked, carefully, at the sepia faded photograph of granpop, in his wrinkled suit and too-tight collar. His look was defiant, as always; the scar on his forehead showed deep and painful.

I touched each of the things with my left hand, saying hello, goodbye to them, while I rubbed the bronze key in the fingers of my right. I looked at it. The shaft was round, and the teeth were filed directly into the billet. The top was flat and shaped like a shamrock. The letters were worn but very legible: *Éirinn go Brách*. "Right, granpop," I thought, " Ireland should be free for ever. So should I." Except in dreams, I knew I would never see Judith's perfect china face and impish grin again.

# 10. VETS

I wasn't really asleep, not really awake. The old dream came again, vivid, palpable, my skin crawled. It was so wet, so dark, so cold. My teeth ached from it. We watched, helpless, as the Royal Ulster Constabulary shot our comrades, one by one. They were having fun, taking their time. Their laughter was hollow, viscous from too many cigarettes. Our lads didn't make a sound. In the yellow glare from the burning shed on the North-South border, I could see an ugly knot of rag-tag B-Specials looking on idly, smiling, as a bottle passed among them.

The pounding on the door brought me to with a lurch. In Philly, you never open the door in the middle of the night, very unhealthy. I crept out of bed and took Toot's 45 from granpop's box. It wasn't loaded, and there was no time, but maybe it might be enough. I crouched by the door in my underwear, waiting. My breathing seemed very loud. The pounding stopped, and then a tiny scratching sound in the dark. Could be anybody: cops, IRA, thieves, outlaws, junkies, what?

I loaded the clip, slowly, and stayed like that, muscles knotted, for what seemed like half an hour; probably more like five minutes. The neighbors wouldn't move, wouldn't call anybody. I knew that. At last, it seemed okay, so I turned on the light. Under the door, somebody had slipped an envelope. On the outside was scrawled: "Kavanagh— Deliver." It was written quickly, in pencil, but there was no mistaking the small, crabbed, old country handwriting the nuns teach in Ireland. Looked a bit like granmom's hand on a shopping list: "Fish, oysters, corned beef." Inside was a standard piece of typewriter paper with a short note: "Jacko, this comm. came for you from an old friend. Pray for us. Watch *An Phoblacht* for news. Sean." A tiny square of folded up cigarette papers lay on the bed. I opened it carefully. There were about a dozen of them, glued edge to edge. The writing was in quaky block letters, very small.

H Blocks, Long Kesh,
April, 1972

Dear Jack,

Hope this comm. finds you well. Mary Daugherty, the saint, smuggled it out for me, wrapped in cellophane. You can guess where. I heard after I was in the Maze a while that you decided not to join us in the struggle. Think again, boyo. We know you're the man for us, the blood of '16 runs hot in your veins. This time we will win. I pray every day to the Virgin Mary that you will change your mind. Here at the Republican University (ha, ha) I've learned how important we all are to the lads outside. It's to us they look for courage. We are the inheritors of Tone and everything that stands for Ireland. Not the politicos in Dublin. Now that Stormont is no more, we have Brit soldiers to deal with in the North, but that suits us just fine. Soon, we'll be taking them on in their own backyard—about time, too. They owe us for the 13 martyred in Derry on Bloody Sunday, and it's a comfort we'll still have enough materiel for July. I guess you wondered what happened to me. Once we had the shipment together in Boston, with the FBI's noses up our bums, I sailed with it because I had been trained in the new detonators. We transferred to the little boat well enough, but they got us in Lough Foyle, off the Derry coast, grassed on we were. The traitor's in his grave as I write. The RUC beat me and my shipmates something fierce. Not a one of us talked. Made them even madder. For a while, my ballocks were the size of footballs. My teeth never were very good, and now I don't have to worry about them anymore. I don't require their services anyway. My comrade and I have been on the blanket on hunger strike for two weeks. Unless we get political status for the IRA prisoners here, we won't wear prison clothing or eat prison food. I've taken a bit of water, but mostly I spit it up. I'm pretty weak, and it shouldn't take much longer. The priest wants us to stop, but we believe we're doing right. My death can only help the cause. My soul can only join all the glorious dead who have gone before. Remember me, Jack, and pray that I stay strong in the face of the grave. Take heart and join us for the good of Ireland.

> Your friend in God's name,
> Charlie Murphy

I don't cry very often, but it stopped when I banged my head against the wall a few times. Even the Sunday *New York Times* ran a big splash. There was a picture of IRA men in balaclavas carrying his coffin and another showing the rifle salute over the open grave in Bodenstown, near to the Wolfe Tone he loved so. Charlie made his point, I guess. The article was pretty hot about how badly the prisoners were treated under interrogation and in the Maze. As usual, though, they were really dumb about the political situation in the North. There was a lot of raving in *An Phoblacht* that sounded like St. Patrick had been crucified. When you think about it, maybe he had.

Later, I put Charlie's letter in granpop's box. Toot's 45 held it down. Sure was some strange collection of spirits in there.

"Well, if it ain't Black Jack Kavanagh. I declare Nate; this boy does get around some, don't he. Kinda dumb not ta stay with Mr. Castesi. Just lookee here, his patch says 'Shop Manager.' Ain't that cute. Where's the owner, Jack? We got to have a little talk about the parkin situation out front. Can't just have you takin up all the spots out there. Can we now, Nate?"

"Absolutely right, Jeeps. Last time I checked, the signs said, 'No parking, loading zone.' "

"Oh, shit, how'd you two find me so fast. Telepathy?"

It was Nate again: "Well, let's just say our guardian angel told us. Right, Jeeps?"

Jeeps with a snort, "Guardian angel, that's a good one. I'll remember that one. So, Jack, do we talk to the owner or you gonna do it?"

"Okay, okay. Don ain't here right now. How much should I tell im?"

Nate did the honors. "It'll be twenty-five a week—each. You make it clear that if we don't see it, Friday afternoons, cash, it's gonna rain tickets. Oh yeh, by the way, Jeeps' Bonny needs some work, and we don't wanna see no bills. You know how it goes, Jack, dontcha?"

"Yeh, yeh. I'll tell im when he comes in."

Jeeps was right, sort of. It probably looked dumb to him, but I was offered a chance to build a shop from the ground up, so I took it. The money was even a bit better. Mr. Castesi looked puzzled, not mad, when I told him I was leaving. "It's a career move isn't it, Jack? Well, okay, but you'll be hearing from me." Jeeps and Nate were right back on me like a dirty shirt. Still didn't know how they found me so fast. Except when I worked at Castesi's, it was always the same squeeze, the same bullshit, no matter where I went. Nate and Jeeps must have bought this beat from their captain, because the last time they had the balls to shake me down was in Germantown and then Fairmount. They had their eyes on me for sure. No doubt, the area around the Inquirer Building would be better pickings for them, what with all the bars and small industries scattered about. Twenty-five a week from each stop added up to more than a cop's entire pension in a single year.

Don, part owner of Philly Triumph, was from Cherry Hill and wasn't connected in the city. He said I could tell the cops to screw off. I told him he couldn't do that, and I wouldn't. "Just give em what they want, or the tickets'll start commin, and then they'll ask for fifty each to cut it out. You'd have to cough it up, too. You gotta play their game, or they'll be all over us. Besides, who you gonna turn to? God?"

He did what they wanted, and, except for Jeeps, the cops mostly let me alone, although I could feel them watching. I was too busy for that crap, anyway, because I was trying to hire some quality help to get the shop off the ground. Vultch said he could give me weekends, days off. Claus, the BMW expert, was lukewarm. Luci got busted for arson during the race riot in 64. He was still in jail after he knifed a white screw, so I couldn't even find anybody to sweep up, not that he'd even talk to me anymore.

There was a lot to do, and I didn't like the daily battles with Don, or his silent partners. "Why do we need a drill press? An air compressor is expensive. The brazing equipment doesn't seem necessary to me. Can't we just open the doors and skip the exhaust fan?" He was full of excuses, and getting anything was like pulling teeth. He was a good enough guy, and a great salesman, but setting up a new franchise was out of his league.

I had a line on a used drill press down on Fitzwater Street, so I jumped into the El Camino I just bought—black naturally—cut over Callowhill and took a right on Broad. The light at South Street turned red, and I pushed in the clutch and started gliding to a stop. A guy sprawled in a doorway caught my eye, so I pulled into the curb lane. I couldn't tell for sure at first. He looked a lot older, and he wore his brown hair hippie style, down to the middle of his back. His Army fatigue shirt and bellbottom jeans were beat up, and one of the black high-topped sneakers had a hole in the sole. I rolled down the passenger side window, anyway. "Hey, buddy." He looked up at me, and then I was certain. "It's me, Jimbo, Jack Kavanagh. Remember? Olney? St. Tim's?"

His light brown eyes were dead, and he looked at me blankly for a few long seconds. Then there was a flicker of recognition, then a warm smile. He stood up, shuffled over to the window and stuck his head in. "Yo, Jack! Course I remember, ya big lunk. How's it goin? Those were the times, huh? That Olds 88 a mine sure could honk, couldn't it? Too bad I sold it. You got any money, man? I sure could use a meal."

"You got it, Jimbo. Jump in, and we'll grab somethin to eat."

We found an Italian mom and pop joint on Carpenter Street, across from the Ridgeway Library. First thing he did was eat all the bread in the basket, even before the butter got to the table. Then he had a huge plate of spaghetti with meatballs and three glasses of milk. Pop was in the kitchen, and mom was serving us. She was a little weird at first, probably because of the way Jimbo looked, but when he cleaned up on the second plate of spaghetti and another basket of bread, the big grin came out. She liked to see men eat; you could tell by her dark eyes.

I got up like I was going to the can, but really I wanted to talk to her out back by the kitchen. "Wouldya mind bringin him some apple pie with ice cream? And anything else he wants. Oh, yeh, and a couple a coffees. I'll pay the bill back here when he's done, kay?"

"That's nice. You're a nice boy to take care of your friend like that. He's sure hungry."

When I got back to the table, Jimbo was staring down at his empty plate. "Yo, Jimbo, still hungry, man? I'll get momma to bring you another plate. Or maybe dessert?"

"No way, Jack. But a piecea pie would go down good." I knew it would.

He ate the pie and vanilla ice cream slowly, like they were the last on the planet.

"Feelin better now, are ya? Man, you looked like you hadn't seen food in a month a Sundays. My granpop would say you eat like a pit pony, boyo. Whatcha been up to, Jimbo, since we used to boogie with the Italian girls?"

"Dumb shit, I volunteered after the Armory to get a better deal, and the cocksuckers put me in the Infantry. I went right from boot camp to the jungle. It was a fuckin mess. When my tour was up, we got stoned for a week on the beach at Da Nang and re-upped. Stupidest goddamn thing we ever did. Charlie chopped us up like dog meat. I gotta a fuckin Purple Heart, man, but when I get back nobody gives a shit. Can't even find a job. You remember Sheltie from Mt. Airy? Lived up near Chubby Checker's house."

"Yeh, you seen im? Good basketball player."

"Yeh, I seen him alright. Point man; stepped on a mine that tore him apart."

"Christ, man. I hate that. I hear too much a that shit these days, so many good guys. You were lucky as hell to get out in one piece. Yer right, though, nobody does give a shit. But if yer lookin for work, I got a job for ya at a new bike shop I'm managin—Philly Triumph—if yer interested."

"Yeh, you always liked the bikes, Jack. Whadyado in the service?"

"Nothin, Jimbo, they 4Fd me. Diddn want no part of me. My brother, Mark, he's still in—Artillery, then Airborne. Just finished up his second tour."

"You always were a lucky fuck. What could I do at this Triumph place, man? I don't know dick about engines."

"You don't have to at first, Jimbo. I'm just puttin the place together, and you could help me bring in the equipment, build the benches, paint, clean the place up. Stuff like that. Later I could show ya how to set up the new bikes. Whaddya say? Deal?"

We shook hands with thumbs locked, like veterans do.

I paid the bill, and we took off for Fitzwater Street. The machine shop was going out of business, and I picked up the drill press and a brazing set-up cheap. We loaded them into the back of the pickup and headed for Philly Triumph. I put some Allman Brothers in the tape deck as we drove up Broad Street.

"You got *In-A-Gadda-Da-Vida*, Jack? It's what me and Chick like best, unless you got *Time Has Come Today*; that's good, too."

"Nope, not here, anyway. Who's Chick? Don't remember him from the neighbahood."

"Naw, he's from Detroit. We served up country together, both tours. We're tight, man. He watches my back. I watch his."

"You got a place to live, or what?"

"Uh, yeh, sort of. Me an Chick got a crib over near 2$^{nd}$ and South. You know, where Head House Square is—the old market. It's real quiet, nobody much around, except for the spy across the street. He lives in a car. Chick says he's with the CIA. But lissen, Jack, don't tell nobody about where we're livin, huh? That would be a definite bummer. We just wanna be left alone right now."

"Sure, Jimbo, sure. Ain't all those buildings condemned over there? I heard they were gonna tear em all down, or fix em up, or somethin."

"Maybe they will; maybe we won't let em."

We took the stuff into the shop and set it up. Don gave me an argument about hiring Jimbo, of course. "Jack, what the hell are you up to? I don't want any acid heads working here. What if Jeeps and Nate get a load of him?"

"No sweat, Don. Jimbo's smart enough to steer clear of the cops. Look, he's an old friend of mine. He's down on his luck, so what? He drops a tab once in a while, so what? The poor sucker spent two tours as a grunt in Nam, man, so no wonder he's screwed up. You don't have to worry. I'll vouch for him. He just needs regular meals and some money in his pocket."

At closing time, I called Jimbo over to my bench. "Here's half a yard, man, buy yourself some good work boots—steel toes and shanks. You're gonna need em. Don't buy em from the shysters on South Street, either. And you better tie your hair back. Could be a problem with the machines. You can pay me back when you can."

"Jesus H. Christ, I've had it with that goddamn car. Jack, you're telling me it's going to cost how much?"

"Five hundred, just for the parts, Don. They must think Lincolns are gold plated or somethin."

"Shit. That's perfect. The goddamn thing falls apart just after the warranty expires. I'm tempted to leave the keys in it, park it in North Philly and collect on the insurance."

Jeeps was leaning against my bench, drinking coffee from a paper cup, taking it all in. His Bonneville needed a valve job, and I was just finishing up so he could go on his Saturday ride with the other cops. He had a slick, little, nickel-plated, snub-nosed revolver on his hip in a leather holster. Naturally, there was no work order.

"Hey, Don, ever tell you about my brother-in-law, Gino?"

"No, what's that got to do with it?"

"Everything, if yer smart. He runs the crusher down at the pound on Route 95. Just might be if you left it out front tonight, it wouldn't be here in the morning. Don't need no keys."

"How much, Jeeps?"

"A yard, man, a hundred. Guaranteed, they'll never find it."

"Okay, it's a deal. See me in front before you leave."

"Tell ya, Jack, you look at me like that one more time, and you'll be back inside quickern shit."

"What trash you talkin, Jeeps? Just got somethin in my eye."

I had Jimbo building a paint booth out the back, and he didn't show his face until Jeeps took off.

"I heard all that shit, Jack. That Jeeps is a slimy mothafucka, ain't he?"

"You got that right. You finish up those motor mounts, yet?" The gorge, the rage, was very hard in the back of my throat. I gulped it down.

"Nope. I had to go out and get some more Red Devil Oil for the drill bits. I'll do it now, unless there's anything else you want first. I been meanin to tell ya, Jack, thanks for givin me the chance. You always were like my guardian angel."

"Fuck off, Jimbo, and get back to work."

"Yeh, yeh, yer ma, too."

I started on a tune up, then went to the parts counter to get some spark plugs. There were five or six people in the show-room, looking over the new bikes, so I answered a few questions and showed off a few features until Don came out of his office.

When I got back to the shop, Jimbo was standing in the middle of the floor with blood streaming down his face and onto his T-shirt. He didn't say anything, just looked down at the blood as it dripped on the newly painted, gray concrete floor. I grabbed a shop rag and got the first aid kit and a bottle of peroxide from the bathroom. I dumped it over his head. A patch of scalp about the size of a silver dollar was missing from his hairline. I unwrapped a square of gauze, and he held it over the wound with one hand while he used the other to wipe his face with the rag. I went over to the drill press to turn it off. Hair and the piece of scalp were whizzing around on the drill bit.

When I got back to him, he whispered: "Medic, medic. Got a man down over here." Then he passed out, but I caught him before he hit the floor. At Hahneman Hospital, they said they couldn't do anything with the piece of scalp. They stitched him up after I said I'd pay cash.

"Yeh, Jack, Chick says it's okay. Wants to meet you. I think he's got plans. Come on down about 10:30-11. We'll have a few toots and lissen to some tunes. We're on Howard Street, between 2$^{nd}$ and Front. It's the one with the condemned sign on the door. You gotta come in the back, though, off Bainbridge. We don't use the front door, causea the spy. Don't bring a bike; too much noise. Park the truck on Lombard and walk down. Oh yeh, there's a little piece a string stickin out from below the back door. Just pull it twice to let us know you're there. And, pick up some munchies, wouldya? I'll give ya the bread when you get here. Catch ya later."

I couldn't find a parking spot on Lombard, so I left the El Camino at 3$^{rd}$ and Pine, right in front of St. Peter's Church, the one with the plaque that says it was built before the Revolution. The college kids, hipsters and high-heeled boys were out in force, diving in and out of the apartments and coffee houses. As I walked down 2$^{nd}$, the streets emptied. The market arcade was boarded up tight to keep out the smack freaks. Most of the broad rowhouses looked like they had been built just after the Revolution. They were boarded up, too, except for a few, where the junkies had gotten in to nod off or rip out what they could. At the corner of South and Hancock there was a street light, but the rest of the block was dark as a dungeon, and the sidewalk was crunchy with broken glass.

Howard was a funny, U-shaped little place, and, except for my footsteps, it was very, very quiet, only the dull city roar far off and hollow. I found what looked like the right door and made a mental note of the location so I could find the back on Bainbridge Street. When I turned around, I looked straight into a weedy empty lot where a trashed, early sixties Ford was sitting on milk crates. Inside, I could see a point of light from a burning cigarette. The driver's side window was open a bit, and smoke curled out slowly into the still air.

"Jimbo's lost it," I thought. "It's probably just some wigged out old black dude with nowhere else to go." Bainbridge had a bit better light, and I counted the doors until I thought I had the right one. I found the piece of string, pulled it twice and waited. There was nobody on the street and no cars parked. The window next to the door had steel shutters on it that looked like they hadn't been opened for years. One of them swung open without a sound, and Jimbo's head appeared in the dark rectangle.

"Yo, Jack, how's it goin, man? Keep it down, willya? Pass the munchies and come on in."

I climbed in through the window and jumped into what must have been the kitchen. When my feet hit the floor, I had a cold feeling up my spine and in my mind's eye saw a quick flash of red. It was so dark in the room I could barely see him as he walked toward the front of the house. He stopped me at a door at the end of the long hallway and whispered through it: "Chick, we're commin in."

We walked into the darkened room. Jimbo closed the door, and the lights snapped on, blinding me for a moment. It was like Christmas: a long string of bare light bulbs was hung around the tall ceiling. On one of the beat up sofas sat Chick in Army fatigues and jungle boots. He was a skinny, fine-boned little black guy with an Afro the size of a bushel basket. He peered at me over the lenses of small, round, gold rimmed sunglasses.

"Ah, yes. Black Jack—high school buddy, angel of mercy, medic and motorcycle dude. Far out, man. Have a seat."

He lit a fat joint and passed it to me. The place was some strange. The door and the windows in the large room were covered with Army blankets, and the inside walls were stacked high with sandbags. An AK 47 rested in one corner next to a green ammunition box.

"Whaddya think a the shit, man?"

"It's got a kick like a horse, Chick. Wheredya get it?"

"Let's just say we got Asian connections. Know what I'm sayin?"

"Yeh. Hey, I saw the guy in the car outside. What's he up to, anyway?"

"He's collectin information for the CIA. Been out there since a few days after we took possession. We will take care of him when the time comes. That is a definite fact."

On the other sofa, Jimbo was dropping a tab of acid, washing it down with the apple juice I brought along. It didn't take long to send him into gaga land.

Chick said: "You wanna trip, man, or just blow some weed?"

"No thanks, don't get along with acid. Had a bad experience with some Window Pane once. That was the last time."

"That's cool, Jack. Let's just put on some tunes and have a chat. Jimbo's out to lunch for a while."

He walked over to the wall where there was a monster Sony reel to reel tape deck and concert-size speakers. He flipped a couple of switches, and Iron Butterfly began their long, slow, meaningless chant. It started low, but I knew the volume would rise, both from the dope and the way the song went.

"Come on downstairs, Jack. We can have a talk and some practice at the same time. Jimbo's okay here for now. He likes to sit in the dark and listen. It's a very safe place for him."

He walked over to Jimbo, put his feet up on the sofa and brushed his hair out of his eyes. The scar on his head was red and white and puckered. When Chick turned out the lights, only the tape deck was glowing in the big room. We walked back into the hallway, and I followed the dark bloom of his hair down the stairs into the basement. A switch cracked, and more strings of lights lit up the long room. A hole had been cut in the brick wall on the Hancock Street side. They had done a good job: electric wiring, water pipe and a phone line led through it into the next building. More sandbags filled the hole and lined the walls.

"It's a good set-up, ain't it? Me and Jimbo spent a week cuttin through basement walls until we got to some hot connections near the street. Gotta be careful with the phone, though. The bitch who uses it sounds suspicious when we lissen in."

*In-A-Gadda-Da-Vida* blared from small speakers in the joists. We were standing in front of an old door set up as a table on two sawhorses. The top was covered with an Army blanket, and on it were handguns of various sizes: two very small, like Jeeps' Saturday ride pistol, but they weren't nickel plated, a large blued revolver with a long barrel, two automatics, a 45 and a Luger. In front of us, down at the end of the basement, were two cardboard human silhouettes with paper bull's-eyes over the hearts. The heads were shot away.

"You know weapons, Jack?"

"Not much, Chick. Used to shoot a 45 once in a while over on Fairmount Street, but that's about it."

"Well, this one here is very fine. It's my favorite, a 9 millimeter Beretta. Check it out, man. It's loaded. I'll use the Ruger. It's a big sucker, 357 mag."

I always knew all that stuff in movies and on TV was crap. The Lone Ranger pulls out his silver Colt and plugs the bad guy from horseback at fifty feet. Nobody can hit shit with a handgun at twenty-five feet—standing still, too. I blazed away; maybe I nicked the cardboard once, but most of the slugs thumped into the sandbags well off target; one even skipped off the floor.

Chick watched with a smile, then emptied the magnum into the center of the bull's-eye. The pistol was loud in that confined space, and it had a big kick he held in check with both hands on the butt. "That, ma man, is how it's done. You need some serious range time, Jack. It's a skill you're gonna need real soon. Just bring your own ammo, and you can use this place when you want. I owe you for takin care a Jimbo, and I don't forget dues or who's right on the street."

> *Oh, won't you come with me,*
> *And we can walk this laa–aah–nd?*
> *Please take my haa–ahh–nd.‡*

"Some of this other shit is very specialized, and we can't fire them in here." He showed me two small grenade launchers; they looked like G. I. Joe toys. Then, he handed me a camouflaged rifle with a big scope on top. I lined up the crosshairs and hit the bull's-eye dead center; when I fired, the round only made a little "zip."

"Yes, yes. A natural for this kind of weapon. Perhaps we have sniper material at hand. Good shot, Jack. I'll introduce you to a pro sometime."

"Lookit, Chick, I don't mean to ask the wrong question or anything, but where'd you guys get all this stuff? I mean Jimbo never has any money, man. When I first saw him on South Street, he hadn't eaten in a while."

‡*Iron Butterfly, In-A-Gadda-Da-Vida, Atlantic, 1969.*

"Jimbo says you're a brother, Jack, so I'll tell ya as much as ya need ta know. The boys in the squad send it back in parts or bring it when they get back. We keep it here until we get together again. Like, it ain't ours. It's the squad's."

He looked at me as if he was making up his mind. "We got some very secure connections: Laos, Cambodia, Thailand. There's lotsa opportunities, Jack, for the smart among us to make some serious coin. One of the reasons I wanted to talk to ya. We bein watched, so we can't do too much on the street. You ain't, I think. How'd you like to deal for us, Jack? We can get as much Thai-stick, hash, opium, smack, what-ever, as you can sell. You make a livin; we get our finances in order. It's all primo shit, man, guaranteed."

"Hold on, man. Jimbo musta told ya about the cops that shake us down every week. I know those two guys from way back, and they know me. They busted me up in German-town, and I did time in Holmesburg. They got their eye on me, man. I'm probably too high profile for what you want, but I'll think about it."

When I left, I stopped at the corner and took a very careful look at the guy in the Ford. Another cigarette was burning. I thought I could hear the faint crackle of a radio, but it was probably the weed talking. On the way up 2^(nd) Street, a Harley chopper flashed by. The rider wore colors, but I couldn't make them out, it happened so fast. As I walked, I kept repeating to myself: "No way. Don't think about the money. No way."

Judith's letter was ringing in my head; I missed her terribly. I snorted when the old *Baltimore Catechism* thing came back to me in the murky, mixed up memory jumble of words, of images, of delight, despair. That old jigsaw puzzle was in pieces all over the floor once more.

# 11. "No Home"

"Hiya, Jackie.  How come you haven't called?  It's really great you keep the money coming, but your granmom and I would like to see your face once in a while, not just envelopes put through the slot in the middle of the night.  Why don't you come over Sunday?  Matt's been in town for weeks.  He got permission from Father Talarico, and he'll be saying a special Mass at 11:00 at our church.  Isn't that great?  He said he expects to see you there.  After that, we can have lunch."

"Sure, mom, I'd like that, but I can't make church.  I'll be over about 1:00.  Got some stuff I gotta do at the shop.  A new guy walked in the other day.  He's from New Hampshire —flat-rate guy says he's got his own tools and a lot of exper-ience.  Have to meet him to see if he's what he says he is.  I sure need some more people."

"Matt will be so disappointed.  You two haven't really seen each other for too long. Did I tell you he's been giving special summer school lectures at LaSalle?  He's really excited about that."

"Yeh, right.  I bet he is.  How's the job?"

"Oh, it's okay. They don't pay me as much as they should, but it's okay. I really don't like leaving granmom alone, though, even though Mrs. Francini looks in once in a while. She's getting so she can't remember things anymore. Let's just have a nice lunch, okay?"

"Promise. I got a customer in the meat business. I'll see what he's got in stock. He owes me a few. Whaddya hear from Mark, anyway?"

"He called last week from Fort Bragg. He got promoted, and Sylvia is pregnant again. I'd sure like to meet her, and my granddaughter. Maybe they'll have a boy this time, God willing. He's doing some kind of instructor work out there."

"Yeh, that's fine, mom. Lissen, see ya then. Gotta go. Lots to do."

On Sunday, I disconnected the speedo cable from a new, three-cylinder Triumph Trident—had my reasons—and rode up Ridge Avenue to Manayunk. It was an old mill town where they used to make rubber and carpets and stuff; now Philly had swallowed it up in a gulp. Terraces of row houses are built into the steep banks of the Schuylkill River, and some of them look over the train tracks, the old stone mills, the canal, and the river down below. Mom's place didn't. It was on Sion

Street and faced northeast, up the hill; it was dark most of the day.

It was just after noon. They weren't back yet, so I used my key to get in. I hadn't been inside since Judith's last letter. The living room was crammed with granmom's stuff from Fishtown: an upright piano and its stool, the round oak dining room table where the brothers argued over dinner, granpop's horsehair chair where I used to sit in his lap, plus everything mom didn't figure was worth selling from Hope Street. Over the piano, the framed color photograph of John F. Kennedy had a red glass votive candle in front of it. On either side, embroidered pictures of Jesus and Mary. Jesus pointed to his heart; Mary pointed to the ceiling with her finger and her big blue eyes.

It smelled stale and hot inside, so I left the front door open a bit. I put the ham I brought with me and two quarts of Bud in the refrigerator; mom couldn't leave off calling it the icebox. Hoping for a cross breeze, I opened the kitchen door to the postage stamp back yard, went down the single step and lit a Camel. In the lane between the houses, two little Italian kids were duking it out noisily over a toy or something. I watched, idly, until Sal Francini came out and chased them off. He wiped his broad hands on his white apron and waved. I waved back. He was a good neighbor and helped mom out when he could, a lot when she first moved to Manayunk. I walked over to shake hands. He was a thin, tough little Sicilian, about thirty. He was sweating, and his black hair was covered with flour, like it seemed to be every time I saw him.

"Hey, Sal, how's it goin? How about momma, huh? Any more bambinos on the way, or did you take the pledge?"

He gave me a broad smile, whacked me on the shoulder and called inside the shed built on the back of his house. "Hey, momma, look who's here. Theresa's son, big Jack. He looks hungry, too. Maybe some wine?"

We walked into the shed. Inside was a low, broad baking oven made from the same dark red brick as the house. Pallet wood crackled in the firebox. He was getting ready to make the best Italian rolls known to man, and it was hot as blazes in there. Early every morning and late every afternoon, his brother Vini's truck would pull down the lane and take away a mountain of them to stock the hoagie joints and restaurants in Shawmont, East Falls and Mt. Airy. This was probably the third batch of the day; his long wooden peel, worn shiny and thin at the edge, stood ready against the wall.

Mrs. Francini came out of the kitchen with two jelly glasses and a Chianti bottle that had been refilled many times. Her name was Angela, but everybody called her momma, including Sal. She put them on the steps, disappeared into the kitchen and came back out, beaming, with a rectangular pan straight from the oven. Momma had the most radiant smile I think I ever saw. It could light up a room. The pan held my favorite, and she knew it. She cut the thick, chewy pizza into large, neat rectangles. On top was her famous, secret pizza sauce and a sprinkle of oregano fresh from her tiny garden. That was it: simple and perfect.

"Jackie, you're thin as a broom. Whatsa matta, lose your best friend or somethin?"

Sal coughed behind me, and momma looked quickly at the dirt floor. She was about five two and broad as she was tall. Her house dress was new and very clean, but the red flowers on her apron were fighting it out with the green flowers on her dress. She made a point of going to the novenas with mom and granmom, but she always went to the 6:30 on Sundays. It was a toss up who was the most devout Catholic.

"Here, have some nice, fresh pizza and some wine." She said with a quaver in her voice. "They'll do you good. Maybe

you should move in with me for a while. Poppa wouldn't
mind. It's time he visited his father in the Bronx." Sal laughed
behind me.

Her head was down, so I bent way over and kissed her
cheek quickly. It smelled of warm talcum powder. "No way,
momma, Sal would pound me into the ground like a stake.
Thanks for the pizza; it's straight from heaven." The wine was
thick, sweet and powerful, the way Sicilians like it.

Me and Sal walked back outside and yakked about what I
was up to. Across the lane, I could see they had come back
from church. Mom was in the kitchen making coffee, and she
waved to us. I finished up the third piece of pizza, shook
hands with Sal, nodded to momma in the kitchen doorway
and started to head back when he put his hand on my arm.

"Look, Jack, momma's sorry for what she said. She didn't
mean it. Theresa told us about your girl. That's too bad, a
real shame." I looked at momma; there were tears in her dark
eyes, so I smiled at her. "We gotta lotta respect for how you
take care a yer mom and granmom. You want anything from
us, you got it, any time."

I walked over to momma in the doorway; she was looking
at her hands, twisting the wedding ring in the deep groove in

her finger. I lifted her chin, gave her a big smacker on the other cheek and said, "You ship him out to the Bronx next week. I'm movin in. We'll make lotsa Irish babies, kay?" She laughed, gave me a teary smile and reached behind her. The paper bag felt warm and delicious in my hands.

In the living room, Matt was tinkling away at something on the piano. He didn't come into the kitchen. I went to the refrigerator, got out a quart of Bud and poured a glass: "Hey, Matt, wanna beer? Just look at you, mom, far out doo. Sure looks better than the gray. You man huntin, or what?"

She was busy at the gas stove, with her back to me. She laughed, shaking her stiff, sort-of-brunette beauty parlor hair. At the kitchen table, granmom was looking out into the yard. I stood behind her, put my hands on her shoulders and kissed the top of her head. She looked up at me with a startled smile. "Danny? Oh, Jackie, I thought it was Daniel. That was just like him. It's a fine thing to see you such a man. But you're too thin." The cataracts were getting slightly worse, and the tight bun of her hair was steel gray. On the table, between her gnarled, arthritic hands, was her tattered missal with the white covers and tarnished gilt.

"Right, granmom, that's why I came over, so you could put the beef on me. Except it's ham this time. Mom, did you get a load of it? It's a monster. I got it from that customer I told you about. He's got a shop over in Tacony."

"It's sure a big one, Jackie. It must have been expensive."

"Nope. I cut him some slack sometimes, so I get a favor sometimes."

"It's probably stolen," Matt said. He was standing in the archway between the living room and the kitchen. We were the same height, so we stared at each other eye to eye. Right then, he looked so much like the Jesuit with the Aquinas questions when I was in high school that I was struck dumb for a moment.

"It is not. I make a stupid mistake once, and nobody forgets. You wanna beer or what? Maybe not, somebody sure has been puttin the beef on you, sport."

"No thank you. Mother, I'll have coffee. You know how I like it these days."

"Get it yerself, man; she's not yer servant. When you start payin the bills, buddy, you can start givin orders around here. Not before."

"You know perfectly well that I don't have any money of my own." I snorted at that one, looking him up and down. "And, please, Jack, spare me the Kensington dialect, will you? You're perfectly capable of speaking the language properly, so why don't you?"

I used granpop's voice and pulled my white forelock: "Fadah, let it never be said this Kavanagh ever put on any lace-curtain Irish airs."

"Oh, fine, that's just wonderful. Now we have a cross between the Dead End Kids and Edmond O'Brien. What an embarrassment. My brother, the ex-con, street hippie and stand-up comedian. What's next, a step n fetchit walk? Mobster lingo? Or is it the Fenian today?"

Granmom's head went up quick, and she turned to me. "Ah, no Jackie, not you, too? Christ have mercy on us all."

I moved closer to him and said flat and even: "You don't have to worry, Matt, nobody at Fordham will ever see the two of us together, so your secret—and your career—are safe. Just say I died of a drug overdose down in the East Village or something. And, please, reserve that 'I am the Word' tone for the women and the high school kids. They buy it; I don't.

What's happened to you, anyway? I'm your brother.
Remember? Or are you too hypnotized?"

Mom got between us. She seemed to be getting shorter
all the time. "Okay, you two, cut it out right now. Matt, Jackie
was generous enough to bring us lunch, so you can be good
enough to say grace over it. He told us where it came from,
and I believe him. Can't we just have a nice family lunch for a
change?"

"Alright, Matt, truce, kay?" I stuck out my hand to shake. I
hadn't noticed the manicure on his soft hands, and he winced
when we shook. "Sorry about that, Matt, didn't mean it." And
I didn't; his hand was soft and very weak.

Jaw set, Welshman rigid, I stared straight at the perfectly
trimmed black hair on his bowed head as he said grace.
When he was finished, his pale blue eyes locked on mine.
The pit of my stomach dropped to my boots when I saw the
pain and fear in them.

When lunch was over, Matt cleared his throat. Same
signal he always used when warming up for a long speech
about how right he was. "Yes, Jack, well now. I stopped in on
campus to listen to a rally for the strikers in Long Kesh prison
about a month ago. The speakers were Sean Guaghan and a

woman named Mary Daugherty; he did the Republican hero routine; she did the Bernadette Devlin imitation. Professor Connor, who teaches Irish literature for us, introduced me to them. They knew my name right away. It surprised me at first. But when they asked closely after you, I wasn't. They said you and they were old comrades. Don't the men in this family ever learn anything? I saw the Daugherty woman's name in the *Times* yesterday, before I came down. She was arrested for her part in the Bloody Friday explosions in Belfast. Three hundred people were injured. It's a fine lot of friends you have. That's just perfect. How long before you're back behind bars, I wonder?"

"Never heard the name Guaghan before in my life," I said. It was a white lie; I never did get Sean's last name. "Sure, I met Mary a few times, down in Kensington. She's not a friend, and I have nothing to do with the Provisionals, or the INLA for that matter. Let it go, Matt. Look what you've done."

Both mom and granmom were crying. I did my best to reassure them, but I don't think they believed me this time. I left Manayunk, relieved, at about 2:30. Didn't like the scene Jimbo was into. Had to check it out. Always did get in trouble standing up for him. Call it friendship; call it stupid.

The Trident belonged to the shop, and I figured I wouldn't be marked if I kept the helmet on. The streets around 3<sup>rd</sup> and Pine were pretty quiet as I cruised down toward Hancock. I pulled a little way into Howard, dropped the side stand, lifted the seat and took out the tool kit like I had engine problems. Through the dark face shield, I could see a black guy about thirty-five outside the Ford cleaning the windshield. Stupid giveaway, that one. Arrogance always got them. He looked toward me quickly, put his stuff away and shuffled over. His clothes were regulation rubby, but he didn't do the walk very well, mostly because you could tell he was in good shape under the torn, loose T-shirt and baggy work pants. The arms were muscled, and the shoes were almost new. They always blew it with the shoes.

"Hey, bro, got a quarter for a coffee, man?"

"Sure, buddy, here ya go."

"That's a nice, new cycle y'all got there. Whatsa matta wit it?"

"Yeh, well, I think I blew a plug. It ain't broken in yet, see."

He bent down as if he was looking at the engine and tried to look up under my face shield. "Man, can y'all see through that thing? Sho looks dark ta this old niggah."

What crap; they couldn't even get the accent right. He sounded like Bill Cosby doing Mississippi John Hirt. Even though the motor was plenty hot, I pulled a plug, put in a new one and started the bike. "That's better. Catch ya later, man." Before I turned the bike around, I took off my leather jacket and draped it over the back of the seat. In the mirror on the handlebar, I could see he wasn't pleased that it covered the dealer plate. There was no shuffle when he made for the Ford.

South Street runs one way toward the Delaware, and I didn't think that was a wise move, because I'd be pretty much limited to big streets like Front or Delaware Avenue. Instead, I headed the other way on Lombard, dropped down onto Naudain at the Graduate Hospital, made a hard left on Taney and took Schuylkill Avenue around behind the US Naval Home. I sat on Fulton Street for over an hour, then made my way back to the shop by the smallest streets I knew in the city. Far as I could tell, nobody followed, but off and on I could hear the straight pipes of a chopper.

"Jimbo, take the El Camino, wouldya, and pick up these parts shipments." I gave him the waybills. "One's got the stuff in it from Paul Dunstall I've been waitin for to fix my Norton. The other one's from Triumph, so we can finally get these motors back on the road. The first pick up is at Camden Terminal; the second is at 30<sup>th</sup> Street Station. Maybe do the Jersey one first."

"Okay, Jack. I'll drop the stuff off for the Norton on the way back. I know how long you been waitin for those parts."

I was looking forward to that shipment from England. I had gotten absolutely nowhere finding authentic parts for the thumper until I took the Brit route. It was expensive, but I'd really have something when the old Featherbed Manx was back in original shape.

Harry Stevenson, the mechanic from New Hampshire, was rubbing his hands. He'd been hung up for two weeks on those Triumph engines, but now he could look forward to a big paycheck. He was a gentle, flax-haired country guy who did his time as a conscientious objector looking after the pigs on a Quaker farm out near Ephrata. Now he lived in up in Whitemarsh Township with his wife and new son. He was a good hand, honest, but luck never seemed to shine on him. I knew the symptoms.

Jimbo came back from Jersey in an hour and a half. Me and Harry had a good time opening the boxes, unrolling the oiled paper and spreading the parts out on my bench. It was like Christmas. On the way out, Jimbo said, "Hey, Jack, if it's okay, I'll pick up some other stuff on the way." I waved to him, not turning from the bench: "Yeh, better get a move on. It's 4:30, and the shipping office closes at 5."

It was dark, and everybody else was gone. I sat alone in the shop, waiting for Jimbo. On the radio, Levon Helm was singing *Stage Fright*:

> *Now, deep in the heart of a lonely kid,*
> *Sufferin so much for what he did.*
> *They gave this plough boy his fortune and fame*
> *Since that day, he ain't been the same.*

"Where the hell is he? If he got all tripped out and wrecked the truck, I'll murder him. No, no, he wouldn't do that. All he said he wanted to do was pick up some stuff."

*See the man with stage fright...*
*He got caught in the spotlight.*
*I got firewater right on my breath,*
*Doctor warned me I might catch a death.*

*Said, you can make it in your disguise,*
*Just never show the fear that's in your eyes.*

"Maybe he just got hung up somewhere, or maybe.... Oh shit, if he used the truck to make a run down to Howard, there'll be hell to pay." I jumped on the Trident, then thought better of it. Instead, I started a customer's bike, a four cylinder Honda I had done a lot of head work on. It was a bullet, and I didn't think he'd mind under the circumstances. Just for insurance, I took a new, full coverage white helmet and a pair of Barrafaldi goggles out of the case in the showroom. No use showing trademarks.

*Now, if he says he's afraid,*
*Take him at his word.*

I thought, "This could be tricky. Be very, very careful, my man. No chances."

The indirect route was best: down Broad, left on Christian and up Darien Street. I parked in the shadows of a vacant lot, about five blocks from Howard.

> *Your brow is sweatin, and your mouth gets dry,*
> *Fancy people go driftin by.*
> *The moment of truth is right at hand,*
> *Just one more night there you can stand.‡*

I spotted the El Camino parked on the corner of Bainbridge and Philip. Not very bright. Once I got the key from Jimbo, I had to get the hell of there. Maybe I could convince him to come with me. The street didn't feel right. I had been down here about a dozen times, but I'd never seen the Oscar Meyer truck parked on the sidewalk at Bainbridge and American before. The double doors on the back didn't have a padlock, and one of them started to open. Four guys in windbreakers

*‡The Band; Album: "The Band;" Capitol Records, 1970; Lyrics: Robbie Robertson, Canaan Music, Inc./ASCAP.*

were coming toward me from the Front Street side. Going for the back door on Bainbridge was out of the question.

Chick and Jimbo had to have broken through to a basement on Hancock Street, so I ducked around the corner and tried all the grates over the window wells in the sidewalk. Sure enough, one wasn't locked, so I jumped down and tried the plywood over the window. It wasn't loose, but it wasn't nailed up tight, either. I lit my Zippo and looked around. The basement was cobwebbed and filthy from the rats, but there was no mistaking where they tied into the utility lines. Followed them through one basement after the other until I could see light coming through the sandbags up ahead. Didn't sense a thing until I felt the gun barrel in my back.

"One sound, asshole, and you'll get a second one right in the middle of yer back. Move!"

The sandbags were pulled away from inside, and I was pushed into the firing range. This time, the music was different: Chambers Brothers, *Time Has Come Today*. There were four guys; one of them was Chick; all were very spaced out. There was an opium pipe on the table. "Oh fuck, Jack, whaddya doin here, man? You ain't no pig or nothin, are ya?"

He had the Ruger hanging loose in his hand, pointed at the floor.

*Time has come today.*
*Young hearts can go that way.*
*Can't put it off another day.*

*I don't care what others say.*
*They think we don't listen anyway.*

"No way, Chick, you know that. If I was, I'd be nuts to come in here this way. Jimbo took off with my truck and didn't show up back at the shop like he said he would. I got worried about him, so I came down here to help him out if he's in trouble. It don't look too kosher outside, man. There's all kinda movement out there. Before they spotted me, I thought to come in through the basements. What's goin on, anyway? Where's Jimbo? I don't want my truck messed up, but how am I gonna get it back? They'll be all over me out there if I move it, won't they?"

*The rules have changed today.*
*I have no place to stay.*
*I'm thinkin about the subway...*

*The love has flown away.*
*My tears have come and gone.*
*I have no home.*

The guy who got me in the other basement frisked me, then nodded to Chick. "Okay, Cat, that's cool. Jimbo's lookout on the roof, Jack. I'll let ya talk to im." Chick picked up a radio from the table and pressed the button. "Red four."

"Red four, here, red one."

"Got a surprise visitor. Wants to talk to ya. What's yer status?"

"No action for about five. Who ya got?"

Chick handed the radio to me. "It's me, Jimbo. What the hell's goin on?"

"Hey, what's happenin, man. Sorry about the truck, but the gooks started to move in fast. Had to get the rest of the ordnance here as quick as I could. Tell Chick I need the other launcher, now! The one I got is fucked. They're movin again. And get Cat up here, goddammit."

> *No place to run.*
> *I might get burned up by the sun,*
> *But I've had my fun.‡*

Chick turned to his buddies: "This dude's okay. He's a tight bro of Jimbo's, but he ain't got no combat trainin." He turned to me: "Right on, Black Jack, yer in it now, like it or not. Take this launcher and the sniper rifle and the ammo up on the roof.

"Now! Do it! Spider, you go wit im."

I felt the threat, and the two other guys watched me closely as I left with Spider. On the first floor, the door to the big front room was open. Except for the tape deck, the lights were off; the big speakers silent. Two more guys were crouched by the windows. The blankets had been taken down, replaced by sandbags, except where slits had been cut in the plywood. "Ssst, Spider checkin in. Got a replacement with me. We're gonna supply Jimbo, up top."

‡*Chambers Brothers. Album: "Shout!; The Time Has Come;" Song: Time Has Come Today, Columbia, 1968.*

"Okay, buddy. Stay on the horn."

We walked up the stairs, me in front. I reached out for the banister and felt an electric cable running up it. On the third floor, there was a trap door to the flat roof. Outside, Jimbo was on his knees behind sandbags, peering over the three foot high false front. A joint smoldered in his right hand. Beside him were weapons and ammo boxes, a flare gun and a large spotlight. His face was covered with camouflage paint, and he wore jungle fatigues, except for the steel toed boots he bought for the shop. This time, his hair was tied back.

"Okay, Jimbo, here's your boy." Spider whispered. "I gotta go down to red three. You okay with this guy?"

"Yeh, no sweat, Spider. He's my bro, man."

"Good to see ya here, Jack. I'm gonna need the good launcher. I got that sucker in the Ford lined up. The sniper rifle's no good without Cat. Where's he?"

"He's in the basement. Maybe Chick figures I'm yer man, but I gotta get the hell outta here. So do you. You guys aren't gonna take these people on, are ya? This is fuckin crazy; you nuts? You got no chance in hell. Come on. I'll take ya back to my place before the blood starts."

"Maybe so, maybe not. When the music begins, we're gonna find out if they can fight or just send other people to do it for em. Lock and load, Black Jack, it's time."

The guys on the first floor must have turned the speakers toward the street. "No place to run. I might get burned up by the sun. But I've had my fun," blasted into the street, then the tape went right into the manic instrumental part of *In-A-Gada-Da-Vida*. Jimbo fired a white flare straight up. It looked just like fireworks when it went off high overhead, then floated down on its tiny chute.

The grenade launcher made a little pop, and I followed the round as it slowly reached the top of its arc. It came down right in the center of the Ford's roof. The windshield disintegrated and the doors blew off with a loud crash and a ball of flame. Couldn't tell whether there was anybody inside or not. The vapor in the gas tank exploded, lighting up street level.

Right away, muzzle flashes came from the roofs and windows across the street. Bullets chipped off the brick and screamed away. Then all hell broke loose. The squad downstairs opened up; right under us there was a deep, slow report from what must have been a heavy machine gun. It was like an acid dream, or a news clip from the barricades in Belfast or Derry. When the helicopter came out of nowhere, I knew it was time move or die. Jimbo was busy lobbing grenades onto the roofs, but when the copter turned on a search light, he picked up the sniper rifle and shot it out.

I tried to grab him, but he pulled away with a snarl and went back to work. He didn't turn when I scrambled for the trap door. All I could see was the side of his face. He was smiling thinly.

# 12. MOCKINGBIRD

The rest of the squad was too busy to notice me, and the
sound of my boots on the stairs couldn't be heard above the
gunfire, the exploding grenades and the music. The pitch
black hallway smelled like gunpowder and fear—mine. Didn't
even have time to think about how bizarre the whole thing
was; it was like my soul was in a meat grinder. I slid along the
wall to the basement door and made it down the steps. Chick
was there, alone, with the Ruger in his right hand. He
wagged a finger of his left hand at me like I was a little kid
caught with his hand in the cookie jar.

"No, no, no. Desertion during a fire fight? That's
punishable, real punishable. Ya, know, man, I really hate
guys like you. You're too fuckin pure to be real. Anyway, I'll
count to ten. I owe you that much for Jimbo."

I dove for the hole in the wall, got up, took two steps and
went for the second one. There were three rapid bangs from
the big Ruger. One of them shattered a brick near my head,
and a piece hit me below the left eye. Then, there was a
loud rumbling explosion up above. I crouched against the
wall for a minute, breathing hard. With my good eye, I looked

around it toward the firing range, but the lights were out. I made for the window well on Hancock as fast as I could. The side of my face was thumping.

Unmarked cars blocked Howard Street, and guys in blue windbreakers were firing shotguns and rifles over them toward the building. Jimbo's searchlight had them lit up. Maybe they didn't know about the basements, because nobody was looking my way. I climbed out of the well and kept my back to the wall as I slid toward Bainbridge Street. I looked both ways. Down the street, I could see that the back of the Oscar Meyer truck was open; the inside was lit up, and two guys were sitting at a wall of radios. To my left, the four guys in windbreakers were at the back door. One of them found the signal string and pulled on it. The plywood came off with a low "karump," and the four of them ended up across the street on the sidewalk.

The guys in the truck looked up quickly and saw me. There was too much noise and I was too far away to hear what one of them yelled as he jumped out the back. The other guy started chattering into his head set. I sprinted across Bainbridge and down 2nd, cursing myself for being such a truck. At Monroe, I headed west, toward the Honda, but I took the cross-country route: down the alleys, over the Cyclone fences and through the vacant lots. I knew where the bike was, but I wasn't completely sure where I was. I stopped in an alley to figure it out. Overhead, helicopters with search lights headed for Howard Street. Sirens wailed. The sound of the gunfire was muted a bit by distance, but the firing hadn't lessened any. "The echo of the Thompson Gun" came to me as a musical phrase and died away.

I walked down to the end of the alley and looked out. The street was almost normal, very dark and nearly empty, with a few cars parked here and there. It turned out to be Pemberton, and I tried to walk normally toward the vacant lot near Schell Street. I heard the rustle of a windbreaker from an entryway to my right. I stepped into it and hit him once before he could move; bone cracked under my fist, he crumpled and went down in a limp heap. Then the centuries of impotent fury came, hot, crazy. It was close, but I didn't kick his head in, just once for good measure.

The helmet and goggles were where I left them. Getting them on over my bad eye hurt like hell, but somebody might mark a guy with a cut face. I started the Honda and rode slowly down into South Philly by the circular route.

I pulled into a gas station on Federal Street and filled up, keeping my helmet on. The kid behind the cash register gave me the key to the rest room without looking at me much. In the can, I took off the helmet and had a look at my eye. No wonder it hurt. There was a ragged chunk of brick stuck in my cheek just below it. I pulled it out, and the blood started. It took a while, but it finally slowed down enough that I thought I could get going again as long as I kept the rest room towels jammed between my face and curve of the helmet's mouth guard. I called Harry from the phone booth outside, careful to keep the door half open so the light wouldn't go on. I kept my face away from the station and toward traffic.

It was after midnight, and he sounded groggy when he answered. I ran down to him what had happened, my part in it, the whole thing. He whistled into the phone: "Holy shit, Jack. You have to get out of Dodge, fast. Did anybody figure it out it was you?"

"Don't think so. The black guy in the Ford never saw my face when I checked the place out. He might suspect, but he can't know. The one guy in the truck was almost a block away. I'm hard to miss, but he couldn'ta seen me very well. The other guy? Not sure. It was pretty dark, and it happened very fast. Course, the El Camino is there, and they'll trace it to me, but it's true that Jimbo borrowed it."

"Where can you go?"

"Don't know. Can't go to my place, or Manayunk, or the shop, even. I'll figure somethin out; maybe down to Margate. I just wanted you to know how things stood before you walked into the shop tomorrow."

"Put some more money in the phone and hold on."

In the background, I could hear him talking to his wife. He came back on: "It's okay, Jack, you come on out here. Linda says it's fine. Neither one of us has any particular loyalty to the feds," he said with a laugh.

"No way, Harry. I'm not puttin you and your wife and kid at risk for somethin you had nothin to do with."

"Just shut up a second and think for a change. You didn't have anything to do with it either, but do you think for a minute they'll believe you? There has been a supreme fuck up, and they will need heads to line up for the papers. Yours will do as well as anybody's. You need an alibi in the worst way. They'll be there tomorrow morning when the shop opens. You call Don at home, first thing, and tell him you decided to take Saturday off and stay with me in the country. This is not a problem for us. The only problem for you is that they won't take kindly to your alibi coming from a conscientious objector. Get out here. Take your time. I've got lots of cold beer in the fridge."

He hung up.

It would have been a lot quicker to get on the expressway, but I had a saying: "If you can walk on it, it's the 'Skookull' River. If you want to die on it, it's the 'Sure Kill' Expressway." Both were true. I crossed the river at Grays Ferry, skirted the University of Pennsylvania on the west side and got onto Ridge Avenue. It wasn't far once I got close to Lafayette Hill. Harry rented a little house near Militia Hill, on the edge of one of the big money horse farms, because he said he couldn't stay away from the smell of good, clean manure for long.

It must have been about 2:00 when I rolled the Honda in behind his house. He came out right away, and we pushed the bike into a tool shed and locked the door. Linda was a pretty little blond from Vermont with a permanently surprised look on her freckled face and an accent you could cut with a knife. Then again, she said the same thing about mine. When I pulled off my helmet, I thought she was going to pass out and slide off the kitchen chair.

"Relax," I said with a nervous laugh, "it's a lot worse than it looks." Harry went to the bathroom and rummaged around for some Band-Aids. I could hear stuff bouncing off porcelain and falling on the floor. She got herself together, ran the tap in the sink until it was hot enough, and washed my face with a kitchen towel. After the stinging stopped, it felt better. Harry came back with the gauze, the peroxide, the adhesive tape and tweezers.

"Hey, hey, slow down. You promised me a beer, Harry. I gotta have at least one beer before I let some ham-fisted motorcycle mechanic work on my face."

He laughed. "Of course, please forgive my rudeness, sir. How thoughtless of me." He draped a towel over his arm like a waiter and got some Rolling Rock from the refrigerator. Even Linda cheered up a bit.

I guzzled the first one; then he started on me. The peroxide fizzed in the wound as it cleaned it out. "Jack, you still have some pieces of brick in there. I'm going to take them out. Close your eye. You need stitches for this. We should really go to the hospital."

"Nope, no hospital, not tonight. You stitch it up."

"You nuts? I can fix engines, but that doesn't mean I can sew. There's only one person here who can." We both turned to Linda.

"Oh, no, no you don't, not on your life. Not me. I'd faint."

"Make them as close together as you can, Linda. That way the scar won't be so big," Harry said as he watched over her shoulder. She was using a tiny embroidery needle and black thread. I was on my fourth beer, but each stitch still hurt like hell.

"Okay, Jack, here's what we'll do in the morning once you tell Don we sat up half the night drinking and we both have wicked hangovers. After we take off the bandage, you will take my dirt bike out back for a few practice laps. But, cowboy that you are, you will not wear a helmet. Linda and I will watch from the porch. The kids riding their horses up at the barn will watch, too. They always do. You will fall down. We will come to the rescue; you will get up holding your face. Sound like a plan?"

"Yep, sounds good. Thanks you two, but I really feel bad. The, ah, manure is really gonna hit the fan tomorrow, and it's my fault. You will feel a lot of heat."

Linda stroked the good side of my face: "Jack, it's okay, really. We've had heat from them before because of Harry and some other things. I'm not very brave, but it's absolutely necessary for the innocent and the honest of this screwed up country to stick together."

The night was hot, breathless, no sleep. How did all this shit happen? It was like I had somebody near who wanted me dead. The crickets, tree toads, night critters took turns in their ordered march toward the robin song dawn as I thought and thought, searching for some thread of sense, of meaning, purpose, cause. No luck. I dozed, finally, with Judith's crooked smile before me, then random, disconnected images of dad, Toot, granpop, granmom, Pat Johnston's yellow teeth. The morning was fine, even a little bit cool. Linda sat in a wicker rocker on the porch with her white robe open, nursing her pink baby, while I smoked and drank coffee to get ready for my accident in the field. I didn't look at her until she said, "Jack, what's wrong? Are you embarrassed? I'm not. Don't be silly. Come over here and see my son." In a dogwood nearby, a mockingbird, gray, black and white, was trilling sweetly, then he started imitating a chain saw, dog barks, cat mewing . Comedian bird.

The three unmarked Fords with standard issue cheapo hubcaps showed up about 10:00. There were six of them; all looking exactly the same in blue windbreakers, chinos and

Ray Bans with gold rims. They probably had a haircut every morning. The two of us sat at the kitchen table as Linda answered the door. They pushed by her and went for me, but she said very calmly, "Just a minute. This is my home. Who the hell are you, exactly? I'm going to call the police if you don't get out of here right now."

The one with the swollen black and blue cheek was in charge. He turned to her, whipped out his wallet and flipped it open: "I'm Agent Moore, and we have business with this man. Just stay out of the way, ma'am. We have no problem with you or your husband; not right now, anyway." His jaw was wired shut, and he sounded a little like Daffy Duck.

She looked closely at his ID. "Excuse me, but that's CIA. What business could you people possibly have with Mr. Kavanagh? You don't have any domestic authority. We all know that. Do you have a warrant?"

Harry looked at me across the table and winked quickly.

"Now, now, Mrs. Stevenson, just calm down. We don't need a warrant; all we want to do is ask him a few questions."

"If he agrees, that's fine. But you do it outside, with us present as witnesses. Otherwise, you can take a hike. We'll have the ACLU on this so fast it will make your head spin."

Agent Moore looked to his buddies and shrugged. Outside on the porch, the grilling started. I'd been through the good cop bad cop routine before with Jeeps and Nate; these guys needed practice.

Moore took a clipboard from one of the Bobbsey Twins and riffled through it until he got to the right page: "Let's see: 'Jack Kavanagh, born 1942, Philadelphia. A.k.a. Black Jack. Lives alone in an apartment in Kensington. Mother, Theresa, lives in Manayunk.' Where the hell's that? 'Brother, Matt, priest. Brother, Mark, soldier.' Nothing on them at all. 'Six two, 200 pounds, white flash in hair above left eye. Moves around a lot. Most recent job, Shop Manager at Philly Triumph. Eight months in Holmesburg Prison for receiving stolen goods and resisting arrest, 1964.' Hmm, that's interesting. 'Known outlaw connections.' Better yet. 'Police informant A says possible drug running involvement.' Ahh, we're 4F, are we?"

He turned to one of the others, rubbing his jaw, and handed him the clipboard. "What else have we got from the FBI?" The other guy sounded like a robot in a low budget space movie. "Right, chief. Let's see: 'Kavanagh, J. Grandfather Daniel Kavanagh (deceased, see attached) highly placed in the *Clann na Gael*. Joe McGarrity henchman. Indicted for murder of FBI informant, 1955; acquitted. Uncles suspected Noraid organizers (see gun-running report, Boston office). Father, also Jack, Irish born, no more info.' A lot of blacked out stuff on the priest, though. 'Brother, Mark, Green Beret, clean record. Jack Kavanagh known to consort with Provisional IRA members and give money to Noraid. Seen with Sean Guaghan, Michael Flaherty and Mary Daugherty at McDougall's Saloon in Kensington (photo on file). Cohort of bomber Charlie Murphy (deceased). Daugherty currently on trial (explosive charges) in Belfast, Northern Ireland.' A lot of this has been blacked out, chief, but that's about it. They didn't give us the gun-running stuff."

Moore had been watching Harry and Linda like a hawk during all this. Linda's eyes were hooded, but Harry's widened just enough when the IRA came up. Moore noticed.

"Well, well, Kavanagh, looks like you stuck your head up once too often. What happened to your cheek? Get cold cocked like I did last night?"

"Dunno about last night. Dumped Harry's dirt bike out in the field this morning. Stupid, didn't wear my helmet."

"That true, Mr. Stevenson?"

"Yes it is. I told him to wear it, but he's a bit of a cowboy. My wife and I both saw it happen. Linda bandaged him up.

I'm sure if you'll check over at the barn, there'll be other witnesses."

Moore nodded to one of the twins, and he beetled away.

"Where were you, Kavanagh, between the hours of 10:00, approximately, and midnight last night?"

"Last night? I was here. Me and Harry had a rough week, so he invited me out here for dinner. We got into the beer some, so I called the boss early this morning and said we wouldn't be in today."

"How did you get here? In your—let's see—black 1970 El Camino? Or maybe you rode a green Triumph?"

"Nope, couldn't take the truck. Lent it to Jimbo; he works at the shop, and he needed it to pick up some stuff. I don't own no green Triumph, man. I came up on a Honda last night. Customer's ride. It's in the shed."

One of the other guys did the hostile routine: "You often take a customer's bike out like that? Some people might call that theft."

"Sometimes, if I know the guy well enough. Let's call it a test ride. He won't mind."

"We'll check on that."

"Fine, ace, you just do that."

The agent came back from the barn and nodded to Moore.

"Mr. and Mrs. Stevenson, do you corroborate everything that the subject has just said about the timing and his whereabouts last night?"

Linda said, "Yes, we do. He spent last night here with us. I don't appreciate it when they sit up half the night drinking beer, but they work hard enough, so it doesn't hurt once in a while." She nodded to a case of Rolling Rock empties on the porch, mostly mine. The mockingbird started doing raspberries from his branch, pretty good ones, too.

"Okay, okay, cut the shit," Moore wheeled on me. "You the wise guy, asshole?" All three of the good guys laughed when I pointed to the tree. The bird let go a big one, then a sort of titter. "Fuck," from Moore, "get the goddamned shotgun. No, check that."

"How about you, Harry? You agree with this bullshit?"

"My name is Stevenson, Agent Moore, and I agree with everything my wife has said."

Moore was back at the clipboard again. "Here, Dave, you read it." The other guy took it up again: "Well, now, let's have a look. Yes, here we are. 'Stevenson, Harold; born, Concord, New Hampshire, 1946. Conscientious objector status granted 1967 following court challenge.' Oh, this is great, just great. Now, what else have we got? 'Linda

Stevenson, née Rutland, born 1947, Montpelier, Vermont. Couple met at Harvard, *circa* 1966; male subject, political science major; female subject, pre-law student, daughter of anti-war proponent, Senator Rutland; suspected activity in the SDS; possible ties to radical civil rights organizations.' What a fine rat's nest we've got here, gentlemen. Just exactly why should we believe anything you say?"

Linda was calm: "Because it happens to be true, that's why. You haven't told us what any of this is about. Why are you so interested in Jack's movements last night? I'd like to know, too, how you got all this information about us. I don't think what you're doing is legal."

The hostile agent came in on cue: "Let's just take them in right now. They're not going to tell us a thing here. They know, all right. When we lay charges, they'll start talking."

Harry snorted, "That's ridiculous. Charges for what? You have no right to take us anywhere, and you know it. If you haven't noticed, there's quite a crowd watching from the barn."

Moore went to one of the Fords and came back with a newspaper. "You upstanding citizens seen this yet?" He threw the paper at me. The headline on the front page of the *Philadelphia Bulletin* was the biggest, blackest one I'd seen since the race riot in June of 1964: "Shoot Out Kills Nine, Wounds Seven." Below it, smaller type read: "Entire City Block Razed."

Harry was looking around my shoulder: "Wow, that's too bad, but what's it got to do with us?" "Waahaha," from the bird.

Moore came up very close to me. He was about five eight, so he had to look up into my face. The green glass of his sunglasses flashed in the mid-morning light.

"Kavanagh, we're going to nail your ass to the barn door. You conspired with James McDevitt for the purposes of transporting illegal arms across state lines. We found the keys in his pocket, and your truck parked outside. You were present last night before and during the fire fight that killed three of my agents and wounded a lot more. We've probably got you for assault, too. You are going to do serious time in a federal pen, unless you tell us what we want to know. Who were these people? What were they up to? Who were they dealing with? Where are the rest of them? We want it all." He started rubbing his jaw again.

"You can check on the fact that I sent Jimbo by himself on a parts run yesterday afternoon. One to Jersey; one to 30th

Street Station. Lookit, he's just an old high school buddy a mine. I gave him a job because he was down on his luck after he got back from Vietnam. He lives with a spade dude by the name of Chick somebody, somewhere down around 2$^{nd}$ and South. That's all I know. Where's my truck? I want it back."

"He doesn't live there any more, Kavanagh."

"Oh, yeh, why's that? Lock him up, did ya?"

"They're all dead. We dropped one through the roof and blew them all away. You better come with us for your own safety."

Linda and Harry stepped in, and Linda said: "Not a chance. We want to see a warrant. You have your suspicions, fine. We have ours, fine. Unless you people can show us a legal document, you can't take him anywhere."

They bitched and complained a lot, but Linda was right. There really was nothing they could do if we didn't cave in. By the open door of his car Moore said: "Kavanagh, you won't be able to take a piss in this country unless we know about it. It's personal, now. One day, it will be just you and me. Anything, anything at all, I can prove, and it's your ass." As he slammed the door, a pigeon flew over and splattered the center of his windshield. The Fords roared off, wipers flicking on one.

It took a long time and a lot more beer to explain the *Clann na Gael* and the IRA to Harry and Linda. Did me good. It had all been bottled up too long since I lost Judith in Egypt. Helped me sort out why I turned down Mary Daugherty in McDougall's and what I had to do when the money was there. Then there was mom and granmom to worry about.

Two days later, Harry was doing what he could with the Triumph engines, while I played with the old Norton. Jeeps came in, whistling. "My, my, Jack, you do like to live dangerously, don't ya. Got yer truck outside. They sure did go over it in detail. Hope you know somebody in the upholstery business. It'll cost ya a yard."

I went to the cash register, pulled out the money and threw it at him. He laughed as he tossed me the keys on his way out.

Jimbo's funeral was on Thursday—closed casket. His parents wouldn't look at me or talk to me at the cemetery. Harry and Linda came, too. The guys in the sunglasses took a lot of pictures. When the three of us turned from the grave,

I mumbled to myself, "Now who the hell is informant A, I wonder?"

"How's that?" from Linda.

"Nothin, nothin, just thinkin out loud."

# 13. BUTTONS

Unmarked cars were all over the place after they bombed Howard Street. They gave me a full-time tail that made me uncomfortable at first, but I got used to it. Besides, I wasn't doing anything illegal. I even felt sorry for them. They weren't Philly cops; they were scrubbed-squeaky feds, and probably had wives and kids and lawns to mow in the suburbs near Annapolis or Georgetown, but here they were following me around the city at all hours.

Once in a while, I'd saunter over to their car and hand them a couple of coffees through the window. They all looked the same: bored stiff. Sometimes, I'd tell them where I was going next to make it easier for them: "Automat, Horn and Hardart's, across from Gimbel's, Market Street." If Moore was with them, he'd growl something like, "Your time is coming, jitbag," and dump the coffee out the window. His partner would do the same, with a sour, disappointed look on his face.

Don was super paranoid right after. He wanted to fire me and Harry, but his business sense got the better of him, and we stayed on. He was silent, though, guarded, around us. On top of my reputation as a mechanic, now I had the street moniker of "dangerous dude." If it wasn't so sad, it would have been funny. Naturally, Matt went ballistic about me to mom when my name showed up in the papers as a possible witness, but I think she almost believed my side of it when I told her the whole story. Far as I knew, Mark hadn't a clue, so I wrote him in Fort Bragg to bring him up to date. When he called, his only real response was "Watch your back."

It was getting easier to keep mom going now that I was making better money, but it looked like granmom might have to go into a home, and I wasn't saving much toward my own shop. I needed more. Always, always, more.

Business was booming during Philly Triumph's second season; the place was usually mobbed on Saturday afternoons. I let the usual "Mechanics Only in the Shop" rule slide for good customers. Maybe it was because the place was clean, well ventilated and well lit. Maybe it was just the mystique any motorcycle shop has. Don wasn't too pleased at first, because of the insurance, but I convinced him it was good customer relations. One Saturday afternoon in early April, there were about ten people hanging around by the benches, talking bikes and racing. Vultch was holding forth as usual about the rectitude of the pushrod to a couple of greenhorns with their mouths open.

The Bonneville I was working on was a candidate for the "noise of the month" award that me and Harry started. Customers would come in with the wildest stories: "Ya know, when I go around corners it makes this funny 'tinkley, tinkley' sound, but only sometimes." Mostly, they turned out to be harmless or imaginary; sometimes they didn't. The goofiest noise imitation won the owner a beer and a greasy hand written award over my bench. The Puerto Rican guy in the fancy clothes who brought this one in said it had a "kathunga, kathunga" noise that was getting worse. Harry considered this an original contribution; so did I.

I kicked the engine over a few times with the key off and the plugs out. There was something very strange going on in the bottom end, so I called the guy and told him it would have to be split down to the last bolt. He didn't seem concerned about the expense, but he did say he'd be in on Monday to have a look. I took the engine out of the frame and hoisted it up on the bench. I knew I could have it apart in about an hour, so I ignored it in favor of shooting the shit with the boys and girls for a while.

First, though, it was time to clean and arrange my tools. It's an important rule I tried to teach inexperienced mechanics, especially new flat-rate guys. If you have to hunt for a screwdriver or a micrometer or your torque wrench or socket, you're losing time. Better to put everything in its place, so you can find it without looking. Something I learned real early— from granpop, from dad.

I felt it while I was putting my hammers back in the big bottom drawer, the faint brush of a feather on the back of my neck. Casually, I reached way in the back for dad's huge ballpeen, let it dangle in my right fist and turned around. The switchblade was ready in the open top of the box, but Toot's unloaded 45 was still in granpop's box in Kensington. All I needed was a weapons bust. Staring at me from the other side of the shop, about twenty feet away, was Iron Mike. First time I'd seen him since he dropped the dime and got me sent to Holmesburg. This I would enjoy, and I started for him. Only Vultch understood what was going on. He kept talking, but the nod told me he was ready to back me up.

"You gotta lotta stones commin in here, shithead. It will be my pleasure to take you out the back and kick your sorry ass." I said it low, right in his face, so nobody else could hear. I knew he'd be armed—he had a rep with a straight razor—but it didn't worry me. He was a strange sight just then. Even with all the outlaw stuff on him, I could tell he was scared—probably heard the Howard Street story. He held his arms loose at his sides and frowned at the hammer in my hand. He looked like a fat little kid. I thought for an instant that I'd known him before he became an Angel, but I shook it off: "Nah."

"Lookit, Jack, what can I say, man? The cops set me up. Nate and Jeeps needed a collar. They were gettin too close to my business, so I hadda give em somethin. Like, I'm sorry, Jack. And you're right, you should kick my ass. I'm tellin ya, though, I didn't have no choice—woulda done ten years. You only did a couple a months. I knew where you were, so I came in to pay my dues."

"Yeh, right. After all this time? You, ya prick, never have more than ten bucks in yer jeans. Whaddya think eight months in the joint is worth? You'll never have that much bread, Mike, so I'm gonna take the time outta yer hide."

He had his hands up with his palms toward me. "I know, I know, I've done enough time to know that. Lissen up for a minute; then you can do whatchu want. My brudder, you— uh—don't know im. Well, he got shot down in San Diego a month back. We buried im there; musta been two hundred Angels at the grave. Some party. He was real high up in the Frisco chapter, know what I'm sayin? Anyways, his old lady kept all his stuff, but she said anything still left on the East Coast was mine."

"All this don't mean jack shit to me, Mike. Yer wastin my time. Spit it out."

"Okay, okay. My brudder had a couplea rides stored up at my sister's place. One a them is a Harley KR still in the box, right from the factory. I know you don't like Harleys much, but this one's a factory race piece, never been ridden. It's primo, man, and all I want is five yards for it. It's worth six times that. You could win some serious bread on the track with it, Jack. Best I can do."

"Whaddya think I am, stupid? Fine, I buy the bike. Fine, the cops show up, and I'm back inside again. Not on yer fuckin life, Mike. You know how much heat I got on me right now? I can't fart without a tape recording it."

"No, no, no bullshit, Jack. I got all the papers. It's absolutely legal. I'll go to any place with ya to sign em, in fronta anybody. No shit, man, I'm tellin ya it's a clean deal."

My mind was running. He was right. KRs were scarce and very fast. I could road race it, of course, and probably do pretty well, but there wasn't any money in that, just glory. No, blood sport, flat-track would be the way. The season was getting underway up in Bethlehem, but I'd have to get a move on to get my AMA license. I thought about it for a bit more and then called Vultch over. He gimped toward me, not taking his eyes off Mike.

"Mike, you tell Vultch here everything you just told me. Any differences, man, and it's yer ass."

After we shook hands on it, Mike's funny, familiar smile returned before he took off. Vultch leaned against his bench. "You trust that shit, Jack?" "No way, Vultch, but it's a sweet deal. Don't worry, I'll keep a real close eye on Mike."

Then a big shit eating grin broke out on his blue-black face. "My son, the ways of the Lord are mysterious indeed. Finally, finally, you have come into the fold, and it's about time. For you, pagan, salvation is nigh. Howsomever, if you wanna flat-track the sucker, we'll have to work on the cam."

"No way, Vultch, I ain't got time to wait for no factory grind from Hardley Abelson. Besides, they'll want a major buck for it."

"Not what I had in mind, my doubting apostle. I will take charge of this project personally."

"Yeh, right, you see a $50,000 cam grinder around here anywhere? Besides, where're we gonna get a billet to machine?"

"The Lord, Jack, and the kindly federal government, will provide. Just might be able to get my hands on some super hard alloy rod, very secret. The NASA boys don't keep the finest inventory around, and my regular shop just happens to have such a grinder ready to hand. They say I'm—um—eccentric, yeh, that's the word." He dialed his finger around his temple for emphasis. "So they let me do my thing in peace. I'll have it finished next weekend. You can handle the gearbox and sprocket sizes, I trust, with a little divine guidance?"

"Yeh, no sweat. Depending on what it's got on it, I'll probably have to buy some dirt tires. Whaddya think? Dunlop or Pirelli?"

"There is no reason to blaspheme, and you know it. Pirellis are made in Spain—a Popish nation. Dunlops come from England—an island of god-fearing Protestants."

"Right, I'll go for the Pirellis."

"Arrgh," he said as he threw up his hands in disgust, turned on his heel and gimped back to his bench. Over his shoulder, he growled, "You will have much to atone for, Jack, when Armageddon comes."

The guy was dressed like Angelo Bruno's boys when he showed up on Monday: shiny, gray silk pants with creases like knives, skinny, expensive black belt with a heavy gold buckle, gray, short-sleeved knit shirt with that round, funny looking collar buttoned to the neck. Only the shoes were different, but then again he was a PR, so he wore the spit-shined, pointy black boots those guys like, not the flimsy Italian loafers the wise guys sport.

Buttons was his name. About thirty, five ten, a lean 175, short black hair combed straight back and held there with lots of Brylcream, face like a bull fighter, full of bright white smiling teeth; very laid back, relaxed but powerful, like a wound spring. On his arm was a knockout twenty-year-old blond hooker type stuffed into a red, poured-on suede number—big hair, stiletto heels, lots of cleavage. Not your average MC shop customers.

"Okay, mahn, run it down to me," he said, while the chick played with my torque wrench.

I showed him where the sludge trap access bolt in the center crank weight had come loose and was carving a deep groove in the bottom of the aluminum engine case. "I figure another few minutes runnin, the cases woulda split and the oil'd be all over yer rear tire. Lucky you brought it in when you did." I sized the guy up. Weren't any Puerto Rican soldiers working for the mob I ever heard of; they were too close knit for that. Maybe he was a pimp, or a freelancer in the smack trade, or a numbers guy. Hard to tell, but he did look well heeled.

"Tell ya what, Buttons, I can have it back together and runnin by Wednesday morning. I'll have to put new gaskets and piston rings in it, so there's some cost there. This is the weirdest thing I've ever seen, and I been workin on these Brit engines a long time. Yer warranty has expired, but I'll cut ya a break on the cost, cause this shouldn'ta happened. Course, now that it's all split down, you got an option or two."

"Like what? Whatchu sellin, mahn? Don't try no con on me. Just ask about Buttons on the street, chump. I already know about you—bike rep and street rep. It's my business to be informed about the people I deal with."

"No scam, buddy. I can put it back stock, or I can build it fast for ya. That's all I'm sayin. Up to you," I said with a shrug.

"Yeh? So how fast's fast?"

"That depends on you: high compression big bore kit, roller cam, port and polish the head, bigger valves, larger carbs, cast rods. There's lots a goodies, man. I can build ya the fastest street piece out there. Yer call."

We went to the front desk, and I pulled out all the speed-gear catalogs. He went for it all without a blink. I started adding up the cost, but he stopped me with a big grin.

"You just do it, Jack. You treat me fair, I treat you fair. I find out you ain't been, then we talk, you an me, one on one. Know what I'm sayin? I'm in no hurry. Do it right, take yer time. I pay cash. Good buck for good work."

Iron Mike's sister lived in a tumble-down, 1950s trailer in Mechanicsville, way the other side of Poquessing Creek. Took forever to get there. It was off by itself on a narrow, dead end dirt road with no name. In the tiny yard where some of the weeds had been mowed down sometime was a collision of wrecked pickups, a ringer washing machine, rusting, rolled up chicken wire and a pyramid of broken bicycles. A little boy with a torn T-shirt and no pants or underpants sat in the clay dust howling as I drove up in the El Camino about 3 on Sunday. As I got out of the truck, somebody screamed from inside, "Shut the fuck up, Tommy, can't you see momma's busy?"

The screen door was broken and hanging from the hinges. Inside, I could hear the announcer belting out the blow by blow of a wrestling match: The Blond Bomber versus King Tut: "Oh, no, the King has the Bomber in the Mummy Death Hug, wrestling fans. It's just a matter of time, now."

I got no answer when I knocked on the peeling aluminum wall of the trailer, so I peered around the jamb. The inside was what you might call from the anarchy school of decorating. The television was large and new; nothing else had any reason to be where it was, except for a very carefully placed rack of souvenir spoons on one wall, next to the two flying plaster ducks. An extremely fat, short woman with scraggly fake black hair and gray roots sat in a pre-war arm chair gazing blankly at the screen: the Bomber had recovered. She wore a kind of muumuu thing with pineapples on it, the origin of Omar the Tentmaker jokes. A green pony-bottle of Rolling Rock in one hand, a Salem in the other. In front of her was a folding metal TV table with an overflowing brown glass ashtray, six empties and a pile of balled up Tastycake wrappers.

"Yo," I yelled, "you Mike's sister?" Her head turned toward me slightly and nodded, mottled dewlaps flapping; her eyes didn't leave the screen. "Mike," she shrieked so loud it made the trailer shake, "get yer fat ass outta bed. Somebody here to see ya." King Tut was being strangled by the Bomber: "Get up, you fuckin asshole," she hissed.

Mike stumbled out of a doorway to my left, bleary and smelly in his colors and run down boots. Looked like he hadn't brushed his teeth for about a year. He grabbed two beers from the tiny refrigerator; we went out the back and followed a well-worn two-tire track into the trees that led to a small old barn that looked like it was part of a farm once. It was solid and locked up tight, with "Keep Out" posters and the skull and crossbones stenciled in many colors.

Inside, there was a new poured concrete floor and fluorescent fixtures hanging from the rafters. On the back wall was the largest Nazi flag I'd ever seen. The two side walls were piled high with wooden crates. Somebody painted them out, but it was hard to miss the US Army markings. In the middle were two choppers leaning on their side stands. Next to them was the crate I wanted. I popped the top and looked in. There was the KR; it looked undisturbed, still with the brown Climolene preservative on it. Mike was right; it was primo, and it was a legit deal far as I could tell.

We finished our beers, then we loaded it onto my truck. Mike wanted me to stay for a few more, but I told him I had to get over to my mother's in Manayunk for my Sunday visit. He seemed to understand that. As I pulled away, Tommy was still howling in the dust, the wrestling was still on, and after giving me a really strange look I couldn't interpret Mike stumbled back to bed.

It took a while to get all the parts together for the motor. Some were Triumph factory gear, and I had to pull a few strings to get hold of them. I stayed late quite a few nights porting and polishing the head and opening it out for the big valves. I chose 36 millimeter Dellorto carbs: Italian, predictable, bullet proof. A street kid I hired for the job polished the outside of the aluminum cases, clutch and rocker covers, first with a cloth wheel on the grinder, then by hand with Simichrome from West Germany. The cylinders I shot peened myself and sprayed them flat black. It was one dangerous looking engine: 800 ccs of 12:1 brute force from the German cast Mahl pistons. Harry whistled when it was sitting on my bench, finished.

"How much has this guy got into this monster, Jack? Must be a bundle."

"Haven't added up the labor, yet, but it's more than a grand in parts. I figure it'll come out more than two. This sucker sure should move."

"Yeah, too bad you have to plug it back in that stock frame."

I rubbed my chin on that one. With so much power, the engine would definitely be too much for the suspension.

Frame flex could be a problem, too, and the swing arm just wouldn't cut it.

Buttons had another hooker with him. This time she was extremely beautiful, black, about six three, with a very tight afro and a one piece leather dress that fit like Saran Wrap. It had a shiny silver zipper running down the center that was open half way to her navel. She looked like one of those Egyptian statues of Nubian slaves you see in museums.

He ran his soft, slender hands over the engine. The nails on his long fingers were manicured and polished. "Jack, I ain't even heard it run yet, but I can tell she is one fast mothafucka. How much?" I gulped and gave him the bad news, ready with the paperwork and my time sheets as back up. He waved them away with a smile. It was two and a half grand. He pulled out a roll of hundreds and gave me three. "The extra five yards is for you, mahn, not the boss. Dig it?"

"Thanks, Buttons, that's really generous man. I ain't puttin no con on ya, but we should talk about the rest of this ride, now. If ya want."

"Means what, Jack?"

I ran it down to him the best I could, how so much horsepower would blow away the stock frame, brakes, wheels, tires, shocks, everything. The ride could get very squirrelly when the power was dialed on, and it could get dicey trying to haul it down to a stop.

We went back to the catalogs again. I couldn't believe this guy. He went for the large diameter nickel tube Rickman racing frame from California, the Cerriani shocks from Italy, the John Tickle brakes from England, the aluminum gas tank and rims, Pirelli tires, the whole thing, right down to the Cibié headlight. With this kind of freedom, it would definitely be the best piece I had ever built. We talked it over for a while, and then I said, "You should start thinkin about paint, too. My info isn't too good, but I've heard about some primo painters in LA. Should I find out about that?"

He gave me the pearly whites. "No need, salesman Jack, I have to be in the city of angels on business in the next few weeks. Just leave that part to me. I have to split for a meeting now. Carla here will be staying with you for the weekend, but she says you have to wash your hands first. No damage, Jack, understand?" He stuffed a couple of grams of coke in my jeans on the way out. That I didn't do; she did.

They weren't too easy to find. I went to Fox's on Sansom Street and struck out. Then I stopped in to the University of Pennsylvania bookstore and hit pay dirt. The students wandering the aisles looked very young and clean and earnest. Yeats' *Irish Fairy and Folk Tales* and the *Book of Irish Short Stories* would definitely do for a start. I figured one of the nuns could read them to her, now that the cataracts were so bad.

Her little room was painted like a prison cell and smelled about the same. At least there were French doors leading out to the broad porch. In the hallway, somebody was moaning non-stop. She sat on the cheap single bed, looking at her hands folded in her lap, palms up, like she always did. On the tacky, tiny dressing table, all her most precious things were arranged in a fan: the ivory brush and comb, the white rosary blessed at Fatima, the missal.

"Yo, granmom, how's it goin, huh? How they treatin ya? Looks okay ta me, I guess. Lookit, I brought you some of the old stories. Member how granpop used ta say we had to know about them? I figured you might want a refresher," I said as I handed her the bag. It was still pretty clean.

She took out the small Yeats first and rubbed the dust jacket with her right hand as she stared vacantly out the partially open doors. I was flooded by a memory of long ago. She was young, raven haired and very beautiful, gazing, clear eyed out the window, waiting for her man to come home. I was sitting on the Irish lace coverlet on their bed in the Fishtown rowhouse, tracing the pattern with my little-boy finger, pestering her about the banshee. My eyes filled up, couldn't help it. They say a lot of things about the Irish; one of them is that we're fierce. When it comes to family and emotions, that part's true. That's why they're so deeply buried—to keep the rage way down inside.

The type on the jacket was large, so she could read it. She looked up at me with a bemused smile and handed the book back. "Jackie, I don't need this one. I already know them all, maybe more, musha." The short stories puzzled her. I started to read her the authors and titles, but she held up her hand when I got to Joyce, "The Dead."

"The nuns won't read such stuff to me, and I don't want to hear it. The church has banned them, and I won't have any truck with such atheists."

Before I could say that books hadn't been banned for years, a fat nun bustled in without knocking. She was all double chins and beads, and said to granmom like she was talking to a five-year-old: "All right, up you get now, Sophia, it's time for prayers before lunch. Dessert is your favorite, cherry Jell-O. Isn't that fine?" The nun turned to me with a frown and said, "Are you a relative? It doesn't matter. You have to leave, and take those awful books with you." I would have stayed for a month if I knew then it was the last time I would ever see her.

Buttons brought in the gas tank and fenders on a Tuesday. They had about nine thousand hand rubbed coats of black lacquer and some sort of Indian symbols in a pearly gray so fine they looked like spider webs. Very small, on each side of the tank was the single word, "Thanatos." "Tacky," I thought, "Too bad to ruin the paint like that." Over it all was another nine thousand coats of buffed clear lacquer. When I put it all together, it was some machine, a cross between a track rocket and a show bike. People stood back from it, walked around it, looked under it, but didn't get close enough to touch. It was that special.

Buttons paid up, right there, another two grand, and another five yards for me, plus one of his girls—a leggy redhead this time that would have done a Vegas stage proud. He seemed to enjoy bringing me different colors. She was a sweet kid from Minnesota who wanted to be in movies. I was feeling slimy about the Carla thing, though she definitely didn't mind: "My job," she said. "You know what they say: 'If you can't be with the one you love, honey, love the one you're with.'‡ Besides, you're kinda cute, for a white boy." With me, it was another *Baltimore Catechism*, milk bottle, left over. So, later, when we were alone, I gave the redhead a smacker on the cheek, fifty bucks and sent her home: "Tell Buttons we had a good time, kay?"

Me and Buttons walked to the glass front door of the shop together. After we shook hands on the deal, he opened it just as Nate got to it. They were on a collision course. Buttons gave him the grin. Nate was in uniform. He jumped back and

‡ *Steven Stills, with Eric Clapton and Jimi Hendrix. Album: "Steven Stills Solo," Atlantic 1970; Song: Love the One You're With.*

held the door for him, looking at the ground, not those rows of white teeth. Buttons kept him waiting.

"It's a fine thing you made in there, Black Jack. I'll send some of my boys over later to pick it up. I think maybe a few of my associates might be interested in your services." Looking toward Nate, he said louder, "Don't forget, you need a favor from Buttons, you got it." He walked by the uniform like it wasn't there.

"Jesus H. Christ, Jack, you one crazy mothafucka. Who you hangin wit now?"

I shrugged and said, "Good customer."

"Yeh," said Nate, "number one hit man in these here United States. You just picked up a lotta points on the street. Not nobody gonna mess wit you now. Even the feds'll think twice."

Across the street, Agent Moore was busy with his notebook, grinning like a madman.

# 14. Paper Whites

Coming out of the first turn, the KR took over and started walking away from Tracy and his Triumph in the straight. I was shouting into my helmet, "We gotta get outta this place, if it's the last thing we ever do. Man, it's a better life for me and you."‡

He got up near the fence before the second turn and came down low to try to pass me on the inside. Out of the corner of my eye, I could tell the line was wrong. His front wheel, or maybe his boot, hit my rear wheel and I went down, hard. The KR did an endo or two and stopped about ten yards away. The pack roared by in a swirl of brown dust.

The crowd went nuts. It was a deliberate drop, pay back time for Pecker's win at Atco, I figured, and I decided just what to do when I caught the sucker. Only problem was my right ankle wasn't working very well and my back hurt like hell. I peg-legged it to the bike, hopped on and dialed in the throttle to catch up with the pack. Of course, the track officials hadn't

‡Song: We Gotta Get Outta This Place, single, 1965. Group: The Animals (with Eric Burdon).

seen a thing. "Just hard racing," I think they usually call it. Through my face shield, my vision narrowed, surrounded by that old red fog. I was very, very pissed off; snapped out; killing mad.

There wasn't a starting system, really, just a rope stretched across the track, held by a guy at each end and dropped when the marshal dropped the flag. Then everybody not racing got the hell out of the way of the flying stones and gravel. All fifteen of us held maximum revs while the flag circled in the air and came swooping down. It was a clean start, and I had Tracy at my elbow sweeping sideways into the first turn at 85, hot shoe bouncing off the ground, knee joint pounding. He didn't have the horses I did, but he sure could ride dirt. It was going to be close under the lights that Saturday night.

Bethlehem was just what you'd expect, a beat up, bumpy, old-time oval flat-track with no place to sit in the pits, except a tailgate, lousy lighting, and spectators looking down from the crummy bleachers hoping for maximum blood. The KR was unbeatable, and I knew it, as I bent down to strap on my metal hot shoe before the final. On a track as cruddy as this, you definitely needed one, otherwise your boot sole would last about two laps.

I deked in and out of the other riders, rocks bouncing off my face shield, helmet and leathers, going in high, coming out low, rear tire sliding out, front almost touching the hay bales and tractor tires surrounding the infield. It was risky, and the bike wasn't handling right after the spill—felt kind of loose— but I was so angry I didn't care what happened, long as I caught him. I could see him with a comfortable lead up front. He kept turning around, trying to mark me, but I stayed out of sight behind the three riders left between us. Timing was critical.

There was a small gap between the two closest to Tracy. In the straight, I dropped to third gear, planted my chin on the tank and gave the Harley everything there was in the throttle. Good old, crazy Vultch; that cam grind came on like gang busters as I shot past them and upshifted to fourth. The bike had a really bad speed wobble that was getting worse by the second.

First, he looked surprised when he found me on his rear wheel. Then he turned around again and looked scared. "Good on you, prick," I thought. There were two laps to go.

In the second turn, I got to his outside and closed him out, slowly riding him into the hay bales. We banged elbows just before his front wheel hit a tractor tire. I backed off the throttle and watched the high arcs. The Triumph did two graceful flips in the air before it landed on its gas tank in the bed of a pickup. Tracy did a few more before he landed on his back and slid head first into somebody's tool box. The crowd was on its feet, sounding like a huge, hungry animal.

The last lap was a piece of cake, so I slowed it down a bit to lessen the speed wobble. Two hundred and fifty bucks for a night of big fun racing. I even won a leather Hardley Ableson kidney belt, the one with the big brass eagle medallion on the back, ugly as sin. The KR had a bent fork, I could see, but that was no problem. A hydraulic press would straighten it. The ankle and the back; now they were problems I couldn't fix.

In the pits, Harry Stevenson sat on the El Camino's tailgate, staring at the ground, shaking his head slowly. Linda looked completely stunned; then she started laughing. Vultch handed me a can of Bud and said, "You Philistine, you goof ball, I thought you were gonna shoot the pushrods to Mars.

Nice ride, convert, nice ride.  Now you're walkin just like me.
Awesome how the Lord works."

Linda said, "Do you really want to die that badly?"  She
watched me gimping around, then took me by the elbow and
pushed me to the ambulance they always have on standby at
races.  Tracy was on a stretcher inside.  He had a neck brace
on and was out cold.  The nurse, a tiny, pretty little brunette
with a pushed up nose and a pouty lower lip under her
starched white cap, started giving me royal shit about the
spill.  "You people are crazy.  You could have killed him."

"Well, he tried ta kill me, lady, but he missed."

 Linda stepped in:  "Listen, nurse ahh?"

"Logan, Sarah Logan.  What's the problem?"

"Looks like Black Jack, the maniac, has a broken ankle
and maybe a broken back.  You better check him out."

She was small and trim, but she had that nurse's manner.
She pushed me around like a little kid.  "It's ER time for you,
you big galoot.  Get inside."

It was weird, sitting next to my victim on the high speed
ride to St. James' Hospital.  Fortunately, he didn't wake up.  It
would have been hard to strangle him through the neck brace.
The doctor put a cast on my ankle and told me to wear the

HD kidney belt until my back felt better; lucky for me, it didn't
for a long, long time. "And no heavy lifting," he said as he
beetled out of my stall and went back to Tracy. His neck was
broken, but he'd be okay. Sarah came in with a look of satisfaction on her face. "You won't be pulling any harebrained
stunts for at least six weeks, now, will you? You city guys are
all alike—angry and nuts."

"Yeh, right," I thought, "no heavy lifting, no racing. Fat
chance."

"You feel okay?" she asked with her head cocked to one
side. "You look pale, probably concussed." She put her
slender hand on my forehead to feel my temperature. A wisp
of fine chestnut brown hair had escaped from the tight bun
under her cap. Her little finger rubbed my banshee's mark.
She was curious, but said nothing, as she looked into my
eyes with a quizzical look, almost surprised.

"Oh, oh," I thought.

"You get a lot of rest and take it easy for a few days. You
might think you're tough, but the real effects of the spill you
took won't really come home until tomorrow."

I didn't tell her how many times before my noggin had hit the road. Anyway, I smiled at her, patted her shoulder in thanks and gimped away.

I had the KR up on a lift in the shop. Took off the front end to straighten it out. Vultch slid over and started looking over the fork stem that was still in the frame. He was just killing time; we both knew how to fix front ends. I had my back to him when I heard: "Jesus H. Christ on a Honda, Jack, take a glim at this shit."

He had has neck craned to look up under the tank at the frame. He reached into my box and pulled out a pencil flashlight. I joined him. There, where the frame meets the front end neck, was a very carefully done, well concealed cut made with a premium hacksaw blade. No wonder the handling was getting so bad at the end of the race: the cut was open like a gaping mouth. Definitely fixable, but I could have been killed on the track.

"No prophecy here, Jack. Mike tried to put your lights out. How come?"

"Vultch, I got no clue." Then it dawned on me. I'm really stupid about paperwork, bores me, don't care, do it fast, get it over. When we did the papers for the KR, all I did was sign my name and pay the money. Didn't look at the ownership. What for? Now, I lunged for my toolbox and pulled it out. There was a greasy thumbprint over the owner's name; cleaned it off a bit, very gently, with some Windex. It was just legible: the first owner of the KR was Freddie Devlin, the same guy I punched out so many times when I was a kid, the same family my dad and granpop fought with, the same Devlins Father McLaughlin liked so much he got the old man into the Knights of Columbus, the name of the guy they arrested granpop for shooting. Damn. That meant that Mike was the fat little kid I used to ignore, even when he mouthed me. What a dumb shit I am sometimes.

Vultch whistled: "That's like right outta the Bible, man. Revenge, hate, feuding through the generations. Maybe you should have a little private talk with this bag a dirt. You think? Don't argue, I'm commin with ya."

We pulled up to the trailer. It was about 9 and very dark. No lights on inside, not even the TV. Didn't knock, just kicked in the door and went for his room. Empty, smelly, but empty.

As I came out the bedroom door, she lunged at me with a kitchen knife raised to stab. The flab, the muumuu, should have been pitiful, but her face was contorted into such rage, such choking fury, I will never forget it. Vultch caught her arms from behind, then she started screaming at me. "Oh, yes, I know who you are, pretty Jack Kavanagh. Too good to be true. With that fag brother of a priest. It was your grandfather started it. He killed my grandfather, that's why we let them know he was coming, so they could get him. You people think you're so special. You can't get even close to the Devlin name. We'll get every one of you, every fucking one, you bastards."

Vultch took the knife and threw it into the yard, then pushed her down in her TV chair. As we made for the truck, she was still screaming: "I'm glad they killed him; glad, you hear, Jack Kavanagh. The Devlins did it. The Devlins of Inniskeen."

Put the word out on the street: "Find me Mike Devlin and there's a yard waiting for ya." Didn't hear a peep. Made sense, I guess, because I was asking for the dime to be dropped. Seemed like Mike just fell off the face of the earth. At least now I knew who Agent Moore's Informant A was.

This was really weird, all these years, Mike nursing his hate like that. If they hid the fact that they were originally from Inniskeen, not Tipperary as we all thought, even granpop, then the feud went all the way back to 1916, when granpop shot Eddie Devlin in the head for informing on him. I knew very well that granpop had killed a few more of them before he left Ireland. If what Mike's fat sister screamed really was true, I better never, ever, get my hands on his throat. I kept looking, though.

The ankle cast was a pain, even after I pared it down with diagonal cutters to about the size of a Band-Aid. I ruined a good pair of work boots so I could get my bad foot in. Three weeks after the crash, I was back at the track. I'd had it with the invalid routine, so I clipped the cast off completely to get my racing boot on. Judith gave them to me, so there was no way I was cutting it. Suddenly, Sarah the nurse was at my elbow.

"You really are crazy, I'm bound. At least let me wrap it up with a Tensor bandage." She didn't pay attention to my foot while she was wrapping it, just looked up at me, kind of surprised, startled.

"Oh, oh," I thought again, "be nice now."

"And don't forget the belt, either," she said, holding up one long index finger, as I got ready for the start.

With Tracy out of it, the race was clean and smooth. I won again and was thankful for the extra cash. If I kept it up at this pace, I could hit a few more tracks and make some serious money. Just couldn't tell mom where it came from. She'd freak. Sarah was back while I was loading up the El Camino. When I started to take off the belt, she held up her index finger again and shook her head. "You keep that on all the time, unless you're in bed, mind."

"Oh, oh," I thought once more and cinched the belt tight.

Every race, she was there, whether she was off duty or on. I couldn't help but notice when she showed up in a T-shirt and jeans that very good things can come in small packages. We talked, had coffee a few times. She even walked into the shop once on a weekend, but you could tell she was definitely out of place, wide eyed, like a child at a circus. I liked her, respected her, admired her, desired her, even, but that was it, I convinced myself. Right then, I didn't want any more complications in my life, and she was much too sweet and human for downtown. Besides, what would happen when she heard about my street rep, or ran into one of Buttons' girls, or noticed my CIA tail?

"What do you do for fun, Jack?" she asked me one Saturday night in mid-June. "You always look so grim and determined."

"I ride, mostly, or listen to music, or find a nice quiet bar with a loud band."

"What about the country, Jack, don't you like the country?"

I winced when I thought about sweeping through Blue Bell with Judith's arms around me. "Yeh, the country's fine sometimes. I'm justa downtown sorta guy, I guess."

She had that look on her face again: "I ride, too, you know."

"Yeh, like a Vespa, maybe?"

"No, horses, you dolt. My folks have a farm, north, up near Egypt."

"Say what? Egypt? Where the hell's that, over near Venus?"

"No, Pluto," she said with a laugh, her hazel eyes sparkling under the track lights. "It's a little town, in the hills, the farm is further north yet. You should see it, Jack, it's beautiful, four hundred acres along the Lehigh River. It's been in the family forever, before the Revolution, even. We're Quakers. The family came over with William Penn. Would you like to see it sometime? Like tomorrow morning? We could have a ride, and some lunch, and a swim. You need some time off from this. Oh, come on. Take a chance; you're good at that." She was very casual, not insistent.

I took a deep drag on my Camel and thought about it. It wasn't just because she was tiny, or nice, or innocent, or very pretty, or any single other thing. I just had an overwhelming sense that I didn't want to see her hurt—by me or anyone, anything. Maybe it was only a macho protection number in my head—a big guy protects little girl sort of thing—but I don't think so. It was like a dark shape lurking near. Besides, Egypt was where I lost Judith.

"Sure, Sarah, sure. I'm kinda short on friends right now. It's nice of you to ask. Just give me a time and very detailed instructions on how to get there. Do I need a passport to go to Egypt? Don't swim very well, never learned right. Never been on a horse. Hear they're dumb and they bite."

She handed me a printed card with "Logan Farm, 1720" on the front and a map on the back. "We give these out when we have a cattle auction. How about 9 in the morning? And by the way, horses aren't dumb; they only nibble, they don't bite. Two more things—favors—Jack. Please don't smoke around my parents; it offends them, though they'd never say anything; and please don't swear, it offends me. Deal?"

She held out her narrow hand with the long, slender fingers. I took it, but didn't squeeze it; I was afraid to. She grinned and gave me a surprisingly strong handshake. "Promise," I said.

Some single buildings, even some clusters of buildings, sit on the land exactly, perfectly, as they should. Logan Farm was like that, nestled in a green hollow by the winding river. The ancient three-storey stone house with the deep porch, the massive stone barn with the musket slits, the outbuildings, the paddock, even the silos, the blinding white board fences, were set in place with careful thought and no flaw. The massive Sycamores knew just where to grow. It was the kind of place where you could sit still in the quiet, breathe deep and smile to yourself.

I had been coming every Sunday as the summer wore on. Her parents were wonderful people: friendly, open, no suspicious looks, no awkward questions. I was probably the strangest man they'd ever seen, bringing the savage outside into their peaceful inside, but I was their daughter's friend; that was good enough for them. I had a good appetite; that was even better for her mother, who liked baking pies. The two older brothers and the two younger sisters were okay, too, but the girls giggled into their hands a lot, peeping around corners at me.

I was terrible with horses, and they knew it. No, they aren't stupid; sarcastic is a better word. I'd get on one; the thing would turn, stare with a big black eye and say, "Nope, I ain't doin nothin for you, buddy. Where's my stall?" Sarah thought it was a riot. Of course, she was perfect on a horse; they seemed linked by telepathy. The riding and the swimming were where the body came from. I kept my hands off, made a half-hearted promise to myself about it. She didn't like it much, but I think she sort of understood when she got to know me and my story a bit better. Some things, like

Toot and Charlie Murphy, Howard Street and the Devlins, I figured, would only cause her pain, so I kept them to myself.

I had come from the track late on a Saturday night in mid-July. We sat in the big kitchen for a while, having coffee with her mother, then Sarah led me up to a cool spare bedroom on the third floor, with its antique rocking chair, huge blanket box, a cherry desk, family portraits and an old rope bed painted red. She unclipped the clasp in her bun, and her hair cascaded down her back before she opened the door for me. I looked in, then turned back to her. She turned her face up to me and pulled me down to kiss her. It took me by surprise; I responded but kept a civil tongue in my head. One of her legs slipped between mine, and I could feel her as she squeezed her legs together. Her mouth opened wider and her pouty lower lip felt even softer. I panicked and tried to pull back, but she had me locked there. Her look was dreamy, but her breath was short. So was mine.

"Sarah," her mother called up the stairs, "would you please look to the horses before you turn in? Your father had to go to the vet's with the dog, so he can't." I kissed her nose before she took off.

Next morning was beautiful, sunny, high puffy white clouds sailing by. The dew still sparkled on the grazing fields, clumps of cattle stood silently, chewing thoughtfully, as they watched us ride by. A thin mist hung over the river. We hadn't taken this trail this far before. We packed a lunch, towels and wore our bathing suits under our jeans. Mine were blue for a change, with a new white T-shirt. I called them my farm duds. I hadn't felt so relaxed in years, even though I was on a horse. Maybe the buckskin felt it, because he just ambled along, side by side with Sarah's dapple gray mare. We didn't speak much, instead we looked around in still time at the broad oak trees, the hills, the sky. If this was Egypt, I wasn't in exile, I was on another planet.

As we rode around a bend in the river, past the family cemetery with the ornate iron fence and the mossy old headstones, we flushed a large flock of mourning doves. They took off together, making that strange whistling wing noise of theirs. Up ahead was a small stone building set right on the bank in a grove of large oak trees.

"It's the old ice house," she said. "Of course, we don't use it anymore, so I turned it into my spot. I come here to think, to read, to be by myself. Do you like it?"

"It's perfect," I said as we dismounted. "Who built the dock and the raft out there?"

"I did," she replied, proudly, "with a very little help from my brothers, who drank beer and laughed a lot. You didn't know I was a carpenter, too?"

"Nope, heard you were a bossy nurse who beats up on the sick and injured."

We dumped our stuff on the dock, stripped off our riding clothes and dove in. Diving I can do; not much else. Kinda fits me. River water in the hills of Pennsylvania is always just about freezing, even in late summer. It felt like a horse kicked me in the chest. I let out a woof of air and headed for the surface, checking out the rocks and the ice house foundation on the way up. She surfaced behind me and pushed me back under. I came up, spluttering, "God damn, that's cold. Oops, sorry, gosh darn it all." "That's much better, thank you. Race you to the raft." I can't swim very good, goes back to the beat up shoulder and the back, of course. That's why I had a Tensor bandage wrapped around the small of it for swimming. She beat me by a long shot.

I hoisted myself up and reached over to give her a hand. She was treading water, brushing her chestnut hair back with her hands, smiling up at me with that look. The water was very clear, and I watched it caress her. She took my hand, and I pulled her up. She didn't let go, instead she planted her feet on the edge of the raft with her arched back leaning over the water. She was wearing a yellow bikini. The muscles in her flat stomach were clearly defined, her thighs were strong and perfectly shaped; they didn't touch between her legs. Her hips were small, and her rear end was so round it made me gulp. The cold water had made her large nipples very hard and prominent. She pulled toward me and put her arms around my waist, with her head buried in the hair on my chest. We didn't kiss, we didn't speak. Her slender hand slid down my stomach into my trunks. Her touch was light but firm, teasing, enticing.

She looked up at me. The expression was different in her hazel eyes: electric, deep. "So much for promises," I thought to myself. She pulled away suddenly with a laugh and plunged back into the water. "Bet I can beat you again," she called as she took off for the dock. I stood with my mouth open, watching, as she grabbed her towel and bounced up the outside stairs to the ice house loft. She threw open the casement windows that looked out over the river. "Now that is really slow, I'd say."

I dried off as I walked up the steps. Inside, the thick stone walls were whitewash brilliant. She had set up a sort of study, with odds and ends of furniture from the attic at the main house. Against the far wall was an iron bed made into a sofa. She was standing on a low, yellow, painted stool, leaning against the window sill, framed in the bright window, combing out her hair. I sat down in an overstuffed chair to finish drying off. "I'll have to rewrap that bandage for you. Why don't you take it off so it will dry?"

"Hold on, you told me not to take it off, except at night."

"Wrong. I said, "except in bed.""

While she arranged her hair behind her with both raised arms, she watched me unroll the thing. "Jack, I think I know how you feel about me. I accept it. It's enough. I have a very strong sense that you don't want to hurt or mislead me. Underneath all that street-smart, hard-boiled, tough guy stuff, you're really a very kind man, but you hide it pretty well from most people. I wish I could heal the damage; I don't know if I can. Sometimes, I think, you just react, don't think far enough ahead, and you have no peace in your heart. I can't tell you exactly how I feel yet, but I can tell you two very plain facts. I want you, and you want me." I opened my mouth to butt in, but she stopped me, holding up her finger in that way she had. "Just sit still for a minute. Don't say anything. Just watch."

Very carefully, she spread her towel on the sill, smoothing out the wrinkles. Our eyes met, in hers the electricity was back, only deeper, more liquid, more hazel this time. She put the antique, chased silver, heart-shaped locket she always wore back around her neck. The chain was braided, thick, heavy, old. Then she looked down at herself. Deliberately, she slid the straps off her shoulders and reached behind her to undo the clasp. She held it in place with a hand cupping each breast, then slid it down over her red-brown nipples. Water beaded on her skin. Carefully, she turned and arranged the top next to the towel. She looked back at me over her right shoulder; there was pride in her eyes. The shape of the side of her breast was astonishingly beautiful in the sunlight and shade.

She turned to me, smiling, and ran her hands down her stomach. Her fingers slid under the band of the bikini bottom and started, oh so slowly, to inch it off. It dropped to the floor, and she bent gracefully to pick it up. Once more, she arranged it precisely next to the top and towel. Once again, she looked proudly over her shoulder at me. Water beaded in the brown hair between her legs and still on her breasts. She picked up the towel and carefully dried off. I was in agony. None of this was coy, no peep show, not even a joyous striptease. It was a tribute to her, a gift to me.

She put the towel back in place and walked toward me. I slipped my hands down her waist and thighs, leaned forward and kissed her stomach. She knelt in front of me, ran her hands up the sides of my thighs, grabbed the waist band and slid my trunks off. I was still wet, so she took my towel and dried me, the delicate rasp of terrycloth.

I stood, pulled her against me, then picked her up. On the side of the bed, I knelt between her legs, kissing her mouth, gently nibbling her bottom lip. When I started kissing her neck, she whispered, "I'm so close, Jack, if you kiss my breasts now, I'll just explode." I did, and she did, with tiny, sweet little murmurs in the back of her throat.

"Stand up, Jack," she said after a while. "Not just yet, my beautiful princess, not just yet." I started at her ankles and slowly kissed my way up the inside of her thighs. This time, the orgasm was deeper, longer, more physical. She twisted, turned, bunched her fingers in my hair and let out a sharp cry as her back arched. I looked up to see her head thrown back and her mouth open in a long "Oh." It was magical. I kissed my way up her belly to her mouth.

Later, I said, "Move over, willya. Give a guy some room." "Yes, sir," she said, and rolled over on the bed. "We have to be careful of your back, so you just lie like that." She was on her knees, lightly stroking me everywhere, then kissing, sucking.

She climbed on top of me. We kissed and touched each other for a while. There was no hurry; I was hoping to regain my composure a bit. I wanted to give her as much pleasure as I could. When I started kissing her breasts again, she raised herself and then lowered, very, very slowly. "Look," she said in a honeyed, hoarse whisper, and we watched as we joined. Then, our eyes locked. Suddenly, hers widened. So did mine.

She was standing on the stool again, elbows propped on the window sill, looking out over the water. Down below, the horses whinnied softly and snorted in the lengthening shade. I was massaging her shoulders, deeply, but gently, watching my hands take over. By the raft, hundreds of paper whites danced in the sunshine. "I know they're only cabbage moths, but I still think they're beautiful, don't you?" "Yep, sure are. Looks like there'll be lots more next year if I'm any judge." She laughed through her nose, spun round to kiss me, and then turned back again. "Umm, that feels good on my shoulders, don't stop." She backed up a bit so she molded into me. "Mmm, that's nice, too. Just like that." Across the river, I saw the glint of a camera lens from the scrub oaks. She didn't notice.

It's difficult to explain. I didn't think I was in love with her, but there was a very deep affection. That's not quite right, either. It kind of snuck up on me. It was very different from what I felt for Judith, that continuous hungry emptiness. With Sarah, it was more racing blood, eye dissolving into eye, tactile, skin on skin, soul on soul. Care for her I certainly did—a lot.

It was the end of August, and the corn was ready. We had a big roast one Sunday. The family was there, of course, some neighbors, looking sunburned, hard working, healthy.

Harry and Linda came. Harry was in seventh heaven and spent a lot of time in the barn talking farming with Mr. Logan. Her mother was singing in the kitchen, hauling pie after pie out of the oven. It was good, perfect. Even Vultch laid off the weird religious stuff, mostly because his mouth was full all the time. Just like the first time I saw her in Norristown, his skinny little wife said practically nothing and ate less. The corn tasted like the meaning of sweet.

After everybody took off and we cleaned up, it was understood by then that we would head to the ice house for the night. Her parents had that Quaker principle deep inside them: "Do not judge, do not interfere." It was an unspoken understanding. We saddled up and rode out just as the sun was disappearing behind the green hills. The buckskin was my friend by then. I guess he thought because I didn't really know how to ride, he'd do the driving. They waved to us from the broad porch. In the light from candles and an old oil lamp we made love twice that night. "Being able to see each other is very important," she always said, and I learned how right she was. The first was quick, urgent. The second patient and slow and gentle. She fell asleep across my chest while I stroked her hair. I thought long and hard that night, about

Canada, about her and about whether I would go alone or not. It was a very big step for me. Marriage, even. Kids? Holy cow.

I was still at it when the sun started to come up, mind revving like a two-stroke engine. Just the slightest change in the darkness at first, as the robins said it was okay for the new day to start. Then a curious sound almost like doves but not, soft, gentle wingbeats. I don't think it came from outside my head. Suddenly, the sun slanted golden into the valley, but the room was still dark. Sarah was lying on her stomach, her head resting on her arm, long chestnut hair covering her face. She stirred, brushed her hair away and smiled at me. "Come here," she said. "I'm cold. Look." In the half light, I could see her thighs were shivering and her nipples were very hard.

With her, each time seemed different. She pulled me on top of her. I was afraid to rest any of my weight on her. She understood right away and put her arms around my neck and wound her legs around me. It was slow and deliberate; we moved as one and came as one. That last part always seemed to be the same, though. It was very new to me and to her. We talked about it, laughed about it, treasured it. "Our timing is exceptional," she would say with that proud, dreamy look in her hazel eyes, her bee-stung lower lip very pouty.

It was becoming broad day, and the light was reaching down the walls of the whitewashed room. A small ruby-red shadfly hovered in the open casement. She was on her stomach again, and I was running my hand from between her shoulder blades down over her rear end. Slowly, lightly, up and down. She loved it. I wasn't looking at her. I was staring out the window, trying to come up with some way of asking her to come to Canada with me that didn't sound too stupid or soppy or goofy. It wasn't easy. I'd never gulped out a question like that one before.

"Sarah," I whispered, still looking out the window, "do you like snow?" "Umph," she replied, "if you haven't checked, it's August out there." "Yeh, I know, but that's now. What about winter time, like in Canada maybe? Think you might like to come with me there, sometime? It's a long way from the farm and your family, but we could get some horses, live in the country outside a city, where I could set up my shop and you could work in a hospital. We could come back to visit. The going wouldn't be simple, and I'm not the easiest idiot to get along with, but....uh. I guess I'm not making sense. What I mean is, I want you to come to Canada with me. If getting married is important to you, fine—er—great, I mean."

There was a long silence, only her breathing, deep, steady. Then her back started to heave, slightly at first, then more and more. She was crying, then bawling like a kid. She grabbed me around the neck so hard I could hardly breathe. "Yes," she said into my neck. "Oh yes, yes indeed, my love."

When we made love it was like the beginning of a sweet, old country ballad about the dawn of a new day, with fireworks at the end. She was astride me, sitting straight up, the silver heart-shaped locket shining between her breasts, palms on my chest. All through it, I was smiling so hard, she was smiling so hard, it was tough to kiss.

She was on her stomach again. I was stroking her back again. We were silent. I looked down at her small, perfect torso. In the brightening light, I saw five or six dark bruises on her back. "Hey, did you fall off your horse or somethin?" "No, why do you ask?" "You've got bruises on your back. It wasn't me. I didn't do it. All I need is your father chasing me around the farmyard with a pitchfork because he thinks I was rough with you." I said all this smiling.

I could feel the muscles in her back tense. "What do they look like, Jack. Be as accurate as you can, please." Her voice was clipped, scared. "Well, they're about as big around as a silver dollar and sort of blue-black. Funny thing is, I swear they weren't there last night. I woulda seen em." She tore out of bed and started pulling her clothes on at a thousand miles an hour. "Get dressed, Jack, hurry. I have to go to the hospital, now! And put your belt on."

We didn't go into the house, just jumped into the El Camino and roared off for St. James'. On the way, she told me in a shaking voice that her family had a history of Childhood Leukemia that showed up every second generation. Hers was it. The symptoms were bruises that seemed to come out of nowhere.

The doctor was the same guy who put the cast on my ankle. He looked me up and down with a sniff, then started to wheel Sarah away. I started to follow. He turned on his heel and said, "Just where do you think you're going, pal? Call her family and get them over here. You just sit down and wait out here."

"Look, sport, we're engaged." My fists were doubled, and I could feel the rage rising from deep inside. "I'm not lettin her outta my sight." I grabbed his white coat by the lapels and got in his face. "Pay attention. Let me give ya some advice. Don't screw up, or you'll have me to deal with outside. Unnerstand?"

He looked at Sarah, and she nodded. There were tears in her eyes.

Her mother and father came. I was sitting by the bed holding her hand. She looked tired; her skin was blue-gray. Her voice was cracking when she said to them, "Mom, dad, Jack and I are engaged. I love him very much. When I get better and things work out for him, we're moving to Canada together. I'd like to get married on the farm, first, if that's okay with you?" She was looking at me. I nodded. There was a very large lump in my throat that I kept trying to swallow away. It was dry and made of hemp. Her parents stood behind me. Each put a hand on my shoulder. They knew. So did I, even before the test results came in.

The doc, the asshole, came up to me in the cafeteria while I was choking down the worst coffee I ever had in my life. I guess he was trying to be nice. There were dark bags under his eyes. "Um, Jack, isn't it? Yes, well, look Jack, it's like this.

The disease is very swift, very rare, 100 percent fatal. It could be a matter of days or weeks. We just don't know."

I started up out of the chair at him. He put his hands up, palms toward me, with a tired, troubled look on his face. No fear. "Look, buddy, I know it's not easy, but there's absolutely nothing we can do. Nothing. Zero. You aren't the only one around here who loves her; we all do. If you have a problem, maybe you should take God outside, but if you come at me again, you'll never get in here again." He turned on his heel and stomped away.

I wouldn't leave the room. Two weeks I sat there with her, mopping her brow with a cool, damp cloth, holding her hand, whispering to her, cradling her beautiful head on my chest. The bone of her skull felt very thin, delicate as eggshell, fragile. One morning at dawn, I must have been dozing. Her hand clasped mine very hard, and I started broad awake. Her lovely eyes were hollow, sunken, but incredibly serene. "I'm so sorry, Jack. We would have been the best ever, you and I. Say it, please. Please say it to me."

"I love you, Sarah, now and always. Please stay with me. Please don't go. Please don't."

She smiled weakly, then the clasp of her hand released. Her eyes were open and blank, still looking at me. At first, I wanted to jump up and get help. It was no use; she was gone. I reached over and closed her eyes. Then I pulled her tiny, light, cooling body to me and held it, rocking, for a long, long time before I went out in the corridor to find a nurse.

Parts of the old song started running in my head and wouldn't quit. I learned to hate it:

*It was down in old Joe's Barroom, on the*
*corner by the square. The*
*drinks were served as usual. And the*
*usual crowd was there.*

*On my left stood big Joe McKennedy,*
*His eyes were bloodshot red.*
*He turned to the crowd around him,*
*These were the very words he said,*

*"I went down to the St. James Infirmary*
*To see my baby there.*
*She was stretched out on long white table,*
*So sweet, so cold, so fair.*

*Let her go, let her go.  God bless her,*
*Wherever she may be...."*

*And now that you've heard my story,*
*I'll have another shot of booze.*
*And if anybody happens to ask you,*
*I've got the St. James Infirmary blues‡.*

Her wooden casket was in a wagon pulled by the buckskin and the dapple gray. We put her in the ground in the old family cemetery, among the mossy stones.  The wind rustled the leaves of the oak trees like feathers; you could almost smell fall coming on.  A red-shouldered hawk circled high in a thermal, screaming.  There was no preacher.  Her father said a few words, then recited "Ashes to ashes, dust to dust."

Everyone stood silently around the grave, heads down, eyes closed, for what seemed forever.  I couldn't stand it.  I fell on my knees by the open grave and started howling like a run-over dog.  No one intervened until it ran its course.  Her mother helped me up.  Her daughter's eyes looking into mine;

‡ Anon., St. James Infirmary, traditional folk song.

serene but now permanently changed. She pulled my head down, put Sarah's locket around my neck and spread her strong, farm woman hand over my heart. "We know you loved her very much, Jack. She said it was the finest gift she ever received. She wanted so much to help you heal and find the peace you needed. Remember her. We will remember you and your kindness to her. She's past care, now. You aren't. Come to terms with it, Jack. Heal and find peace inside yourself."

I had come to the farm on the Bonneville. On the way back to Kensington, the engine screamed like a lost soul. It was a miracle I didn't die.

Don't remember much. I was in the parking lot at McDougall's taking on two Italian guys, one of them had a tire iron. Then Vultch pulled me off; he had a pistol in his hand. One of the them said, "Yeh, thought so, asshole *and* nigger lover. Don't come back here, chump, ever." Took a lot of guts for Vultch to set foot in Kensington, black man on very dangerous turf. The wrong people get named as saints.

I sat in a booth at the Salty Dog in Margate, looking out the window at a dusk of wind-driven drizzle, slanting south like bullets. Gray-backed gulls hunched wet by the sea. Beach season was over. I was the only customer, and the bartender was waiting patiently for me to finish the bottle of Jameson. The plate of food was untouched, congealing into garbage. Voices, unintelligible, contradictory, mad, manic, argued, hissing, in low, angry whispers inside my skull.

The motel room was ugly. Day after day, the beach was deserted, except for noisy, skittish flocks of south heading birds, wanting warmth and the beating hearts of their own kind near. I spent hours and hours walking up and down, up and down, in the sand. The rest of the time I spent getting as much Jameson into me as I could. Pizza and the Irish, great diet, but it was what I needed to dull the pain.

Harry and Linda tracked me down after about ten days. I wasn't sure how long I'd been there, or how they found me. Maybe Vultch. They didn't say much, just stacked up the pizza boxes and threw out the empties. "Jack, you look like shit," Harry said. "Right," from Linda. "You're coming with us." I didn't resist, and stayed with them up in Militia Hill until the motorcycle season slowed down. I laid off the whiskey and tried to get my head on straight. It wasn't working. The voices remained, more strident, never silent. The feds were still with me; probably thought the three of us were hatching some kind of plot to blow up the White House. Went to my mother's place once, to drop off the envelope, but I think my look, my wild talk, scared her.

Finally, I went back to my apartment. First thing I did was haul out the white oak box granpop made for me. The wood was darker still. I took off Sarah's locket and opened it. On one side, her mother had coiled a lock of her chestnut hair. On the other side was a shaky note she probably wrote in the hospital: "I love you forever, Jack. Remember." I closed it, slowly, staring, memorizing the incised lines in the old silver, finally putting it in the box with the other past, precious things. It rested on Charlie Murphy's comm. from Long Kesh, next to the pure pearl handles of Toot's 45, beside Judith's yellowing letter. Inside the lid, granpop had written a verse with what must have been a very fine nibbed pen. The lettering was ornate, like you see on the diplomas hung up in the doctor's office:

*Cast a cold eye*
*On life, on death.*
*Horseman, pass by!*‡

I never understood why he did it, until then.

"Later," I thought, "maybe I can wear her locket again." I stared into the box, no focus, my hands balled so tight, one broken nail drew blood. Then it rang in my head like the deep toll of a bell: "'*Éirinn go Brách*.' Right, granpop, Ireland should be free. So should I." A clear voice, no contradiction. Next thing I did was start making some traveling tapes for the truck. I began with *Up the Country*, by Canned Heat, then *Off to Dublin in the Green*, by the Wolf Tones, and finished with Velvet Underground, volume at ten out of ten.

‡W. B. Yeats, "Under Ben Bulben," September 4, 1938.

## 15. Big Pink

"Yo, Mr. Castesi, how you doin?" It was December, and I was in the shop working on my Norton. The bike was just about finished, almost perfect. Couldn't decide whether to sell it or take it with me. "How'd ya know to call here? What can I do for ya?" The call surprised me a little, because I hadn't heard from him in a while. I knew he still had the shop up at Five Points in North Philly, one of his many businesses in the city. Tried not to think about Toot, but it was hard to stop the flashback to the bathroom. Through my black T-shirt, I touched Sarah's locket, heavy against my chest.

"Oh, I have my sources, Jack. You okay? Heard you've had a lot of trouble. Not the kind of stuff you should get involved in. All sorted out now? Sorry to hear about your girl. By the way, I rode the piece you built for Buttons. Very fine work. Very impressive. *Mucho gusto*, as we say in Italian."

"Thank you, sir. She was very special to me. The other stuff? Oh, yeh, guess so. Lotta people thought I was a bad guy or somethin. I ain't." I didn't want to tell him the feds were still with me; probably knew anyway. Another bonehead move.

"No, you aren't," he paused, "perhaps. Listen. I'm expanding. I'm getting a few more franchises for next year, another location, and I really need a good shop manager. Interested? I know you left because you had the chance to build a shop the way you wanted it. From everything I hear, you did a fine job. Now you can do it again, for me, and you'll have more freedom and more money to do it. We can work out a sweet deal, bonuses and so on, as long as you bring your people with you. I could have another little talk with your friends Jeeps and Nate. I'm sure they could be persuaded to be much, much more polite. The other situation, I'm afraid, I can't help you with, not right now, at least. I've spoken to your uncles about that. Later, we could probably sort it out, but it would take time."

This was really awkward. I'd already made my decision to leave Philly. Had most of my stuff stored in Manayunk, in Sal Francini's shed. Did it late, when I was pretty sure I wasn't being followed too closely. Still had the apartment, but there wasn't much left in it I wanted. Now, granpop's box was never out of my sight. The deal with Bombardier was close;

Triumph said we could talk about a franchise once I got set up in Canada. The money was there; for a start anyway, once I took care of mom and granmom. It looked good. Problem now was how to get out of the offer without sounding disrespectful to Mr. Castesi, or tipping my hand too soon. The first part would be a definite mistake—a big one that could get painful. Linda, Harry and Vultch were the only ones who knew what I was up to, so the second part might let the news out on the street. Wouldn't be long before Agent Moore heard it.

"Mr. Castesi, I'm really sorry, sir, but I set this place up for Don. You know im?"

"Yes, I know his family, but we aren't exactly what you would call close friends." His tone was very level.

"Whoops, careful," I thought. "Well, sir, I really wouldn't like to let him down. He stuck by me through all the trouble, and it would be, like, disloyal, I think."

He understood that: "That's just like you, Jack. Just what I would expect—fair and loyal, just like your uncles. That's why I called. You're sure, are you?"

"Yes, sir. Thanks very much for the offer. Can I call you if things change?"

"Certainly, Jack. You're a pro, and I like using pros. Call me anytime."

"One more thing, Mr. Castesi. I'd be glad to do anything you might want."

He chewed on this for a while, knowing why I said it, understanding I knew there was nothing I could do for him of any value. It was the offer that counted. "Well, now that you mention it, Jack, there is one thing. The boys in the Mummers' club I support are working hard down in South Philly trying to get their costumes ready. There have been a few problems, and they're running late. There's a shipment of stuff for them coming in from Europe next week. I would appreciate it very much if you would go down to the docks, pick it up and deliver it. How about it?"

"I'd be glad to, sir, glad to." He gave me the name of the boat and the delivery address. "Whew," I thought when I hung up, "got outta that one clean." Bonehead again.

The stevedores loaded four big boxes directly from the hold into the bed of my truck. The inspectors had the day off, I guessed. I had beefed up the suspension, and the El

Camino took the load well. It was raining, so I covered them up with a tarp for the trip to South Philly. Two feds were there in their Ford, of course, and I waved to them as I drove away from Philadelphia Tidewater Terminal and headed down Delaware Avenue for Oregon. I kept the speed pretty low so they could keep up without working too hard. On the radio, The Band belted out *The Weight* from "Big Pink." "Have to add that to my traveling tapes," I thought. Canadian boys, mostly. Then I thought with a snort, "How about, *I've Got a Friend in Jesus*?" I rejected that one; too much like Vultch, or maybe Matt. No, Vultch for sure.

I drove along, past Marconi Plaza on my left. On my right, street after street of small, clean, polished, fixed up row houses and trinities with phony Permastone fronts stuck on over the brick to dress them up. You had to go north, through Chinatown, before everything fell apart. Oregon curves around the US Army Depot and turns into Vare Avenue. I was headed for Point Breeze and a street called Emily.

The warehouse was large, pretty new, with a door tall and wide enough for tractor trailers. There was no name on it, but I had the street number. Down the block, I could see the feds finally made it, but this time there were two cars. "That's weird," I thought; the change made me uncomfortable. I pushed the big red bell button. A small panel in the door opened with a click. The guy had a beak like a hawk, curly black hair and a voice like a chainsaw: "Yeh, whaddya want?" "Mr. Castesi asked me to bring some stuff for the Mummers. Got it in the truck." His manner changed, sort of. "You gotta name?" "Yeh, Jack. Lissen, you want this stuff or not? I got places to go." The panel shut, and the tall door opened quickly with a whirr from the electric motor on the rail above it.

Inside, it was just an ordinary warehouse, but there was something funny about it, a familiar smell I couldn't pin down. It was very hot, overheated. The guy who opened the door was wearing a strap undershirt, it was that bad. "Sorry, Mack, gotta frisk ya. Mr. Castesi's orders." The El Camino was idling roughly, because of the race cam I put in it when I worked the motor. After he did his thing, and looked around inside the truck, he turned to me: "Nice short, buddy, clean ride. Who does the body and engine work?" "I do. Know a PR named Buttons? I built his piece, too." He looked at me sharply, nodded, but didn't reply.

He told me to drive along the wide central aisle that led to another loading door at the other side of the building, back the truck down Number 27 and then knock on the double doors I'd find at the end. You could have blown me away like a feather when one of them opened. It was Jeeps. He was wearing a strap undershirt, too, and had a White Owl stuck in his unshaven face, but the rest of the outfit really did me in. Couldn't help it. I started laughing to beat the band. Over the undershirt, he had on a scoop-necked top in gold sequins. Around his waist was a frilly yellow tutu. On his fat legs, yellow tights. On his feet, gold sequined pumps with little bows on the toes. He was the most ridiculous sight I'd ever seen.

"Shut the fuck up, Jack. Ain't you never seen a wench before? One a ours has appendicitis, so I gotta do his bit in the parade. Course, he's just a kid, so we hadda make a lotta alterations to this outfit. I think it looks good on me," he said, peering over his beer gut. "Aw, come on, cut it out, willya?"

I almost had it under control. Gasping for breath, I said to him: "Jeeps, you ever hassle me again, I'm gonna drop the dime to anybody who knows you on the street. You'll never be the same." I started laughing again, hoarse, manic.

"Okay, okay, so you got one on me. Just stop laughin, willya? Let's get this stuff unloaded." When the tarp came off, he said, "Hey, there's four boxes. Only supposed to be three. Oh, yeh, now I see." He started to walk to the back of the large room, tutu bouncing, past the headdresses and gold skirts the musicians wear in the Mummers' Parade along Broad Street on New Year's Day. I was planning to hit Times Square for New Year's Eve, a kind of farewell party, but now I would definitely have to be back for the parade in Philly. Too bad I didn't have a camera with a telephoto lens. I could take a shot of Jeeps, get it enlarged and give it to Harry to hang up over his bench. Maybe the feds would lend me one, just for the day. I made a mental note to ask.

He knocked twice on the door in the far wall. Another panel clicked, and he talked through it. The door opened, and two guys came out, taking off the surgical masks they were wearing. Then it hit me, the drowsy talc smell of heroin. It came wafting out of the back like the long, bony claw of the devil. "Shit," I said to myself, "this I definitely don't need to know." They pushed the door shut with a bang, walked over, eyeing me, loaded the box on a dolly and headed back to the door. That's when the first pistol shot rang through the building, not loud, just an unmistakable pop; a lot more followed very quickly; then splintering wood and shotgun barks.

I dove into the El Camino and burned rubber down the aisle to the intersection. The nose of the truck was sticking out far enough so I could look to my left. The door was bashed in and blocked by five or six fed cars. They were firing from behind them at the guy who let me in, plus a few more shooting pump shotguns from the catwalk above. One of the guys up there got his knee blown apart by a shotgun round; he bounced back against the wall from the impact then fell forward, head first over the railing to the concrete below, all smashed upside down at weird angles.

Moore was there, in the thick of it. He marked me with a tight grin. In the rear view mirror, I could see the two guys from the back room running toward me with automatics in their hands. Jeeps was nowhere to be seen. No time to get Toot's 45 from the box I brazed up for it under the El Camino's battery. Crazy, anyhow, I'd be dead meat.

I gunned the truck to the right, got to the other door, jumped out, punched the button and roared into the street, just missing the door as it opened. A single fed car was on my tail. I screamed around a corner just as a step van drove out of an alley. I swerved around the hood and slid to a bumpy stop against the curb. The van kept coming and had the road blocked completely. I looked up at the driver. Didn't know him, but I could spy an Irish face a mile away. He grinned, winked and waved bye-bye to me. The feds were blowing their horn from the other side. He climbed out of the cab slowly to see what all the fuss was about.

I drove right on the speed limit out to the scrub hills near Wings Field and stayed put for a couple of hours, thinking, considering options, possibilities. "Maybe I should just score enough smack that it would all stop—quickly—peacefully." The old definition of mortal sin ran in my head. "Give your head a shake, nitwit. What dumb bastard came up with that stupid line, 'The Luck of the Irish'?" I wondered, finally, "What else can go wrong?"

Strangely, very strangely, nothing happened. I laid low in Jersey for a few days, stayed away from Margate, Cape May instead, watched the papers, the TV, made a few calls. My mother would hardly talk to me. Sal Francini was the most helpful. It was a really big bust—200 pounds of street-ready smack—but only a few little fish got fried, no big guys were mentioned. Neither was Jeeps. Me neither, even as an unnamed suspect. *The Inquirer* quoted Agent Moore: "We put a really big dent in the heroin supply for the East Coast. Of course, our investigations are continuing to find the organizers of this ring. We believe it's the biggest in the country." Nothing else.

This was not good, not good at all. Felt like I had a vise on my head. Now it really was time to get out, but I needed more to get all my stuff in order. If they didn't grab me as an accessory, I'd leave on the second of January, just like I planned. If they did, well, I'd just have to wait and see. The El Camino was stored at Vultch's place in Norristown, with the Norton and enough tools to work in the back. Now I carried Toot's 45 in my waistband, the switchblade in my back pocket. I was as ready as I could be. At night, just on the edge of sleep, hoofbeats and dark shapes in the dark, far off. It would be very, very close.

The feds were outside my apartment, just like I expected. Like I didn't expect, they didn't jump out of the car and hassle me. Instead, they waved, just like I used to wave to them. Not good. I decided not to go to Times Square to "dig the worms," as Hose would say, but I wasn't going to miss the Mummers' Parade. I thought about going out to Arizona to join up with him and Chica, but it didn't last long after I used the signal and talked to him: "They'll find you, and they'll find me. Not cool, Jack, not cool at all. You gotta get out of the country. Far out." Judith's letter was running in my head; Sarah's peace was far, far away.

I stood on the wide sidewalk at Broad and Sansom watching the bands go by, eating a soft pretzel, drinking hot coffee. If you aren't a native, the Mummers' Parade is really weird. Well, even if you are, it's pretty strange: grown men and teenagers strutting like high-heeled boys in satin, sequins and feathers, playing lousy music on banjos—*Oh, Dem Golden Slippers*—stuff like that. The competition is really fierce, and the guys aren't what you'd call Main Line types, so you don't laugh unless you can't help it. They're riggers and stevedores, plumbers and cops, carpenters and iron workers: Irish, Italians, Polish. What drives them, year after year, generation after generation, since the 1700s, is beyond me.

It was cold and damp; a light dust of snow fell from the lead sky. I looked up at Billy Penn in his green-bronze suit and hat on top of City Hall. He wasn't laughing, either.

Jeeps' band started coming by, but he wasn't there. Didn't
have a camera, anyway. Besides, it wasn't funny any more.

Across the street, I saw Carla in the crowd; hard to miss in
her red fox fur hat. Her voluptuous mouth was set in a hard,
cruel line; she was looking beyond me. Close behind her,
Moore was looking directly at me, sunglasses off. There was
a very big smile on his face; it was lopsided, though, because
the jaw never set right. When the hoof clatter from the mounted cops went from real on the street to haunting in my head,
the music muted and the parade looked distorted, like through
the wrong end of binoculars. My old friend death was near.

Looking down, inside my jacket, to find my Camels, I saw
them, right beside me, the spit-shined, pointy-toed boots.
Buttons had his left hand on my shoulder: "Sorry, Jack, but so
long." The ice pick went through the back of my jacket, but it
hit the brass eagle on my kidney belt and skidded sideways,
away from my spine. I elbowed him hard in the gut, reached
into my back pocket for the switchblade, flicked it open and
stabbed him in the thigh. He grunted, but this time the pick
went over the brass and got me deep enough to hit a rib on
my left side. I think it stuck in the bone, because I could feel

him pushing on my back with his other hand to pull it out. It released.

I dropped to my knees and had a vision of those smiling, voracious, unforgiving teeth and the ice pick aimed at my neck. I cocked the 45, pressed the muzzle against his foot and fired—didn't make that much noise above the banjos. Pieces of sidewalk whizzed by my head. Then I took off, sprinting through the crowd, around the mounted cops, through the pretzel and chestnut vendors, stuff flying all over the place. The bike was parked on the sidewalk on Juniper Street. I jumped on and headed up Ridge Avenue fast as I could, blowing red lights, passing into oncoming traffic, over the sidewalks to get around lines of cars. My side didn't hurt at all—stone terror will do that to you.

With tears in her eyes, Momma Francini gave me some pizza and wine in the kitchen, but I was too charged up to eat anything. Then she noticed the dark red drops on the linoleum. Centuries of blood, retribution, binding shattered men in hiding, took over. Her eyes dried up and my shirt came off, quickly, efficiently. Then came the basin of water, the rags, the cool, keen, evaluation of the wound. Now it hurt.

"Looks like it went right through the rib, broke it," she said, rather professionally, "but it's not so bad, not so bad, considering. At least it didn't come through your front." Iodine was invented by the devil, make no mistake. She bound me up with a ripped up old sheet. Felt better. "If there's no infection, no hospital could do any better. I'll pray for you, Jackie, so the blood stays clean." The old momma snapped back in place once I had my shirt on. "Here, have something to eat."

Sal was on the phone. I didn't dare go near my mother's house, even though I could see it out the window. He hung up. "Jack, this is really bad. My cousin sez you got set up becausea da bust in South Philly. This fed guy's really got it in for yez. He put it out on the street that you was his snitch. Mr. Castesi heard it, they cut some kinda deal, and he put out a contract on ya. That's why this Buttons guy tried to ice ya at the parade. He is one very bad man, and he don't give up. Far as anybody knows, he never missed before, and you wounded him. It's pride, reputation, revenge, now, even though he's a spic. Castesi's soldiers will be all over Philly lookin for ya.

"We gotta get you outta town. Vini will come down the lane with his truck like always at 5 in the morning. We'll get you out that way. Don't worry, I'll square everything with yer mom and yer friends downtown when I can. You won't be able to come back for a long, long time. Momma, go over to Theresa's and get Jack some clothes without blood. Come right back."

I had a grand in cash in my jeans. Too dangerous to go to the bank. Later, maybe, I'd send mom a letter so she could send me some money, wherever I ended up. Anyway, I had the Norton, and that was as good as cash—about four thousand, I figured.

Vini let me off on the road outside Vultch's place. It was very dark, very cold, after the warm-bread air inside the back of the truck. Nobody was around, not a headlight in sight. I hoped momma and Sal and Vini would be okay.

I wanted to go to Egypt and say goodbye to Sarah, but it would be way too chancy, and it might get the Logans in trouble. Christ, what about my uncles, my mother, granmom? I'd really done it this time. I called Uncle Joe and ran the situation down to him. "What a fuck up, Jack. You just got us all in a lot of trouble. Nice work. Castesi knows where we all live. I'll do my best to blame it all on you. Hope you don't mind. Castesi's a businessman, though, so it might not be too bad. The *Clann* won't like this much. You've jeopardized a relationship that goes back a long way, and we've got a lot of plans going that involve him. Do me a favor. Don't come back anytime soon."

Best to get out of the state, quick. With the lights off, I headed, slowly by the circular route, toward the Pennsylvania Turnpike. I sat, idling, on the side of the road, short of the on-ramp, checking out the situation. Just a few trucks went by, nobody else was up yet—maybe. "Right," I muttered, strangling the steering wheel, "time has come today." I switched on the headlights and drove very legally to the automated ticket gate. The sun was trying to come up and shine through the low black clouds. I could feel it; knew it. There were eyes on me.

Once I cleared the entrance gate, I opened the El Camino up, flashing by Willow Grove and Fort Washington at 90, heading for the Northeast Extension, New York State and the border. As I started the long climb toward Scranton and coal country, I was worried about the State Police, of course, but I was more worried about Buttons. Toot's 45 was under my seat; the open switchblade on the passenger seat was stuffed in the middle of a tied up bundle of orange shop rags. The gas gauge read half full, enough to get me to the HoJos plaza at Hickory Run. When I roared by the exits for Allentown and Bethlehem, I waved to Sarah, "I'll be back, princess, promise, one last time."

I blew through the Lehigh Tunnel all by myself, duals roaring, twin Holley four-barrel carbs sucking air with a moan, engine growling like a caged black panther. Unlike Vultch, I didn't see the light, no revelation was at hand.

The Norton was on its side in the back, handlebars off, resting on an old mattress, tied down tight, covered with a tarp, tonneau cover over it all. I pulled off at Hickory Run, south of Wilkes Barre, to gas up and get something to eat—parked way out the back, behind the big rigs—like maybe a famous Howard Johnson's hot dog. No, better yet, scrapple and eggs as a last meal. Afterwards, when I walked out of the can, I saw them at the counter, talking to my waitress. Mob soldiers—they always looked the same. I deked back in, jumped on a sink and dove out the back window just as the door banged open.

"God damn," I thought, "this is gonna be some run," as I screamed sideways down the ramp and back on the highway. When I felt my side under my jacket, the fingers came away bloody. It was a dull, dark day, and I couldn't see any cars or headlights behind me, but that didn't mean a thing. Then I saw them on the overpass near Bear Creek, two guys in matching parkas, marking me. Couldn't be sure, but it looked like Mike Devlin standing with them. The State Police had taken the day off, I figured.

I was flying around Scranton spread out in the valley down below when they caught up with me, probably sitting at the last on-ramp, waiting for the signal on the radio. It was a big, silver Cadillac that must have had a worked engine. They were about a hundred yards behind when the muzzle flashes started out the windows. "Can't hit shit with a handgun at that distance," I snorted. Then I thought about just one ricochet hitting a tire, or a rifle slug. My foot went all the way to the floor, and the big motor started walking away from the Caddy. The speedo needle was buried.

At Clarks Summit, the Northeast Extension ends with one of the wickedest right-hand turns around. Big signs say "25 MPH," and they mean it, maybe fifteen would be better. First time I went through it on my way to Mosport, I nearly lost it into the concrete divider. Good thing was, I knew it was there. Maybe they didn't.

I got as far outside the beginning of the turn as I could, nailed the brakes, downshifted to third and dumped the clutch. The Caddy started closing—fast. I dumped second gear, got to the apex and mashed the gas pedal, just as the Caddy hit the divider and flipped over on its roof, all broken glass and sparks. The guy in the collection booth took one look at me coming for him with the skidding Caddy close behind and dove under the counter. The wooden bar across the road didn't last long, and I screamed up Route 81 toward New York State. There was a ways to go yet, though, and I kept the hammer down, racing by the slag heaps of the old, forgotten coal towns, into the Endless Mountains near Lennoxville. I knew I had to get off the highway soon, but not yet.

I let out a whoosh of air as Great Bend came and went and the "Welcome to New York State" sign swept by. Got off the highway at Binghampton, went west toward Endwell, then headed north on 26.  Didn't know the road, but it didn't matter, long as I was going north all the time.  Did the speed limit. Cut back over Highway 81 and wound my way north and east, up to Chenango County, past Norwich, Kenwood, Durhamville, between Syracuse and Utica.  The traveling tapes were a good idea; kept me going—and half way sane.  So much death, so much running, so much bad luck.  It had to leave off soon.  I yelled along sometimes:

> *I rest my feet*
> *While the world's in heat,*
> *Blue collar.‡*

> *Take a load off Fannie,*
> *Take a load for free,*
> *Take the load off Fannie,*
> *And put the load right on me.†*

> *Goin up the country,*
> *Got to get away.*
> *Goin up the country,*

*Got to get away.*

*So much fussin and fightin, man,*
*You know I sure can't stay.*

*I'm goin, I'm goin,*
*Where the water tastes like wine.*
*I'm goin, I'm goin,*
*Where the water tastes like wine.*
*Jump in the water,*
*Stay drunk all the time.§*

I turned west, north of Oneida Lake, pretty country, clean, cold air over the ice, and stopped near Mexico, New York. It was time to hole up, but I didn't want to be too far from the highway if things got dicey. I was standing at the urinal in a gas station. On the wall, some freak had written: "Young farmer wanted for some fun. Into barn boots and Levis. Call 723-1640 for a date."

‡ *Blue Collar, single by Bachman Turner Overdrive, Mercury, 1973.*
†*The Weight, from "Music from Big Pink," Robbie Robertson and The Band, Columbia, 1969.* § *Going Up the Country, from "Living the Blues," by Canned Heat, Liberty, 1969.*

The motel was cheap and clean, run by a Dutch couple with thick accents. They weren't interested in me at all. I tried to rest, get my head together and plan the run through Watertown to the border. I stayed two days, keeping a careful eye on my side. I cleaned it up and bound it up. The bleeding stopped, outside at least, didn't know about internally, but there was no swelling and I felt okay, long as I didn't laugh.

Seemed to me that Moore would have it figured I was making for the border, and there feds did have a lot of pull. I'd have to be quick, smart and lucky to make it. Didn't want any trouble on the Canadian side, either. Their customs' guys seemed friendly, polite even, and didn't wear guns, but that might change if they knew the feds wanted me.

Then, again, how was Moore going to explain a Caddy full of damaged mafia gunsels at Clarks Summit? I started out at 5:30 AM. Didn't want to go in the middle of the night—too suspicious—so I timed it to make the border about 6:30-7:00. It was snowing hard, harder than I'd ever seen in Philly. "Just my luck," I thought with a frown. Then it dawned on me that it *was* lucky, very lucky indeed.

Around Theresa and Lafargeville, the rolling valleys in the middle of the state give way to flat farm country marked by gray sandstone along the road.  The plain leads right up to the St. Lawrence River, where the multicolored granite of the Canadian Shield starts.  North of Watertown, it's almost deserted, nothing much visible from the road, trees full of black-headed hawks looking cold, feathers plumped out, run down trailers, abandoned houses.  That's where the white-out started.  Couldn't see more than twenty feet in front of me.  Speed down to twenty miles an hour; rear wheels of the truck squirming around like they were on an oil slick.  Looking through the windshield was eerie, like driving in a flour sack, or maybe a tub of lard.  Suddenly, the snow seemed to coalesce into a long trailing shape, a figure in a white cape.  Then a face formed, fleeting, the eyeless skull, just before I almost drove right into the back of the tractor trailer.  Didn't even see the running lights until I cleared the plume of snow coming off its rear tires, then the draft made a still, clear bubble where I could see, but, I hoped, not be seen.  Stuck right in behind him, about ten feet off the bumper.  My hands were brazed to the steering wheel, eyes wide, nose open, legs out straight and aching.

The crossing at Thousand Islands is really two bridges.  The first is still on the US side, then you come down on

Wellesley Island for a little. The second crosses the border. I got over the first one okay, tucked in behind the rig in front of me, high over the frozen river on the pale green bridge. My mouth was very dry when I approached the second one, tasted like Saltines. The border is right in the middle of the center span. If I could get on, I could make it.

We were down to fifteen, the wind howling across the road. Dimly, like shadows, I could see two cars and five or six men on the left side of the road. They were covered with snow. Couldn't tell, but it was probably Moore who was hopping up and down, pointing in the direction of the first bridge. He didn't see me, but I waved, smiled and gave him the finger, just the same. Made me feel better as we started onto the bridge.

The snow cleared all at once. I let off the gas even more and looked down at the little islands in the frozen river. There were big, expensive looking summer places on some of them. I smiled a lot; my muscles released as if somebody snapped off a switch. Then, after a silent word with Toot, I threw the 45 out the window. It spun slowly, silver metal and ivory handles, out into the gray sky, hovered, and dropped away.

When the ice melted, the pistol would sink into oblivion. Toot's burial at sea.

On the far side of the river it wasn't snowing at all, very little on the ground. Didn't find out until years later that the river and Lake Ontario further west often stop storms south of the border. Right then, it seemed miraculous.

The customs' guy was young, blond, with a pony tail, no gun belt. "Morning," he said, "what's your citizenship." "Merricun," I replied. "Well, we all are, actually, considering this is North America. What state, please?" "Pennsy, er, Pennsylvania." I handed over my ID, and he took a squint. "Okay, what's the purpose of your visit to Canada, and how long will you be staying?"

That part I had worked out. "Well, see, there's this big motorcycle show in Toronto, and I want to show my Norton Manx there. Featherbed thumper; it's in the back. Want to find out about these new Ski-Doo things, too. I'm in the business, see, shop manager. Might stay two weeks or so. Maybe learn to ski," I said with a grin. He wasn't amused.

He pulled me over and rummaged around in the back of the El Camino for a while. I didn't mind one bit. "Nice bike," he said. "I've never even seen one of these, except in pictures. It's very well restored, isn't it." "Yep, absolutely like it was new," I said, "did it myself." "Well, don't even think about trying to sell it here, unless you get the proper papers. Have a good trip. Welcome to Canada. You really should get that smashed headlight fixed on the left front. It's a shame to not to repair such a nice vehicle. By the way, what punched the hole in the tailgate?"

I stopped in Kingston; it's a small university town right where the St. Lawrence and the lake meet. Found a restaurant for breakfast on the main drag, Princess Street; they didn't have whole wheat bread, only brown. Turned out to be the same thing. The thick, fried back bacon was new to me. Heading west, toward Toronto, through the rolling farm country, I sang to myself: "Till a sudden thought came to my mind that I should roam away/For I'm sick and tired of slavery since the day that I was born." Then I thought, "Nice spot, woulda been perfect for me and Sarah." My eyes cleared after I banged my forehead on the steering wheel a few times, her locket bouncing against my breastbone.

# 16. DARK AS A DUNGEON

The hiss of the black plastic air pipe was the only sound in the darkness.  Old Bill sat on a stack of shoring across from me, an unlit Number Seven hanging from his lips.  He nodded the miner's lamp on his yellow helmet to me as he twisted the handle of the small detonator.  There was a pause, then came the long, familiar, muffled kaarump from the working face of the raise, about a hundred and fifty feet above us.  We stood up quickly. "Okay, pard, let's go fuck the dog at the lift until 4:30," he said, "lessen you wanna breathe some a that refreshin powder smoke."  We grabbed our lunch boxes and clumped up the drift in our black, high-topped, steel-toed rubber boots, talking about the bonus we'd make for the week.  For Cariboo Mountain, the ground was pretty stable, the timber had been holding and the vein of silver we had been following was rich.  I was a long, long way from Philly, even Toronto.  Best of all, far too far away to be followed.  I had convinced myself of that.

After we'd gone about a hundred yards, Bill stopped, turned and looked back down the tunnel.  He grabbed my arm. Our lamps lit it up; toward us rolled a thick, white cloud of smoke, slowly, inevitably, like a churning tidal wave. Both of us clumped off just as fast as we could go; the lights on our hard hats making crazy patterns on the dripping drift walls and shiny, narrow-gauge train rails.

Five hundred yards more, and we both sank down on our knees, sweating and wheezing, in the wet rust-red muck underground. "Okay, pard," he said, "that awtta do'er, you think? Shouldn't come no futher." He started to laugh, yellow teeth in his grimy face. "Oh man, shit, that's about the funniest thing I ever seen. Musta put bout forty pound too much powder in that round. Ain't done that in years." He was a good miner and usually didn't make mistakes. The problem was always greed; more ore meant a bigger bonus; more ore required more dynamite. But how much was too much? In a way, we were a bad mix. Both of us thought a lot about money. The timber shoring was probably blown away, and we'd have to clear it before we began with the jack-leg drills once more. I just hoped the mill hole wasn't plugged again; you could die real quick in that 45 degree shaft.

When we got to the lift at the 600 level, the haywire boys were already there among the other guys: Waco, Tobacco Can, Fuckhead for Short, Red and Goose. Off by himself, as usual, was Pole, leaning against a wall of pure white quartz. Red and Goose had been drilling a stope; their faces were black and greasy with lead and zinc dust, eyes very white in the dirt, lower eyelids sagging, showing dark purple mucus membrane. Classic symptom: silver poisoning.

"Hey, Jack," Goose yelled, "goin to the dance tomorrow night, or what? Should be a good old time, eh?" "Yeh, what for?" I answered, "And who'im I gonna dance wit, you?" Tobacco Can stuck his fingers in his ears, always said my Philly accent gave him a headache. He'd see me heading toward our table in the beer parlor and say, "Here comes the Yank. Hold on to the glassware when he starts talkin, boys." I always gave it the classic Kensington try, just to piss him off. Old Bill looked at his watch and walked into the lift. We followed, and he pulled the signal wire for the long hoist up top.

Outside, it was dark, sort of, not like the ink underground that's darker than any dungeon I could imagine. With your helmet light off, you could touch your eyeball without seeing your finger coming. Outside, it was so cold your boot soles froze and cracked. After a while, so did the cloth of your overalls where your elbows bend. If you had to come out a lot from the dampness below, driving a battery powered lokey pulling ore cars to the crusher, overalls didn't last long. Neither did fingertips.

It was January, dead center in the twenty-four hour Arctic night, second winter I'd been in the Yukon. The moon hadn't risen in the sky for some time now. The air was so pure, so clear, so dry, the randomly scattered camp buildings, the enormous, craggy Ogilvie Mountains, the stunted little boreal spruce, and the frozen snake of the Chandindu River in the valley far below, looked like they'd been cut from cardboard and stuck there in some absent-minded kid's game.

Where heat escaped from the buildings, mushrooms of white ice fog hung in the still air. Anybody who says dry cold is better than damp cold is nuts and never been north of the sixtieth parallel. Fahrenheit or Celsius, fifty below reads the same and will kill you fast, wet or dry. Sixty below is only ten degrees different, but it's a lot worse. We were at the sixty-third parallel, just short of the Arctic Circle. Sixty below was average that crushing winter.

We fell into a ragged line making for the mine dry, a shower in the steaming, iron-hard water, some cleaner clothes and dinner at the cook shack. Most of the guys walked with their heads down. Our boots squeaked in the few inches of snow on the ground. Only snowed during a heat wave, like twenty below. Hadn't seen any for a month. The snow gets so cold, so dry, so packed, it turns to sapphire ice that's hard as diamond. You need a bull gang and a lot of torch-hardened, sharpened miner's picks to get rid of it.

Anybody who says starshine can't cast a shadow is nuts, too. It's that bright from the indigo-black bowl above: filling it, huge planets spinning red, topaz, yellow, emerald, monster cold stars twinkling fierce blue ice. An army of pale ghosts followed us along on the whiteness. I looked up just as the show started: way in the west, a long, rippling wave of silver Northern Lights began shimmering toward us from the Alaska border eighty miles away. Overhead, fingers of current shot out to fill the sky, turning to vivid orange, crackling like a shorted electric cable heard from a distance. The tide turned blue-green to the east and died. Then it started over from the northwest, purple this time. Mostly, nobody stopped to look. "In spring," I thought, "first time I see the rim of the sun over the mountains, I'm gone, no matter what."

Got to the camp by the roundabout route, via Toronto. Good thing, too. Toronto's small compared to Philly: compact, tight, ordered along the lake; streets in a grid— north-south, east-west, Manhattan turned sideways. Found the area in the West End like I had a compass in my head. Rented a dingy room in the Edgewater Hotel, but I figured that was too public. Maybe it was paranoia, maybe not. True enough, I was in another country, but the mob has a long arm. They were in Montreal, for sure, I knew. Wasn't certain about here. And what about Mike Devlin? I was strolling up Roncesvalles Avenue, buying fresh bread and dynamite kielbasa in the Ukrainian and Polish stores, doing the tourist number. The laughing ladies in aprons behind the counters didn't speak English very well. In one window a handwritten sign advertised a room and kitchen for rent. Well, really, it said, "Room and Chiken," but I got the idea. I wondered what sharing a room with a chicken might be like.

The house was further north, away from the shore of Lake Ontario, in the Junction, as they call it. It's blue collar, but it wasn't that run down then. A few rough edges, a few tough guys, junkies, but clean, swept up, cared about. You could only smell the meat packing plants when the wind was right. It was my kind of place. Even the rubbies were polite when they panhandled you. A lot of people I talked to called it the roughest place in the city. I snorted to myself at that one. The big, fat, smiling Ukrainian lady, Mrs. Lukowski, rented me the room on the third floor of her big brick house, and a garage out the back for the El Camino. Didn't use it. Too conspicuous: Pennsy plates, works motor, fancy paint and pinstriping. Took the trolley and the subway instead. Good system: cheap, fast and safe. I put the switchblade away in granpop's box.

One good thing about the Edgewater, though, it had a really nutty bar, with all kinds of weirdos doing their thing. I looked forward to the little old bag lady in the wig. On Fridays, she'd stop by for gin in a tattered, strapless blue chiffon evening gown under her greasy green parka. After about twenty shots, she'd stand on a table, pull up her skirt and flash the crowd, quickly, front and back, giggling. She wasn't into underwear. Everybody liked her.

The beer was cheap and powerful as hell, but the food would give you a fast trip to the can. Fell in with the regulars in the afternoons there. Friendly bunch, mostly, from all over the country, all over the world: Germany, Hungary, Croatia,

Portugal, Scotland, Russia, Northern Ireland and every Canadian province I could name, then. Not that many, really. Got into some nasty arguments—beer driven—with Orange- men from the Six Counties about who owned Ireland. The day I sat under the picture of the Queen and sang at the top of my lungs, "And we're off to Dublin in the green, in the green/Where the helmets glisten in the sun," I ended up in the parking lot taking on two guys. Seemed I liked it.

The guy who pulled me off them worked sometimes as a bull cook in mining camps, cleaning up the bunkhouses. Native, Dog Rib from the Yukon Territory, good guy. First Indian I ever knew. His name was Johnny Two Axe. He drank too much, but, then again, we all did. "That's fuckin stupid, Jack," he said. "Come on back inside and buy me a drink." He was right. It was stupid, useless. What if the cops showed up? I kept my mouth shut after that.

He was a strange, gnarled, dark little man with some kind of skin disease that made it fall off in chunks. He'd get up from his seat to hobble to the can, and there'd be a snowfall of it on the floor around his chair. He always wore a Cat Power baseball cap; mostly because he was bald and his angry red scalp was peeling. A long, limp, black ponytail streaked with gray and flecked with dead skin hung down his back. "I'm goin back to the camps, Jack, soon as the money runs out, eh? See my brother in Edmonton. Wanna come? Lotta money to be made on the rigs, in the mines. You're big enough and strong enough, I'd say. Work two years in a camp, you won't have to work for two, less you bet the nags like I do. Don't mean to get personal or anythin, but I think you got a lotta trouble chasin behind you, eh? Enahways, nobody, but nobody, gonna find you up north."

He was a comic, in a wicked sort of way. We hit it off immediately. He'd start two guys going at each other, then sit back, chuckling, and watch them argue each other blue. I asked him once whether he was born with a little stick in his hand. "Yep," he said, "You sound like my mother. Always said I was a born shit disturber."

Unless they were immigrants like me, Toronto people didn't have much of an accent I could hear, except some of them pronounced it, "Tranna." Mostly, it was very flat, like a CBC newscaster. Johnny's, though, was deep, forced from the back of his throat, halting, not fluid, harsh from the straight-end Export As he smoked non-stop.

He introduced me to Spadina Avenue. We'd hang out in the Silver Dollar sometimes. Downstairs, it's mostly a native bar, Indians on one side, Inuit on the other. They all call it "The Buck," but the Indians and the Eskimos didn't mix. Johnny told me it went a long way back, to disputes about hunting territory. Some tribes didn't mix, either. The Cree thought the Dog Rib were lower than coon shit. "Niggers of the north," they called them. The Mohawks didn't like the Cree: "Bush Indians, right outta the rat camps on the Mackenzie Delta."

Other times, we'd walk down to the El Mocambo, if a group like Ian and Sylvia, or Neil Young and Crazyhorse, was headlining. Or, we'd cross the street to Grossman's Tavern for blues. The music was really, really fine. Went to Kensington Market to buy fresh food. Seemed appropriate. Stayed out of Yorkville in midtown; too flower power time warp. It was like 1968 in Philly—only with a scrubbed face, no record, no guns, no needles.

Walked into a motorcycle shop on Dundas Street to find out how much I could get for the Norton. No sense letting it rot in the back of my truck, and money was running low. Once he saw it, the owner was interested, very interested, until I told him it had a Pennsylvania registration. "No way, buddy, the import duty would be way too high, the paperwork would be a hassle. And if I don't pay it, they'll take it away from me, and I'm out the money. Anyway, how'd you get it across the border? They'll ask, you know. Sorry, smells illegal, can't do it."

The outlaw clubhouse was further west on Dundas. "Quicksilver MC," they called themselves. I talked to the prez; his name was Gerald. He was polite, too, sort of. "This is crazy," I thought. I wanted four thousand for the bike. We haggled a lot. Finally, I took three and a half, because he'd have to pull a lot of strings to get legit Ontario papers. "Expenses," as he put it. We shook hands on the deal. He paid cash, US bucks. On the way out, I felt better, safer, somehow. What a bonehead.

I'd been in the Junction a while, head down. I had to find out what was going on in Philly, but how? Couldn't call; they'd tap it and find out where I was. Same reason I couldn't write. Mom must be going nuts. Granmom? What about Harry and Linda, Vultch? The brothers? I hadn't forgotten the number or the signal. "Warlock for Ramirez," I said into the phone, gave the number of Johnny's apartment and waited. The next day, me and Johnny were half way through the "twofer," Canadian for "case of beer," when the phone rang. Johnny answered, talked a bit with a surprised look on his face and handed me the phone. Hose was the same bebop, laid back beatnik I remembered and missed. My spit had a bitter taste. "Greetings, young wizard, what's happenin in the wilds of wherever it is you are currently? Didn't know there was a 416 area code on the planet." I looked over at Johnny with a frown. He understood. "Back in ten, Jack. Gotta get some chips. You want gravy on yours, or just salt and vinegar?" "Salt and vinegar, Johnny, and ask them to cook em crunchy. Nothin worse than soggy fries." Hadn't had a real hoagie or a cheese steak since I crossed the border. Nobody knew what they were; still don't.

Unlike the last time, I ran the whole thing down to him, all of it. Where I was, how I got there and why: Judith and Jimbo and Sarah and Charlie, Buttons and Moore, the mob and the Devlins. The words were flour and water in my throat; my tongue felt fat.

"Humm," he said, "I haven't had any heat for a long time now, so nobody's gazing in my direction from the East Coast. Did I tell you me and Chica did the dirty, man? We've been hitched two years. She still digs older men. Life is unfolding as it should. Seems to me I could make some discreet inquiries for you. Who's this Francini guy? Give me his phone number; Harry's and Vultch's, too. I'll get in touch through channels with your mother. We always got along. Once I have the situation scoped out, I'll get back to you. Is this number cool? And by the way, what kind of accent was that I heard? Interesting."

"Yeh, it's okay, Hose. I'll stay here until I hear from you. My buddy's a Dog Rib Indian from the Yukon Territory. Name's Johnny Two Axe."

"My, my, Jack. You always were the one for myths and legends, poetry and prose. Now you're into the gods of earth and forest. Far fucking out."

"Yeh, remind me to tell ya about the Jersey Devil sometime. Thanks, man, thanks a lot. I knew I could count on you. Catch ya later."

It took a week. About 9 on Thursday, Johnny was smoking a spliff on the sofa, and I was sitting on the floor, drinking a Molson Canadian, watching the Maple Leafs lose again. I was almost beginning to understand the game. When we first got to know each other, Johnny was puzzled when I turned dope down. "Bad karma, Johno, too many scary flashbacks, so I'm layin off." He shrugged and passed on it with that blank, stony look of swallowing the inevitable native people have.

Hose sounded out of breath. "Jack, bad scene, man, really bummed out. News travels fast. That Norton you sold in Toronto made a lotta noise. Whoever you sold it to sold it right back across the border. Not a smart move, too pure, too trademark. Pecker, your Jersey Devil compadre, tipped me on it. Says it's back in Philly and his dues are paid in full. He was scared to tell me any more.

"Sal says Buttons has got you marked; don't know how. You didn't tell me you stabbed *and* shot the guy. I trust it was necessary. He's probably on his way right now, so get outta town, far, far outta town, fast as you can. Your mom's fine, just worried sick about you. Says she's praying for you. Your downtown friends say to stay safe and wait. Vultch said to consult Revelations. What's that supposed to mean? When you come to ground, call me. Remember, if you hear hoofbeats in the air, duck your head. Take very, very good care of yourself, my man, and watch your back." He hung up.

Didn't like doing it. I'm not a thief, but I didn't have much choice. Way north of Toronto, in French River country, I stole black and white Ontario farm plates for the El Camino. Back to the old *Baltimore Catechism* and milk bottle thing again, like an itch you can't scratch. Johnny thought it was funny. We stuffed everything we needed into the truck the same night Hose called and headed for Edmonton. I made sure granpop's box stayed with me, behind my seat. "What's in there, eh?" Johnny asked. I started, but answered in a level voice: "Nothing worth anything to anybody but me. It's just the past." It spooked him badly, I think, because after that he gave the box a very wide berth, wouldn't come near it, let alone touch it. But he did keep a slanting eye on it, probably hoping it wouldn't open by itself and let Pandora's playpals fly out.

We swung around Georgian Bay, got to the top of Lake Huron and kept right on for Manitoba, through Espanola, Blind River, Iron Bridge. It was the coldest weather I'd ever felt.

Johnny thought that was funny, too: "You ain't seen nothin, yet." Didn't stop to rest until we got around Marathon, right on the water on the north shore of Lake Superior. They say it's the biggest fresh water lake in the world. Maybe it is. The country up there makes you feel tiny anyhow; it sweeps away from the shore, rocky and limitless, to the boggy lowlands of Hudson Bay. The lake did look like a frozen ocean. Closer to shore, the surf pounding on the stony beach kept the water open. The spray coated the pink and red granite boulders with slick, glistening, transparent ice. Coils of mist spiraled into the clear, pure air from the white ice far out.

In the morning, we started again. Wasn't speeding, just running level. Anyway, in the north people don't pay much attention to speed limits, 80 is okay for a spin, even the Ontario Provincial Police and Mounties seemed to think so. We got around Thunder Bay, through Dryden and Kenora in the Lake of the Woods. The spruce, jackpines and tamarack looked black, hunched down, blasted. Branches didn't grow on the north side. Johnny said they were spirits of the dead, centuries old. It was eerie. I put Janis Joplin, *Ball and Chain*, in the tape deck, pulled it out, put in Velvet Underground: Lou Reed and *Sweet Jane*. Pulled that one, too. Jethro Tull,

*Locomotive Breath*, was just crazy enough; "Somebody stole the handle. The train it won't stop goin, no it couldn't slow down."‡ Images of Ian Anderson hopping around on one foot, playing the flute. Finally, just the whistle of wind over the window seals. More running. I was very, very tired.

Manitoba looked like a frozen Ohio: flat, white, boring to drive through. We stayed over with some Metis breed guys Johnny knew in Winnipeg—drank a lot. The wind at Portage and Main almost tore the skin off my face. Saskatchewan was about the same, only it was colder, and the land started rolling close to the Alberta border. To keep awake, we talked about what it was like to be Irish, to be Indian. There were absolute, unbridgeable differences, but some scary similarities, too: tribal, drunken, robbed and angry about it. "Don't think you know it, Jack, but you've been in the home of the Orangemen. Shit, Toronto used to be run by the Orange Order. They'd think you're a Fenian." Didn't really know much about the border raids in the 1860s until he told me about the Philly boy, Luke Dillon, who tried to torch the Empire by blowing up the Welland Canal. Didn't work. Mental note: "Find out more."

‡*Jethro Tull. Album,* "*Aqualung,*" *1971, Reprise.*

He started it, and I responded, verse after verse. "Well, I don't care if it rains or freezes, long as I got my plastic Jesus, ridin on the dashboard of my car." "Well, I don't care come hell or calamity, long as I got that Blessed Family, ridin on the dashboard of my car." "Well, I don't care bout no big twister, long as I got that sainted Christopher, ridin on the dashboard of my car." "I don't care bout no big killer fog, long as I got that tiny Infant a Prague...." There are about a zillion of them; we quit after fifty.

We blew through Edmonton, too high profile, and stopped in a wrecked native village north of Calahoo on the Sturgeon River. Johnny's brother lived in a tiny green and white bungalow with his wife and three kids. He found us a cabin to use with a wood stove and an electric plate to cook on. Johnny introduced me to Indian steak—fried baloney. "Some people call it prison food," he said. We drank strong tea from the kettle at the back of the stove. The trees outside creaked, snapped, moaned like tormented spirits in the non-stop February wind.

Johnny was in his element. Very quickly, he found out that a mine north of Dawson City was hiring. Cariboo Mountain it was called. In two days, we could fly from Edmonton to

Whitehorse, catch another flight, and be in the camp in four. Johnny arranged to rent a shed to store the truck. I rubbed my chin on that one, but what else could I do? "It'll be okay, Jack, 'promise,' like you would say. My brother'll make sure nobody messes with it while we're gone." A lot of the native guys gave me the hostile hairy eyeball, but Johnny would say over a twofer, "You guys fuck right off. Jack's with me; that's all you need to know. Besides, he bought the beer." The women were harder to read. I called Hose and brought him up to date.

I found him, as usual on a Saturday morning, finishing up Friday night's poker game. His eyes were glassy, but he was still sharp as a tack. The ashtray in front of him was full of Export butts; two short roaches rested on the rim. The five other guys were boozy and out of it; two were missing fingers, I noticed. Johnny had quite the pile in front of him; the other players pretty little. I was terrible at cards; they bored me stiff, so I didn't sit in on any of the games. Besides, the pots were large, sometimes five grand a hand, tempers were short and everybody carried some kind of weapon, mostly well used, very sharp skinning knives in sheaths on their belts. Johnny said I could have made a lot more money at poker than underground, but I doubted it, not lucky. Instead, I shot eight ball for a buck a game in the beer parlor.

He looked up from his cards to me from under the brim of his Cat Power hat and tipped me a wink that said he was ready to call it quits. There was a snowfall of skin beside his hands on the green blanket they used for the table top. We both coughed with the first breath outside. "God damn, that's cold," I said to him. Then mentally, with a smile, "Gosh darn it all."

"You really serious about this dance thing, Jack? Don't know what the company's got in its head. Everybody knows there's always trouble. Me, I'm gonna play again tonight. Been on a roll. But enahways, mebbe I'll show for a bit— before the bottles start flyin. Right now, I'm gonna turn in."

When we got to the outer door of the bunkhouse, Waco and Tobacco Can stuck their heads around the corner of the building. "Psst, hey Jack, you hungry? Today's Pole's day. Come on. We can scoop all that stuff before the critters git it." Johnny just sniffed, stepped in and opened the inner door. The three of us walked between the bunkhouses and headed toward the dump. Tobacco Can was a Cree, just about the only native guy up there who would go underground. Mostly, they worked topside, in the crusher and the mill. It was some kind of superstitious thing, Johnny said. "Why you hang around with that cripple, Jack?" It was TC asking. "He's nothin but a dog fuckin, card shark Dog Rib, anyhow."

I gave him the best Kensington had to offer: "That, mah man, ain't none a yer fuckin bizness." He held his moosehide mittens over his toque covered ears. "Ouch. Okay, okay. Just don't say 'wudder' or 'cawfee' would ya?"

We skirted the dump. It was only a small clearing where the trucks unloaded; when there was enough of a pile, stuff would start sliding down the mountainside toward the valley floor far below. Not smart to get too close without firepower, even in winter. The Cinnamon Bears were hibernating— probably—but you never knew with all the heat in the build- ings and food from the dump. They were really big, really nasty grizzlies, and they loved mayonnaise. Any other time, there'd be stunted, barrel chested little caribou, heads not much more than belt high, rooting around, along with the foxes. The brown and red foxes were left alone for the most part; the blue Arctic foxes were shot quickly for their pelts. In the autumn, the native guys would take a caribou and have a feed, a party, really. Cooked outside over sapwood and broken up shipping pallets, the meat was the color of pork; tasted gamy, like deer, but better.

When we saw Pole in the little stand of spruce next to the shed, we ducked down behind the utility corridor. It was square, made out of wood, insulated, elevated about three feet above the ground, and it snaked all through the camp. Had to be elevated and insulated: in winter, water pipe running from the boiler house would freeze solid in no time; broken pipes would short electric and phone cables. In late fall, the frost would heave anything buried right out of the ground. In summer, when the permafrost melted a bit, stuff would sink out of sight in the muck and mosquitoes. That's why mostly there weren't any telephone poles, except on solid rock.

Pole had a bunch of paper grocery bags from the company store crumpled up around his feet. Arranged in a circle of snow before him was enough food for five guys, even five miners. In the center was a case of Old Style beer, brewed in British Columbia. He surveyed the feast, looked satisfied and started to amble back toward the bunkhouses.

Snickering, Waco watched him disappear into the star-
shine, many shadows following along. "Okay, boys, let's have
at er." We put all the stuff back in the bags: loaves of bread,
a cottage roll, bacon, a Sarah Lee cake, Red Rose tea, two
dozen eggs, butter, Kraft Dinner, orange juice. There was
even a head of freezing Iceberg lettuce that probably cost him
five bucks at the mine store. TC took charge of the twofer.
Just like always, we cut a few branches and swept our boot
marks away. Pole would be back to check if the little people
had come out of the trees to enjoy his gifts, his tribute, his
atonement. He was that bushed; hadn't left camp in ten
years.

We took the stuff, but not because we wanted it. There
were mountains of steaming food at the cook shack, much as
you could eat. Thing was, if his payment didn't disappear,
Pole would be dead certain sure they were coming for him.
He was a very large, very strong, usually gentle moron. Gone
haywire, anything might happen.

In the bunkhouse, over beer and fried egg sandwiches, I
thought back. "You become what you behold," Judith said.
And Sarah, "You just don't think far enough ahead." I
definitely had to leave—soon.

Johnny was right. It really was nuts to have dances once a month at Cariboo Mountain. Two hundred horny single drunks with cabin fever, plus about fifty married miners who lived far from the bunkhouses, on the valley floor, with their wives and daughters. It was worse than a powder keg; more like handling a case of CIL dynamite with a burning smoke in your mouth when you knew damn well the nitroglycerine was sweating right through the brown paper wrappers, like slippery silver beads of crazy mercury.

Johnny showed up about half way through; had had a few toots. The bunkhouse boys were standing on one side of the dance floor, leering at anything not male. Age didn't matter at all. Then Johnny got out his little stick and started on Tobacco Can. "Hey, TC, check out the little girl in the tight white sweater and the brown jeans. Nice bum, eh? Why don'tcha go ask her to dance? What are ya, chicken? Mebbe you don't fancy girls? Go ahead then, away you go then." If TC was sober, there'd be no way he would have crossed that floor. Besides, it was a Stompin Tom Connors song, not exactly dance music. The girl was sixteen at most, the daughter of the Steelworkers' Union steward, a big, burly guy with a handlebar moustache and arms like tree trunks. It wasn't long after he tapped her on the shoulder that TC got slugged hard enough to slide him back to our side of the floor.

Everybody was laughing except Fuckhead for Short. "Hey, TC, that Dog Rib prick set you up for that." TC went for Johnny with a yell. I got between them, pushed Tobacco Can down on the floor, picked up Johnny by his belt and made for the door. Suspended, Johnny started swinging at the air: "Come on, all a ya, fuckin Indian assholes. I ain't afraid a any a you pricks." In the morning, nobody would remember.

I was seriously out of touch with what was happening in Ireland. Didn't think it was  smart to subscribe to the *Irish Voice* from New York just yet, even if I used a phony name. The CIA and the FBI had long noses for lots of reasons. I tried, though, by watching the news from the Canadian Broadcasting Corporation, the only channel available in the North, very colonial, Commonwealth. Worse, there was just one television in the camp, at the "Drop-In Centre." I'd go by at noon on Saturdays, get a coffee and wait. You could start a fight, easy, if somebody wanted to watch hockey or football instead—reruns, mostly.

Got there early one day. Right in front of the screen, sitting on metal folding chairs, was a whole family of Inuit, in thick caribou hide winter clothes, just off the tundra. Weirdest thing I ever saw. They sat there, mesmerized, only moving to eat more orange Cheesies from a big bag. They were watching "Little House on the Prairie," hanging on every word. Couldn't figure out why. Tried to ask, but they didn't speak English. Didn't find out until much later. An Inuit guy who worked in the mill asked in Inuktitut and translated for me: "It's the trees, man. They think it's magic. They can't believe trees get that big. Or that the white man can make them grow in a box."

When the show was over, they stood up and walked out, their mukluks making not a sound on the plywood floor. I watched them through the window. The father started the snowmobile, mom climbed on behind, and the two kids jumped into the wooden dogsled hitched to the back. They took off, who knows for where. I had the place to myself.

Part of the news was a long clip from Belfast. The Falls Road looked like a war zone. Behind the droning English newscaster, British soldiers in helmets and flak jackets lobbed tear gas into the jeering crowd; they lobbed the smoking canisters back among the hail of paving stones and Molotov cocktails. Rubber bullets were fired. "The troubles are continuing here. There were more deaths this year than since the fighting started in 1971. Eight British soldiers have died here, many more civilians. Property damage is running into the millions. There seems to be no end, no solution in sight."

The show cut to Ian Paisley shouting from a podium: "Ulster is British. Ulster will remain British. Even if it means shedding the last drop of loyal Protestant blood." Nothing, nothing at all from Dublin, from the other side, let alone the IRA. It was a very different point of view than what I was used to. Either way, the whole thing was a crime.

The El Camino was back in shape after a tune up and new tires. The Alberta plates were borrowed from Johnny's brother, not exactly legal, but I'd take care of that somehow when I got there. When we blew across central Canada the last time, everything was frozen solid. Now it was sunlit June, turning luminescent green, soft and beautiful. On the prairies, fields stretched out so far it made your eyes hurt to look for the horizon. Lake Superior was gray-blue, choppy, immensely strong, completely pitiless, in the soft blue, horizontal northern light. Green and orange and silver-gray lichen covered the granite. It felt free, like the end of a long sentence or a dumb country western song.

It was just as I promised myself. When a sliver of sun showed over the Ogilvie Mountains, I settled up with the mine store, said my goodbyes to the haywire bunch over a drunken weekend in Dawson City and got my stuff together. Last guy I talked to before the Twin Otter was due in from Whitehorse was Old Bill.

"Thanks, Jack," he said. "You and me been good pardners, made lotsa good bonus money morena year runnin. You were strong as an ox when you got here. Figure now yer strong as a yoke of em. Hope everything works out and the trouble stops. Bout time for me to head back to Kamloops anyhow. Think I might try a little placer minin for gold up in the hills, just like my old man did when he was done with hard rock." We shook hands. He was a Chris Kringle fireplug of a guy about sixty. Even though he only had half a thumb and no little finger on his right hand, his grip equaled mine.

I carried granpop's box beside me during the flight. Inside now was a chunk of near pure silver crystal big as my fist. When I found it underground, it was a deep, deep purple under my miner's lamp. In the air and light topside, it quickly turned black and tarnished. Johnny took one look at the box and moved to an empty seat further back.

It wasn't much of a place, really, a large, peeling, two-storey 19th century clapboard farmhouse and a big, pretty sound barn, north of Kingston in Ontario's Sydenham Township, right in the heart of Loyalist country. Couldn't have been more British heritage. Both buildings needed work, but Johnny's hands were so crippled up he couldn't be much help. They were even worse than Sean Guaghan's right hand. Johnny could deal cards and push a broom, but he couldn't hold a hammer, so he concentrated on cooking, wearing silly yellow Playtex gloves. Five acres went with it. "I'll take it," I said to the agent, "but I want a break on the rent for repairs. And I want to know if it comes up for sale." Johnny thought I was nuts. Probably was, when I think back.

Right away, I called Hose. I kept in touch, month after month, when I was up north: in the starshine cobalt bright of winter or the twenty-four hour summer blue-air day, sun circling your head like a top. Both make you feel strange, sleepless. The ravens know this and don't shut up cursing you—ever. Christmas was the worst, or maybe the best, don't know; I dreamed deep, detailed images of Judith and Sarah. There was no contradiction, no disloyalty, in this.

Only one was bad, sort of. It only came once. We ran for our lives, holding hands in the dark of the dungeon: Sarah on my right, Judith on my left. In front of us, lit by flames, I could see the Customs' shed, my comrades kneeling in the muck. Behind us came the Jersey Devil wailing, the banshee keening, hoofbeats pounding. The flash in my hair burned like hot brass. Sarah yelled to me, "They're all the same; they're all the same." The women ran ahead of me. I stopped, turned to fight, but there was nothing but the dark of the mine. Judith and Sarah were gone when I turned back to the shed. The fire still burned; my comrades waited.

Hose didn't have much to report for the longest time. Buttons and his boys lost my trail in Marathon. They kept on west for a while, found nothing after Winnipeg and took off for

Philly.  I thought of him on crutches at Portage and Main:  a pointy boot on one foot, a big cast on the other, silk pants. Hoped he froze his balls off.  Jeeps was still missing.

The signal stayed the same.  I'd leave it, and he'd call back.  Never knew from where.  This time it was Chica: "Jack, you handsome devil, glad to hear you're back in the land of the living.  You still aren't married, are you?  You should try it; good for the soul. Hose isn't around just now.  He's back east sniffing around in the city of brotherly gunfire.  I think you'll be getting some good news soon, but don't get your hopes up too high until you hear from him, kay?  Hey, remember the old days in the Big Apple? Sure was a hoot.  You and Rene, me and Hose, Wheels and his old lady, Van Ronk, the high-heeled boys across the street.  Remember?"

I did, indeed I did.

The roof of the farmhouse had about ten layers of shingles on it and leaked like a sieve.  I bought a ladder, carpentry tools and bundles of shingles from the farm Co-Op.  Early one Saturday morning, I was kneeling on the roof hammering away when I heard the ladder rattle.  I spun around and sat down on the steep slope.  The hammer and the shingle knife were the only weapons I had.  A John Deere hat showed above the eaves, followed by the lined, sunburned face of a guy about fifty-five. "G'day," he said in his farmer's twang, "how are ya now?"  When he climbed on the roof, I could see he was wearing overalls, a leather nail pouch and steel-toed Greb Kodiak boots.  He was followed by his spitting image, only the son was about thirty.  Together, they said, "Got any nails?"

Bradley was their name.  They lived close by; their fields bordered my house.  From the roof, I could see it through the maples: the dove gray, squared limestone farmhouse, the green and white barn, the silos, the white fences.  There was a tall blond woman near the barn playing fetch with a dog. Somehow the light seemed to gather, intensify, around her. I shook it off as a trick of early northern sunshine. No dope to blame for years.

The place wasn't as old or grand or large as Logan Farm, but that didn't stop me from wincing.  The Bradleys were dairy farmers.  Except for hay and silage, there wasn't enough topsoil on the Canadian Shield for much else.  The farm had been in the family since 1820.

The men didn't say a whole lot more, just worked away like a couple of beavers.  Around noon, Johnny put together some sandwiches and beer for us. I brought the stuff up, and we ate on the roof. They chewed silently, slowly, looking out over their fields with a soft pride in the lines around their weathered eyes. The father said to the son: "Never seen it from here. Pretty good, eh?" "Yes, pretty good, pretty good," from the son. The father asked me: "You mind if we come up here sometimes to look?" "Nope, anytime, anytime at all. I'll leave the ladder by the side of the house for you."

About four, the roof was finished, and we climbed down. Johnny brought us cold Labatts, and we stood around on the porch drinking in the slanting light that would last until ten. They didn't talk to him at all; instead, they cocked their heads and watched him. He sat on the railing, apart from us, studying the label on his bottle. It was awkward. Didn't know what to say. Should I offer to pay them? The son, Luke, went inside to get more beer. Country people are pretty casual about stuff like that. When he came back, he said, "Hey, mister, that's an awful lot of serious lookin tools you got in there. You a mechanic, maybe, eh?"

"Well, yeh, I am. Mostly motorcycles, but I'm good with just about any kinda engine. Prefer four-stroke, but two-stroke's okay, too. Been at it a long time." The father, Chris, took the cue. "Well now, isn't that lucky. I got this gasoline tractor over the barn that just won't fix. I take it to the dealer, but those guys mostly work on diesels. He charges me a bundle, and it still doesn't run right. Maybe you could have a look sometime, Jack, ah?" "Kavanagh," I said, "Jack Kavanagh. I'd be glad to, anytime." He cocked his head at me while we shook hands. "Irish?" "Yep, green as green," I said. "Whoops," I thought, "probably Orangemen," but both of them kept on smiling, their faces open, expectant, friendly.

I was standing at the bench I was building in the barn, with my back to the large square of brilliant sunshine from the wide door. Hadn't contacted Bombardier yet, or Triumph. It was still too risky, but that didn't mean I couldn't start setting up the shop, or take in engine work. I could always buy parts in Kingston or Toronto, just like any Joe off the street. Money wasn't a problem after Cariboo Mountain. Too chancy to send any to my mother, but she had control of the Philly bank account anyway. Still had to sort out the Irish news supply. Kingston was out. The town was so monarchist British it

positively squeaked; the Orange Lodge was very active.
Maybe Toronto?  Probably not.

The framework for the bench was getting there.  I had a
guy in Kingston making up a steel top for it.  Sawhorses, four
by fours, the saw, the square, the smell of cut spruce, brought
granpop back to me.  The last song on the tape suited my
mood just fine as I lit the torch to braze the bar stock cross
braces. The blue point of flame through the dark goggles
flashed me back to my father at Eddystone:

> *And I followed her to the station*
> *with my suitcase in my hand.*
> *And I followed her to the station*
> *with my suitcase in my hand.*
>
> *Well, it's hard to tell, it's hard to tell*
> *when all your love's in vain.*
> *All my love's in vain.*
>
> *When the train, it left the station*
> *with two lights on behind.*

*When the train it left the station*
*with two lights on behind.*

*Well, the blue light was my blues*
*and the red light was my mind.*
*All my love's in vain.‡*

The first side ended; the second began. I didn't sense any threat—it was a very different feeling, like being out in a warm mist—but I knew there were eyes on my back—close. They certainly weren't Johnny's; he was in the city taking care of business at Woodbine Race Track. Besides, he was much too smart to come up behind me silently. I turned off the torch, pushed the goggles up on my forehead, held up my hand without turning and did my Hose number: "You lookin for somethin, mebbe, pilgrim? Or are you just gonna stand there?" There was a sharp intake of breath and an "I ah" over the hiss of the tape leader. Van Ronk started into *Black Mountain Blues*:

‡Robert Johnson, *Love in Vain*, ©1990, King of Spades Music.

"I say on Black Mountain, well, a child will spit in your face./
All the babies cry for whiskey, all the birds sing bass."

I turned around slowly.  Framed in the open barn door was
the sunlight woman from the Bradley barnyard. She was in
her late twenties, five nine, 120.  Her kinky, curly,
Uncontrollable hair was the color of ripe wheat with
strawberry highlights.  It was pulled back tight as it would go
and exploded in a big bush of a pony tail at the back of her
head.  She wore a checked cowboy shirt with pearl buttons,
straining in the middle, skin tight Wrangler jeans and tan
western boots; the origin of hourglass.  How she got into
those clothes without doing herself an injury was a mystery to
me. Her face was blushing red to the roots of her hair.  When
it subsided, I could see how healthy, how radiant, her oval
face and small chin looked in the halo of light from outside.
The skin was perfectly smooth, lightly tanned, almost
translucent, without line or scar. A band of small brown
freckles ran from one cheek to the other over her small,
straight nose.  It might seem strange, but she reminded me of
a newborn calf. Her eyes were green, like mine.

*I'm going back to Black Mountain, me and my razor
and my gun,
I'm going back to Black Mountain, me and my razor
and my gun,
I'm gonna cut her if she stands, shoot her if she
runs.‡*

"Well, I guess so," she said with a raised reddish eyebrow. "Luke sure was right; he said you listened to really weird music."

"You'd like Guess Who and *American Woman* better, I guess?"

"Not really, I like country, Loretta Lynn, but Carly Simon's okay."

"Not in my line, lady, but if you'll hang on a second, I'll go get a bottle of whiskey, jump in the truck, turn on the CB, put the pedal to the metal and run over a good old houn dawg or two for y'all, before I shoot myself about momma." I turned off the tape. "Waylon Jennings for president, that's what I say."

‡*Black Mountain Blues, from "dave van ronk sings ballads, blues & a spiritual," Copyright* ©*1959, Folkways Records.*

"Ha, ha. Very funny, I'm sure. In this country, it's prime minister, by the way."

I bowed deeply in apology to the national honor. "Okay, okay, how about Judy Collins for PM, then?"

Without a break for breath, she said: "Humpf, dad says you're supposed to come over for dinner, mom's making chicken, Luke says to pick up some Old Vienna, we're out, what with the milking equipment down again, they don't have time to go to the beer store, mom's cooking, I'm busy."

"Hey, hey, slow down, freckles. You gotta name?"

"I do, and it's not freckles, thanks very much," she said with a grimace, a stamp of her small boot and a flash of anger in her eyes. "I'm Annie Bradley. Dinner's at six. Don't be late." She turned on her heel and bounced out. "Not the friendly type," I thought, scratching my head, and headed for the house and the shower.

# 17. Black Jack's

"You sitting down, Jack?" It was August, and he was calling out of the blue. "Hey, Hose, where you been all this time?"

"Down in easterly climes, Jack, doing the Sergeant Friday thing: 'Just the facts, mam, just the facts.' Get ready for it. First really solid news I've found. Everything turned sour for Buttons after he missed the hit and couldn't finish it off. Behind his back, his nickname was "Two Toes." Anyway, he got way too big for his boots and tried to muscle some territory. Somebody wired a bomb under the seat of his Caddy and blew him into messy little pieces. They had to pick him up in a bucket. Seems right, doesn't it?

"Very tricky to get all the details without sticking my head up too much, but there's some kind of very bloody turf war going on in Philly. A humongous dime dropped on Castesi. He went down hard: life for murder, drug trafficking, the whole schmear. Somebody wanted him out of the way—big time. His family's in ruins. Your nemesis, Agent Moore, got shipped out to Nicaragua. Seems the agency has a beef with him over something. Nobody's heard from him for more than six months, and the drug enforcement people want him bad. Like I told you, your good friend Jeeps disappeared after the warehouse ruckus. He hasn't turned up yet. Word on the street is he's wearing cement shoes in the Delaware. Looks like you're in the clear, but I wouldn't go back for a while, even for a quick visit. Let it cool, man, let it cool down. Phone calls should be okay, but don't write yet. You never know.

"Oh, yeah, one more thing. Ran into Pecker. He says for me to tell you you've still got a very bad angel on your shoulder. Know what that's about?"

"That? Right, I know what that means. I'll fix it. Everything you've done, what can I say? Can't say I owe you, cause you wouldn't buy it. I just hope, some day, I can do as much for you."

"Yipes, Jack, don't wish me into a cauldron of turmoil like you've been in just so you can pull me out. No thanks. Rub your forelock, warlock, and take the thought back. Tell you what, though, we haven't been out of the state together in eons. Next summer, we're coming for a visit. You can kill the fatted calf and lay on the suds. Deal? I'll even get the Shadow out of storage for the trip. It'll be just like old times."

I really hoped it wouldn't be *just* like old times; like new times would be better. There were tears in my eyes when I croaked out, "Yeh, that's solid, that's a solid deal. Plan for July or August, when the light's really fine."

Dropped everything and got on the phone. Didn't have the guts to call my mother just yet. "Hey, Vultch, what's happenin, snake oil?"

"May the Lord be praised. You made it, son of thunder. Where the hell are you? Been talkin to your western mentor over the last while. He, I think, helped in parting the waters by eating honey and locusts. When you cummin back? You need further instruction. I still have the KR at my place, waitin for you to take up where you left off on the path to salvation and the moral pushrod Harley Davidson."

"I'm up north—Ontario. Don't want to be too clear on that right now. Glad to hear you haven't changed a bit. Howsomever, I'm settin up my own shop. Lookin for a job? It's pretty quiet here, man, just like I always hoped. No tail, no hassles, no more runnin. All I gotta do is get my papers sorted out."

"Unfortunately, young acolyte, I am seriously engaged in the work of the Lord. Got my own tent, the whole thing. It's a very cool way to reach the unknowing and make some coin at the same time. Can't desert the flock, know what I'm sayin? But, that don't mean we can't visit sometime. Hear them Canadians are all Protestants. Righteous."

"Yeh, you're right on, there, Vultch. Check it out. My western friend and his old lady are cummin next July or August. How's that?"

"Sounds perfect. My wife will bake a cake, and we'll bring the Jell-O."

"Yeh, thought so," I said with a laugh. "Just come. I'll keep in touch."

Took a while to get hold of Harry and Linda Stevenson. They were back in Vermont. "It can't be you," she said. "We thought you were dead until we talked to your friend in the desert. Are you okay, you crazy person?"

I ran it down to her, including the papers snafu. She promised to talk to her father and find out about immigration stuff. My record would be a problem, so she said she'd work on getting it wiped. "Can be done," she said. Then Harry got on the phone, out of breath and excited: "You son of a bitch, don't ever, ever, put us through this again. God damn, it's good to hear your voice. I really missed that Kensington, punch you in the face accent."

I went over it again, in more detail. "Hmm," he said, "Ontario in July or August. You got a date. The partners idea? Well, Linda and I will talk about it. It's a big step. Hear the winters are softer there than in Vermont. True?"

"Depends a lot on how far north you go. But down here, yeh. I'll tell ya all about that when you two get here. It's a new day, Harry."

"Great. You deserve it if anyone does. You can meet our second son. His name's Jack. We dress him in black on special occasions. Drives my mother-in-law crazy."

Johnny was out the back, stoking up the barbecue. The Bradleys were really good about helping us out. They kept a few beef cattle, pigs and chickens for their own use. Luke would bring over a pile of hamburger, steaks, chickens, bacon, whatever. Chris wouldn't take any money, but, then again, during the summer I'd been looking after the tractors and the baler and a lot of the other machines that are always broken on a farm. Johnny liked taking care of their pigs and chickens. He'd just hobble over and do it, then walk away. I thought it was a good trade and told him so.

He sniffed and said, "Ever tell you the one about the white guy who forgot to get his wife an anniversary present until the last minute?"

"Nope."

"Well, he dove to a liquor store and bought her a giant bottle of Crown Royal in the fancy blue bag. On his way home, he picked up an old Ojibway hitchhiker. The native guy kept lookin down at the bag as they drove. The white guy thought he better put a stop to it, so he said, 'Sorry, Chief, can't share that with you. Got it for my wife.'

"The native guy thought about it for a long time. Finally, he turned to the white man and said, 'You got that big bottle for your wife?' The driver nodded, and the Ojibway said, 'Good trade.'"

"Okay, okay, put the stick away, Johnny. Let's get the burgers on. I could eat a horse."

I sat in the living room after dinner, sucking on a beer and a Rothmans. Couldn't find Camels anywhere, except the city, so I started on them in the Yukon. Didn't smell right, burned slow, but I was getting used to them. "Now," I wondered, "how'm I gonna do this?" I shrugged and dialed Manayunk; not prepared, but no use waiting any longer.

I thought she was going to pass out on the other end of the line. In the background, a hockey game was on the television. "Jackie, thank God you're safe. I've said novena after novena for you. Are you in one piece? Where are you? When are you coming home?"

"Can't do that just yet, mom. I'm in Canada. Got some stuff to sort out. Nothin illegal, nothin a little time won't fix. I'm very, very clean. None a that trouble was my fault. You gotta believe I didn't do anything wrong. How's granmom and Sal and momma, huh? What about Mark—and Matt?" There was a long silence.

Outside, I could see Annie walking along the fenceline with her dog; he was a slobby, muddy mutt named Goof. It was almost dark, but the light still seemed to gather around her, like a personal flashlight.

Mom was pretty stiff. "I had many talks with your old friend from Rising Sun. I'd really like to believe you. Sal and momma are just like always. They miss you. Momma's just started to smile again. Granmom? Of course, you couldn't know. She passed away in May in the home. She just gave up, I think. The nuns were really great. We buried her next to your father and his father. Matt said the funeral mass, and

Mark came from Fort Bragg with his wife and kids. She gave everything she had to the Little Sisters of the Poor in Africa. That was wonderful. I'm sure she's smiling down at us right now. I have a few of her personal things put away for you."

The gorge rose in my throat; my left fist doubled and the knuckles of my right turned white on the phone. "Yeh, no doubt the nuns were mighty fine." I thought, but didn't say, "Takin a little blind old lady to the cleaners for the few bucks she had." Aloud, I said, "I'm very, very sorry I wasn't there. She was my favorite; very important to me. I'll miss her badly." That's all I could say just then about granmom and stay sane. I took a deep breath to steady my voice. "How about the brothers? What's up with them." My voice sounded tired. There was another silence. Annie was far off on a rise, looking toward me.

"Mark is doing great. He seems to get promotion after promotion out there. He's been helping out a lot with money since you went away. I still have all yours, haven't touched a penny. He said it was your responsibility for much too long."

"You didn't have to do that, but okay. We'll sort it out once I get a chance to come down for a visit. I'm stayin here. Had it with Philly. You can come to me, though, anytime you like."

"Leave here? No, I couldn't ever do that. They're all here."

"Who's here?"

"The graves. Holy Cross."

"Right. Of course. Wasn't thinking. Anyway, at least you could visit sometime. You haven't told me about Matt." There was another, longer, pause. Annie had disappeared.

"Well, ah, Matt's been having a few problems. Overwork, his psychiatrist says. They gave him a leave of absence from Fordham, and he's been staying at a seminary up near the Delaware Water Gap since Sophia's funeral. At the grave is where it all seemed to start. He'll be fine. He even asked after you, but I didn't know what to tell him."

"Right, mom, that's a shame. Tell you what, I'll get back to you when I know more about my plans. See you soon."

September ended, October began. The corn was over. Too bad. The hay was in the Bradley barn for the winter. The interior of the shop was almost finished. I really went at it once I bought the place: poured concrete floor, drywall, peg board, lights, ventilation fans, paint booth, the whole deal.

Johnny helped out as much as he could; so did Chris and Luke, when they had time. Looked like I could go back to Philly and get the rest of my tools, the stereo, the bikes; see mom, the Francinis, Vultch.

Did the sign myself on a sheet of steel, even though I didn't have the franchises yet: "Black Jack's♠Triumph♣Ski-Doo." It was a confidence thing. Didn't hang it yet, though. The temporary plywood one outside said: "Sydenham MC Repair." Bought a Ski-Doo and the manuals. Watched my hands take over. Took it apart and put it back together a few times to get the hang of the two-stroke engine, the track, the tensioners, the idlers. Different, but not too complicated. The kids from Queen's University heard about me and started coming in for tune ups. They were polite, well spoken, no accents. It was a slow start, but that was alright. I had a shop, and it was mine. In my mind, I blessed Judith again and again.

The hydraulic system in the Bradley's front-end loader was possessed by a really mean troll who had no intention of getting out. I'd pull the hoses, replace the seals, fill it up and start it up. In about two seconds, there'd be hydraulic fluid all over everything, including me. I was in their barn, underneath it on my back on a creepy. "Goddamn thing never works," I muttered, rolled on my side, and reached for the ratchet and sockets again, when I saw her small boots. I really wanted to see her, so I slid out from under the loader too quickly and really creamed my head on the heavy frame. Too many MC spills, I guess. I saw stars and almost blacked out. My stomach was churning. At first, Annie laughed, but then she took a good look at my face and put her hand over her mouth.

"Oh, sorry, Jack, are you okay? You really aren't, are you? I didn't mean to laugh. You do look funny, though. You're supposed to put the fluid *in* the loader, *not* in your hair and on your face. Here, hold on a second." She walked over to the work bench along the far wall, rummaged around in the jumble and pulled out a rag. Holding it up to the light from the barn door, she looked it over, dropped it on the floor in disgust and pulled a blue bandanna from her back pocket.

She walked back to me, smiling. The light was behind her; the Indian Summer wind coming in the door blew her shining pony tail around. Now she looked like a young colt, all eyes, skin, innocence and energy. The air smelled fresh, clean, like dry hay and fallen leaves. When she knelt down next to me, she smelled the same, but warm, vital, feminine. The perfume was overpowering. She put her left hand on my shoulder while she wiped my face and hair with the other. There was blood on the bandanna from where I cracked my head. "Sorry bout that," I said. "I'll buy you a new one."

"Uh huh," she said, absorbed, looking down at my forehead. The skin of her neck was smooth as pearl, same color. There were small, fine freckles below the hollow of her throat. She never wore bras or buttoned up her shirts very high. The skin between her breasts was so pure, almost translucent, it made my head spin even more.

She must have looked down at my eyes, because I saw the blush rise from her chest right up her neck. I looked up into her green eyes; they were flashing, sparky. "You, you, don't you...," she whispered, leaning toward me, hand squeezing my shoulder, eyes on my mouth. I shook my head to clear it. Our lips were very close together. "It's okay, Annie. I just shouldn't bang my head anymore. Did it too many times." I put my hand on her shoulder. "Help me up, wouldya? I gotta get outside." She put her arm around my waist and helped me to the barn door. We stood there, looking out over the falling, fading crimson maple blaze, the stubble in the fields, the rattling cow corn drying brown in sun and wind.

I reached over and pulled her head down on my chest. "I can't Annie. Something bad will happen to you for sure." I kissed her hair. She pushed away from me, head down. "I'm a lot stronger than you give me credit for. Besides, who says I'm interested?" she said, and took off for the house.

I was in the living room, looking out through the wavy glass of the old, six over six  pane windows, thinking, making plans, dreaming, remembering, counting the losses, the sins of omission, commission, fighting the pain. Behind me, I felt she was there again. More than once, I told her not to come up behind me like that, but she seemed to think it was fun, like spooking the cats in the barn. I put up my hand without turning again. "Hi," she said, "what's in this thing, anyway. It's locked." I spun around. Annie was standing in front of the bookshelf that held my *Cycle World* magazines, Irish books, Yukon sanity novels. She had her hands on granpop's box.

"Get the hell away from that right now," I growled, low, level and angry. "That's none a yer bizness, now or ever. Don't ever, ever, touch it again." Johnny stuck his dark face out from the kitchen, looked from her to the box to me, gulped and disappeared.

She jumped away. "Well, now, Mr. Black Jack. I'm very sorry, I'm sure. I didn't know you had so many dark secrets. What's so precious about an old box, anyway? Maybe you have a bunch of secret IRA papers in there."

"Don't be silly. Decided against that long ago. Being free is one thing, firebombing people with napalm when they're sitting in a restaurant is another. Like I said, it's none a yer affair. Let it be. Sorry I got mad."

"Oh, really?" she said with a sneer. "You don't look it. All I did was to come over to tell you dinner's at six—roast beef. Didn't want to, but dad made me. Oh yes, he says Johnny can come too, this time. I'm sure I don't give a damn what you do. Him, either."

She didn't look at me during the meal, just stared at her full plate. Johnny slid his eyes quickly from me to her and said nothing. He knew better than to stir this one up. I think her mother understood what was going on. All Luke said, mouth full, was, "Hey, sis, what's wrong with you? Sick?" Afterwards, I went out on the porch to find her. She was sitting on an oak press-back chair, wearing a thick, gray, man's cardigan against the chill. On the back was a knitted pattern of a maple leaf and crossed hockey sticks with a puck between the blades. She was looking out over the fields, back straight, strong farm-girl hands balled into fists in her lap. "Hey, lookit, Annie. I'm sorry, kay? You surprised me, that's all. My grandfather made me that box a long time ago. It's very important to me, very private. He, not me, was tied up with the Brotherhood and the *Clann*. He had his reasons. I've had a world of trouble in my time, and I get jumpy when people get behind me. How about it? Truce?" I held out my hand.

She looked at it, then up at me. Tears brimmed in her green eyes, and she was shaking. She shot out of the chair and stomped off toward the barn.

Johnny was in Deseronto, down the line toward Toronto. He didn't say much, but I thought he had a girlfriend there. I worked on him a lot, and he finally agreed to go to a skin specialist. The doctor gave him some ointment and told him to lay off the rye. At least he got as far as using the stuff. For a while, he looked like a greased pig, but his skin was getting a lot better.

I phoned Harry and Linda regularly. Seemed like everything was okay, so finally I gave them my number. She called one evening in late November. "Jack, tell me something? Now that you're settled, when the hell are you going to get married?" She was smiling, I could tell. "Not any time soon, I'm thinkin. Not a lotta opportunities out here in the boondocks. Maybe I'll put an ad in the paper: 'Big guy wants submissive, obedient, angelic young bride.' You didn't call to ask me that, anyway. What's up?"

"Very good news is what's up. My father talked to a few people in Washington and Harrisburg. As of today, you, you certifiable lunatic, have no record at all. You're free to go get started on your immigration papers. You're sure, are you, you want to go through with this?"

"Oh, yes indeed. Indeed I am. Except for you guys and Vultch, my mother and brothers, the Francinis, Hose and Chica, there's nothing left for me there, except a lot of hassle and too many bad memories. Here, at least, I don't feel trapped anymore, just foreign."

"Okay, then. Dad said all you have to do is cross the border again, turn around and come back. You apply for residency right there. Just be careful to explain you own property in Ontario, how much money you have and that you plan to open a business. Bring proof. But don't tell them how long you've been in the country. They want immigrants who work, so it should be easy. "

And it was. Chris Bradley was in on it. After he got over being surprised about my story, he thought it sounded like fun. We put his farm plates on the El Camino and got over the Thousand Islands bridges in about an hour. It was a windy, damp day, and there was a big knot in my throat when we pulled up to US Customs. The cop looked like a shave-head former Marine: lots of creases in his shirt, big automatic on his hip. "Where you two guys from?" "Tranna," I said. Chris said, "Kingston." "Both Canadians?" "Yep," Chris answered for both of us. "We're going down to Syracuse to look at some farm equipment for a day or two." "Okay," the cop said, bored, "take off."

We stopped on Wellesley Island for a few hours; pulled off into a rest area and ate the lunch Johnny made. My ears were drumming. Chris was curious. "Tell me something,

Jack. I don't want to pry or anything, but why are you doing this?"

I chewed on the sandwich for a long time, thinking. Didn't swallow, turned to mush in my mouth. Washed it down with coffee from the Thermos. There wasn't a simple answer. "Well," I said, finally, "I guess everybody is lookin for peace, you think? On this side, I'll never find any. I know it as sure as I'm sittin here. Up there," I nodded north, "I think it's possible, not certain, but possible." The Pennsy plate was still hidden under the rug behind the seats. I put it on and slid the farm plates in where it had been.

The guy at Canada Customs looked exactly like the first one: young, pony tail, no gun. "Nice truck. So, you want to stay with us, do you? Who's your sponsor?" "I am," said Chris. I filled out the forms and listed all the stuff I wanted to bring in from down south. The El Camino was officially legit for the first time in a long time.

I dropped Chris off in front of the farmhouse. Me and Johnny planned a big spread over at our place later to celebrate. Besides, it was my birthday. Annie was looking out the window at me. I smiled broadly and waved, excited.

She turned away and didn't show up for dinner. With a grin, Luke said she had a headache.

"Mark, for Christ's sake, I can't believe it. How'd you get this number? Mom?"

"No, I've gotten a bunch of calls from a guy you know. He sounds like Jack Kerouac. What sort of name is Hose, anyway? Last time he called, he gave it to me, said 'the heat is definitely off.' At first, he wanted my help in getting some government information. He convinced me it was important for your safety, so I did it. Took the circular route, around official channels. Didn't get a lot, but he said it helped. 'Another piece in the cosmic puzzle,' he called it. Peculiar guy. Then again, you always did hook up with some weird people. How the hell are you, anyway, you big lug?"

"Mark, right now, I couldn't be better. I'm openin my own shop up here, with franchises from Triumph and Ski-Doo, they make these snowmobile things. They're startin to get real popular with farmers and hunters. I bought a big old house and some land in the country. How many kids you got now, ten?"

He laughed. "No, just four. You have to meet my wife, Sylvia, she's a peach from Louisiana. Accent like molasses and just as slow. We haven't seen each other in how long? Only about a dozen times since dad's funeral, right?"

"Yeh, I guess. It's great to hear your voice again. What are you doin next July or August, huh? How about a vacation in foreign climes. Whaddya say? There's lottsa room in this old house. It's still a bit rickety, but I'm gonna fix up the bedrooms this winter and put in another bathroom."

"Whoa, slow down. Tell you what, I'll think about it, talk to Sylvia about it. How's the fishin up there?" I didn't have a clue. "Don't know, but I can sure find out."

His tone changed, lowered. "Jack, what do you hear about Matt from mom?"

"Nothin much. She says he's in a seminary up on the Delaware. Had a few problems with overwork, so he took some time off from Fordham."

"I'm sorry to say, Jack, it's a lot worse than that. He's in Pennsylvania Hospital in Philly right now. Shrinks always piss me off. Seems to me they have no idea what's going on in the real world. Anyway, they say he has severe problems with unresolved anger, whatever the hell that's supposed to mean. They say he's manic-depressive and can't keep in touch with reality, as if they knew how. There's nothing we can do about it, but I thought you should know."

"Thanks for tellin me, Mark. We never did get along, but I don't want to see him hurtin. How's mom about it?"

"Not good, Jack, not good. If everything is okay with you and the law...."

"I got no problems with the law, Mark, none at all. Only thing left is the Devlins."

"What? Come on, Jack, you must be shittin me. That still goin on after all this time?"

"Fraid so. Mike Devlin's been on my case for years. Freddie bought it in San Diego, so he's outta the picture. The sister? I can't see her bein much of a problem. I'll just have to take care a Mike when the time comes. There's one more thing. We always thought the family came from Tipperary. They came from Inniskeen."

"Holy shit, so they're related to the guy granpop executed with granmom there. That means they set granpop up in Belfast, the bastards. Don't forget the step-brother, Jack. He's older, smarter and meaner than Mike. We'll do it together. Promise?"

"Promise. Never met the step-brother. You?"

"Oh, yeh. Name's Tracy. Used to live in Ambler, years back. We had a few run-ins before I went overseas. Tell you what: Mike's yours, Tracy's mine. Deal?"

"Shit," I thought, "Tracy. The fuck." To Mark, "You got it. We gotta settle it some time."

"Okay, Jack. About mom, I think you should go see her. She said you offered to take her in up there. That was kind, but she wants to stay on this side of the line, so I'm going to ask her to come out here. That, I think, she might be able to deal with, except she'd have to leave her idols behind."

"The graves at Holy Cross in Yeadon," I thought to myself. Into the phone: "Idols? What idols?"

"Yeh, you wouldn't know. She thinks the sun rises and sets on the Philadelphia Flyers."

"Holy cow, your mother, the hockey groupie. Amazing," I said, smiling broadly. Then, seriously, "What do you really think?"

"We haven't sat down to talk and get roaring drunk in a long time. You're out of touch with me; I'm out of touch with you. But, I think you're doing what you think is right. If that's how it is, I'm for it. You've had a very rough time since dad died and things fell apart. I'll never be able to repay you for looking after mom and granmom like you did."

Like he didn't, too. I tried to interrupt. "No, no, let me finish. I don't blame you for getting out. It's probably the only reason you're still alive. Crossed my mind, too—until Sylvia— and then the kids started coming. I don't regret my decision at all, even though the politics stink and the cities are falling apart. You been to Philly lately? No, guess not. It's a mess. North Philly looks like it's been shelled. Even the cops won't go into parts of West Philly. The Army's been awful good to me, but sometimes I wonder what would've happened if things were different. Anyway, it's all water under the bridge now. Hey, guess I just talked myself into that visit after all. Count on it."

"Great, Mark. That's good news. Do me a favor though, wouldya? Get me a subscription to the *Irish Voice*. Don't want to send anything from here right now." I gave him the address of the paper in New York. Then I told him the post office box number I had set up in Kingston. Originally, I was going to use Johnny's name for it, but I thought Charlie Murphy's would be better.

"Still at it, huh?" he said.

"Yep, still at it.  Just can't turn my back on it."

It was 3 in the morning on a cold, raw night in early December.  I'd been tossing and turning, trying to shut off the pictures in my mind.  I dozed, finally, and the dream came again.  As I watched through the hedgerow, I could taste whiskey on my breath.  The Royal Ulster Constabulary had the last man on the ground, face down.  The sergeant leaned over him, laughing, and shot him through the temple.  The body jumped.  Still laughing, he turned it over with his boot.  At first, I thought it was granpop's bloody face.  Then I could see clearly.  It was mine.

The phone was downstairs, and it must have been ringing a long time.  I untangled myself from the balled up blankets, jumped out of bed, ran down the stairs and grabbed it.  "Jackie, Jackie, you have to come quick.  It's Matt.  He's gotten out again, and nobody can find him."  "Okay, mom, sit tight.  I'll be there just as soon as I can."

It was dawn.  I talked to Johnny.  He wanted to come, but I told him to forget it; zero big-city street smarts could get him in  trouble.  Then I went over and found Chris and Luke in the barn, setting up the milking equipment for the restless, lowing cows. "I'm gonna have to be gone for a while. Thought I should tell you. Don't know how long. Maybe you could look in on Johnny once in a while, please? Thanks, you guys, thanks a lot for everything. Say so long to your wife, Chris, and tell her I'll be hungry when I get back. Oh yeh, if it won't make her too mad, say goodbye to Annie, too."

I jumped into the truck and started it with a roar from the duals. A light snapped on in a window at the side of their house. It was cold, but she opened it anyway and leaned out. Her hair was down in a bushy halo around her head. She was wearing a white flannel nightgown with frills at the neck. I wasn't smiling when I held my hand up to her, palm flat and unmoving. She wasn't smiling, either, when she held hers up in return.

I slid out of the truck and walked over to her. "I have to be away for a while, Annie. Take care. I'll be back soon as I can." Her hand was warm on my cheek. I was terrified of getting involved with her; terrified of love, of bad luck, of death. She knew it without my telling her. I started to walk away, then stopped and went back. I took her smooth, sleepy, perfect face in both my hands, kissed her pink lips quickly, turned on my heel and started for the El Camino. She grabbed the back of my jacket, pulled me to her and wound both arms around my neck. She felt light, soft, yet muscled, strong, delicate, all at the same time. "Be bloody careful," she whispered in my ear, "and come back in one piece. I'll be with you the whole time." She kissed my neck and pushed me away.

# 18. "WHAT ROUGH BEAST?"

We were pounding up the black slate sidewalk on Spruce Street just as fast as we could go. At the corner of 16$^{th}$, we stopped under the street light, out of breath, hands on our knees. "Hey," Mark said, "don't you think it might be a smart move to go get the truck, instead? It's ten more blocks, and I don't think he'll give us the slip this time." We'd been chasing him all over the city. He always seemed one cunning step ahead of us, playing hide and seek in the dark, like he knew we were after him. We both started laughing, then turned around and headed for the El Camino.

Picked Mark up at the airport the day before. Driving down Route 95 past the police pound gave me some wicked Jeeps flashbacks, but I threw my head back and laughed when I remembered Lintoff up on the not so high wire doing his threadbare act on the little Honda, Marta showing him off like a new Chevy. The afterthought of Luci's vacant eyes made the permanent frown return.

Mark was far away, down the long, crowded corridor, and at first I almost didn't recognize him, lean and tough in his uniform. His green beret had the sword and shield insignia.

Each collar had a single silver oak leaf. On his left sleeve were six yellow stripes. Above the three rows of ribbons on his chest was a small silver parachute; below them, a silver bullseye with four bars hooked to it. He walked toward me, very erect, quick, confident, with his pant legs tucked into his high black boots. There were soldiers all over the place. They took one look at all that stuff on his uniform, stood still and saluted sharply as he passed; he returned them with a snap, not taking his eyes off me.

We were about four feet apart. He dropped his suitcase. I saluted with a smile. He returned it, then grabbed me. "Get a haircut, wouldya, huh? Whaddya think all these grunts will make of a Lieutenant Colonel hugging a long-hair in broad daylight? Could ruin me." He slapped me on the back, then held both my biceps in his hands as he looked me up and down. "Jesus H. Christ, Jack, you are one hard son of a bitch. Where the hell have you been? Want to join up? I need a good hand to hand instructor." We laughed together.

From the corner of the big plate glass window, we could just see him sitting by himself at a round table for two in the back. The ring of tables near him was empty. Mark said, "You go in and get him. I can't stand it. I'll call the cops."

"You crazy? Don't call no cops. I'll talk to him, and we'll take him quietly back to the hospital."

I walked in. It was a very fancy seafood restaurant with a big reputation, prices to match. At the front was a desk for the maitre d', screened from the patrons. I had on my usual black clothes, boots and a plain leather jacket. She was wearing a very expensive indigo cocktail dress, low cut, well made. "Excuse me sir, may I help you?" "Yeh, that's my brother sittin by himself  back there. Come to collect im."

"Thank God. Who's going to pay his bill? It's a big one. He's been buying drinks for everybody." She shoved it toward me; a hundred bucks. I slapped down a yard and a half and pushed by her.

As I walked toward him, Matt shouted to the room. "Ah, gentlemen, hang on to your ladies, protect them from rape and pillage. Here comes my Visigoth brother. Don't let him hurt me, please, oh please." The last bit was said with a melodramatic roll of the eyes. I looked over at the waiter. He was a black kid about twenty with eyes round as saucers. I held up my hands and gave him my "no problemo" shrug. He wasn't convinced.

I sat down. Matt turned to the kid: "Bring this distinguished Irish nobleman a Remi Martin, if you please, *garcon*. I will remunerate you handsomely for your trouble." I shook my head to the waiter. In front of him was a half eaten piece of dark chocolate cake, a full ashtray, an empty wine glass and a large, lead crystal paperweight; it was faceted. He turned back to me. "Yes, it's fascinating, hypnotic, isn't it? I've been staring into it for hours and hours. All the secrets of the universe are in there, and I've been pulling them out, one by one, pulling them out, one by little one. Did you know there is no one up there, whizzing around in the sky? There's only a slow-thighed woman named Thelma who dusts the furniture, washes the dirty laundry and sweeps up the dirt. It's all a ruse, a big joke. Isn't that funny? We are but specks on a flea on a dog's back. He scratches; we die." He picked up the paperweight, laughing, and turned it, gazing into the sparkles. His fingernails were painted gold. Then he looked at me quickly, almost furtively: "You're my brother, aren't you?"

"Look, Matt, why don't we just step outside for some air, huh? Then we can go back so they can help you. Mark's waiting for us on the sidewalk. It'll be just like old times downashore at Margate. Come on, big brother, lead the way."

He looked at me directly for a long moment, one black eyebrow cocked. His pale blue, whitish eyes were wild, empty, bottomless. "Oh, what a lovely idea, a walk with the brothers in the City of Brotherly Love. How fitting, like a play about the Trinity." We stood up to go. Every eye in the restaurant was on us. "Good bye, good night, sweet princes and princesses. Life is such sweet sorrow, don't you agree? Quick to spring, soon to fall." He draped his coat over his shoulders and swept out like Liberace, or maybe James Brown. The maitre d' stopped breathing as we passed her. When we walked around the screen, both of us could see the flashing red lights and the uniforms outside. "*Ta an garda ag teacht,*" he said, twice, once loud, once under his breath: "The cops are coming." I didn't know he cared about the Gaelic. Granmom and granpop spoke it, but, except for phrases like that one, only to each other.

It was really tough for both of us, maybe all three of us, hard to tell. They had Matt in the locked security ward, same one he busted out of and mom panicked and called me. A long, long time ago, Rice Crispies had one of those offers where you got a prize for sending in a bunch of box tops and a quarter taped to a piece of cardboard. I was hooked. Mine was a cheap little ring with the rubber face of Crackle, I think, on the front. You twisted his nose to make him look funny—all squished and out of proportion. That's what Matt's face looked like.

"Well, well," he said, "the gunsel and the baby killer, again, what an honor. What have I done, oh Lord, to deserve it? Have I told you, brothers mine, that the Pope suggested I become a cardinal? I turned him down flat, of course. It's really his job I want. Think of all that power, and the robes. Oh, the robes."

They had taken his belt and shoelaces. I knew what that felt like. Everything was bolted down. There was nothing in his tiny cell of a room that could be used as a weapon. It was useless, trying to talk to him. Outside, the guy on duty told us they found him the first time he escaped, wandering around down by Penn Treaty, yelling at himself and some invisible other about ashes and dust.

"Who the fuck is in charge here?" I roared. "You assholes let him get out again, and you'll be dealin with us outside. Unnerstand?" The cop at the desk looked up with a snap from the papers he was filling out. He didn't like that much. He peered at my face closely, shuffling through the mug shots in his head. Mark quickly hustled me out the heavy door with its shatterproof glass. The stainless steel lock snapped shut with a loud click.

Parking stinks down around that hospital, so we pulled the Camino up on the sidewalk in a narrow alley about four long blocks away. It was dark, lined with beat up, overflowing trash cans, dumpsters alive with squeaking. We leaned toward each other, over the roof, talking options about Matt. Neither one of us heard the pops over the city noise, but we saw the muzzle flashes from the corner, about fifty feet away. Crazy, nobody can hit shit with a handgun at that distance. At the other end of the alley, a Ford pickup squealed in, lights off, and the driver jumped out. Trapped. No way out except through them. Both of us knew right away who they were: Tracy and Mike.

At first, we crouched behind the hood of the Camino, then Mark signaled me to go for the guy in the truck. That would be Mike; guns weren't his style, he preferred the close up approach with a straight razor. The shooter would be Tracy.

Mark got Tracy's attention as he dodged through the trash cans and dumpsters. Four more shots made six total. I knew Mark would be counting: eight max in the clip, one in the pipe made nine. I kept my back against the wall, out of sight, making for Mike. The switchblade was open in my right hand. Funny thing was, I wasn't scared at all, just mad as hell, centuries of rage alive in my right hand. Two more rapid shots from Tracy. "He's down to one," I thought, "God help him when he runs out." Mike was about ten feet ahead of me, walking carefully, in full view, looking for me.

"Pop," then Mark was on him. Fastest thing I ever saw in my life. Tracy cocked for a pistol whip. Mark hit him once in the gut, got around behind him and snapped his neck like he did it every day. The body slumped on the cobblestones.

"Time has come today," I thought, stood up and started making right straight for Mike. He'd seen what I saw, and he was breathing hard. We were about five feet apart. "You muthafuckin Kavanaghs been on my family too long. You and yer fuckin *Clann*, yer asshole granpop. I'm gonna cut you first, then take carea yer brudder, then the other one, the fag, then yer mudder. It was you who killed my granpop; it was you who fucked up my family, made everybody turn on us. Now you're gonna pay for Tracy, too."

He started for me with the straight razor in his hand. This was not going to be easy; Mike was good and very crazy.

We circled. A switchblade is a stabbing knife, not great for slashing. Mine had an eight inch blade, good steel, needle pointed. I'd have to get in close, inside his arms, maybe take one before I could get him. He'd be going for the throat, of course.

I deked to his right, toward the razor, he slashed out and just missed my face. I could hear the whistle and feel the wind. He was off balance, so I gave him a left jab straight in the eye. That rocked him back. We were silent, bent on killing, noses open, mucous flowing. We circled again; him feinting toward me with the razor. I flipped the switchblade for a downward stab, butt toward my thumb.

He took a run at me, flailing with the razor. I pushed him by me and gave him a shot with my fist, just under the ear. Still not close enough to get at him. We squared off once more. No doubt Mark was near, but he would know I wouldn't want any help. Mike held the razor up to go for my neck. I countered with my left arm, and he got me good, right through the leather of my sleeve. Close enough. I grabbed his right arm with my left hand, bent it back almost to breaking, and drove the blade, haft deep, right into his heart. He let out a long "ahhh." His eyes rolled in his head. I couldn't let go of his arm, and it snapped as he fell to his knees. Only took about twenty seconds for him to die. I put my knee on his chest, pulled out the knife and wiped it on his greasy colors. I felt no pity at all. "Last demon down," I thought.

Mark grabbed me. "How is it?"

"Can't tell, but there's a lot of blood."

We were making for my truck when a beat up Ford Fairlane screamed around the corner where Tracy took his first shots. Dead center, full bore, right at us. Through the windshield, I could see the contorted witch's face of the sister. We dove to opposite sides of the alley. How she missed us, I don't know. She must have seen Mike's body in the center of the alley, because she made a panic left, directly into the corner of a dumpster.

We walked over. She'd gone right through the windshield, head first into the hinge of the dumpster lid. It was messy, bloody. Her head looked like a ripe cantaloupe dropped from four floors up. She was very, very dead.

"Don't touch anything, Mark. Let's get the hell outta here."

On the way to Manayunk, Mark driving, we figured that the cops would think it was a domestic: two guys, one woman. But there wouldn't be a knife left behind, so maybe they'd figure it was an outlaw beef. Anyhow, we didn't see how we could be connected to it. Mike was a career snitch, probably against his own MC club, too, just like his father and grandfather before him, and the cops would probably think some of his victims caught up with him. Which, in a way, was true.

Mark went into mom's house first and came back with a field dressing kit, a big bottle of Jameson and one of my shirts. "Can't let momma Francini do it, too risky for her." He gave me a shot of something in my arm, then got me about smashed before he stitched me up. Very professional.

"You had a lotta practice with this?"

"Yep, much as I ever want."

In the living room, the hockey game was on, loud, and she just sat in front of the tube, staring. Don't think she heard much. The Broad Street Bullies were making Alpo out of some team from the west. Me and Mark sat at the kitchen table until the second bottle of Jameson was empty and the sun came up. We needed it, but neither one of us could get drunk.

I was out the back in the tiny yard, smoking a Camel. On the sagging electric wire above my head, a single mourning dove turned her black eye on me, cooing softly. Sal Francini stuck his head out of his shed and let out a loud whoop. He ran over, grabbed me by the arm, the right fortunately, and pulled me across the laneway. Momma gave me a big hug and about a hundred kisses. We ate fresh bread, drank wine out of the same old Chianti bottle and talked and talked. "See," he said, as he pulled the tarp away, "all a yer stuff, just like ya left it. Now ya can come back and start all over again, fresh. We're gonna find ya a sweet little Italian wife who knows how ta cook."

"Thanks, Sal, momma, you two are the best. But no, I don't think I'm ever coming back. Maybe sometimes, to visit, but not to live. No, no, not to live, not to live. It just won't work, just won't work, just won't." I snapped out of it. "Howsomever, I think you two need a vacation, so you're commin to see me. Before I leave, I'll get you all the details. No backin out now, Sal, or I'll take momma with me by herself."

Suddenly, I looked over at the back door of mom's place like I had zoom lenses in my eyes. Mark was standing there, face like lumpy gray putty, gold eyes wide, afraid. Couldn't tell right away whether it was inside my head or outside my head. First the blood pounding in my ears, then the mixed up, disjointed sounds of whinnying horses, jingling halters, hoof-beats. The noise stopped. Then the hollow, heavy thump of a blackthorne banging three times on the thick oak door of a cavernous stone room, reverberating in the emptiness. I ran over. The dove was silent now, but she didn't move from her perch.

"In cases like these, we normally don't allow burial in hallowed ground. Certainly not in the Order's cemetery, of course. But we have decided to make a partial exception here at Holy Cross Cemetery. So tragic. He was a fine priest with a wonderful future with us. Such an investment, so hard to replace." The Jesuit was about fifty, sleek, manicured, well fed, very right, used to being treated with deference. I wanted to drive his perfect teeth right through the back of his head. So did Mark, I could tell; the muscles in his jaw stood out proud. Mom was crying softly; her body looked caved in. It seemed like a crazy, senseless thing to do, jumping off the Tacony-Palmyra bridge like that. Much later, when I could think calmly, it became very clear what a logical, fitting way it must have seemed to him.

We laid him in the ground with granpop, granmom and dad. The plot was arranged by the *Clann* when granpop was gunned down. Holy Cross had a section that seemed like a Fenian, Irish Republican Brotherhood monument. Nearby, Joe McGarrity was buried, a bit futher off the dynamiter Luke Dillon. The Francinis were there, and mom held hands with momma. The same Jesuit started the routine. I elbowed him out of the way and recited "Ashes to ashes, dust to dust." It was from the King James version that Mr. Logan read over Sarah's coffin, not the *Douai*. His face turned very red and puffy; looked good on him. When everybody else went back to the house, I stood by the graves, still, silent. Promised to visit Jimbo; it hurt I didn't know where Toot was; for sure I'd go to Bodenstown to see Charlie. After the coffeecake and tea and condolences from people I didn't know or could barely remember, me and Mark picked up four big bottles of Jameson Irish Whiskey, a bunch of beer, and got very, very drunk with dad's brothers. They watched me, friendly enough but stone-faced; Derry, the Devlins, the IRA, even Castesi, weren't mentioned. Maybe they hadn't seen the *Bulletin* article that talked about gang warfare in Center City. Later, Uncle Joe, pretty stewed, asked Mark to tell him some war stories. My brother looked him in the eye and gave him a quiet "No."

"Call it, Mark. Heads it's Pat's, tails it's Red's." He called tails and lost. Pat's it would be. Before we went to the airport, we headed down Delaware Avenue to South Philly. Pat's had been there forever, so had Red's. Each had its specialty: Pat's for the best steak sandwiches on the planet; Red's made hoagies that tasted like manna.

"You sure about this, Jack? From what you've told me, maybe 9th and Wharton isn't the, ah, most secure position for you."

"No sweat, Mark, the Lanzettis are in the driver's seat—for now, anyhow. I never did know any of those guys. They got no reason to be lookin for me. Sal checked it out with his cousin. Besides, I've been away a long time now, and they got other problems to put down. They've been shootin each other so fast, there won't be many left in a few years."

The rolls, the paper thin beef, the fried onions, the melted provolone, the sauce, all were absolutely perfect, just like I remembered. When you squeezed them, they even leaked onto the plate as they should. It was a real blast from the past, like Jerry Blavat, the Geator with the Heater, broadcasting Frankie Lymon's *Why Do Fools Fall in Love?* from Camden, like the boys outside the boxing club down on the corner singing do-wop imitations of Little Anthony and the Imperials.

On the street, the wise guys were still there—same clothes, same hair, same shoes. Two young ones were leaning against a bright yellow Sting Ray, hanging out, trying to fill out their black Ban-Lon shirts and look as bad as the older heads. One of them poked the other and gestured to us with his thumb. At first I thought it was me, but then I could see it was Mark's uniform that attracted his attention. The one who got poked shrugged and turned away to watch the big-haired girls strolling by.

I felt bad about the coin flip, sort of, so we swung over to Red's and picked up two monster hoagies, with the meat and cheese and onions busting out of the long rolls. The olive oil made the waxed paper transparent. One was for his flight home; one was for my trip—home. We shook hands, hard, before he took off, dry eyes locked. "I'll see you, Jack, with my whole gang, in the summer. I don't think you know what you're letting yourself in for." "Maybe not, but I'm gonna have a lot of fun teachin you how to respect Canadian beer."

"Hello, Sarah, my love. It's been too long, princess, I know. I promised I'd be back. Couldn't come any sooner, honest." It was just coming dark, and I was on my knees by her headstone, under the broad oaks. Her epitaph was one word: "Remember." "Yes, princess, I'll always remember, always. Promise." The old silver of her locket felt warm, heavy, against my skin.

Above, in the falling gold sky, two red-shouldered hawks flew far apart and low over the oaks, screaming. I looked down at her stone and said, "Please, princess, please help me. I need you to tell me what to do. I don't know how anymore. I don't think I can anymore." Slowly, almost beyond perception, I was surrounded by a light, delicately sweet perfume, like lying on your back in a warm, wind-swayed field of wild flowers, looking up at fluffy clouds strolling across the sky. Her silver peace touched my chest softly, released me and drew away, the fleeting, sure caress of her warm, narrow hand.

The buckskin and the dapple gray were side by side in their stalls. The mare was near to foaling time. They turned their coal-lashed eyes on me, whinnied softly and nuzzled my shirt in greeting and farewell, as I stroked their muzzles, their velvet ears. Except for their oats-rich, fecund breathing, there was no sound anywhere in the world. As I stepped out the door, the whistle of dove wings slid by my ear.

The El Camino isn't exactly what you'd call quiet, so I had parked it well away from the house to avoid disturbing the family. Even so, all the Logans stood on the porch watching me as I walked toward it to leave. I smiled, held up my hand to them and said "Yes," silently, into Mrs. Logan's Sarah eyes. Mr. Logan had his hand on her shoulder as I drove away.

"I seem to be seeing a lot of you. Tell me, do you want to sell your truck? It's a classic. But you have to get this crease in the roof fixed first."

"Nope," I patted the dashboard. "This old warhorse needs some serious R&R. I'm gonna put it up on blocks for a while, rebuild the motor, bang out the dents and repaint it. No more winters for this guy."

"Look, here's my home number. If you change your mind, call me. Okay?"

"Sure, sure. Hey, aren't you supposed to be a Customs' guy?"

"Oh, right. Forgot. Sorry." In his official voice, he said, "What do you have to declare. What's all that stuff in the back, please."

He wanted the KR, too, but I wasn't selling. The Bonneville didn't interest him as much. On the tank of the KR, I had written "Sarah" in white paint; "Judith" on the Bonneville's, near where I had written "Trusty" so long ago. I decided then and there to call the El Camino "Elmo." An Annie, maybe, with luck and a lot of patient help, just maybe, I could start building.

I hadn't seen her since I got back, three days ago; afraid to, really. At first, I meant it as a joke, and a way to show her what it felt like. Luke told me she was in a walled-off section of the barn they used for preparing the cows for shows. There were ribbons and photographs all over the walls. Annie had a degree in animal husbandry and was in charge of the breeding and the show preparation. Winning at shows is very important to dairy farmers, means a lot, and she was really good at it.

She seemed to have a gift for concentration. I think she talked to cows in her head; they talked back. Annie was facing away from me, grooming a huge Holstein with electric shears, leaving a ridge of hair along the spine that stood up like a brush cut. Except for the cud chewing, the Holstein didn't move; portrait of the contented cow. She fixed her big black eye on me as she chewed, steam coming from her wet nostrils in the chill.

"That's my girl," Annie said, "you'll be the most beautiful one at the show. The judges won't be able to take their eyes off you, you're so pretty." She ran her powerful hands along the cow's flank; the hide rippled. Her shoulders were broad for a woman, but maybe it was her small waist and delicate hips that made them seem that way. I still couldn't figure out how she got into her jeans, they were that tight. Jumped into from a great height when still wet? Possible. "Maybe I should ask her," I thought. "Yeh, and get knuckles between the eyes for noticing."

Outside, there was snow on the ground. The horizontal light coming in the window was dull silver-blue. She knelt to shear the cow's belly. The two of them became one at that moment, inevitably outlined, deftly, perfectly colored, like a painting etched in memory. My ears were buzzing, no hooves attached. Without intent or thought or desire, I was drawn into the frame. The sunlit perfume surrounded me once more, but now it did not withdraw. It held me, pressing my chest, the old locket felt very heavy. "Sarah," I thought, "Annie would be the third. Would it be okay?" The picture, perfume, pressure vanished. "No, no, no. Don't be an idiot." I shouted in my head. "Everything would fall apart again, and she'd get hurt. Just forget it."

As she pivoted on one knee to put the shears down, she saw me. Her lovely oval face turned red again. When she jumped up, the cow's head snapped back and rattled the chain clipped to her halter. Annie took a run at me and started pounding me on the chest. Surprisingly hard, too. I pinned her arms in a bear hug. "You son of a bitch, why haven't you come sooner? Don't you ever sneak up on me like that again, or I'll, I'll...."

"Uh huh," I said, "or you'll what? Now you know how it feels."

I let her go. Both of us were breathing hard, puffs of steam hanging in the still air. "How was it?" "Bad, Annie, the worst yet. But I'm home now. Just hope nothing followed me. Look, can't we have that truce? Can't we be good friends? You know damn well how much I like you. We just seem to light a fuse every time we're together. I don't mean to get under your skin; you don't mean to get under mine. I, ah, I'm, ah, really burned out right now. Can't think straight. How about that truce?" My big right mitt stretched out to her all by itself.

She cocked her head in that Bradley way. Her eyes were mysterious, dubious, sparky. All the wonderful curves of her chest were heaving. She took my hand in hers, then in both of them. "Truce, Jack. We've got all the time in the world, musha."

Grief is a strange thing. It doesn't stalk you with purpose, like death, a yellow sulfurous fog swirling just at the edge of your peripheral vision. Grief is a big, sloppy rubby that hides in the bushes and waits to jump you for kicks when you aren't looking. It was late spring, and I'd just gotten back from Montreal. Annie went with me; we had separate rooms. We went shopping on St. Catherine's Street, feeling European, drank too much wine at dinner and ate bagels together in the morning. Everything was settled about the franchises; I'd even been talking to Kawasaki about another one. I gave her an argument, but mom turned all my money back to me. She didn't say whether she'd come up with the Francinis come summer.

I thought about colors for the house: yellow clapboard, blue trim, red doors. Good, solid, old-time colors. Maybe I could have it finished by August if I hired some kids from the Farm Pool to do the scraping. I considered changing the sign, calling the shop "Philly MC," instead, but I rejected it. Some baggage I didn't need.

The alfalfa was just poking out of the ground in the Bradley's field beside the house. I was smoking, pacing up and down, looking out over the pale, pale, delicate green, so hesitant yet so tough. The butt arced into the field and hissed out in a damp furrow. I really wasn't thinking anything at all, but all of a sudden the tears came like an old milk can was kicked over in the barn. Grief, that rubby slob, thought it was funny.

"Hey, Jack," she called. She had started making enough noise before she came up on me that I wasn't spooked. It was part of our truce. I didn't turn, didn't hold up my hand. The tears felt warm on my face; the flood wouldn't stop; no sound, not a sob. She looked around my shoulder with a blinky little smile on her healthy face. It looked a little like Raggedy Ann come to life. Told her that once; she didn't like it. I meant it as a compliment.

"Oh, no. Oh, no. Oh, no, don't, Jack, don't. I'm so sorry. I'll just leave you alone now. Didn't mean to intrude." She touched me gently on the arm.

Her boots squished away on the damp lawn. I whirled around, mind made up to go with dad's "nothing tried, nothing happens." Call it an act of faith. "Hey, freckles, hold on a minute."

She spun around with her hands on her fine hips, green eyes flashing. "What, then? What? Don't worry, I won't tell anybody."

"Annie, it's not that. Don't care. You wanna get married, or what?"

Raggedy Ann looked like somebody poleaxed her. "You bastard, don't you fool with me like that. Why, I'll, I'll...I don't know what I'll do to you for that."

"You could start by givin me an answer. Yes or no. Your choice." I turned back to the fields again.

I could hear her running, plashy steps behind me, but I didn't move. She tackled me, and we rolled around on the ground. I was laughing; she was slapping me on the arms, playfully but sharply. She got on top of me, pinning my arms to the ground with her knees. "It's about time, I'd say, about bloody time. Of course I will, you big, dumb Mick. My grandmother will roll in her grave, eh? She always said no Bradley ever married a horse thief or a Fenian."

She released my arms. I pulled her down on my chest, then we kissed, hungry for each other, on the snow-melt lawn. "This is nuts." I said. "We're soaked. Let's go inside." There was world enough and time. No hurry. I got some towels from the bathroom, and we dried off as best we could. She untied her golden hair to pat it dry. I pulled granpop's box off the shelf and handed her the shamrock key. The silver crystal from the mine made the box heavy. She was sitting on my lap, her head on my chest. One by one, in order, I took out the past, precious things and told her what they were. Not the whole story, more like an introduction. Sarah's locket glowed dull silver light. The white missal, the ivory brush and comb, were on the table. When I got to granmom's engagement ring, I watched my steady hand slip it on her finger. All the past, precious things: forever and a day.

Johnny stuck his dark face out from the kitchen. He looked from her to the box to me again. "Holy shit," he said under his breath, gawking. Then he smiled harder than I'd ever seen him smile. The kitchen door banged. He was on his way to Deseronto.

With her, it wasn't the same as Judith or Sarah; it was both together—more so—if that's possible, almost as if she knew them, how I felt, how they felt, touched, breathed. She was like a bright cloud whose waist you could encircle with your hands—lightness, the brush of a feather, the strength of spring steel, the heat of a torch. The first time each of us almost tore muscles, then almost passed out—together.

We walked beside the lichen-covered, glacier-rounded stones piled along the fenceline—generations of aching backs around the kitchen table, too tired to lift the fork. A black front was blowing in, low, from the east, rain full, ozone heavy. Goof, the slob, ran ahead, looking for a woodchuck to torture. I stopped, lifted a heavy piece of orange granite and put the switchblade away for the last time. It was a burial alright, but the rock wasn't a headstone. I wanted that shield to hold the knife down.

The *Kingston Whig Standard* treated it like Armageddon. Maybe it was: front page, huge type, grainy photographs of the wreckage, the state funeral. The Provos blew up Mountbatten, his yacht, a woman and two young boys, at Mullaghmore, County Sligo. Between the lines in the *Irish Voice*, I could read shock, disbelief, confusion. The fact that the explosives came from a water tunnel being built in Manhattan didn't help any. I wasn't shocked at all, just sickened.

I didn't plan it that way, but it turned into something like when all the players come to the front of the stage at the end of the show at Lincoln Center. We decided to get married the last week in August, when everybody, even mom, would be there.

Harry and Linda showed up the third week. Couldn't have been better for Harry: a shop in the country, next to a farm, near a small city. Linda liked the colors I put on the house. Used the compressor and the paint gun from the shop. Did a good job. All four of us talked long and hard. Annie had enough trouble with my accent when I got excited; she tried, but mostly she was out to lunch with the New England ones.

Well, really, three of us talked long and hard, anyway. Harry couldn't handle Canadian beer yet. He'd have four and get a bit sloshed. They decided quickly; they were staying; we were partners. Linda had passed the bar in Vermont, so she could hang out a shingle in Kingston once she sorted out the regulations. Because we were so near the St. Lawrence River and the lake, Harry seemed to think we could do better if we handled outboard motors, too. We all agreed on that one. Mental note: "Call Evinrude? Maybe Honda?"

There was a stone house with a stone drive shed and a few acres for sale not far down the road. It needed a lot of work, but the price was right; they wanted to raise chickens and horses. Everything looked so good, I got worried, uneasy, tossing and turning at night, waiting for the crash, hearing glass breaking and metal tearing in my mind. Annie would switch on the light, lay my head on her finely marbled breast, pry my fingers flat from fists and stroke the bump of broken rib on my back until I fell asleep. Around her neck was a fine gold chain for the bronze key. Finally, I had a real personal angel; the wings of a slender dove; she smelled like sunshine.

It was a wacky mismatch of a wedding party when you think about it. Vultch in a home made dog collar, blue-black face shining; his skinny wife with a bandanna over her hair, looking like a starving African missionary. The cake had "This Beginning of Miracles. John ii. 11" squirted on top of the white icing in that red decorator junk you should never eat. The Jell-O was green, of course. Smiling and humming "do dah, do dah," he gave me the sign of the cross blessing in the air. His close cut hair was grizzled stainless.

Mark arrived in a GMC van made over for traveling with a crowd. His kids piled out like an army of screaming monkeys. Luke, bless his heart, took them all over to the barn to check out the cows. It wasn't just. Matt would have made the fourth. The winged man didn't make it, so we had to go on with the lion, the ox and the eagle.

Sylvia was extremely beautiful, a raven-haired, stunning Cajun, near enough, now, to her Acadian homeland. Her smile was liquid, voice like warm, dark honey, gleaming walnut-brown eyes. "Now, Mark," she drawled, "you nevah did tell me haow haaansome youah brautha was. I think, maaiybe, we should just run away togethha rahht naow." Annie got a bit sparky around the eyes when Sylvia slipped her arm around my waist and got up on her toes to linger a kiss on my cheek, just below the Howard Street scar.

"Aaargh," I said into her golden hair, "cut it out." She took off
with her mother and Linda to get ready.

Once I got dressed, I felt pretty spiffy, that's for sure.
Hadn't been in a suit since the senior prom in high school. It
was black, naturally, but this time I went for the crispest white
shirt I could find. I gave up on the tie, so Annie bought it:
silver with black stripes. Chris tied it for me with his thick
farmer's fingers. I forgot how.

It began when I was looking in the mirror, straightening the
tie. It wasn't the first time. In my mind—no, somewhere
else—the whistle of wind blowing steady over white-caps.
Last time I heard it this way was what must have been the
instant granpop was gunned down. The *Clann na Gael*
shipped him over to Dublin for some important meetings in
'56, just after the border campaign began. I never did find out
why he went to Belfast, but he was shot walking out of the
Green Man pub, point blank, died instantly. Granmom told
me they put pennies on his eyes over there and had a wake
that lasted three days. The *Clann* had his body shipped back
to Philly, and there was a huge funeral with lots of IRB guys in
heavy suits, the burial at Holy Cross and a traditional band
after at the Legion hall in Kensington: tribute to one of Michael

Collins' Twelve Apostles in 1919, Captain in the IRA, 1922, Irish Civil War prisoner in Kilmainham Jail, 1923. The Devlins set him up as payback for the execution of Eddie Devlin in Inniskeen and because granpop was on the tribunal that condemned their grandfather for ratting to the FBI on an important arms shipment out of Philly. A British agent did the job. The IRA caught up with him in a Birmingham phone booth in '58, shot him in both knees with a pistol, then blew his head off with a shotgun.

I could hear the distant, solitary keening of the penny whistle that played for him so long ago. Silence, then the whirr of lens' vanes opening. There they were, the past, precious people, forever and a day: dad, sitting on the beach at Margate, massive arms stretched out behind him, face lifted to the sun; granpop, with his Sunday hat on the back of his head, standing beside granmom clutching her missal to her chest; tiny Sarah, turning with a radiant smile to look at me from her dapple gray mare; Matt, a young seminarian in a white alb, hands raised in benediction. Even teenaged Jimbo, looking out the window of his red Olds 88. And Toot, lumpy and chocolate fed. And the shy urchin, Charlie Murphy. It was good to see Judith wasn't there. Except for Sarah, they weren't smiling, but I could feel approval, peace, serenity, forgiveness, maybe even salvation, all around me for the first time in my waking life. The lens shut with a snap. Picture taken.

I walked downstairs and out into the sun, kind of dizzy. Sal and momma and mom pulled in. Sal was driving a shiny new Chrysler, very substantial. He was some proud of it. Don't know how he managed with the Customs' guys, but he lugged two huge, wicker covered carboys of red wine out of the trunk and a big bag of pizza dough. He wiped his hands on his dress pants; momma cuffed him on the arm. She could duke it out later with Mrs. Bradley later about who was in charge of the kitchen. Momma was all over me; I didn't mind one little bit. My mother was restrained, lost; she was having trouble with the idea of a Protestant daughter-in-law—Orange Irish to boot—and a United Church minister marrying us. I was sure once she got one good look at Annie everything would be fine. She'd never give up on the conversion pitch, the novenas, the holy cards at Christmas, but that was just her way.

I shook hands with Sal for a long time, clasped is a better word. He was smiling, misty-eyed. He looked me up and down: "Hey, Jack, you need a violin case to go wit dat outfit."

Me and Harry and Vultch heard the Shadow before anybody else; we nodded in unison. He always had a flair for the dramatic entrance. Hose and Chica climbed off. Hose took off his helmet. His hair was shot with more gray than black now, snaking through it like lightning, but he was the same beanpole beatnik I used to know. He held up his flat palm to me and said, "Greetings from the desert to all and sundry revelers in the northland. Far fucking out." His eyes swept the crowd like lamps. He looked at me and nodded with a bright grin. Me and Chica held each other hard, eyes closed, quiet, for a long time, her cheek against my shoulder, until Hose pulled us apart. "Careful with the old lady, pilgrim, she's hot to trot." Chica punched his chest, laughing. She got better looking with age. Annie, I thought, would understand.

The wedding wouldn't be complete without Johnny. Hadn't seen him all day. He'd been very mysterious for the last while. Not because of Darlene, his black eyed, roly poly, grinning Mohawk girlfriend. She'd been with him steady at our place almost a month. I half-kidded him about a double wedding until he said, "No way, white man, I ain't the marryin kind. Course, then again, I might need to make a good trade some day."

The brick-red front door opened, and they walked out, hand in hand, into the bright, straw-yellow sunshine on the lawn. They wore traditional clothes: a very soft, beaded deerskin shift and moccasins for her; for him a deerskin shirt, a black leather vest and a choker of bear's teeth. He wore a black, flat-brimmed western hat, like Clint Eastwood's, with a band of turquoise studded silver. His pony tail was braided; in it was a single eagle feather. Everybody was gaga over them. Hose took one look and said, "Aha, the gods of earth and forest appear. Mystical." Not sure what mom thought; she was just getting used to Vultch. The Bradley relatives and friends —there was a whole slew of them—were bug eyed.

"Where the hell is he, Dar?" Johnny said. "I told him 11:00. Ain't payin im if he don't show on time." Darlene shrugged. The minister drove up in a dusty Ford F-150 with farm plates. His name really was Sam, couldn't have been funnier. Hose gave him a long once over, one eye shut.

Weddings seem to bring out some kind of flocking instinct in women; men act different. All of them, mom, Darlene, Sylvia, momma, Chica, the Bradley side, even Vultch's wife, fluttered around for a while then took off for the farm in a V, like migrating Canada Geese. It was time, I guessed, for them to play with the ribbons, look at the bride in the mirror and say "ohhhh" a lot.

The old Indian got out of the Pontiac Parisienne very slowly. He wore jeans and a plaid western shirt. Around his neck was a string tie held by a silver medallion with a large blood-red stone in the center. His craggy, lined face was the color of dark brown saddle leather; it looked exactly like the one on the Indian Head Nickel. Two long, steel gray braids rested on his chest. In his hand, he carried a worn, undecorated moosehide pouch. As he walked toward us, Johnny whispered to me: "He's from the Sarcee tribe, Jack, a famous shaman, very holy, very respected. It took some doin, but I got him here for you two. It's my gift. After your ceremony, we'll have another one. He'll burn sage and then sweet grass for you, then say the words in his head that will keep you both safe forever." My eyes filled up, couldn't help it.

Johnny introduced us. The old man opened his bag—it was smoke tanned, I could smell it—and took out a long white feather; didn't know from what bird. "Yes, now I understand, Johnny Two Axe," he mumbled. "This man is white," he touched the white flash in my hair with the feather, "but we know each other since a long, long time." I guessed the Sarcee had their own warlocks.

Johnny had a problem. He whispered in the old man's ear. "Sorry, Johnny, forgot." He turned away from us, rummaged around in his pockets, ducked his head, then turned back. He flashed me a big grin with his false teeth and shook my hand: "Sure am thirsty."

Chris Bradley called all the men over to the table with the cake and the glasses on it. Women flock to preen; men herd to feed. He pulled up the tablecloth and reached under. It was the biggest bottle of Jameson I'd ever seen—gallon sized. He cleared his throat, awkwardly, and ran a finger around the tight collar of his white shirt, just like the father of the bride always should.

"I'm a farmer, not much for speeches. Just like to say I think Jack here is a very good man, and he'll make a fine son-in-law. Besides, I need somebody to fix the equipment for nothing. I've never seen anything like it. From the first moment Annie saw him, my wife and I could tell by the look on her face that this day would come. Only it took a bit for them to stop scrapping long enough to figure it out. Just one more thing—between us—Jack."

He poured two glasses of the amber and handed me one. "Éirinn *go Brách*," he said, holding his glass up to me. "Ireland for ever. Up the Republic," I responded. "All of us should be free. Here's to King Billy, too—I guess." In my mind, unbidden, "For her, for them, for me, for all those who didn't make it, the past, precious people, there's a personal peace from today—south and north." Our empty glasses hit the table as one. Chris and Luke poured drinks for everybody while we waited. Finally, after all these years, finally, I got the right answer to the how many angels dancing on the head of a pin question. Easy, only one—for the lucky millionth customer.

The guy I hired in Kingston to play the keyboard was pretty good, but he didn't know anything much about rock and roll or blues. I loaned him some tapes, so he could get the music down. When we saw the women coming, Annie hidden in the middle of them, I nodded to him. He started the melody from

*The Weight*, by The Band. Annie's head shot out from between Darlene and Chica for an instant. Her look was like dark, black-green thunder. I turned to the musician, laughing, and slashed a finger across my throat. He quit right away and started tinkling some country-western ditty, simple chords and stuff, no lead, no statement.

It went by in a many colored blur. Like driving a bike at speed in the rain on a strange road. *The Wedding March* started. Annie had her arm through her father's. Then we were standing together. Good thing there weren't any flies around; I'dve had a mouthful. She wore her grandmother's wedding dress, all white lace and seed pearls. The red glass in granmom's engagement ring twinkled on her finger. Her waist was tiny. I don't know how they figured out getting her hair to stay put under the veil. She was trembling, electrocuted. So was I, same plug. Harry's son, little Jack, was the ring bearer. He wore black. Mark was the best man, ramrod straight, in a dark blue suit. Her cousin, Rachael, was the maid of honor in fetching, off the shoulder, deep yellow satin.

In a thermal high above, two red-tailed hawks, turning and turning, widening and widening, then swooping close together, dancing, wheeling, wing tip to wing tip, silently. The old Indian watched them, lips moving, no sound. The silver and the stone of his medallion very bright. Vultch watched, too, hands pressed together like Mahatma Gandhi, a single silver tear glistening on his blue-black cheek.

Marrying Sam started: "Do you, John Sebastian Kavanagh, take this woman, Annabel Margaret Bradley, to be your lawful wedded wife?" "Yeh, I, Black Jack, take freckles here...." She pinched my arm, hard, so I said it right the second time. Through the fine lace, her eyes were the deep, deep emerald of flashing star-shine planets heated to flesh— this new day, new hour, this clear diamond instant come round at last.

After my hands took over and didn't drop the ring, her lips opened like a pink flower when we kissed. "Promise, my angel," I said into her beautiful hair, "Promise, my love." Three times I said it, magic, an incantation. "Goddamn thing does work," I thought with a start and a smile.

While everyone, even Annie, was still outside, I opened granpop's box. It hadn't been locked since I gave her the old bronze key. Everything was in order, year by precious year. I left it that way—open to the light—the oak inside uncolored by stain or time. I read the verse on the lid again:

*Cast a cold eye*
*On life, on death.*
*Horseman, pass by!*

I stepped to the window, looked out over the fields and thought about it. Then I said to him, "Not today, granpop, not tomorrow, either, and that's a promise." For the briefest instant, there was the rumble of a Harley engine. "No way," I said out loud. I knew for sure there was a little Annie being built already.

Afterwards, we were going to Minaki Lodge for two weeks. It's up in the Lake of the Woods, near the Manitoba border. The water would be clear, deep and cold. No ice at all. We were flying up there. Elmo the Camino was resting in the shop with Sarah the KR and Judith the Trusty Bonny. It had been a long, long running road. They deserved it.

Made in the USA
Charleston, SC
13 July 2010